ANNE STUART

Ruthless

THE HOUSE OF ROHAN

MIRA®

MIRA

ISBN-13: 978-0-7783-2848-3

RUTHLESS

Recycling programs
for this product may
not exist in your area.

For questions and comments about the quality of this book please contact us at
Customer_eCare@Harlequin.ca.

www.MIRABooks.com

Printed in U.S.A.

For my darling middle-aged editor who's very tolerant, and my brilliant agent who's very fierce.

Beginning

The visit with the lawyer had not gone well. Elinor Harriman arrived home just as her sister, Lydia, had finished dealing with their landlord, and she ducked out of sight so the old lecher wouldn't see her. Monsieur Picot had no patience for either her or her mother, but her baby sister was a different matter. All Lydia had to do was let tears fill her limpid blue eyes and make her Cupid's bow mouth tremble and M. Picot was destroyed, awash with apologies and assurances. He didn't realize he was being played until the door was firmly closed behind him and Elinor could sneak up the stairs, grateful that she hadn't had to defend Lydia's honor if M. Picot got carried away.

He never did. None of the landlords and butchers and greengrocers ever took advantage of Lydia's delicate beauty. She radiated such an exquisite innocence that no one would dare. Even in this less than felicitous area of town, no one would even think of offering her an insult.

"Told you," Lydia said with an impish grin far removed from her Madonna smile. "It works every time."

Elinor flopped into the nearest chair, letting out a groan as an errant spring poked her backside. During their last enforced move they'd had to relinquish all but their most wretched of furniture. The tiny parlor on the edge of one of the least savory neighborhoods in Paris held three chairs and a meager table that served as a desk, a dining surface and a dressing table, and the chairs were barely functional. The bedrooms were as bad. One sagging bed in the first room held their mother's snoring body, in the other there was only a shared mattress on the hard floor. She refused to think about how Nanny Maude or Jacobs the coachman slept in the back area that served as kitchen and servants' quarters.

And how absurd it was to have a coachman when it had been years since they'd even had a horse, much less a coach. Not since their very first days in Paris, when their mother had been in love and the two sisters had reveled in their new adventure. But Jacobs had come with them from England, under Lady Caroline's spell as most men were, and nothing, not even a total lack of wages, could induce him to leave.

The lover and the money had disappeared quickly, to be replaced by someone almost as wealthy. In the last ten years Lady Caroline Harriman had been working her way down to a state Elinor couldn't bear to consider. At least right now her mother was too ill to cause trouble, to go looking for another bottle of blue ruin, another game of chance, another man to finance her more important needs, which had never included her daughters.

"So how much time have we got?" she asked, reaching for her knitting. She was a wretched knitter—her handwork was atrocious but she convinced herself she could do something useful, even if her socks and vests were full of dropped stitches. Nanny Maude had taught her, but as usual she was proving less than adept.

Lydia sighed. "He'll be back in a week, and I don't think I'll be able to put him off again." Sweet Lydia was perfect in every way, pretty and darling and clever, and her handwork was flawless. She could dance perfectly with only the cursory lessons their mother had once paid for, she could paint a pretty picture, sing like a bird, and any man who met her became her willing slave, from Jacobs, their elderly manservant, to the wealthy young Vicomte de Miraboux whom she'd met at the lending library. For a brief time Elinor had hoped their problems were solved, until the Vicomte's family caught wind of what was going on and the Vicomte had been swept away on a grand tour of Europe.

They'd offered her money, Elinor thought, rubbing her chilled hands, and she'd probably been a fool to throw it back in their smug faces. As if a Harriman would ever stoop to being bribed. But at that moment, with M. Picot just walking away, she suddenly thought she could do almost anything if it ensured safety for Lydia and their little family. Even for their reckless mother.

Lady Caroline had been too ill to cause trouble recently. They had no money for a doctor or medicine, and the flush that had covered her body and disordered her never clear mind was a mixed blessing. Ill as she was, at least for the time being she was bedridden, unable to get them deeper in debt.

"So tell me about the lawyer, Nell," Lydia said, calling her the pet name only she used. "Has our father left us some vast fortune to ease *Maman's* final days? Or at least a minor pittance?"

"He's left us something, though a vast fortune might be too optimistic," Elinor said morosely. "His title and estates have been left to a Mr. Marcus Harriman, and another, undoubtedly smaller amount for us. He probably wouldn't have left us anything if he could have helped it." She carefully avoided the fact that whatever inheritance existed belonged, nominally, to her. Lydia's parentage was cloudy, but most definitely had nothing to do with Elinor's father, and everyone knew it. Though British law declared a child born within a marriage to be the legal offspring of the husband, her father had been infinitely inventive in denying either child or his ex-wife any kind of support.

Lydia sighed. "Perhaps M. Picot would be put off another week if I allowed him a few liberties. A kiss would hardly compromise my soul if it kept a roof over our heads."

"No!" Elinor dropped another stitch, and tossed her knitting aside in frustration. She looked up at her sister. "The lawyer definitely said our father had left us something, though apparently there was some ridiculous stipulation that I would have to go to England to receive it. I just wish we'd known of his death sooner—we could have put this in motion months ago. I expect the death notice would have gone to our former residence, and since we left in the middle of the night with our bills unpaid they would have been unlikely to pass along any correspondence that might have showed up. I'm sure it won't be too miserable an amount. He wouldn't let his daughters starve."

Lydia's brief smile was wry. "Don't try to sweeten things for me. He always said he wanted nothing to do with the spawn of the harlot he'd had the misfortune to marry. Why should he change his mind on his death-bed?"

"Well, he was still angry. It was only a few years after mother had left him, and he was the laughingstock of London. Sooner or later he must remember that we are his blood and he has some responsibility to us."

"I thought he claimed we aren't actually his children, didn't he?"

Elinor could barely remember their father. He'd been a tall, singularly unpleasant man with little interest in anything but his horses and his women. It had always seemed patently unfair to Elinor that his wife had been denounced for following similar interests, but she'd learned fairness had little to do with reality. "Of course we're his children," she said. At least Lydia had never suspected the truth about her own parentage. "I'm as tall as most men, and I have his wretched nose."

"It's a very nice nose, Nell," Lydia said gently. "It

gives you character, whereas I'm just a pretty little nothing."

"There are times when I would have given a great deal to be a pretty little nothing," Elinor said morosely.

"No, you wouldn't. I don't really think you want to be anyone but yourself, if truth be told," Lydia said.

Elinor forced a laugh. "You're probably right. I always was wretchedly strong-minded. I'd like to be exactly as I am, only fabulously wealthy. That's a reasonable enough request, isn't it? Unfortunately the only way to obtain a fortune is to marry one, and The Nose precludes that."

"A very good man would appreciate you, elegant nose and all," Lydia said firmly. "And I have every intention of marrying someone fabulously wealthy, so you don't need to worry about it. You will be free to marry for love."

Elinor snorted in disbelief, a very unladylike reaction. "A lovely thought, dear. But how are you going to meet this very rich man when we're living on the edge of the Paris slums? The next move will put us in the heart of them. It's going to come to that, eventually, and I'm not quite sure we'll survive."

"I have faith," Lydia said simply. "The answer will be provided when we need it." On top of everything else Lydia was a devout Christian, whereas Elinor had lost her faith years ago, when she'd met Sir Christopher Spatts, and now she accompanied Lydia to church only as a matter of form.

"I think the answer is long overdue," she grumbled. "If you could make it hurry up I'd appreciate it."

She heard the commotion coming from the back of the apartment, and Jacobs burst into the room, his hat in his hand, his weathered old face creased with worry, Nanny Maude close behind him.

"She's gone, miss," he announced.

There was never any question who he was talking about. "What do you mean, gone?" Elinor said, jumping up. "Is she dead?"

"No, Miss Elinor," Nanny said, her voice thick with worry. "Your mother managed to find the last of the money I'd had for food, and she put on her fancy dress and left."

"Oh, dear God. How did she manage that? I thought she could barely move," Elinor said, chilled. "We can find her, can't we? She can't have gotten far."

"I almost caught her, miss," Jacobs said miserably, crushing his hat with his big, strong hands. "I thought I recognized her running down the streets, but she got in a coach before I could catch her."

"A coach? Are you sure it was my mother? I didn't realize she still knew anyone with a coach."

"It was her," Jacobs said grimly. "And I recognized the coach. Even in the streetlights I could see the crest."

"Oh, Lord," Elinor moaned. "What new disaster has she gotten us into? Whose was it?"

"St. Philippe."

"Bloody hell," Elinor said. "Don't look at me like that, Nanny Maude. I know you raised me better, but if any occasion deserved a curse then this one does. You know who St. Philippe's friend is, don't you, Jacobs?"

"I don't," Lydia piped up, her blue eyes shining with curiosity.

"You don't need to know," Elinor snapped.

"It's that devil, isn't it?" Nanny said, her voice grim. "She's gone and taken herself off to the devil's lair, where there's orgies and such, and she'll lose the tiny bit of money we have left and probably end up sacrificed to the dark one."

"I don't think they do sacrifices, Nanny," Elinor said in her most practical voice, trying to ignore her own racing heart.

"They do," Nanny said, nodding her head so vigorously her lace cap slipped off her silver hair. "Women go in there and are never seen again. They kill virgins and drink their blood."

"Well, if it's virgins they kill then I think our mother's safe," Elinor drawled, determined to take the terrified look off her sister's face. "And I doubt anyone will be so besotted with her that she'll disappear. She'll gamble away the money and then come crawling home, sick and helpless."

"You don't understand, miss," said Nanny. "It's the only money we have left. And she took the diamond brooch."

A cold chill ran down the center of Elinor's body. It was the last thing of value they owned, a poor piece with tiny, flawed diamonds that was worth very little, but she'd kept it hidden for an emergency that didn't involve their deliberately self-destructive mother. She straightened her shoulders. "Then I'll simply have to go after her."

She ignored Nanny's howl of protest. Jacobs said nothing—he knew there was no other choice. Lydia rose. "I'm going with you, Nell."

"You certainly are not. If I walk into that den of iniquity I know I'm safe. They'd be on you like a pack of ravening wolves."

"I think you overestimate my irresistibility," Lydia said with a grin.

"And I think you underestimate it. Nanny said they drink the blood of virgins, remember?" she said with just enough lightness to allay her sister's fears.

Unfortunately Lydia could see right through her. "You're a virgin too, darling, unless you've been keeping something from me. They'll drink your blood too."

Elinor didn't even flinch. "They won't be drinking anyone's blood. They thrive on scandal and secrecy, but I suspect they're not nearly as dangerous as they pretend to be," she said in a matter-of-fact voice.

"They murder babies," Nanny contributed helpfully.

"Hush," Elinor said. "I'm hardly a baby. Jacobs will take me to the house of the Comte de Giverney and we will extract our mother and be back before midnight."

"Begging your pardon, miss, but they were heading out of town," Jacobs said. "I think they've gone to his château."

Elinor remained calm. "And how far away is that?"

"Not far, miss. An hour out of town if we hurry."

"Then we'll be back by dawn," she said. "Safe and sound, and this time we'll tie mother to the bed when we can't watch her."

"And how do you intend to get there?" Lydia said. "Last I heard we had no coach, nor horses, nor money to rent them. Are you intending to walk?"

Elinor shared a knowing glance with Jacobs, who backed out of the room without another word. "Jacobs will handle it," she said smoothly. "In the meantime I'm counting on you to make certain Mother's room is clean and ready for her. We'll probably have to use the restraints we had from the time she was raving. It will depend on how much gin she's drunk and if she's been fed anything else dangerous."

"I don't want you going there alone."

"I'll go with her," Nanny said, bless her elderly heart. She was so crippled with the rheumatics that she could hardly walk, but she'd fight a dragoon of soldiers for her babies.

"No, Nanny," she said gently. "I need you to look after Lydia." She met Nanny's gaze for a moment, and a world of understanding passed between them. If by any bizarre chance Elinor didn't come back Lydia would need someone, and Nanny was their only choice.

Nanny nodded her head, and Elinor could see tears shining in her eyes. "Don't be ridiculous, you two. I'm not walking into the gates of hell. The Comte de Giverney is just a man who throws decadent parties, not Satan himself, and I'm hardly the type of female to inflame his darker passions. Besides, Jacobs carries a pistol, and he'd shoot the first man who tried to harm me. I'll go in, ask for my mother, and they'll probably be happy enough to get rid of her. So there's nothing to worry about."

"Except the diamond brooch," Nanny said grimly.

If Elinor had been closer she would have kicked one of Nanny's painful shins. The old lady had a very gloomy outlook on life, and right then Lydia needed to be hopeful. She didn't need to learn their last hope of rescue had vanished, and if the jewelry was lost they were well and truly doomed.

But right then she couldn't afford to waste any more time. Apart from the orgiastic goings-on at the Comte de Giverney's notorious house parties there was high-stakes gaming. The brooch would be gone in a matter of moments, and if anyone were fool enough to extend her mother credit they'd have to start hiding from a better class of creditors, the aristocracy as well as the greengrocers.

She grabbed her threadbare cloak and the rough shawl she wore over it for added warmth, kissed Lydia and Nanny Maude goodbye, trying to appear insouciant and brave. Nanny clung to her like it was a final goodbye, but Lydia simply sat back in her chair and calmly took up her knitting again. It was an act—she knew just how dangerous Elinor's task was, and she knew the best thing she could give her sister was not having to worry about her. The sight of her brave, bowed head of blond curls made Elinor want to cry.

But she didn't have time for crying. Moments later she was out in the cold night air; her fingerless gloves, which were more darning than original weave, were pulled on, the shawl over her ordinary brown hair, and she started down the street, determined to ignore the more unsavory denizens of the neighborhood.

Jacobs would be at the nearby café, where horses and carriages were stabled. Circumstances had forced them to "borrow" a carriage once before, when Lady Caroline had proved herself unwelcome at a masked ball, though they'd fortunately been able to replace it in time with no one the wiser. Tonight they might not be near as lucky, but she couldn't afford to think of that. For now all she could concentrate on was getting her mother safely out of the devil's lair. One thing at a time.

Jacobs did better than she'd expected, appearing with a small traveling chaise large enough to hold two females and not much more. She scrambled inside before Jacobs could get down to assist her, and a moment later they were off.

It was a cold, moonless night in early February, and if the modest carriage had ever held lap robes they were long gone. She pulled her shawl from her head and wrapped it around her shoulders, shivering. It would take an hour to reach the comte's château, if she didn't freeze to death before she got there.

Still, if she was half-frozen it could only help matters. It would give her something less daunting to concentrate on. She held on to the seat as it swayed back and forth. Jacobs was driving at a dangerous pace, but she had complete faith in his abilities. They would arrive at the château in one piece; the rest was up to her.

She had no qualms. She knew exactly what she looked like. She was tall, a bit too thin thanks to the state of their larder, with plain brown hair and eyes, and that unfortunate nose. It wasn't that bad, she mused, it was narrow and elegant, and when she was an old lady she would look quite striking. Still, that didn't help when she was young and wanting to be pretty.

But she was past all that. If she ran into the wretched comte he'd take one look at her dowdy clothes and hair and never even see her. Thankfully that was the way with most men. She had no doubt she could find her mother in no time at all, spirit her away and the strange goings-on at the château would be a distant memory.

If she still believed in God she would pray, but she'd lost that particular comfort six years ago. Besides, Nanny and Lydia would be praying for them like mad—if there really was a god he'd certainly listen to the two of them. Lydia was too charming to ignore, and Nanny too fierce. Perhaps it was only Elinor he paid no attention to.

She closed her eyes. The day had been disastrous from beginning to end, with the unlikely hope of a small inheritance being a mere pinprick compared to the far greater disaster of their future prospects having vanished with the succession. For now she'd hold that knowledge to herself. Nanny Maude and Lydia didn't need the worry.

The lawyer, Mr. Mitchum, had suggested she meet with the new heir, the stranger who'd have control over her inheritance, but she'd left the office in a fit of temper.

She'd have to meet with her distant cousin eventually, and she'd been a fool to storm off. If there was, in fact, even the most pitiful of bequests she couldn't be proud enough to refuse it.

But first she had to find her mother.

2

Francis Alistair St. Claire Dominic Charles Edward Rohan, Comte de Giverney, Viscount Rohan, Baron of Glencoe, leaned back, letting his long pale fingers gently stroke the carved wooden claws that decorated the massive chair he sat in. He let his head rest against the velvet cushioning, surveyed his eager guests and allowed himself a faint smile. The vast supply of tapers lit even the dark corners of the salon, and he could see them all, his so-called friends and acquaintances, practically quivering in anticipation of the revels that stretched in front of them. Three days and nights of the most libertine indulgences—gaming and coupling with anyone agreeable, whore or lordling, male or female. Mock satanic rituals to make participants feel truly wicked, calling on a dark force that no more existed than did a loving god, but babbling Latin in front of an inverted cross gave them even more license to indulge themselves. There was opium and brandy and wine and even good Scots whiskey, and by the time the party was done he expected every drop to be gone, every body to be well pleasured, every soul drained of any illusion of morality.

And he would watch it all, indulging when the urge struck him, overseeing it all with veiled interest. He always wondered how far people would go in pursuit of pleasure. He knew his own appetites were extraordinary, and there were times when he needed more than his own pleasure to satisfy him. He needed the wicked delight of others, and his willing acolytes provided it.

There were women and men awaiting his word, some dressed in clerical garb, some wearing little at all. He could recognize Lady Adelia dressed in a diaphanous chemise better suited to a dancer half her weight, and her husband would be somewhere among the gentlemen dressed in feminine splendor, their carmined lips pursed in anticipation.

He let his gaze drift over them, his disciples in the art of sin, and he sat up, tossing back his long, unpowdered hair.

"My children," he said in the French they all understood, English and French and German émigrés who'd come seeking pleasure. "Welcome to the revels of the Heavenly Host. You will partake of each other as you would partake of the holy wafer, you will drink the wine as if it were the blessed blood, and you will take your fill, with no one to judge. For the next three nights the paltry rules of society are forfeit. Our motto stands… 'Do what thou wilt.'"

"Do what thou wilt," they intoned with deep seriousness, like novices taking their final vows, and he let a faint smile dance around the mouth they all craved. They were so determined in their pursuit of wickedness that it made him laugh.

He waved his hand, the layers of Mechlin lace floating. "Then go and sin once more," he said, his deep, rich voice echoing in the huge salon.

There was a cheer, and the great doors to the rest of the château were opened. The revels began, and Francis Rohan leaned back in his chair, wishing he were back in Paris with a glass of brandy and a good book and no eager sinners seeking his attention.

He was bored. He'd witnessed almost every depravation known to man, participated in a great many of them, and he'd yet to find anything to pierce his interminable ennui. True, he could still find physical pleasure, but it was no more than a brief respite. When he so desired, he would wander through the rooms of the château and observe acts prohibited by church and state, he would watch fortunes being won and lost at the turn of a card. He would watch men give in to the most base instincts with no fear of repercussion, and in the end, he would return to his opulent chair and he would try to summon up some interest.

One woman had separated herself from the hearty revelers, and she glided toward him, a demimasque on her face, her lush body spilling out of the artful gown she wore. It laced in front, and beneath the loosely tied strings he suspected there was nothing but ripe flesh. He would enjoy loosening those strings— Marianne had quite the most spectacular breasts he had ever seen. And she knew the rules. He wasn't fond of kissing, and she would seldom make the mistake of putting her lips anywhere near his face. She would instead use that magnificent mouth elsewhere, and it would while away an hour or so, while the more timid of his guests watched.

He signaled with his hand, and she approached, a sly smile on her lips. Lips devoid of rouge—she knew what he preferred from her. She came up the small dais his idiot followers had built him, and he noted with approval that the lacing went down to the hem, and indeed she was wearing nothing at all underneath.

He pulled her onto his lap, gently, and began playing with the laces, loosening them until her milky-white breasts spilled out into the cool night air. Her nipples beaded with the chill, and he had the sudden urge to suckle her.

"Lean back," he said in his bored voice, and she immediately did so, arching over the arm of the chair, presenting herself to him, and he moved his head down to let his tongue graze the pebbled mound, when a sudden noise caught his attention, and he sat up, annoyed, drawing Marianne with him.

"You've got trouble, Francis," Charles Reading said in his rough, lazy voice. "And it's early times for you to be sampling the banquet."

Marianne turned and smiled at him, cheerier than Rohan felt at that particular moment.

"What kind of trouble?" he said. "I'm not in the mood to be seconding duels or even stopping them. If they want to kill each other then let them go ahead. I have servants to clean up the blood."

"Not that kind of trouble. I think you'll like this one. I myself find it rather irresistible."

It was enough to get his attention. There was very little Charles Reading found entertaining, and whatever did had to be unusual, and therefore possibly of interest. "Then don't keep me waiting. Bring forth the trouble."

"One of your footmen has her. Willis was going to send her on her way when I intervened, knowing you'd be entertained. Shall I tell him to bring her in?"

"I should go," Marianne said, attempting to pull her gown together over her breasts. He was having none of it.

"You should stay," he said in the cool voice. He turned to Charles. "A her, is it? An interesting 'her'? I find that hard to believe. But by all means bring her in. If nothing else, we can toss her to the gentlemen and ladies in the green room."

Reading was a handsome man, if you could discount the scar that had been slashed down the right side of face, turning his smile into a twisted grimace. He made a sketchy bow. "I am yours to command, my lord." He backed away in a parody of servile humility, and Francis watched as he called out to a servant.

Charles Reading was one of his most amusing companions. Charles had as little regard for propriety as he did, but he viewed things with the fierce passion of youth, making Francis feel every one of his thirty-nine years. In truth, he felt eighty.

He could feel Marianne squirm, trying to reach for her gown, but it was a simple matter to capture her hand in a viselike grip. He remembered she liked pain, and he deliberately kept his grip gentle but unbreakable. If he was going to enjoy her later in the evening, as he expected he would, he didn't want her becoming too excited too early. She would go spend that energy on someone else, and he did rather like to be first.

One of the footmen appeared, with Willis, his servant from a lifetime ago, on the other side of what was undoubtedly female and undoubtedly not one of the prostitutes imported from the city. This *was* going to be entertaining. He leaned back in his chair and gestured them closer, waiting as they approached, waiting as Reading stood in the background watching him.

"What have we got here, Willis?" he asked in his mildest voice. It was too much to hope for anything truly entertaining, but it might provide a few moments distraction.

She lifted her head, the dowdy creature, and he found himself looking into warm brown eyes filled with such loathing that for a moment he was charmed. Few people ever showed their dislike of him.

"And who is she?" he inquired lazily. "Don't tell me—someone thought dressing a whore as a ragpicker would provide added entertainment. Or no…I think perhaps she's supposed to be a young lady fallen on hard times. Or perhaps a shopgirl. Though I fail to see how a shopgirl could add to our entertainment. Tilt her head up a bit."

The footman moved to do his bidding and the wench snapped at him like a wild bitch. The man made the very grave mistake of hitting her across the mouth, and when she lifted her head there was blood on her lip. "No," Francis said calmly. "I don't think she's a whore, Willis. Not with a nose like that. Whores have pretty little snub noses—this young lady has a nose of consequence. Perhaps you should simply send her on her way."

She glared at him, the frowsy little creature. Though in fact she wasn't particularly little—she was taller than most women of his acquaintance. She tried to speak, but Willis pushed ahead of her. "She says she's looking for her mother, my lord."

Francis threw back his head and laughed. "She's the daughter of a whore? What will we come to next?"

"My mother's not a whore," she had the temerity to say, and his interest grew. She had a good voice, solid, low pitched, and undoubtedly from the upper classes of England. He'd been exiled from that land twenty-two years ago, but he'd entertained enough titled visitors to know the difference. It was the same voice he spoke in, when he cared to speak English.

"Then she's not here," he said. "The only women here are whores. Even lovely Marianne here. Granted, she's a titled whore, but a whore she most definitely is." He waited, hoping that Marianne might pull away, but she sat still in his lap, her breasts in full view of the interloper.

The girl—no, the woman—looked at him. She was past her girlhood, perhaps somewhere in her twenties, and her lip still bled.

"Release her, Willis," he said lazily. "And take the

footman in hand. I'm afraid he's going to have to be taught a very harsh lesson. No one is struck in this household unless they find it arousing. I can tell that Miss Lumpkin is not aroused."

He could hear the footman's alarmed intake of breath, and the fool tried to apologize, tried to explain as Willis hustled him out of the room, another sturdy footman appearing and helping with the disposal of the rubbish. Rohan released Marianne's wrist, and she carelessly pulled her provocative gown together, hiding her treasures. "You may leave us, Marianne," he murmured. "I find I have better things to do tonight."

He paid absolutely no attention as she scrambled away from him. She'd be very angry with him, which might make things more exciting if he decided to avail himself of her later on. At that moment he was doubting it.

The child in the middle of the room was glaring at him, for child she was, no matter what her advanced years. She was a virgin, untouched, unkissed, innocent and angry, and he was prepared to enjoy himself immensely. "So tell me, little one. What really brought you here?"

She clearly wanted to tell him to go to hell, but young ladies didn't do that. She brought her fury in hand with a visible effort, yanked her pathetic cloak more tightly around her and squared her shoulders, obviously determined to be calm. "I'm looking for my mother," she said again. "I realize you have trouble understanding plain English. Perhaps your dissipations have begun to affect your mind, in which case you have all my sympathies, but it's my mother I'm concerned about. I believe she arrived here with Monsieur St. Philippe, and it really is imperative I get her home as quickly as possible. She's not well."

"St. Philippe?" he said. "I believe he had a female companion, but I paid little attention. Clearly you're of an advanced age, which leads me to believe your mother must therefore be old enough to make her own decisions on such matters." He snapped his fingers and a servant immediately materialized from the shadows. "Bring mademoiselle a chair. She looks weary."

"No!" she said. "I have no interest in conversing with you, Monsieur le Comte. I simply need my mother."

"And I need to prove myself a proper host," he returned.

"You've managed to overcome your more proper urges so far," she said pointedly. "Why change now?"

There was enough of a barb in her voice that he was amused. He rose, setting his glass of wine down. "A good point, mademoiselle...?"

"You don't need my name."

"If I don't have it how am I to produce your mother?" His voice was eminently reasonable as he started down the short steps from the dais. She didn't move—he had to grant her that. She was courageous enough to walk into the lion's den and not shrink from his approach.

She hesitated. "Harriman," she said finally. "My name is Elinor Harriman. My mother is Lady Caroline Harriman."

He froze. "Holy Christ. That poxy old bitch is here?

Don't worry, my precious. We shall find her immediately. I have no intention of allowing her to stay
among my guests. I am astonished St. Philippe had the
temerity to bring her with him. Unless it was simply
to gain my attention."

"Why would he do that?" the young girl asked, bewildered. He usually found innocence to be tedious.
Mademoiselle Elinor Harriman's innocence was
oddly appealing.

"Because he has a tendre for me, and I've shown
no interest."

"He has a tendre for you? He's a man."

"He is indeed," he said gently. "And how have
you lived in Paris for so long without knowing about
such things?"

"How do you know how long I've lived in Paris?"
she retorted.

"Lady Caroline Harriman left her doltish husband
and came to Paris with her two daughters some ten
years ago, and she's been in steady decline ever since.
I'm surprised she's still alive."

"Just barely," the girl said grimly. "Could I please
go look for her instead of standing here talking to
you? She's probably gaming, and I'd like to stop her
before the last of our household money is gone."

"A laudable notion, child. I'd like to stop her before
she spreads the plague amongst my guests. I'm quite
adamant about the health of the whores…"

"My mother is not a whore!"

There was a charming flush to her pale cheeks.
She was too thin—she hadn't been fed properly in the

last few months, and he allowed himself the briefest fantasy of feeding her tidbits of meat and pastries while she lay naked across his bed.

His mocking smile was half meant for his own foolishness. Virgins were far too tedious, and even the fiery Mademoiselle Harriman would be more trouble than she was worth.

"Any woman in this house is a whore, my child. So, for that matter, are the men. Let me get you a glass of wine and we can discuss this."

"You *are* as addled as my mother," she snapped, spinning on her heel. "I'm going to look for her."

He wasn't in the habit of letting any woman turn her back on him, and he simply took her arm, ungently, and spun her around to face him, fury on her face and a nasty little pistol in her hand, pointed in the general direction of his stomach.

She would shoot him, without a qualm, Elinor told herself, willing her hand not to shake. If he saw her quaking he would assume she was harmless, and then she might be forced to actually fire the wretched gun. Which she most assuredly did not want to do, unless she had to.

He released her, encouraging her hope that he was a reasonable man, but he didn't take a step back, and he seemed more amused than alarmed.

The King of Hell was everything they said he was, both less and more. He was reputed to have the ability to seduce an abbess or the pope himself, and she could see why. It wasn't his physical beauty, which was considerable. He had dark blue eyes behind a fringe of ridiculously long lashes, pale, beautiful skin, the kind of mouth that could bring despair and delight—and what the hell was she doing, thinking about such things?

He looked younger than his reputed age, around forty, and while his long dark hair was streaked with silver it only made him seem more leonine, more dangerous. He was tall, and he moved with an elegant grace that put dancers to shame. He was standing far too close to her, to the gun she'd stolen from Jacobs while he was busy with the carriage, and he was looking at her with far too much interest and absolutely no fear.

"You aren't going to shoot me, my dear," he said calmly, making no effort to take the gun from her shaking hand. And it was shaking—she couldn't disguise it.

"I don't wish to. But my mother's safety is paramount…"

"Your mother is a walking dead woman," he said, his voice casual and cruel. "You know it as well as I. Why don't you return home and I'll find her and send her after you?"

"You don't understand. I can't afford to let her game away the rest of our money," she repeated. It shamed her to admit how little they had, but then, most of his guests would be capable of losing a fortune on the turn of a card. There was no need for him to guess just how little they had left.

"Then we shall see that she doesn't," he said in that

caressing voice of his. It was little wonder people fell at his feet—his voice could charm angels. "You know you don't want to shoot me. Think of the mess. Not to mention the explanations." He reached out and gently took the pistol away from her. "Very pretty," he said, glancing at the elegant pearl-handled thing. "If you're so hard up for money you could always sell this."

"Who says we're *hard up* for money?" she demanded.

"Your clothes, child. You dress like a ragpicker. What's your mother wearing—sackcloth and ashes?"

"She'd hardly be allowed in here if she was."

"Oh, on the contrary. Sackcloth and ashes could be deemed quite appropriate. After all, this is a gathering of the Heavenly Host, you know."

She tried not to react to the shock of him actually mentioning the forbidden words. Everyone had heard rumors of the Heavenly Host, that covert gathering of wicked aristocrats with too much time on their hands. The stories went from the ridiculous to the disconcerting—there was word of black masses and virgin sacrifice, orgies and blasphemy and the like, but no one ever admitted the existence of the group. Until Rohan's offhand comment.

She looked up at him, unnerved by his height, his glittering, gilded glory. He was dressed in impeccable black satin, with elegant clocked stockings on his well-shaped legs, high-heeled, bejeweled shoes only adding to his already impressive height. He wore a long, heavily embroidered waistcoat unbuttoned, but no coat. He had heavy rings on his long, pale fingers, even a sapphire in his ear like a Gypsy, previously hidden by his long, unbound hair. Most men wore wigs and kept their own hair cut short. The Comte de Giverney was clearly too vain to utilize such shortcuts.

"Looked your fill?" he inquired pleasantly. "Would you like me to turn around so you can observe my backside?"

She didn't blush. "I like to know my enemies. Either let me go look for my mother or take me there yourself."

"Oh, definitely the latter. And I haven't decided whether we're enemies or not." He tossed the pistol back onto the dais, where it landed, with unerring accuracy, on the cushioned chair. "I'm afraid, my dear Miss Harriman, that you would never find your mother amidst the…celebrations. You'll have to accompany me through the nine layers of hell in order to find her."

"I am not a child, Monsieur le Comte."

"That's my French title. To the English I'm the Viscount Rohan."

"Someone else bears that title," she said, repeating one of the bits of gossip she'd overheard.

"Indeed," he said pleasantly. "How kind of you to remind me. The man is a pretender, nothing more." He reached up for his elegant neck cloth and began to unfasten it, and she watched his long, pale, bejeweled fingers in something of a daze.

He pulled the cloth free, his shirt coming open, and she averted her gaze from the disturbing sight of his bare chest. She heard his laugh, and then his hands were on her once more, catching her shoulders and turning her around. "Don't worry, my pet. You won't be seeing anything that might shock you." And he pulled the neck cloth over her eyes, effectively blinding her.

She wanted to fight back, to struggle, but that would give him an excuse to touch her further, and the less she felt the brush of his cool fingers the better. "That's right," he said, his voice soft and approving. "Now give me your arm and we'll give you a taste of damnation."

"Do you really find blasphemy that entertaining?" she said, trying not to start when he took her hand and placed it on his arm.

"Always."

She'd never put her hand on any arm that wasn't covered by layers of clothing, including a coat. The devil who oversaw these revels, be he Monsieur le Comte or something else, wore only a thin shirt made of the finest lawn. In her sudden world of darkness she was acutely aware of the feel of his arm beneath her fingers. The sinew and bone. The unexpected warmth of his skin, when his hands and his heart were so cold.

"Are you ready, my child?" he asked, and there was no avoiding the humor in his voice.

But she wasn't about to show her panic. People like Rohan thrived on fear, and if she were to have any chance of survival she needed to hide hers.

"As I have been for the last, tedious half hour," she said in a bored voice.

"*Allons-y,*" he murmured, and she didn't need

to see anything to know that he wasn't fooled. "Let us go."

And she had no choice but to allow him to draw her deeper into the very depths of hell.

3

The heat and noise and smell assaulted her when he led her through the doors. A dozen different perfumes, wax tallows, spilled wine and wood smoke, cooked meats and human sweat all fought for supremacy, and the voices were loud, giddy. One man's voice broke through the babble.

"What is that on your arm, Francis? Your dinner?" He followed his ridiculous inquiry with rough laughter.

"Don't be absurd," a woman's voice floated to her ears. A Frenchwoman, of indisputably high upbringing, given the quality of her voice. "He's going to auction her off later on. May I put my bid in early? She really looks quite delicious."

Elinor couldn't keep from starting at the words, and her fingers tightened on his arm reflexively. He put his hand over hers, but whether it was meant to comfort her or imprison her, she couldn't be sure.

"Don't be ridiculous, Elise," another man, much closer by the sound of him, broke through. "He's not giving her up. See the way he looks at her."

Elinor hadn't noticed anything in the way Rohan had looked at her, but the very notion made her even more unsettled. He kept her moving through the shuttered darkness, their procession marred by continuing licentious catcalls, and by the time they passed into another room she was grateful. This one darker still, no light filtering through the white neck cloth that blinded her.

"What about my mother?" she whispered. "You didn't ask…"

"I could see quite clearly that she wasn't there, my child. That was only the second circle of hell, though I must admit we don't adhere to Dante's definitions too closely."

"What was the first circle of hell?" she asked.

"The anteroom, my love. Where we met. Better known as Limbo, where no real sin takes place." His voice was low, contemplative, and out of the blue she felt his cool hand gently stroke the side of her face, making her jump nervously. "My footman broke the rules, of course, and he'll be punished appropriately."

They'd paused at what she assumed was the entrance of the room. "Will he be punished because he broke the rules or because he hit me?" she asked. "You can tell me the truth—I won't be offended."

His laugh was so soft she might not have heard it if she weren't blindfolded. "And I do *so* desire to keep from offending you, mademoiselle. In fact, he'll be driven off the place because he broke the rules. He'll be beaten beforehand because he raised his hand to you. I'll make arrangements for you to watch if you care to."

"That's horrifying! And no, I don't want to sit and watch."

"You're very different from most of the women here, including your mother. They'd watch and probably lick the blood from his skin when I'm done."

"Oh, that's foul!" she whispered. And then the rest of his words sank in. "When *you're* done? You're going to administer the beating?"

She knew he smiled, even without seeing it. She knew his mouth already, the way it curved with just a touch of mockery. "Perhaps I need my exercise," he murmured. "I doubt your mother is in this room, but I wouldn't want to miss her due to a misguided sense of propriety." He raised his voice. "Is the Lady Caroline Harriman here?"

No answer, just the strange, muffled sounds that she couldn't quite identify. The rub of silk on silk, the whispered laugh, low and intimate, the curious mix of grunts and curses, and her curiosity got the better of her as she reached for the neck cloth.

His hands were ahead of hers, stopping her. "You really don't want to look," he said, and she believed him. They must have reached the level of lust, and clearly Francis Rohan's guests had leeway to enjoy that particular sin.

"She's not here," Elinor said. In the last year, her mother had lost all her previous obsession with fornication, replacing that desire with a need to gamble. In truth, very few people would recognize the great beauty she had once been, and very few people would have been willing to risk their health for the sake of a cheap tup. In the darkness of these rooms they might not recognize her diseased skin and addled mind, but clearly there were better choices if they chose to take them. Her mother would be gaming, not...

She knew the word for it, the rough, rude, indelicate word for it. *Fucking.* Her father had used it, her mother had screamed it in her endless rages, the people on the street used it, and the lower they sank the more that despicable word abounded.

Indeed, it was probably as good a word as any for her mother. It had been lust that had driven her away from her husband, lust and greed and anger. It had been lust that had changed Elinor's life forever, a strange, dark feeling that she couldn't comprehend. Didn't want to. There was an ugliness to it that spread through this room and indeed the entire château, and the longer she stayed the more unclean she felt as old memories fought to crowd their way back into her brain.

"Could we move on?" she said coolly.

In answer he propelled her forward. It was a strange sensation, moving across the floors in darkness, the man beside her closer than a man had been in many years. And not just any man—the King of Hell himself, or so he was called. In fact, she couldn't really fault him. He'd done her no harm, and seemed intent on helping her. Which was unlike anything she'd heard about him. The Comte de Giverney, the Viscount Rohan, the leader of the Heavenly Host, did nothing that didn't include self-interest. And despite his polite behavior so far, her undeniable nervousness moved up a notch.

She heard the sound of doors being opened, though the man beside her hadn't moved. Servants, stationed throughout this orgiastic celebration—of course there would be. Not one of these pampered creatures had ever had to fend for themselves. They didn't worry about finding enough money to eat, about protecting their beautiful younger sister, about keeping their mother from destroying what small safety they had left.

"You're rumpling my shirt," he whispered in her ear. "Relax your grip. I promise I won't let anything harm you."

If she were the emotional sort she would have wept at the words. She would have sold her soul to have someone simply take over the constant worry that beset her, but then she remembered where she was. Who accompanied her. Selling one's soul was de rigueur in such circumstances.

"I'm in a hurry," she said, trying to sound calm and practical.

"Why?"

"We need to get the carriage back…" The moment the words were out of her mouth she regretted them. He wasn't a man who missed anything.

"That brings up an interesting point. You hardly seem wealthy enough to keep a carriage in Paris. In fact, I doubt you were able to hire a carriage. What did you do, steal one?"

"Hardly," she said with a shaky laugh. "I'm charmed that you think I'm that resourceful, but I could hardly have gone to the nearest hostelry, pretended I was the coachman and taken off with one."

"I am astounded at your resourcefulness, Mademoiselle Harriman. But no, you must have had help." He suddenly released her arm. "Stay here for a moment and don't move."

She had to keep herself from reaching for him. From crying out, "Don't leave me." It took all her self-control to simply nod, not even knowing if he saw it.

It was a strange and dizzying sensation, standing alone and blindfolded in the crowded room. No one seemed to be paying her any mind in this one, and she knew from the noise that his guests must be caught up in gaming. This was the place her mother was likely to be, and she reached for her blindfold, pushing it off her eyes.

And froze. Some were gaming. A few were even partially dressed, and in her brief glance she saw them writhing on couches and in chairs, performing acts that should have been foreign to her.

But she'd lived too long in poverty, and she'd seen those same acts and more performed in side alleys, for pay. She should have been shocked. But in truth, she was more concerned that it might be her mother's mouth on the young gentleman's—

The blindfold was pulled abruptly back over her eyes, shutting out the disturbing sights. "You're a very disobedient creature, aren't you?"

She dismissed the shocking image, simply because she must. "I'm here, am I not? If I were obedient I would be waiting at home for my mother's safe return. Which, times have taught me, is unlikely."

Rohan didn't reply to that. "I've sent your coachman back with his pilfered coach. With luck it will be returned to the Bois d'Or before anyone knows it's missing. I presume he ventured into such a seedy part of the city in order to increase his chances at getting away with it, but he really should have stolen one closer to home. The neighborhood of Rue du Pélican is no place for a young lady, and any coach found there would have been exceedingly uncomfortable."

She was getting tired of this. "Where do you think we live, my lord? Jacobs had only to walk a short way to steal from that particular inn. We live on the edge of ruin. Our lives are disastrous enough without your mockery reinforcing the misery." There was something liberating about finally saying it out loud. She was tired of pretending that things were better than they were. That they didn't spend their days and nights cold and hungry and afraid of what might happen next. "And how do you suggest I get home, once I find my mother?"

"I'll arrange a carriage for her. In the meantime I've found St. Philippe, and he should provide us with the information we need."

"A carriage for *her...?*" Elinor echoed, but he'd already moved on, steering her through the noisy room. At least in this one the inhabitants were too busy with their licentious behavior to bother with catcalls.

"How many circles of hell are there?" she demanded, breathless, as the next set of doors opened.

"Nine, child. Haven't you done your reading? I'm beginning to wonder whether this isn't all a ruse. Whether you've come here on your own, on a trumped-up excuse."

"Why in heaven would I do that?" she said, mystified.

"To ensnare a husband, perhaps? Or at least money. You're not pretty enough to be a whore, but perhaps you heard that the members of the Heavenly Host prize innocence before beauty."

It shouldn't have hurt. She'd never had any delusions about her beauty. She was the plain one—too tall, her hair too brown and straight, her nose too aquiline, her nature too outspoken. She was made for spinsterhood, and she'd accepted it long ago. But hearing her attributes dismissed so lightly in Francis Rohan's pitiless voice was a cruelty she'd not expected.

"Do you get pleasure from inflicting pain, my lord?" Her voice was calm and practical, denying the hurt.

There was a moment's silence. "Occasionally," he said after a long moment. "There are times when hurting and being hurt are the only way to feel anything at all."

"Pray, excuse me from my part in that game then. I'm certain you'll find any number of people here who would enjoy being hurt by you," she said.

"Did I hurt you? You seem so very calm and practical."

"You simply spoke the truth. It was, perhaps, unnecessary, but I would be a fool to let my feelings be hurt by something so insignificant." There, she thought. That should convince him.

Or perhaps not. "You're an interesting child, Miss Harriman."

"I'm not a child. I'm twenty-three."

"Such a great age," he said, mocking. "From my viewpoint you are very young indeed." He started forward, and she wanted to pull back, but he was too strong, drawing her into the next room.

This one was overheated. The sounds were muffled and still—the sound of cards being dealt, the roll of dice. They'd found the room for serious gaming, at last.

She reached up for the neck cloth again, but this time he stopped her, wrapping his hand around her wrists and imprisoning them. "St. Philippe," he said, his voice barely raised. And suddenly the overheated room felt cold and still.

"Monseigneur?" Came the answer, the voice slurred, drunken.

"I've been informed you've brought an unwanted guest into our midst. Where is she?"

"I don't know what you—"

"Where is she?" He didn't raise his voice, but the room grew colder still, and for a brief moment Elinor wondered how Rohan's control of his followers was so absolute.

"Gone," St. Philippe said, his voice sulky. "She had barely enough money to game, and once that was gone no one was willing to advance her credit. I expect she's out in the stables, trying to earn enough on her back."

Elinor couldn't help her instinctive flinch, both at the thought of her mother and at the loss of their only money. It was a disaster, total and complete, and she tried to yank her hands out of Rohan's grip. He tightened his hand, and it hurt enough to make her stop struggling.

"You've displeased me, Justin," he said calmly. "May I suggest you get dressed and come see me in the anteroom? In a few minutes, shall we say?"

"Of course, monseigneur," he stammered, sounding terrified.

Rohan released her wrists, snaking an arm around her waist, his grip unbreakable. "Then I will take my prize back with me," he said, his voice more pleasant. "The rest of you may continue."

"I don't…" Elinor began, but he moved her so swiftly her words died away. She expected him to move her back through the series of rooms he'd brought her, but a moment later they were in the pitch darkness, someplace enclosed and silent, and he pulled the neck cloth off her face.

They were in a hallway, lit only by torches, and he no longer touched her. She found that for the first time she could breathe normally. "The problem is solved," he said. "Your mother is here after all. It won't take long to locate her—my servants are very good. I'll take you somewhere to await her."

She looked at him doubtfully. "I could accompany your servants…"

"No, you could not. You heard St. Philippe. There's no telling what kind of condition she's in. I only hope she hasn't infected half the servants—it's hard to get a decent coachman."

Elinor drew in her breath swiftly. "Don't be absurd!"

"Your mother has the French disease, child. Or as we call it over here, the Spanish disease." He shrugged. "Perhaps even the English disease. She's going to die raving, and I suspect you know that as well as I do. If you want, I can do you a favor and have her tossed off the nearest cliff."

"Joking about such matters is in very poor taste," she said stiffly.

"Why in the world would you assume I'm joking?"

She could barely see his face in the dimly lit corridor. In such an enclosed space he seemed even larger, and she was uncomfortably aware of the fact that his white linen shirt was open. He wasn't joking about anything, she realized.

"I made the mistake of assuming you were a responsible human being," she said stiffly.

"Oh, heavens, a very grave mistake indeed. I'll take you somewhere to wait. You'll be pleased to know I have a very English housekeeper who'll see to your comfort." He held out his arm for her to take, and she didn't move. She didn't want to touch him again. The fine linen weave of his shirt was too thin, she could feel his arm too clearly, feeling the strength of him, the corded muscles, the heat. It distracted her—she wasn't used to touching men at all, and certainly not with such intimacy.

"If you don't take my arm you might trip and break your leg and then what good would you be to your poor mother?" he said in a bored voice. "This corridor is a back way to the private wing of the château and seldom used. There may even be rats."

She grabbed his arm immediately, taking heart in the fact that she hadn't climbed on top of him. She had a horror of rats, which was unfortunate given her family's living conditions. "Let's go," she said hurriedly, trying to control her shudder.

"I take it you don't like rats," he said, drawing her down the hallway.

She kept imagining them running up her skirts, and with her other hand she held them tight around her legs. "I don't care for them, but then, who does?" she said in her most reasonable voice.

"Oh, I think it's a little more than that. Rats are a fact of life, and yet you…"

"Could we please discuss something else?" She'd given up trying to hide her distaste. "Anything else?" The muffled sound of groans leeched through the walls, and they moved on before she could make the mistake of asking what those noises were. If anyone was in pain. Because a moment later she realized what those moaning, grunting sounds were. Remembered.

Her companion seemed oblivious to it all. "We can discuss your plans for the future. What do you plan to do after your mother dies raving?"

Not much of an improvement over rats, but she'd take it. "I don't even know what I'm going to do for the next week," she said, perhaps unwisely, but she'd used up almost her last ounce of courage.

There was a moment of bright light as a door opened into the hallway, and then they were plunged into darkness again. The smell of perfume and heated skin was overwhelming, and she looked at the two who'd managed to breach the viscount's private hallway.

"I thought you'd be here, Francis," the gentleman said, looking at her out of hooded eyes. He was the one she'd first met, with the handsome, scarred face. "Veronique thought you might be interested in a trade and promised her I'd find you."

"A trade for what?" Rohan said lazily.

"The little dressmaker," the woman said in a husky voice. "You know as well as I do, Francis, that she's the most delicious thing to appear at one of our parties in a long time, and you can't just expect us all to ignore her. It's hardly reasonable."

"Veronique, have I ever struck you as a reasonable man?"

"I, too, am not reasonable," the woman, Veronique, said. "I can be extremely difficult when thwarted." Her voice was a soft purr.

For some reason Elinor moved closer to Rohan, her fingers clutching his arm tightly.

"And exactly what are you suggesting?" Rohan inquired.

"I've tried to distract Veronique with my humble charms," the man said with deprecating candor, "but she insists she's in the mood for a woman tonight, and she's never had a virgin. Assuming the little waif still is—she's been in your company for more than an hour, so there's no guarantee of anything."

"Very true," Rohan said. "So Veronique gets the girl and I get you? That hardly seems fair."

The scarred man cast her a wary glance. "She doesn't understand us, does she? Her French was atrocious."

"Oh, I think she understands us well enough, looking at her face. And I think we'll have to forgo the pleasure of your company." He dismissed them.

"When you're done with her then, Francis?" the woman said, looking at her avidly. "I could have a lovely time schooling a lamb who has strayed."

"I think you'll have to find another stray lamb, madame," he said, placing one hand over Elinor's. "You're already aware of the motto of the Rohans— what I have I keep. Reading can find you another innocent."

"Hard to do when you won't let us invite children," Veronique said with a pout.

"A foolish inconstancy on my part," he drawled. "But it's not up for discussion. I'm certain the two of you will find adequate distraction back in the green room."

Veronique spat a very nasty word, one that Elinor had only heard a few times and then from the worst gutter whore in Paris, and she started with shock as the door slid open again, and the woman flounced through, her straight back expressing her disapproval.

The man, Reading, paused a moment longer. "Best be careful, Francis," he said.

"I'm hardly afraid of Veronique."

"She's not the woman I think you should worry about," Reading murmured. And a moment later the door slid shut, leaving them in cocooning darkness once more.

Rohan looked down at her. "You see, my dove. There are creatures far more terrifying than rats who wander these corridors."

"You're known as the King of Hell, Monsieur le Comte," she said. "What else would I expect from your guests?"

He laughed softly, but she had the sense she'd annoyed him. "Next time you wish to call me names you might consider what I've saved you from. Veronique is not very nice to girls—she is one who takes pleasure from hurting people, where most of the whores simply fake their distress."

"I'm ever so grateful," she said with cloying sweetness.

"Of course you are, love. Unfortunately I desire that you show your gratitude before I release you. Just a small token is all that's needed."

"I beg your pardon?" she said in an icy voice.

They'd reached what appeared to be a blank wall. The rest of the corridor disappeared into darkness, and there were no embarrassing animal sounds. He moved, and suddenly she felt her body pressed up against the wall, quite firmly, his hands on her arms. And then a moment later, before she realized what he intended, he moved closer, his tall body covering hers in shadows, and all she could do was feel him, hip to hip, his chest against hers, his heart, slow and lazy against her racing one, as he filled all her senses, and she was drowning.

Endure, she reminded herself, and closed her eyes, holding very still. He moved his head down, to the spot at the base of her neck, and she felt his mouth, his teeth, just the lightest of bites against her skin, and she quivered. Endure, she reminded herself again, trying to breathe normally. He was much too strong to fight.

His body held her still, and he released her arms to

slide his hands up, the fingers stroking the pulse at her neck that was racing so wildly. "Ah, child," he murmured. "If only you'd been lying."

A second later he pulled back, no longer touching her, and she knew she should run. And run she would, as soon as her senses regained their proper order.

"I...I do not lie, monsieur." The stammer was faint, and she couldn't help it. Those few seconds in the darkness had been...overwhelming.

"Alas, you don't," he said. "I had hoped you were more like your dear mother. That you'd seized upon this opportunity to find a protector, as Lady Caroline was prone to do. But appearances, unfortunately, are not deceiving. You're an innocent, and you have no more interest in partaking of our unholy pleasures than you do in becoming a holy martyr."

"It's better than rats," she said frankly.

Silence, and in the darkness she could only see the gleam in his hard eyes. "Child," he said faintly, "you unman me. If I am ever in the position where I wish to seduce someone I will simply assure her it's better than rats."

"Why wouldn't you be in the position of seducing someone?" It was an impertinent question, but she was still oddly light-headed, here in the darkness with him.

"I don't have to make the effort. They all come to me, sooner or later," he said simply.

"How boring," she observed.

"Indeed." He reached up behind her to touch something that was out of her line of vision, and a moment later a door opened, and he guided her through.

It was like stepping into another world. The small salon was warm and cozy—a fire burned in the grate, the walls were covered in pale green silk and the furniture looked sturdy and comfortable. There was no sign of revelers or indeed, any of the kind of jeweled ostentation of the first room she'd been in. No false throne and dais, no gilded walls and cherubed trim. She might as well be in a family drawing room in England.

"There's a seat by the fire," he said as she pulled away from him.

There was indeed, a large, tufted chair that looked so comfortable she wanted to weep. "Isn't that yours?"

"Much as it pains me to tear myself away from you, I have other responsibilities, as well as the party I seem to be hosting," he said. "My guests will wonder where I've gone."

"I must get home. My mother…"

"When your mother is found she'll be taken back to the city in comfortable accommodations. You will follow, and you'll never have to see me again."

"I prefer to go with her."

"I prefer you to follow. Which of us do you think will triumph?" he said.

She almost mentioned Lydia. Her younger sister would be panicked if she didn't return home. Already she must be half-mad with worry.

But her younger sister was just the sort of toy these libertines would take and destroy. She needed to make certain they knew nothing about her, and if surviving a night of worry was the price for her sister's safety, then so be it.

"Never see you again?" she said. "You're fulfilling my wildest dreams."

"If those are your wildest dreams then you need to work on them. Mrs. Clarke will be here in a minute. Go get warm."

In fact she was freezing to death. Now that the immediate fear had passed, and there was nothing more she could do to salvage the situation, the warmth seemed to have left her body. Her feet in the too-tight shoes were cold and damp, and if she didn't hold herself very still she'd start shaking. And she bloody well wasn't going to do that in front of the Antichrist.

She headed straight for the armchair. It was even more comfortable than it had looked. It seemed to enfold her, and she couldn't suppress the sigh of sheer delight. She looked up, ready to say something disparaging to her host.

But he was already gone.

4

Elinor leaned back against the chair, finally alone, trying to regain her balance as the world whirled about her. She'd been in rooms like this, years ago when they'd lived in England. Warm, cozy rooms, with bright fires burning and comfortable, slightly worn furniture.

Which didn't make sense. The notorious Francis Rohan was as rich as Croesus, and the ornate glory of the rest of the château attested to that. The red damask upholstery on the sofa opposite her had worn patches, and the floor was scuffed. She must have slipped into some sort of dream, and when a stocky woman appeared a few minutes later Elinor decided she was simply a manifestation of her deepest longings for the warmth and safety and comfort of a life long past.

"There you are, dearie," the apparition said. "I'm Mrs. Clarke, the housekeeper. You look exhausted. And no wonder, all this chasing around you've had to do. Mr. Willis says to inform you that your mother has been found, she's perfectly fine, and Mr. Reading is taking her back home."

Elinor struggled to her feet. "I need to go with them."

"They've already left, dearie. We have orders from Master Francis. You're to rest for a while and then be sent home in the second-best carriage. Your mother will be fine. Mr. Reading's a good man for all that he's mixed up with this lot."

The woman looked like Nanny Maude's younger sister. Plump, pleasantly rounded, just the kind of woman you might find in English households everywhere. Just not in the household of the King of Hell. "But I need—" she began, but Mrs. Clarke calmly interrupted her.

"I know you do, dearie. But there's no arguing with his lordship. You just sit back and rest and I promise you, all will be well. You're still wearing your cloak? What was that man thinking! It's raining outside, and you're all cold and damp."

Before Elinor realized what the housekeeper was doing, Mrs. Clarke had managed to strip the cloak and shawl from her, laying the patched garments carefully near the fire. "I hadn't planned on staying," she said. "My mother…"

"Now, don't you go defending him," Mrs. Clarke said. "He's a sweet boy but he can be so thoughtless! And your shoes are soaked as well." She made a disapproving clucking sound as she bent down to untie Elinor's too-small shoes.

"I'm not…" Before she could deny defending him, the woman's words sank in. "You must be confused," she said, trying to pull her feet away. "It was the Comte de Giverney who brought me in here."

"Exactly. I was the one who brought him up. Came over from England after he was exiled and I've been looking after him ever since." She pulled off one shoe and set it near the fire, then the other. She must have noticed how worn they were, that they were too small, but she said nothing, treating them like jeweled slippers. She sat back and looked up at Elinor for a moment, her gaze sharpening. "You need some hot tea and something to eat."

"I'm not going to be here long," Elinor said, ignoring the fact that she was ready to faint from hunger.

Mrs. Clarke was as good at ignoring protests as her master. "Won't take me but a minute. You just sit there and warm up. Master Francis's chef is a stuck-up Frenchman, but he does know how to make cinnamon toast and a good strong up of tea. My girl's bringing it up—won't take but a moment. Just rest, Miss Harriman. You look like you need it."

Indeed she did. She couldn't remember when she'd last had a full night's sleep. Her mother had a tendency to wander—just a week ago she'd found her two streets away, dressed only in her nightgown, babbling something about being late for a rout. She'd brought her back and slept sitting up on the corner of her bed, just to make certain her mother didn't wander again. If she'd had any sense she would have tied the woman up, but Lady Caroline made such distressed noises when they did that it was almost worse than the worry.

A moment later Mrs. Clarke was back. There was steam rising from the tray she carried, and she could smell the cinnamon and butter from where she sat.

"There we are," the housekeeper said cheerfully, setting the tray down beside her on a slightly battered table. "All nice and cozy, are we? I'm going to find a throw to put over you—that's a nice enough fire, but you look like you've got yourself a chill."

She didn't deny it. She was so cold and disoriented that she wanted to weep. What had happened to her? Had he managed to drug her? There were rumors that he and his band of degenerates did that to unsuspecting young women, but the brief glance she'd had of the half-clothed women parading around the château told her that he had no need of a plain, over-tall spinster with a nose.

A moment later a thick cashmere robe was tucked around her, at odds with the shabby furniture. "You poor thing!" Mrs. Clarke said. "I'm just going to forget about manners and sit right down beside you. You don't look like you've got enough strength left to pour yourself a decent cup of tea. And Master Francis has never been a man who pays much attention to ceremony. You don't look like you do either." She plopped herself down in the chair beside her, pulled the hand-knitted cozy off the earthenware teapot with capable hands.

"You're looking at the teapot, aren't you?" Mrs. Clarke said as she proceeded to pour her a cup of tea, with lashings of heavy cream and sugar. "I brought that from England when I came here. I thought Master Francis would need something to remind him of home. So young he was, poor boy, to have lost his family, his home, his country."

Elinor wasn't going to ask. She'd heard rumors, but the vagaries of the titled émigré population of Paris had never been of particular interest, and even in the best of times her mother seldom talked to her. "Indeed," she said in a noncommittal voice.

"Indeed," Mrs. Clarke said cheerfully. "You don't want to talk about him, and I can understand that. He's a very bad boy, he is. But he has reason."

"I cannot think of anything that would excuse his—" she was going to say "licentiousness" but thought better of it "—his behavior."

"No, I suppose not. You're too young to remember." She shook herself. "We'll get you warm and fed and taken care of and back home right as rain," she said firmly.

It took all Elinor's self-control to keep her mouth shut. Too young to remember what? What reason might he have for an exile that was far from voluntary? Some scandal? But none of it mattered, she reminded herself. This wasn't her world.

"You look like the kind of girl who's been drinking her tea black," Mrs. Clarke continued, "but right now I think you need some sustenance."

The housekeeper was right—she'd given up sugar and milk more than a year ago, insisting she preferred her tea undiluted. In fact, she preferred her tea just as Mrs. Clarke was making it, but of late it had become more important to ensure that her sister got enough to eat and drink. Any cream and sugar they could afford went to Lydia.

The tea was ambrosia. Manna from heaven, milk

and honey—the biblical terms danced through her foggy brain. It was so wonderful that she would have happily trampled over her sister's delicate body for it.

"Let me get you another cover," the housekeeper said, rising from her seat. "I don't know what's come over me. It's just been so long since I've had a proper young English girl to look after that I let my tongue run away with me."

Elinor struggled to be polite. "Don't you miss England?"

"Of course I do, child. But I could never abandon Master Francis. Not until he gets past this playacting foolishness and marries."

"I believe the Heavenly Host has been holding their revels for many years," Elinor said. That much gossip she'd heard. "Perhaps you should give up waiting."

"Foolishness," Mrs. Clarke said firmly. "Eat your toast, dearie. I'll be back."

The thin slivers of cinnamon toast were wonderful. She tried to eat slowly, but she was so famished she devoured them.

She really must be in a dream. In a moment the King of Hell would come in and chop off her head or something equally bizarre. It would be worth it.

She closed her eyes, the teacup still in her hand. It was old, eggshell-thin china, with myriad tiny cracks in it. Another anomaly, but for a moment she wasn't going to think about it. She was going to keep her eyes closed and let herself drift into this strange, wonderful, magical world, where everything was safe and familiar, where there were no raving mothers, no sisters in need of protection, no servants who needed to be fed, and most of all, no Francis Rohan.

She heard the door open, heard the measured footsteps approaching her. Mrs. Clarke must have returned. She felt the teacup being taken from her slack fingers, and she knew she should open her mouth, insist on a carriage and a ride home—Lydia was waiting for her—but right then it was impossible. Two more hours wouldn't make that much difference. She'd sleep for that long and awake refreshed and reasonable, and this magic room would make sense. By the time she got home her mother would be in a dull, stupefied state, and they wouldn't have to deal with her for a few days at the least. She always slept deeply after one of her sorties.

And all Elinor would have to worry about was what in heaven's name they were going to do next.

He took the teacup from her hand and set it down on the small tray. Mrs. Clarke was watching him, a suspicious look on her face. She knew him too well—she was the only person who saw him clearly, with all his flaws and vanities and wicked indulgences. Saw him and loved him anyway, like an exasperated parent.

In truth she wasn't that much older than he was. She'd come into service at the age of twelve, and her first task had been the care of the Viscount Rohan's youngest son, Francis. He'd been born a sickly, angry child, prone to noisy displays of temperament, and young Polly Siddons had been saddled with him. But even at age twelve she'd known how to deal with him, and she'd been with him ever since, following him to Paris after the debacle of 1745. When her husband died, she'd simply replaced him with a Frenchman, but she still was Mrs. Clarke to all and sundry. His lifeline and his conscience. For all that he listened.

"And what exactly do you think you're doing with this young lady?" she demanded. "If you brought her here you know as well as I do that she's not one of your fancy pieces. She has no place here."

"True enough," he said. "And I'll send her home safely, untouched. You've been around me long enough to know that I have no interest in innocents. And she's hardly my style, don't you think? I insist on beauty."

"In the rest of this godforsaken place, yes. But these rooms are different, Master Francis. Here you're more likely to value real worth. And I don't like seeing her here."

I do, he thought, surprised. "Don't worry, Mrs. Clarke. I'll be sending her back to her misbegotten family as soon as she awakens. Which looks to be a while."

"Poor thing was worn-out," his housekeeper said. "She needs a rest without you harassing her."

"I'm not going to harass her," he said. "I'm simply going to take a nap myself. She'll probably wake up and start beating me with a fire poker, but I'm willing to take that risk. You can go back to bed."

She gave him that doubtful look that always made him feel twelve years old, but then she nodded. "You behave yourself, Master Francis. The girl's already got too much to deal with. She doesn't need you complicating things."

"Trust me," he said airily, heading for the settee opposite his sleeping guest. "I only intend to make her life simpler."

With a disapproving sniff Mrs. Clarke departed, leaving him alone in the room with the sound of the fire crackling in the fireplace, the lash of rain on the windows, her steady breathing as she slept.

He kicked off his elegant shoes. The settee wasn't the most comfortable of beds, but it was long enough to hold his frame, and he couldn't ask for much more. He'd slept on it when he was younger and it had resided in his father's house in Yorkshire, and he'd always found it surprisingly comfortable. He stretched out, his arms behind his head, and stared at her.

He could be kind, he could be generous, if he had reason. He had his reputation to consider, but he doubted anyone would know he'd done an act of charity in seeing to Miss Harriman's mother. If anyone heard, they'd assume he had wicked, ulterior motives, and that was good enough for him.

This girl before him wasn't a beauty. Her dark brown hair was unremarkable, her body, what he could see of it beneath the shabby clothes, could hardly compete with Marianne's lush pleasures. The pleasures he'd turned his back on to lie on this shabby sofa staring at this shabby girl.

Her face was…interesting. She had a smattering of

freckles across her cheekbones, something he'd always found irresistible. A surprisingly lush mouth, which clearly hadn't been kissed enough. And the nose.

It was narrow and elegant and only slightly longer than beauty required. In fact, it gave her face a certain piquant charm. Without it, with the requisite button of a nose, she'd be boring.

Boring was the one thing Miss Elinor Harriman couldn't lay claim to. She'd stormed into his life, and she was still here, long after she should have disappeared.

He could have handed her off to Reading. She would have much preferred accompanying her mother's drunken body back to Paris, but he'd kept her here instead. She was better off this way. Lady Caroline had proven combative, and he'd sent two strong footmen to keep her contained in his traveling carriage, with Reading to oversee the transfer.

No, this stern young woman would be better off arriving home after her mother was properly settled. He'd given Reading orders to make certain one of the footmen remained until they were convinced Lady Caroline had returned to her senses.

Which was no certainty. He'd been watching when they'd wrestled the woman into the carriage, her curses and her fists flying. The pox had driven her mad and nothing would change that. The sooner she died, the better for all concerned.

He could arrange it, of course. As he lounged on the settee he considered the possibilities. The wretched hag would have little connection with him, and there'd be no reason for him to be accused of orchestrating her death. Any of the Heavenly Host who happened to have noticed her presence here tonight would never breathe a word of it, or risk being ousted from their hallowed little group.

The police in Paris were fairly lax, but they might pay more attention to the death of a titled émigré. Then again, they might not. They let him do anything he wanted in his mansion in Rue Saint-Honoré, but then, no one had died. At least as far as he knew.

No, his charitable instincts would be better off curbed for the time being. Wretched as Mademoiselle Elinor Harriman's life might be, it was hardly his job to fix it. To remove the major obstacle to her happiness.

Though the poxy wretch might annoy Reading so much that he stabbed her. Reading was notoriously quick-tempered, rash and impulsive. Perhaps he'd take care of things of his own volition.

In the meantime, here he was, ready to sleep with the perfect virgin. He let out a soft laugh. Miss Harriman would hate that, making it all the more delightful. They would sleep together, albeit a chaste three feet apart, and it would annoy her for the rest of her life.

And with that he closed his eyes and slept, a smile on his face, malice in his heart. He slept.

It was past five in the morning, and Lydia Harriman was already up and dressed, having spent a wretched three hours in bed, tossing and turning, before giving up completely. Her mother's disappearance wasn't that unusual—Lady Caroline would vanish for days at a time, and there was nothing they could do about it.

But she'd gotten much worse recently. Her conversations were sprinkled with curses, and there was a strange, otherworldly look in her eyes that no one could break through. She complained constantly of the cold, even with the warmest fire, and when things were really bad they tied her to the bed lest she hurt herself.

Or them. When her mother was raging there was no telling what she might do, and Nanny Maude kept the knives hidden just to be safe. And there were times, which Lydia would never admit to, that she hoped her mother would simply not return from her next escapade.

But this time Elinor had disappeared as well.

It was an eerie, ice-cold dawn. She'd been careful not to put too much wood on the fire. What little fuel they had must last as long as possible. Elinor tried to shield her from the harsher realities of life, and Lydia had stopped arguing. If it made her elder sister happy to think that she was ignorant of the truly desperate circumstances they were living in then Lydia could pretend. Elinor had always been a bossy sibling, in the best sense of the word, and she wouldn't hear of Lydia shouldering her share of the burden. Sooner or later she'd have to give in, but for now Elinor was happier pretending that she had everything under control, when control had vanished months ago.

She heard the noise in the kitchen, and she jumped up, almost knocking over the chair in her relief. Nanny was already there, in her robe and nightcap, as Jacobs came in. Alone.

"Where are the others, you auld idiot?" Nanny Maude demanded before Lydia could speak.

The old man hung his head. "We followed her ladyship out of the city to the devil's own playground." He turned to Lydia. "There was no stopping your sister, miss. She took off before I knew what she was doing, and they wouldn't let me follow her. I tried to fight them but there were too many of them, and I'm an old man. Not as strong as I was."

"You couldn't have done anything," Lydia said in a soothing voice, while Nanny made a derisive noise that could almost be called a snort.

"They wouldn't have been stopping *me*," the old woman said bitterly. "You're a fool and a coward."

"You crazy old bat, no one would dare to touch a harridan the likes of you," he snapped back, their lifelong battle flaring up.

"Stop it, both of you!" Lydia said sharply. "You still haven't told me where they are. Did they go to that man's château?"

"They did indeed," he said. "Your mother had gone there to gamble. I hadn't been there an hour, still trying to find my way into the house, when they came and found me. Told me to take the coach and get back to town, and your mother and sister would be following."

"What coach?"

If Jacobs had been looking shamefaced before, he looked even more devastated now. "The coach…er… I meant to say…er…the coach…" He cleared his throat. "I had to borrow a coach…"

"You had to steal a coach," Lydia interrupted him gently. "That's all right, Jacobs. I'm not as blind as my sister wishes me to be. You've done it before, I know. So you stole a coach in order to go after my mother. Well done. Did you get it back before anyone noticed it was missing this time?"

Jacobs lifted his head, clearly relieved. "Not quite, Miss Lydia. But I managed to sneak away before they caught me. And they're not going to make too big a fuss since everything's been returned."

"Everything but my mother and my sister," Lydia said.

"The viscount's men promised they'd be coming home in a fancy coach," he said desperately. "I never would have left if I didn't think they'd be better off with his lordship."

"The man everyone calls the devil? The one who runs satanic parties and drinks the blood of virgins?" Lydia said, trying not to sound panicked. "You need to steal another coach, Jacobs. I have to go after her."

"Miss, it's daylight. I canna steal a coach in broad daylight."

"Then I'll walk," she said fiercely. "I'm not going to sit by and let my family be—"

The noise at the front door interrupted her, and she turned around and flew down the hall, flinging open the door with relief. "Oh, Nell, I was so worried about you…!"

Her voice trailed off, as she realized she was looking at someone a far cry from her sister. He stood in the doorway, silhouetted by the sunrise over the rickety buildings, and she couldn't see his face, even though he doubtless could see hers quite clearly.

"Not Nell, I'm afraid." He had a deep, English voice, and for a moment Lydia was flooded with a host of memories of a life lost long ago. "I assume you're her sister? I have your mother in the coach. If you'll show me where I can have my men bring her I'd be greatly obliged."

"Yes. Of course." It took her a moment to gather her wits. "In the front bedroom." She could hear the howls and curses coming from behind the stranger, and her heart sank. Her mother was in one of her full-blown bouts of madness, and Elinor wasn't around. She was better at calming Lady Caroline than any of them. "We'll have to see about restraints. I'm not sure where anything is."

"You needn't be concerned, Miss Harriman," he said smoothly. "My men can handle things." He turned and made a gesture behind him, and for a moment she could see his face.

It was a handsome face, or it would have been, if not for the scar running from eyebrow to mouth on one side, giving him a faintly sinister look, quirking his lips up in a parody of a smile. He was dressed exquisitely, and he'd doffed his hat to expose unpowdered tawny hair. For a moment she couldn't move.

This must be the devil they talked about, and for the first time she could understand the lure.

"Miss Harriman?" he said gently, and she shook herself out of her abstraction.

"You're very kind," she said, racking her brains for his title. All the ones she could remember were vastly insulting. She backed out of the way and he followed her into the shabby little house, and she mentally thanked God she was already up and dressed. Nanny was bustling around, clucking like an agitated hen, clutching her robe around her plump frame.

He took her arm with the finesse of a prince. "Why don't we get out of their way and leave them to take care of things? Your housekeeper can show the footmen where to put her."

"That's Nanny Maude," she blurted out as he drew her into the tiny front room with its sullen excuse for a fire. It was a ridiculous thing to say, but she didn't want Nanny relegated to the role of servant when she was so much more.

He smiled, the move jerking his smile up so that he looked even more ruthless. "Nanny's got things well in hand," he said smoothly. "And I've been remiss—I haven't introduced myself."

"I know who you are, my lord," she said. Finally his name came to her. "You're the Comte de Giverney." She was determined not to show any fear. "Apparently you consort with the devil, have orgies and drink the blood of virgins. According to gossip you're sin itself."

The smile, which had been oddly pleasant and even

comforting despite the scar, turned cool. "Sorry to disappoint you, Miss Harriman. I realize I look like the very devil, but in fact I'm nothing more than an untitled gentleman with an ugly face and empty pockets. Charles Reading, at your service."

She could feel the color flood her face. "You're not the demon king?"

"I'm afraid not." He shook his head. "No, he's busy entertaining your sister."

5

For a moment Lydia didn't move. "You're not ugly," she said. Before he could respond to that she went on. "And what's the comte going to do with my sister? I presume the stories are just that—stories made up to scare children into behaving."

"Do they work? Are you properly terrified?"

"I left my childhood behind years ago, Mr. Reading." At that moment they were interrupted by the procession of people carrying her mother into the house. She was struggling, swearing and spitting, her waif-thin body unnaturally strong, and one of the men carrying her cursed when she managed to land a blow. A moment later they disappeared into the bedroom, Nanny Maude following them and closing the door behind her.

She turned to look back at Reading. He had dark eyes, and he was watching her with curiosity and no pity whatsoever. "How long has your mother had the pox?"

"I don't know," she said, unable to pull her gaze

away from him. For a penniless gentleman he was quite elegant, from his high cheekbones to the glossy boots he wore. The left side of his face had an almost unearthly beauty; the scar on the right had healed badly, turning that beauty into a travesty.

"A duel," he said.

She blinked. "I beg your pardon?"

"You're wondering what caused the scar. Don't be embarrassed. It's what everyone thinks when they see me."

"I'm not embarrassed…because in fact I wasn't thinking about that at all. I was worried about my sister."

"I stand humbled and corrected. Though in fact I'd prefer not to stand. I had no intention of riding in the coach with your mother casting up her accounts all over the place, so I rode, and I'm quite tired. However, I can't sit down until you invite me to do so and sit down yourself, and since you don't seem about to I thought I might offer a little hint."

"Please, sit," she said, rattled, taking the small, hard chair and leaving the more comfortable one near the fire for him.

He shook his head. "Not likely. Change seats and I will."

"I'm fine where I am…" Before she realized what he was doing he'd tossed his hat onto the small table, clamped his gloved hands on her arms and lifted her, dropping her into the seat by the fire as if she weighed no more than a bird.

He must have thought as much. He frowned. "Have you been eating properly?"

She thought about the thin soup Nanny had managed to stretch for the week with the careful addition of more and more water, and her stomach knotted. "Of course," she said.

"Because you don't weigh more than a child."

"How many children are you in the habit of picking up, Mr. Reading?" she responded. "Oh, I forgot, the devil sacrifices babies, does he not?"

"He doesn't..." He stopped protesting. "You're teasing me, are you, Miss Harriman?"

"Just a little bit," she allowed. "I shouldn't—things are hardly humorous right now, but since I've seen the difference between gossip and reality firsthand I have little doubt that the Comte de Giverney is nothing more than a self-indulgent hedonist."

He took the seat across from her, and she held her breath, afraid it might not hold his firmly muscled weight. It creaked, but survived, at least for the moment. "As is his best friend," he said, his voice less than reassuring.

"Really?" she said, her voice bright. "I've never seen a self-indulgent hedonist before. I have to say I'm a bit disappointed. You don't look very dissipated to me. Maybe you haven't been at it for a terribly long time."

"Long enough," he said beneath his breath.

There wasn't much she could say to that. "Could you tell me where my sister is? Why didn't she return with you?"

"Again, there's the problem of the carriage."

"Oh, dear. I forgot. Your poor carriage. We can't

afford to have it cleaned, but Jacobs and I can see to it."

"It's not my carriage. And Rohan has more than enough servants to deal with it. More than enough carriages for that matter."

"Rohan?" she echoed.

"The King of Hell. The Comte de Giverney, the Viscount Rohan," he clarified.

"The man who has my sister."

"He'll return her safe and unharmed. Francis doesn't waste time with innocents. Unless your sister's shabby clothes and stern manner hide a lurid background."

It shouldn't have bothered her, but she pulled her shawl closer around her shoulders, hiding some of her own shabbiness. Her only clothes were those passed down from Elinor, one stage closer to the ragbag, something this exquisitely attired gentleman had no doubt noted and inwardly mocked. "I'm afraid we're living in straitened circumstances, Mr. Reading," she said, lifting her head. "We're awaiting word from our father, who will doubtless come to our aid, but in the meantime there is no denying that our fortunes have suffered of late."

He said nothing more than, "Indeed."

"I get the uneasy suspicion that you're holding something back, Mr. Reading," she said. "Or were you simply going to cast more aspersions on my threadbare wardrobe?"

"I'm afraid you're so pretty that I hadn't even noticed your wardrobe, Miss Harriman. Your sister doesn't have the advantage of your beauty."

"If that's supposed to make me feel better it's failed," she said, finally getting angry. "My sister is very striking, and only shallow gentlemen would fail to realize that."

"I'm very shallow, Miss Harriman. You enchant me. Your sister terrifies me."

"Good," she said. Then realized how it sounded. "I mean, good that my sister terrifies you, and I would certainly wish that I could do the same."

He looked at her. "In fact, you do terrify me, Miss Harriman, for quite different reasons."

"I can't imagine why."

His twisted smile was far from reassuring. "I think you would prefer I not mention it to you," he murmured.

"I don't understand."

"You don't need to. I believe I should make certain your mother is settled." He rose, and he suddenly seemed a great deal more alarming. He took her hand, so small in his large one, and pulled her to her feet, with such strength that she practically flew into his arms, only her presence of mind and his quick thinking preventing such an absolute disaster. He lifted her hand to his mouth, that twisted, scarred mouth, and kissed it. Leaving her to stare after him, momentarily distracted.

Elinor awoke in a dimly lit room deliciously warm for what seemed like the first time in years. Her stomach was pleasantly full, her feet didn't pinch and for a few brief moments she felt almost…peaceful.

And then she opened her eyes and saw a man

sleeping on the sofa across from her. And not just any man—King Rohan himself. Her quick intake of horrified breath was almost silent, but he opened one eye anyway, looking at her.

"Yes, you slept with the devil, Miss Harriman," he drawled. "And lived to tell the tale."

She sat up, shoving down the cover that someone had thoughtfully draped over her, then realized her shawl was gone as well, and during her sleep the threadbare bodice of her ancient dress had shredded just a little bit more, exposing too much of her chest. She needed a fichu as well as her shawl, but woven cloth was a scarcity and she'd thought the shawl would give her modest coverage. She was wrong.

She started to yank the cover back up, but he was closer than she realized, and his indolent pose was clearly just that, a pose. He caught the blanket before she could cover herself, tossing it to one side. "There's no need to be excessively modest, Miss Harriman. You still err on the side of decency."

"My shawl," she said in a strangled voice. "It's over on the chair."

He glanced that way. "Is it? And why would you assume I'd be interested in waiting on you? Particularly when I don't wish to have you cover up your surprisingly delightful charms."

She started to get up, feeling desperate, and he simply pushed her back in the chair again. "All right, if you're going to be tiresome," he said, moving over to her discarded clothing and fetching her thin shawl. She could see the light through it, but it was better coverage than what she was wearing, and she snatched it from his hand, wrapping it around her shoulders and waist so that it stayed firmly in place. "That's better," she said, breathing a sigh of relief.

"Terrible. And it doesn't change the fact that you spent the night sleeping with me."

"Don't be ridiculous. I had no idea you were there, and I'm not quite certain why you chose to fall asleep on such an uncomfortable piece of furniture. You're in the midst of hosting an orgy—shouldn't you have been frolicking with courtesans?"

"It's a three-day revel, child. I seldom frolic until the second night. And besides, I've already…frolicked with any of my guests who interest me. You're a novelty."

"A novelty who shall remove herself forthwith," she said. "I cannot believe I let myself fall asleep in such circumstances. Where is my mother?"

"Back home. I had Reading see to her, and since he has yet to return I'm assuming he's had a bit of difficulty."

"The poor man with the scar?"

Rohan laughed softly. "Oh, he would be distressed to hear you call him that. He thinks his scar makes him a very dangerous character. So tell me, Miss Harriman, what will he find when he arrives at your home? Besides your hapless, larcenous coachman."

"No one." Lydia was much better at opening her eyes wide and looking innocent, but Elinor gave it her best try.

"Don't attempt to play games with me," he said lazily. He strolled over to the window, looking out onto the early-morning landscape. "I'm a master at them. Who else resides in your household besides you and your mother?"

"My old nanny."

"And who else?"

"No one."

He turned his head "You're not an adept liar, Miss Harriman. If I remember correctly, Lady Caroline Harriman had two daughters."

"My sister died."

A faint smile touched his mouth. "If you're going to continue lying you really need to do a better job of it, my pet. I'm certain I could find someone to teach you the fine points. It's a useful skill."

"I'm not lying." She glanced toward the door. If she caught him off guard she could make her escape, and if she couldn't find a carriage or a horse she could simply walk the five miles to Paris. Except that her tattered shoes were nowhere to be seen.

"Don't be tiresome," Rohan said. "You have a very pretty little sister, do you not?"

She wasn't going to show her terror. She'd always known she'd be safe enough—she hadn't the face to drive men to distraction, and a determined libertine such as Rohan would have beauty at his fingertips. But her baby sister was a different matter. She'd already done everything she could to keep her safe, and she had nothing left to barter.

Except rage. "If you or anyone touches my sister I'll kill you," she said in a cold, determined voice.

He flashed her his exquisite smile. "Now, that was

said with real conviction. Your sister must be quite extraordinarily pretty."

"My sister is none of your business." She quickly came up with a more believable lie. "As soon as my father arranges it we'll return to England and she'll be happily married…"

"You expect your father to arrange a marriage for her?" he asked, leaning against the wall of the study. He still wore his long silken waistcoat, unbuttoned, and during the night his white shirt had opened even more. Exposing his chest. Women weren't meant to see men's bare chests, and for the first time she could understand why. There was something deliberately enticing about that expanse of flesh, and it could lead a girl to sinful thoughts.

Not that she was a girl. And she was impervious to sinful thoughts. "She won't have an arranged marriage," she snapped. "I intend to make certain she marries for love."

His look of astonishment wasn't feigned. "My dear child," he said softly. "You cannot tell me you still believe in the existence of love! Not after the life you've been forced to live."

"My life has been just fine," she said coolly. "And I'm not thinking for myself, but for Lydia, absolutely. It's no less than she deserves."

"And why don't you deserve it?"

She didn't flush. She'd trained herself not to show any reaction, and she was a far better liar than he gave her credit for. "I have no interest in it. Lydia's a different matter. As soon as our father…"

"You know as well as I do that your father is dead. The new Baron Tolliver is in town, looking to make your acquaintance."

She kept her expression calm, her hands gripping her skirts, out of sight. "How do you know that?"

"I am kept abreast of everything that goes on in émigré society, poppet. Lord Jasper Harriman died of an apoplexy several months ago, and the heir who has taken his place is now in Paris. He's yet to make my acquaintance, though I assure you that time will come if he stays here long enough. I doubt there's any rescue coming from that direction."

She wasn't going to let him get to her. "Then Lydia will simply have to marry a handsome, kind, wealthy Frenchman," she said calmly.

He moved away. "And what will happen to you and your mother? If your sister is as pretty as I suspect she is, from your fiercely protective mien, then a good marriage isn't out of the question. A deranged *belle-mère* and a sister-in-law are less appealing."

She flushed, knowing he spoke nothing but the truth. "We both know that my mother won't live for much longer," she said. "As for me, I am perfectly capable of being independent. I can become a governess. I can teach English and the pianoforte, or I could obtain a position as companion to an older lady."

"Not once she discovers you spent the night with me."

She rose. Huddling in the chair was a sign of weakness, and standing he still towered over her not inconsiderable height. But sitting gave him an even greater advantage. "There's no reason that would happen. You have nothing to gain by spreading such vile rumors."

"They aren't rumors, my pet. It's the simple truth. As for what I have to gain, I'm afraid you put far too low a price on your charms. I've told you, you're a rarity in these parts, and I find myself reluctantly fascinated."

"Listen to your reluctance," she said briskly. "I'm not worth the trouble. And charming though this conversation is, I need to get home and see to my mother."

"But what if I don't want to let you go? You can hardly walk all the way back to the city, and you continue to fascinate me." He flicked an imaginary speck off the snowy-white shirt he wore.

He moved closer, and she moved back, surreptitiously, putting the chair between them with a casual air. Not that she seriously distrusted him—this was a game he was playing, nothing more. Like a great hungry tomcat playing with a little white mouse. Or so he thought.

"I've walked more than five miles before, I can do it now."

"In bare feet?" he said pointedly.

She immediately crouched so that her threadbare skirts covered her feet.

"Now, that distresses me," he said. "You have quite lovely feet. Most women have fat little toes and broad feet. And dancers—God help me, they have the ugliest feet of all. But you really have exquisite…"

"I would appreciate it if you would stop rhapsodizing over my anatomy and summon a carriage," she said, mortified. He might well have been talking about her breasts, and she wondered what else he'd been observing in such a familiar manner.

"Your hands," he said, startling her. "You're quite ridiculously easy to read. You were wondering what I was going to go on about next. I'm quite fascinated by your hands."

She immediately tucked her hands into her shawl, but he wasn't deterred. "They don't look particularly soft. Not the plump, white, useless hands most women have. You have long, beautiful fingers, narrow palms, and yet there's strength in those hands. I rather think I want to feel them on my body."

She let out a hiss of breath, ridiculously, undeniably shocked. So shocked she forgot to move as he came closer. Dangerously close. "Don't look so horrified, sweeting. Surely you didn't mistake my interest in you as any humanitarian behavior on my part. I don't give a damn if your mother dies, and I don't let myself be distracted from my activities unless there's something I want more. That would be you."

She stared at him. "And how long have you suffered this disorder of the brain, my lord?"

"And how long have you disregarded your worth, Miss Harriman?" he replied.

Six years, she could have told him. But she didn't. That time was over, long forgotten, and she didn't have to think about it.

He was playing a game with her—he'd already

admitted he was very good at games, and she'd seen the women who surrounded him. "If you will please summon your housekeeper I have no doubt she'll be able to retrieve my shoes and then I'll be on my way." Her manner was brisk and practical, the perfect counterpoint to his absurdly seductive manner. To prove her point she rose to her full height again, exposing her bare feet.

"Miss Harriman, are you possibly so unwise as to call my bluff?" he asked, his voice silken.

"Certainly not, Monsieur le Comte. I simply choose not to play this little game of yours." There was a bellpull by the door, and she crossed the room and yanked it.

She half expected him to come after her. To catch her hand as she reached for the bellpull, to pull her into his arms, tight against his body, as he had last night.

He took one step toward her, and then halted, his self-deprecating smile back in place as he dropped back down on the settee. "So be it." He waved one pale hand in her direction. "Mrs. Clarke will see you to the carriage."

The door opened as he spoke. "Mrs. Clarke will do no such thing," that lady pronounced. "You will get up and take this young woman home, like the gentleman you once were."

Elinor expected to see him explode. Instead he merely leaned back with a sigh of acquiescence. "Call me when the carriage is ready."

"This is no way to entertain a young lady, Master Francis," Mrs. Clarke said in a scolding voice.

"Then remove her," he said in a bored voice.

"Master Francis." Mrs. Clarke's comfortable Scots voice held a note of warning, and he opened his eyes again.

"Why I ever brought you with me to France is a matter beyond my comprehension," he said wearily, sitting back up.

"You didn't bring me. We followed you, against your express orders. Which should make it clear that I'm going to do what I think is right, at least in my part of the house, and anyone you bring here will have to be treated respectfully."

"Yes, Mrs. Clarke," he said in a mockingly subdued voice. "You will allow me to change before I escort the young lady home, won't you? I have standards I need to uphold. And for that matter, she seems to be in need of shoes."

"I have them with me, sir," Mrs. Clarke said, perfectly obsequious now that she'd gotten her way. "Go ahead and change. We'll be waiting for you."

"We? If you're going then there's no need for me…"

"I'm not going, Master Francis. You know I have a grave aversion to Paris. I'll merely be keeping the young lady company until you change your clothes. And it would behoove you to hurry—the longer we're together the more things I could tell her."

She expected Rohan to look more than a little disgruntled, but he simply laughed. "I doubt anything you tell her would surprise her. She already knows I'm a total wastrel."

"If you take too long, I'll be telling her all the good things I know of you."

"Good god," he said in tones of absolute horror. "I'll be as quick as the devil." He'd reached the door, then stopped for a moment, looking back at Elinor, staring at her.

"Master Francis…" Mrs. Clarke said in a warning tone.

"I just wanted to take a last glance at her exquisite feet before you covered them up again. It might be a while before I see them again."

"It will be never," Elinor said, crossing her arms over her chest.

"Don't count on it, my pet. Whatever scurrilous lies Mrs. Clarke spreads about my so-called goodness, she'll have to admit that I always get what I want."

And before she could say another word he vanished, closing the door quietly behind him.

6

"There's really no need for him to accompany me," Elinor said hurriedly, suddenly able to breathe again. "In fact, I'd be much more comfortable traveling back to Paris alone. If you could just help me find my shoes and direct me to the carriage you could tell his lordship that his assistance was not needed."

"Don't you worry, Miss Harriman," Mrs. Clarke said briskly. "He'll behave himself. And I've got my girl Janet finding some nice warm boots for you. The ones you wore have fallen apart, and there's snow in the air."

"Find some boots for me?"

On a less dignified personage, Mrs. Clarke's smile would have looked positively mischievous. "Lady Carlton looks to be about your size. Whenever she comes she brings several trunks of clothing and shoes, which seems ridiculous, because according to Janet she spends the entire time wearing nothing at all. She'll never notice if one of her pairs of boots has gone missing."

"I can't wear stolen boots!" Elinor said, scandalized.

"Of course you can."

The door opened and Janet appeared, bearing a tea tray with a pair of kid-leather boots under her arm. She looked like a younger version of Mrs. Clarke, and she set both her offerings in front of Elinor. There were toast strips on the tray as well as tea, and a pair of silk stockings with the boots, and Elinor gave up being virtuous.

"No disasters, pet?" Mrs. Clarke inquired of Janet.

"They're all sleeping it off, most of them starkers," Janet said. "No worries."

"I never do," her mother said. "Drink your tea, Miss Harriman. The doings of this household, while shocking, needn't concern you any more than they concern me."

"They don't concern you?" Elinor said with a mouthful of toast.

"I never venture into that part of the château. His lordship likes to misbehave, but as long as no one is hurt I keep out of it. This part of the house is small but cozy, with no strumpets allowed."

"You don't think I could be a strumpet?" She poured her tea and put obscene amounts of sugar in the cup. She might as well enjoy it while it lasted. "I suppose it's The Nose," she said resignedly.

"The nose?" Mrs. Clarke said, her forehead wrinkling. "You mean your nose? What's wrong with it?"

"It's the Harriman Nose," she said gloomily. "Strumpets are pretty."

"Strumpets are tarts. As for your nose, it's nothing that extraordinary. It gives your face character, something those foolish girls lack."

"Lucky me," Elinor murmured. She took another toast sliver. Then jumped, as she realized Janet had knelt before her and reached for one bare foot.

"I'll take care of this, miss," Janet said. "Me mother wanted me to train as a lady's maid."

"Unfortunately there are never any ladies at his lordship's house parties," Mrs. Clarke said grimly. "And Master Francis should be returning momentarily—you wouldn't want to be flaunting your bare feet in front of him, now, would you?"

Trapped. "Thank you, Janet," she said. "You're very kind to help me."

It was almost seductive. The warm, sweet, rich tea, the toast slivers with lashings of butter and a sprinkle of cinnamon sugar, a maid assisting with her clothes. It had been so long since they'd had a lady's maid that she could barely remember what it was like. Janet drew the silk stocking up her leg for her, and the feeling was decadently wonderful, too splendid to fight. Besides, she could give the stockings to Lydia, who'd delight in the extravagance. She'd have to somehow convince her younger sister that she herself couldn't wear them—Lydia had grown suspicious of Elinor's stratagems. Her sudden dislike of sugar, her inability to drink cream, the discomfort of the one decent pair of boots between them. She'd be hard put to come up with a reason why Lydia simply must accept the silk stockings as her own, but she could prevaricate with the best of them. She'd had her mother as an example.

The boots were a perfect fit, roomy for her less-than-dainty feet. By the time she'd finished her tea and toast and had the kid-leather boots neatly fastened she felt she could face any kind of ogre. Including the one who'd reappeared in the door of the cozy drawing room, looking enigmatic.

"I've had the carriage brought round," he said. "Where's your cloak?"

"Here it is, sir," Janet said, reappearing from behind him, carrying a fur pelisse. The sort of thing that was shockingly expensive and deliciously warm.

Elinor set the tray away and rose, speechless for the moment. Janet came up behind her to assist her into the pilfered cloak, and Elinor whispered a protest to the maid. "I can't take this."

"There you go, Miss Harriman," Janet said in a loud voice, taking one of Elinor's arms and shoving it into the sleeve. She could either have a wrestling match with the maid, something she might very likely lose, or give in. She was taller than the sturdy Janet, but Janet was very strong.

"Are you two going to fight?" the King of Hell asked in a lazy tone. "There are few things more entertaining than watching two females try to tear each other apart, but if you're going to go at it you might give me time to get my own tea and perhaps find a better venue."

Elinor stopped struggling, and the cloak slid up her arms. Janet stepped around her and began fastening it, and it took all of Elinor's self-control not to bat at her hands. Stolen boots and silk stockings were one thing, a rich fur cloak quite another. But the garment was so blessedly warm.

"No catfights? I'm shattered. But then, I've learned to live with disappointment. Come along, then, Miss Harriman. The sooner I leave you in Paris the sooner I can get back to vigorous dissipation, since you seem determined to resist my blandishments. And frolicking with my guests. Or was it trifling?"

"As long as you don't frolic with Miss Harriman," Mrs. Clarke said sternly. She turned to Elinor. "Goodbye, miss. I'll look forward to seeing you again."

That was most certainly not going to happen, Elinor thought, thanking the woman.

Rohan held out his arm, and she hesitated for a moment. He simply took her hand and pulled her to his side, ungently. "You must at least pretend to be on speaking terms with me, Miss Harriman," he drawled.

"Why?"

He simply glanced down at her. It was an unnerving experience. She was so very much taller than most of the men, particularly the French ones, that having to look up into those hard, merciless blue eyes only added to the sense of unreality.

But if she didn't want to wrestle with Janet for fear she might lose, fighting with Lord Rohan would be even worse. Because she knew he wouldn't be following any of the rules of civilized behavior.

There was a light snow falling when they stepped outside the massive front portico of the château, and Elinor drew the stolen fur cloak closer around her, trying to ignore her guilt. The liveried footman immediately opened the coach door for her, and she pulled away from Rohan and scrambled up before he could assist her. He'd barely touched her, but she didn't trust those large, beautiful hands.

A moment later he was inside as well, dwarfing the spacious interior, and they were on their way. It had been so very long since she'd been in such an elegant coach, perhaps never. Her father had been wealthy but not on the scale of Rohan, and he had never sent his young daughters out in his best carriage. She tucked her hands in the folds of the pelisse, lifting her eyes to look at her reluctant companion.

Stretched out on the seat, perfectly comfortable, he was eyeing her with calm curiosity.

"You should have had Mrs. Clarke steal you some warm gloves and a bonnet while she was at it," he said. "Lady Carlton would never miss them."

She'd been warm enough before, but the heat that flushed her face was uncomfortable, and she immediately reached up to unfasten the cloak. One look at his face stopped her. "You really don't want to get into a wrestling match with me, now, do you, my sweet?" His voice was amused. "I'd like nothing more than an excuse to put my hands on you in the privacy of the carriage. It's a long, cold drive into Paris and I can think of any number of things that would make the time pass more quickly, all of which involve touching you. Lady Carlton has a dozen fur cloaks, and your shabby cloak was probably infested with vermin."

"It was not!" she said, incensed.

"If you say so." His eyes narrowed, and he yawned. "I assume you aren't interested in…er… frolicking with me?"

"No!"

"Trifling? We've already been flirting…"

"We have not!" she said, aghast.

"Oh, yes, child, we most certainly have, even if you don't recognize it. Why don't we simply dispense with all the pleasantries and descend into hot, nasty fornication?"

For perhaps the first time in her life Elinor was at a loss for words. And in the end, only the most foolish ones escaped her mouth. "In a carriage?"

He laughed. "Oh, most definitely in a carriage. Though if you prefer a bed we can always return to the château, though we'd have to avoid Mrs. Clarke's evil eye."

His words were shocking, disturbing. No doubt meant to be, she realized. He had no more amatory interest in her than he had in Mrs. Clarke, but if she charged him with it he'd doubtless strive to prove her wrong. She managed to meet his dark, wicked gaze with a deceptive calm. "You promised her you'd behave with propriety."

"Such promises, had I made them, would have been hollow, but in fact I did no such thing. Mrs. Clarke has known me for decades, Miss Harriman. She has no illusions about my true nature—she simply never gives up hope." His eyes narrowed. "Are you really so inured to temptation? I've managed to seduce nuns and Sapphists, and I'm unused to having my attempts ignored."

Curiosity got the better of her. "Sapphists?"

"Women who prefer the love of other women, child."

Her brow wrinkled. "How?"

"Allow me to explain." He moved to her side of the carriage before she realized what he was doing. She tried to leap to the other side, but he managed to catch hold of her, one arm tight around her waist, keeping her beside him.

She glared up at him. "You seem to have spent a great deal of time mishandling me, my lord, and I don't like it. Take your hands off me."

"Then don't fight me. I'm just trying to improve your education." He took one of her hands in his gloved one. It was pathetic—small and rough beneath the patched fingerless glove. He stripped it off and sent it sailing to the other side of the coach. "I'm surprised that Mrs. Clarke didn't come racing after us with a pair of gloves for you."

"It wasn't my idea."

"Of course it wasn't, my pet," he said soothingly. "Mrs. Clarke is a hard woman to argue with. No, just settle back and I will proceed with your education."

"I don't…"

"Hush," he said softly, putting one gloved fingertip up against her mouth. "This isn't going to hurt."

The soft leather that shielded his flesh from hers should have made his touch less intimate. Unfortunately everything he did and said was intimate. He held her hand in his, his thumb rubbing against the center of her palm. It had a curiously calming effect.

"Now, I assume you understand the mechanics of male and female coupling. Most properly brought-up young virgins would be totally ignorant, but your upbringing leaves much to be desired. You know what men and women do, and how their parts fit together with such splendid neatness?"

She wouldn't have called it that, she thought, biting her lip. "Of course," she said in a cold voice. She didn't bother trying to pull her hand away—it would have been a waste of energy. He was so much stronger than she was, and she couldn't believe he intended to hurt her.

"Women, of course, are unequipped with the necessary equipment to complete the act of love. So they employ alternatives. Some use equipment they can strap on that makes them appear masculine."

Elinor squirmed on the seat.

"Others use their mouths, as men and women do with each other. I imagine you've seen something of that, living as you have."

"Yes," she said in a strangled voice.

"But the simplest thing, particularly in a semipublic occasion, is to use their hands upon each other." He was still stroking her palm, and then his fingers moved up, carefully curling all but her two middle fingers down. "You know about this, don't you, my pet? How to pleasure yourself?"

She didn't...couldn't say a word. The thought of willingly engaging in anything that resembled coupling, even on one's own, seemed the height of madness.

"No?" he whispered, moving her hand down. "This is how it's done." And he put her hand between her legs.

She fought him then, shocked, but her efforts made her legs part, and he moved her hand closer to the center of her, holding her fingers steady. "You touch," he whispered, "just lightly as first. Delicately, like a butterfly. Pleasure can't be forced, it must be coaxed." He pushed her hand a little farther into her skirts, so that her fingertips touched that center core of herself, and she felt an odd shiver of reaction, one that frightened her.

"Please, don't…" she protested, but he simply ignored her.

"Now, my love, you mustn't be shy," he whispered in admonishment. "If you knew how to do this by yourself I'd leave you alone. Trust me, you'll thank me once you master the trick of it. It makes many a long night more engaging, and it will help if you decide to turn to women for comfort."

He pushed her hand again, so that it rubbed between her legs, and this time the jolt was stronger, and oddly enough she could feel her breasts tingle. Again, he pushed, and it seemed to have nothing to do with her. It was simply his hand, moving hers, as strange feelings began to build inside her, and she squirmed, moving her legs farther apart, and he laughed softly, increasing the pressure.

"After a while you can be more forceful," he whispered against the side of her neck. "What first you wooed must now be mastered, or it might escape completely, leaving you restless and distraught." He pushed harder, much harder, and she made a small, whimpering noise, not of pain. "Just as you feel it will never happen, the first blush of pleasure sweeps over you…"

She had stopped thinking, as a small, exquisite jolt stirred her body.

"And then you push it farther…" His mouth was hot against her skin. "And deeper…" She could feel something dark and terrible approaching, and she tried to pull back in sudden fear. "And you don't let anything stop you."

With his other hand he pressed her face against his greatcoat, and he moved her hand with sudden force and speed, and the dark place opened and pulled her in, and he muffled her cry against his shoulder as wave after wave of exquisite pleasure washed over her.

Finally he drew her shaking hand back from between her legs. He brought it to his mouth and kissed it, then put it on her lap. He still held her face against his shoulder, his arm around her, and as the wicked jerks of pleasure faded, shame flooded in around it.

When she yanked herself away he let her go, and she stumbled as she landed on the opposite seat, her face red, her breath coming far too quickly. "You animal!" she said in low fury. "How dare you!"

"How dare I what, my precious?" he said in an entirely equable tone of voice. "I did nothing. It was your hand."

She wanted to scream at him. To cry bitter tears and rage at him. But the time for that was many years past. She cleared her throat. "Clearly you have some great need to debauch everyone who comes within your circle, my lord. You may consider yourself the victor."

"I didn't take your virginity, little one," he murmured. "And self-pleasure is hardly debauchery. It's in the Bible."

She couldn't bring herself to look at him. The flame of color still rode high in her cheeks, and she couldn't think how he'd managed to do that, to take her distrustful self and make her…

It was appalling, and she didn't want to think about it. He was a degenerate, a notorious one, and the sooner she escaped from his presence the better she would be.

"That's all I'm going to get, isn't it, *ma petite?*" he said lazily. "I expect you want more, but you'd never admit to it. I shall now endeavor to catch some much-needed sleep and spare your maidenly blushes, unless you'd consider having a second lesson. No? I thought not. I have two more days of carousing left and at my advanced age I need my strength." He smiled at her with angelic innocence. "Cat got your tongue, my pet?"

With supreme effort she pulled herself together, looking at him with acute dislike. "If you sleep you'll stop talking, which would be a blessing," she said. "And at your advanced age I can see that you would most definitely benefit from it."

There was a sudden, charged silence in the carriage. "My dear Miss Harriman, if you continue to amuse me it will be extremely difficult for me to keep my hands off you. There are very few people who don't bore me, and I tend to be possessive about those I find entertaining."

"I shall proceed to snore," she said, snapping her eye closed.

She heard him laugh. It was a wicked sound, soft and low and for many women, irresistible. But she wasn't many women. Her body still trembled from the aftermath of what he…what they had done. She folded her bare hands beneath the fur pelisse and stared out the window, ignoring him.

It was the noise that awoke her. The carriage clattered over the rough cobbles of the city streets, and her eyes flew open to meet his.

"Once again, Miss Harriman, you have slept with me," he said. "Once might be forgiven by a disapproving society. Twice puts you quite beyond the pale. I think you should give up any pretensions to modesty and return to my château with me. Or my town house is quite large— you could wander around there for days and never see anyone. We could spend hours in bed…"

"Don't be tiresome, Monsieur le Comte," she said sharply, the last traces of sleep ripped away. How could she have fallen asleep in his presence? Particularly after what he'd done to her? How could she have been so foolish? She straightened her shoulders. "In fact, we're not far from my house, and I believe this carriage is too wide for the narrow streets. Why don't you let me down here and I'll walk the rest of the way. I'm certain Mrs. Clarke will forgive you."

"Dear child," he said. "I have no intention of abandoning you in your hour of need. Besides, I have to find out what exactly you're so desperate to keep hidden. A strapping live-in lover? Perhaps you live in a brothel and your sainted mother is one of your most lucrative whores? No, that does seem unlikely. But there's most assuredly something at your home that you don't want me to see and I'm surmising it's your exquisitely beautiful and most definitely not dead younger sister. You must know my curiosity, like all my appetites, is insatiable."

"I don't…" She slapped a hand over her mouth, bending over. "Stop the carriage!" she said in a strangled voice.

Her companion didn't move. "Are you unwell? You turned quite a shade just then."

"I'm going to be sick. If you don't stop and let me out I'm going to cast up my accounts all over your expensive carriage!" she said in a harsh, muffled voice.

"That would be a great deal too bad, but carriages can be cleaned. I have servants for that."

She looked up at him, her hand still clamped over her mouth. "Do you want to ride back to your château in a closed carriage filled with the results?"

"An excellent point." He rapped on the carriage wall behind him, and the conveyance came to an abrupt stop, hurtling her forward.

She caught herself in time, just before she ended in his arms. He'd unfastened the pelisse at her neck at some point during the wicked play he'd forced on her, and she thrust it off her shoulders, scrambling for the door just as the footman let down the steps.

With one hand clamped to her mouth and another against her stomach, she let the footman help her out of the carriage as she groaned piteously. A light snow was falling, making the wretched area look almost pretty. She felt the ground beneath her feet, and for a moment she began to sink to her knees in order to relieve herself of her last meal. She leaned toward the footman, making a gagging noise, and he drew back instinctively, releasing her.

It was all she needed. In a moment she was gone, disappearing into the throngs that crowded the main thoroughfare of that miserable part of the city.

She could bless the new boots, and thank Mrs. Clarke most heartily for them, she thought as she raced through the streets, turning corners, making her way deeper and deeper into the seedy underbelly of Rue du Pélican. He would be no match for her, she could outrun anybody when she so desired, thanks to her long legs and determination, and besides, she knew this area well. The footman would be at a loss.

No, Monsieur le Comte would have no choice but to return to his den of iniquity, and Lydia would be safe.

Elinor slowed down to a brisk trot, pulling her shawl more tightly about her. He would have had to get out and walk—that, or have his coachman find a sedan chair in order to reach the back alley that held their wretched little house, and even then he'd have a hard time finding it. Granted, one of his coachmen knew of the place, since Jacobs had been forced to direct him there in order to return her mother, but by the time Francis Rohan got home he would have lost interest in a plain woman with a secret.

The alleyway that held her small house looked

even more dismal than usual, and as she scrambled up the two steps to the entry she felt the cold begin to reach into her bones. That pelisse had been lovely, and would have looked beautiful on Lydia. But safety was a far greater treasure.

She pushed open the door and froze, momentarily afraid that somehow Lord Rohan had managed to defy the laws of nature and arrive there before her. A tall man was standing over her sister, and even in the shadowy light she could see her sister's vivid smile, and she let out a groan, a real one this time.

The man turned, and it wasn't Rohan. Of course it wasn't; it was the scarred man from the night before, the one who had had a half-clad demimondaine on his arm. A man who was talking to her sister, looking at her. A man who was no better than Rohan himself.

Lydia jumped up, her smile wider than ever. "Nell, I was so worried about you!" she cried. "Mr. Reading told me there was nothing to be concerned about, but you were gone all night, and ever since that time you went away to Italy I've been…"

"I'm fine, darling!" Elinor said swiftly, forestalling Lydia's artless comments. Even if Lydia hadn't been able to put two and two together, a more jaded member of society would have no trouble jumping to conclusions, and she couldn't afford to let that happen.

"This is Mr. Reading, Nell. He was kind enough to escort Mummy home."

Only Lydia called Lady Caroline by the cozy "mummy." If their mother had had any favorite besides her own dedicated self-interest, it would be her lovely younger daughter. Elinor herself looked too much like her father's branch of the family, and she had what Lady Caroline considered to be the disconcerting habit of giving her opinion when asked. She hadn't bothered sugarcoating it for her mother in years, and Lady Caroline hadn't thanked her.

"Very kind," Elinor murmured. "But we can handle things from this point." She couldn't quite hold the door for him, but she still made her point that he needed to leave, and now.

His smile tugged at the ugly scar on his otherwise handsome face. "Rohan would expect nothing less from me. Your mother appears to have quieted, but I'm not sure I should take the footmen with me, even though I'm being summarily dismissed."

It was a challenge, one Elinor met smoothly. "It's starting to snow, and it's a long way back to the château. I wouldn't want to be responsible for you getting caught in a snowdrift."

"Only if you pushed me in, Miss Harriman, which you look tempted to do." He caught Lydia's small hand in his and gave her an extravagant kiss. There was no missing the look in her sister's eyes, though Elinor hoped and prayed Reading wasn't alert enough to read it.

"Let me just check on our mother," Elinor said. "I would expect from the blissful silence emanating from the bedroom that she's well settled and we have no more need of your so-generous assistance."

She turned, trying not to shiver in the cool morning air. There wasn't much of a fire in the grate, and she had no idea where they'd get more wood. But first things first, and getting rid of the man standing far too close to her baby sister was utmost. She had no choice but to leave them together long enough for her to see to Lady Caroline, but then she could shoo him out quite handily.

Two of Rohan's liveried footmen stood in the hallway, almost on guard, and at Elinor's approach they moved out of the way, bowing. She pushed open the door to see Nanny sitting beside her mother.

Lady Caroline lay still in the narrow bed, with only the fitful light of the winter morning to pierce the darkness. "She hasn't moved since they brought her back, poor thing," Nanny said. "I washed her and tried to make her more comfortable and told the gentleman that he can safely leave. Your poor mother probably won't be up for days." She looked back at her charge. "If ever."

Elinor looked down at her mother. Her skin was bluish, with deep circles around her eyes, but for the moment she was at peace. "Has she taken any food?"

Nanny Maude knew better than she did just how little food there was in their larder. "Some weak tea. And a bit of gruel. She spat out more than she took in."

And they couldn't afford to waste what little they had. "I'll send Lydia in while I get rid of our visitors," Elinor said.

"What are you going to do, Miss Nell?" Nanny said plaintively. "I've sent Jacobs out to see what he can find, but there's nothing left for me to make a dinner out of. No wood for the fire unless we take this bed apart."

Elinor wanted to put her hands to her face and scream, but her calm expression showed none of it. It was up to her to see to things, and even if she hadn't the vaguest idea what she was going to do, she didn't need to share that.

She couldn't even sell her body on the streets for money. Paris was filled with beautiful whores—she'd barely make enough to keep them fed. If that.

Jacobs could sell the boots and the silk stockings. She'd been a proud fool to have left the fur pelisse behind—that could have supported them for weeks if they were careful.

She was going to have to go back and meet with that wretched lawyer, petition her unknown cousin, her stupid pride in the dust. She could hear the noise from beyond the closed door and she breathed a sigh of relief. The intruders were leaving. Men were such noisy creatures there was no mistaking their footsteps or the sound of their flimsy front door closing. "I'll go find Jacobs," she said calmly. "We're not out of options yet."

Elinor pushed open the door. "Lydia, my dear, could you…" Her voice trailed off as her worst fears came to fruition. The scarred gentleman stood off to one side, an unreadable expression on his face. And Francis Rohan, the Prince of Darkness, the King of Hell, stood over her sister, holding Lydia's small, delicate hand in his.

7

She wasn't pleased to see him, that much was evident, and Francis Rohan bestowed his most charming smile on her. "You forgot to wait for me, Miss Harriman. I had quite a time catching up with you."

He didn't miss the momentary panic in her fine eyes, quickly replaced by that same maddening calm she wrapped about her more fiercely than the ragged cloak she'd worn. "There was no need for you to come all this way, Monsieur le Comte. I know these streets very well, and no one would dare accost me."

"Now, that doesn't surprise me in the least. You'd terrify the king himself. But you left your cloak behind, and despite my many failings I have exquisite manners. Haven't I, Reading?"

His friend bowed slightly in agreement. "Exquisite."

"And I've just met your lovely sister…"

She moved with astonishing speed, somehow managing to come between him and the pretty little chit whose hand he'd been holding, and everything suddenly made sense, which pleased him. He preferred his life with a certain order, and anomalies, while entertaining, needed to be explained, before one could move on.

Though the anomaly that was Elinor Harriman was going to take a bit longer figure out.

"Thank you so much for coming," she said, her voice brooking no opposition. "You've been extremely kind, but we wouldn't think of keeping you from your guests."

She was tall enough, and solid, but he could simply pick her up and move her out of the way if he had any interest in the pretty little sister.

He had not. He'd had enough pretty girls and beautiful women to last him a lifetime. This other one, however, was proving interesting. He was still aroused from their time in the carriage—if he hadn't pretended to fall asleep he would have had her skirts up over her head in a minute.

She was standing too close to him for her own comfort, but she was determined to shield her sister from his lascivious eyes. And Reading had looked a bit…abstracted when he'd first walked in, though his young friend would never make the mistake of wasting his time on an impoverished virgin. He had a fortune to make, and he'd always been dependable.

"Yes, Miss Harriman?" he said, not moving. Wondering how far she'd go to get rid of him, if she'd put those pale hands on him. Wondering how he would react if she did.

"We thank you for your help, my lord," she said in her most polite voice. "I believe we can dispense with it at this point."

A faint smile touched his mouth. "You're an impressive guardian, and my curiosity is satisfied now that I know what treasure you're so determined to protect. You may rest assured that I'm far too jaded to be attracted to mere beauty. Your sister is safe from me."

"Nell," the young girl said in an irritated voice. "Would you stop being so ridiculous?"

"Nell?" he echoed, ignoring everything else about the conversation except what interested him. "That's quite charming. I…"

"Good day, my lord Rohan," Miss Elinor Harriman said firmly.

"Come on, Francis," Reading said. "We have the revels to return to. We wouldn't want them to have too much fun without us."

"Ah, yes," he said, finally moving away from her. While he would have been very interested to see if she really would go so far as to push him, the thought of her hands on him was far too…enticing, and the circumstances were far from ideal. There were too many witnesses.

Lydia managed to move from behind her sister's imposing presence. "Thank you again for all your help, Mr. Reading. And my lord Rohan." She curtsied prettily enough, and her older sister frowned.

It was never his nature to let an opportunity slide by. "It was my pleasure, Miss Lydia," he said in his most flattering tones, relieved that he remembered her name. "The sight of your beauty is reward enough."

Her older sister reacted exactly as he wanted her to, stiffening. If he were younger and more foolish, her dragonlike protection would have ensured his eventual debauchery of the pretty little thing, but at this point it just seemed too tiresome. Besides, he had the impression that Reading wouldn't like it.

"Miss Harriman, your servant," he said, giving her a bow of such extravagant proportions that she'd know she was being mocked.

But she'd already turned back to her sister, and his gesture was wasted.

He waited until they were back out in the narrow alley that held the tumbledown house. His carriage was only a few steps away—she'd lied about the difficulty in getting there. His blue silk shoes were quite ruined by the snow and the filth in the street. "Quite the interesting family, are they not?"

Reading frowned. "I think you should keep your hands off her, Francis. There are more than enough women at the château to occupy your time."

"But I'm not going back to the château. My honored guests will doubtless notice I'm gone, but it won't make much impression on them. This was only a casual weekend—we still have the Spring Revels to plan. Besides, I find her oddly enchanting."

Reading was obviously not happy with him, a curious event in itself. "She has a hard enough lot. The place was freezing, and if they had firewood hidden somewhere I'd be very much surprised. And while she's pleasantly shaped I suspect she doesn't get much to eat. I think the best thing you could do is arrange a marriage for her."

Francis turned to look at his old friend. "Charles, there are times when you astonish me with your perspicacity. That is exactly what I should do. The only problem is finding a willing partner."

"Don't be ridiculous. She's exquisite. Any man would be honored to have her."

They'd reached the carriage, and Francis paused as he was about to ascend the steps. "Dear boy, I believe we're talking at cross-purposes. Is it Miss Lydia you're protecting so fiercely?"

"Of course. Are you going to tell me you don't have designs on her? She's an absolute diamond and you know it." He was sounding particularly glum.

"I fancy the diamond's sister," Francis said, half amazed at the truth of his words. "Though you're absolutely right, she'll be much easier to handle if she's married. I think my cousin should do nicely."

He climbed into the carriage, and Reading followed him. "You mean the doctor?"

"Who better?" He settled himself on the leather seat, draping his long coats around him with great care. "He needs a wife to help him with his practice, and she needs a doctor to attend to her mother. I'll send him over this afternoon."

"Is this the sour young man I met? As I recall he's not too happy you have the title. Is he likely to want to do you any favors?"

"It's true," Francis said, picking a speck of dirt from his sleeve. This area of the city was truly atrocious, but as yet there was nothing he could do about it. "He thinks the French title should belong to him.

Unfortunately he was born on the wrong side of the blanket, and the old title had to devolve onto an émigré Englishman. I've been more than generous with the boy, and he's wise enough to know that following my wishes is the best way to get his hands on at least some of the family estate, if I don't work through it first."

"You have more money than God, Francis. It would take a superhuman effort to lose all your money, and even you couldn't accomplish it."

Francis gave Reading his seraphic smile. "Don't doubt me, dear boy. I can do anything I want if I set my mind to it."

Reading's reluctant laugh was encouraging. "That I don't doubt. I stand corrected. What say we return to the party after all? The Spring Revels won't be for another few weeks, and I see a long dull period stretching in front of us."

"I have every intention of entertaining myself, Reading. You should know me well enough to realize that celibacy is no more for the likes of me than monogamy. And I've decided to celebrate Lent this year on a grand scale."

"Oh, bloody Christ," Reading said.

"Precisely. And I'm going to have Miss Harriman to entertain me."

"You don't think your cousin Etienne will have something to say about that? Presuming you manage to marry her off?"

"No. He'd give me his own sister if I asked for her. In fact, I'd offer his sister to you, but she's alarmingly fat and fecund. And you don't want any offspring until you've bagged your heiress."

Reading's sardonic smile tugged at his scarred face. "Indeed. But what makes you think that the dragon will lift her skirts for you once she's married? She's the frighteningly respectable sort. Why would you suppose she'd succumb to your evil machinations?"

"They always do, dear boy. And Miss Harriman…" He paused. "Good heavens."

A moment later there was a loud crack from outside the carriage. "That's something I don't hear from you very often," Reading said. "Good heavens, what? You have the strangest look on your face."

Francis glanced down at the fine blue satin of his coat. "First my shoes are ruined and now this," he said in a faint voice. "I'm afraid we're going to have to see my cousin sooner rather than later."

"Because?"

"Because I do believe I've been shot," Francis said. "Tell the coachman to hurry, would you?" And he closed his eyes to the sounds of Reading pounding on the carriage wall and the whole conveyance came to an abrupt halt.

Lydia loved her older sister more than any human being in this world, but at that moment she was more than a little cross with her. "Was that entirely necessary?" she said. "You were being ridiculous."

Elinor lifted her head, and for the first time Lydia noticed how pale she was. "You don't realize how very bad Viscount Rohan is," she said in a subdued voice.

"I assure you, Nell, he has absolutely no interest in me," she said. "Don't you think I'd be able to tell by now? Any attention he paid to me was simply to annoy you."

Elinor flushed. Which was odd—she was unused to her calm older sister looking disturbed. "You mistake the matter," she said. "He's the very fiend of duplicity. To lower one's guard around him would be courting disaster."

More and more interesting. "Did you lower your guard around him, dearest?" Lydia said. "Because he was certainly watching you quite closely. Did he...do anything to you? Offer you an insult?"

"Of course not," Elinor said with a shaky laugh. "Do I look like the kind of woman to interest a libertine like Lord Rohan? He merely has a peculiar sense of humor, one he uses to torment others. You may be right—he certainly has his choice of some of the greatest beauties of Paris. I still insist you be careful if you happen to encounter him again. I would presume that we shan't be bothered by him any more in future, but it would be a mistake to assume that fate would be kind."

"I think we'll see him again," Lydia said, not bothering to cover her small smile.

Elinor caught it. "If you find something amusing about this situation I would be most grateful if you would share it with me. Because the humor of it escapes my attention entirely."

"He likes you, Nell. And why shouldn't he? Any man with sense would see what a wonderful woman you are. He won't be able to keep away from you…"

"Stop it!" Elinor said in a sharper tone than Lydia had ever heard from her. She took a deep breath. "For one thing, you're very wrong. Yesterday I was a curiosity, nothing more. A…a virtuous woman in a land of whores. He's a shallow man, easily bored."

"He doesn't strike me as shallow, Nell."

Elinor ignored her. "Secondly, even if he did harbor some demented attraction for me, his intentions would be worse than dishonorable. You know the gossip we've heard about the Heavenly Host. It's true."

"They drink the blood of virgins?" Lydia shrieked, horrified.

"Of course not," Elinor said in a cranky voice. "The other rumors. They gather together for the most licentious of activities, wearing strange garments and behaving like…like animals. You wouldn't want me to be part of such a world, would you? Even if he wanted me?"

Lydia looked at her sister's brown eyes, more troubled than she'd seen them in many years. "I'm sorry, love. I've been thoughtless. I hate to see you judge yourself so unfairly, but you're right. That kind of interest would be disastrous."

"That goes for Mr. Reading as well, Lyddie."

Lydia knew how to bat her eyes and fool landlords and creditors. She could fool her sister as well, particularly since Elinor was so distraught. Besides, he'd been nothing but polite, that twisted, beautiful face of his mostly devoid of expression.

Just as Lydia knew how to fool people, she could also read them better than most. Charles Reading was different. Beneath his determinedly distant behavior, she knew he was feeling the same odd, irrational pull that was knotting her stomach and making her knees shake. She who had flirted with any number of handsome young men and remained untouched. All it had taken was a scarred, unhappy man and she was dreaming…

No, she was losing her mind. The house was cold, the last bit of the fire almost out. Elinor didn't know, but Lydia planned to meet with Monsieur Garot the greengrocer this evening when he closed up shop. And she was going to do whatever she had to do to shoulder some of the burden that Elinor took on herself.

She was calm, determined, undespairing. She knew as well as Nell that Charles Reading wasn't for her.

It didn't mean that she couldn't dream.

"Of course, Nell," she said absently. "He's of no interest to me. I'm waiting for a wealthy prince, remember?"

And Elinor smiled back at her, too abstracted to realize that for the first time her sister was lying to her.

He really wasn't in the mood to deal with all this, Rohan thought several hours later from his exceedingly uncomfortable position on the narrow cot in Etienne's well-equipped surgery. That had been money well spent, he mused dreamily. In fact, it had been simply to occupy a hotheaded Frenchman from being an annoyance. He never thought it might save his life one day.

They'd given him laudanum—he was familiar enough with its delightful effects to recognize it, and he welcomed the drugged daze. He could remember a few unhappy moments when Etienne had dug around in the flesh of his upper arm for the bullet, and no doubt the young man had taken a fair amount of pleasure in inflicting pain on his so-called usurper. But that was all in the hazy past, and if he could just get a bit more comfortable…

"You're coming around, cousin."

He turned his head to see Etienne de Giverney looking at him in pinched disapproval. He'd be a handsome young man if only he didn't have the unfortunate tendency to sneer, and Francis considered informing him of that when he realized it was the effect of the laudanum.

"Saved my life, did you, Etienne?" he murmured. "That must have gone against the grain."

"Hardly. The bullet was in your arm, not your heart. Whoever shot you did a very poor job of it."

"Which must sadden you tremendously."

"I do think assassins should know what they're doing," Etienne said in his clipped voice.

Francis was emerging from the drugged daze, reluctantly. He struggled to sit up without any aid from his unwilling doctor. "You think that was what it was? An assassination attempt?"

"Since you were in town I doubt it was a hunting

accident," Etienne said coolly. "And I imagine there are a great many people who would like to see you dead."

Francis straightened his back. His arm was wrapped in layers of gauze, and despite the drugs the pain was more than annoying. He was going home to soak himself in brandy until it stopped. "Perhaps. But none of them are crack shots."

"Whoever it was missed his target," Etienne pointed out.

"He came close enough, considering the circumstances. A busy city street, the protection of a carriage. I imagine we should look for a talented marksman. Perhaps someone newly discharged from the army."

"Well, should you ever discover him you can give him your compliments on his marksmanship."

Rohan controlled his irritation. "Where's my shirt? And where's Reading?"

"He's been doing your bidding. You had quite the list of commands before you finally succumbed to the laudanum. A servant should arrive with fresh clothes momentarily—I had to shred your coat and shirt. They were soaked with blood—there would have been no salvaging them anyway."

"*Tant pis*. I can always buy more," he said deliberately, just to see Etienne's brow darken.

"And just who is it you're trying to corrupt at the moment?"

Francis smiled pleasantly. "Anyone who comes near me, Etienne. Did you have someone in mind?"

Etienne made an annoyed click of his tongue. "You had Reading dispatching firewood and food to someplace in Rue du Pélican. Don't you realize you could have anyone from that area raise her skirts for a few sous?"

"I agree, it's not a very savory area, but you'll find there are a couple of very virtuous young ladies in residence. With their ill *maman*. I'd like you to call on them, see if there's anything you can do for the poor woman," he said, trying his best to look saintly.

"Charity is unlike you."

He laughed. "Oh, acquit me of any such motives. I have nothing but the most impure thoughts when it comes to one of the young women. I'd like you to see to the mother's swift and painless passing and marry the older girl. She'll provide you an excellent wife—commonsensical and plainspoken. She'll organize your life and your practice and give you a dozen hopeful children."

There was a moment's silence. "You still have the capacity to surprise me," Etienne said finally. "I'm not going to kill some old woman for you. Nor am I about to marry some woman so you can debauch her younger sister."

"In fact, the mother's not that old. But she's dying of the Spanish disease and her mind's gone." Rohan poked at his arm, then winced. "She'll be dead in a matter of months anyway. And it's your future wife I wish to debauch."

Etienne stared at him. "There are times, Francis, when I wonder if you're quite mad."

"In my own way. I take it you don't fancy the idea of aiding me?"

"No."

"I would be most grateful if you'd consider it," he said. "You know I tend to express my gratitude in tangible ways." He could see the light of greed in his cousin's flat black eyes. "And the mother could do with a doctor's care. I could send someone else, of course, but I thought I should offer such an opportunity to my dear cousin and heir."

Etienne drew himself upright. "I'll go see the poor woman. Because I swore an oath to attend the sick. And you're not going to see me inherit the title— you'll marry on your deathbed and beget an heir just to spite me," he said in a voice that wasn't far from a whine.

"What a wonderful opinion you have of my virility," Rohan replied. "As it is, I have no interest in begetting anything. Assist me in this matter, at least as far as the woman goes. It's always possible that you might suddenly become enamored of her daughter. You need a wife, and she'd be a lucrative pick."

"You'd settle money on her simply in order to get her into bed?" Etienne said, aghast.

"Don't I do the very same thing with the beautiful whores who attend me? Even the grand ladies offer up their charms for a price, be it jewels or flattery. Sex is always some kind of transaction, and I have no hesitation in paying the price."

Etienne shook his head. "You're an extremely cynical man, cousin."

"As are you, *mon fils*." With great difficulty he managed to swing his legs over the side of the small cot. For a moment the world swirled about him most unpleasantly, and then it came back into focus. "I believe I hear a commotion outside. I expect it's Reading, back from his errands of mercy. Direct your man to assist him."

"I have no 'man,' cousin. Just an elderly widow who helps me in the surgery, and I'm not about to have her wait on a spoiled aristocrat."

Francis smiled his most angelic smile. "You'd be very happy to be a spoiled aristocrat yourself, Etienne, admit it. This man-of-the-people air you affect is simply because of circumstance, not preference. And you'll have to get rid of the woman. I think Miss Harriman might tend to be the jealous, possessive sort, and she wouldn't want you in close quarters with a comely widow. And don't try to pretend she's not comely, Etienne. I know your tastes too well."

"If the woman you desire is the jealous, possessive sort then why are you interested? Those are qualities that have proved anathema to you in the past."

Rohan was struck. "You know, you are quite right. I have no idea why I am so intent on debauching a young woman who will give me nothing but trouble. But then, I've never spent overmuch time examining my motives. I want her. That's enough." He looked up as Reading was ushered into the room, indeed by a buxom young woman who could only be Etienne's "elderly" widow. "Have you come to rescue me, dear boy? There's only so much of Etienne's disapproval that I can bear."

"The carriage awaits. The food and wood have been delivered, with furniture and rugs and bedding to follow. Are you certain you want to bother? You can dress a pig up in satin and lace and it's still a pig."

Francis smiled hazily. It had been a long day. In fact, a long pair of days, though he usually survived sleepless nights quite well. "Are you calling my intended a pig, Charles?"

Charles raised a dark eyebrow. "Intended what, Francis? You surely can't be having respectable inclinations toward this girl. The bullet hit your arm, not your head."

"No such thing, my boy. I'm too old to change." He turned to look at his sullen cousin. "Etienne, do you have more of that lovely laudanum? I think I'll need medicinal assistance for the ride back to Maison de Giverney."

He wasn't so far gone that he missed the pinched expression Etienne always wore at the mention of the Paris mansion that should have been his. "You've had enough."

"But if you give me more I might accidentally take too much and die. And then where would you be?" he said sweetly.

"It will take but a moment."

The moment he left the room Rohan turned to Charles. "The two women will be removed from the sty as soon as it's feasible. These things must be handled delicately, with finesse, and I've never been a clumsy man. Give me your arm. This place smells of cabbage and death. The sooner I return to my own bed the happier I shall be."

"Your cousin has gone to get you more laudanum."

"I merely got tired of his sour face. He can send it later. Perhaps we ought to send someone to cheer him up. Marianne, for instance." He rose to his stocking feet, unsteadily. "Get me out of here, for mercy's sake. I have evil plans to hatch. Are you with me?"

"Every step of the way," Reading said, taking his arm. "We're going to hell, you know."

"That was ascertained many years ago, Charles. Thank God."

"Thank God," Charles echoed heartily.

But even in his drugged state Rohan could hear the faint thread of doubt in his friend's voice as they headed out into the snowy evening.

8

As far as days went, this one was looking as miserable as the day before. Once Rohan had left, Elinor had waited only long enough to make certain her mother and sister had no need of her, and then she set off to find the lawyer, Mr. Mitchum. Her proud departure yesterday had been put in perspective. There was no room for pride when Lydia was at stake, no room for pride when the Prince of Darkness had set his sights on her sister. Elinor had been a fool to walk out without seeking an appointment with her father's heir, but the disappointment had been too deep. Without a generous inheritance they were doomed.

She never would have thought she'd be so impulsive. In the last six years she'd considered herself calm, practical, thoughtful. Now in one rash moment of temper she might have put her sister and her small, motley family in danger, and her self-contempt knew no limits.

Mr. Mitchum was no help at all. At least the new Baron Tolliver hadn't left France, but for the moment he was out of town, visiting friends in the country. There was no telling when he'd return, or even if he'd still be willing to see his poor female relation at that point. Perhaps if Miss Harriman were to return in a week's time an appointment might be arranged?

They might be lost in a week's time, Elinor thought grimly, scurrying through the wintry streets of Paris. The snow was falling, swirling down in pretty patterns, and at another time she might have appreciated it. Not on this bitterly cold evening. Once she'd left the lawyer she'd walked for hours, more of her fruitless quest for employment. In this area of Paris people could barely find enough to survive—no one had the money or the interest in learning the fine art of playing the pianoforte or stitching a perfect seam. Particularly since no one could afford to own a pianoforte, and needlework was kept for more practical applications. Just as well, because her needlework was appalling and it had been years since anyone had been forced to listen to her on the pianoforte.

She pulled the shawl around her more tightly. Her own cloak that she'd left behind at the château was warmer than the flimsy wool. Rohan had brought the stolen fur-lined cloak, but Elinor had enough sense not to wear it into the streets. Chances were it would have been ripped away from her in a matter of minutes. One did not display items of such worth in a desperate neighborhood such as this.

And indeed, she'd left Lydia wrapped in it, warm and comfortable in the icy house, so it served its purpose. She just had to hope Lydia didn't have an attack of guilt and cover their mother with it. Lady Caroline was beyond knowing if she was hot or cold, and she'd thrown everything away. She didn't deserve the one bit of comfort in their barren home, Elinor thought with fierce bitterness.

Tomorrow she would sell the cloak. Tonight they were going to have to break up the furniture in order to keep from freezing, and she wasn't sure where to start. Her mother's bed would be the obvious choice. The rest of them were already sleeping on the floor. But if Lady Caroline had a pallet on the floor there'd be no way to restrain her, and that was even more dangerous than freezing to death.

It would have to be the chairs or the table, and she couldn't decide which was more necessary. They were young enough and agile enough to sit comfortably on the floor, though Nanny and Jacobs had a much harder time of it. Nanny Maude had frequently napped as she sat beside Lady Caroline on the bed, her back against one of the posts, but that could hardly serve as her main mode of sitting.

Darkness was falling, and what little safety there was in the streets that surrounded them was fading fast as well. She had no choice but to head back, having failed in the most simple of quests. She thought back to that tray of cinnamon-toast strips and wanted to cry.

There was an odd light coming from the small windows that looked out onto the street, and Elinor paused, momentarily confused. One house did look much like another, and she might have mistaken where she was, but no, she could hear Lydia's voice raised in laughter, and she burst through the door, suddenly terrified that her nemesis had returned.

The room was warm—waves of heat coming from the crackling fire in the hearth, with stacks of wood waiting to one side. There were candles lit all around, putting a temporarily pleasant glow on their poverty, and she could smell the unbelievable scent of roasting chicken from the small room that served as kitchen and servants' quarters.

She looked around, somewhat desperately, but there was no tall, dangerously beautiful man in sight. No one at all but Lydia and Nanny Maude.

"Isn't it wonderful, Nell?" Lydia cried, jumping up. "The wood arrived just an hour after you left, more than enough to keep the kitchen fire going as well for weeks, and then the food. You wouldn't believe it— flour and sugar and tea, fresh cream and butter. And chicken, potatoes, sausages. Nanny's already made us scones. It's heavenly."

Not quite, Elinor thought, remember Rohan's satanic smile. "There'll be a price to pay for all this," she said in a dour voice, stripping off the threadbare shawl and advancing into the cozy room.

"One I'll gladly pay," Lydia said cheerfully. "If I have to trade my innocence for a warm bed and a chicken dinner then I'll do so without hesitation. This scone itself is worth any number of indecent favors."

"Don't make light of it, Lyddie," she said sharply. "This isn't an act of disinterested charity."

Lydia popped the rest of the scone in her mouth, then smiled beatifically. "No, I suppose it's not. But for some reason I doubt Lord Rohan would be the kind of man who'd force you, no matter how wicked he likes to think himself. I think he likes the thrill of the chase."

"Lyddie darling," she said, crossing the room and taking a scone. "He's a heartless, soulless libertine. I doubt there's anything he'd refrain from doing, simply for moral principles. He has no moral principles."

"Perhaps not. I suspect he's not the villain he pretends to be. He likes the challenge, the power. Using force would be too clumsy for him—he'd consider it failure."

"You're right about that much," Elinor said. "But it's not me he'd want. And I'm not letting any man—" she took a bite of the scone "—take liberties with you…" She took another bite. "I'm here to protect you—" she closed her eyes "—and, damn, you're right. This is enough to make one surrender one's honor in a trice."

"Don't use such language, Miss Elinor," Nanny Maude said. "You've been spending too much time in these awful streets and around your mother."

"Our awful mother," Lydia said with a giggle.

"And I didn't make the scones—they arrived along with everything else. Real Devonshire clotted cream, strong black tea from China, fresh strawberry preserves. Even the chicken was already butchered and dressed, ready for the pot. Someone thinks I can't cook," she said with offended dignity.

"Someone thinks you have way too many things to worry about and thought you deserved some assistance," Lydia assured her. She twirled around the room, practically giddy. "Don't you see, Nell? We have a guardian angel, and who cares if he's a fallen one? I'm not afraid of him. You're wrong—he has no nefarious designs on me, and you're more than a match for him. If he has wicked motives he's going to be sorely disappointed."

Elinor couldn't help it—the fire called to her with its siren warmth. She sank down on her knees in front of it, holding out her chilled hand, as Lydia brought a cup of tea—real tea—over to her and sat down beside her.

The heat was sinking into her bones, and for a brief moment she simply wanted to put her head down on the rough floor and weep.

"There's someone at the door," Nanny Maude said in her customarily cranky voice.

"Tell Lord Rohan to go away," Elinor said. "We're not entertaining guests at this hour."

"It's not him," she said darkly. "There are a bunch of them. Probably come to take the things back. They were brought here by mistake."

"Then definitely tell them to go away," Elinor said, feeling somewhat giddy herself. "They're not taking my fire or my tea."

Jacobs stomped in from the kitchen, clearly annoyed with the lot of them, and opened the door. "More fripperies," he said in a dour voice that couldn't disguise his pleasure. "You watch where you put those things, laddie." He moved out of the way, as a line of men entered the house, bearing furniture, rugs, mattresses and arms of linens.

Elinor sprang to her feet. "You can't bring those in here!"

"Sorry, miss, but we've got orders," one man said as he dropped one end of the settee to the right of the fire. "We're not taking these things back. Just tell us where you want us to put it. We've got orders not to leave until you're satisfied."

"And I won't be satisfied until these things are gone," she said sharply.

"Watch yourself," said Nanny Maude, slapping at a young man carrying a small desk.

"I can't help you there, miss," he said. "I'm a lot more frightened of his lordship than I am of you. He told me to come back and report to him and I don't like the thought of what he'd say if I brought anything back."

Elinor turned back to Lydia. "This is impossible. Next they'll be delivering clothes and undergarments."

A wistful smile crossed Lydia's face. "It would be so nice to have pretty undergarments again."

"Don't be ridiculous. I'm going to put a stop to this right now." She pushed past the man carrying the rug and reached for her shawl.

"You can't go out now!"

"I can and I will. It's still early—I can inform his lordship that his inappropriate gifts should be removed immediately."

"Not the chicken?" Lydia said in a plaintive voice.

Elinor paused. "No, not the chicken. Or the scones. Or the firewood," she added with a shiver. The constantly opening door was spreading blasts of cold through the house.

"You're not going out to that château again!" Nanny Maude said in a shrill voice.

"No need. He's at his town house. Over on the Rue Saint-Honoré," said the helpful man, who seemed to be the leader of this never-ending line of furniture movers. "I'm Rolande, in charge of the comte's household possessions. I can promise you these things are merely castoffs from his overfilled house."

"It is still unacceptable. I'm going."

"I can take you there if need be," Rolande offered.

Elinor looked at him suspiciously. "Did *he* tell you to bring me?"

"I don't talk to the comte, mademoiselle," he said. "Just his steward. And no one said anything about bringing you back. Just trying to be helpful."

She looked at him for a long moment. It was a cold, dark night, snow was falling, and finding Lord Rohan's town house could be problematic at best. She had no choice—the more things he sent the harder it would be to get rid of them. It wasn't simply the fact that if anyone heard of it Lydia's reputation would be ruined. This was how their mother had lived, how they had lived, dependent on the largesse of a man with wicked plans. She was not going to follow in her mother's footsteps, she simply was not.

Rohan wouldn't listen, of course, no matter how she tried to explain it. If she had any sense she would sit back by the fire, in one of the new chairs the men had brought, and accept it for the sake of her poor family. What was honor if your family was starving to death?

But there was still her missing cousin. They weren't devoid of all hope. They could accept this, and nothing more, and she would make that clear.

"Let's go," she said. *"Allons-y."*

The ride from the gutter to the elegant streets of Paris was surprisingly short, given the disparity between the residences. A good thing—Rolande's mode of transportation was a wagon, the only seat being beside the helpful driver, and the wind seemed to grow colder with each breath she took. She tried to concentrate on his stories of his grown son, his grandchildren, his bad leg, but by the time he slowed the horses she was shivering.

"Here we are, mademoiselle," he said, coming to a stop. "Would you like me to come with you? This isn't the sort of household that welcomes people like us, not at the front door."

People like us? she thought, startled. And then the truth hit. In fact, this servant was better dressed than she was—his old clothes were worn but patched. She'd had to put on her last dress when she'd arrived home earlier that day, and she'd torn the skirt on a loose nail.

For a moment she wavered. Someone of Rohan's wealth and stature would hardly have nefarious designs on a young woman who lived in worse surroundings than his own servants.

But then she remembered that Rohan didn't have a charitable bone in his body. He lived for his decadent desires—altruistic gestures were beyond him. It didn't matter what had happened in his youth to wound him. He was the man he'd become, and that man was dangerous.

"He'll want to see me," she said with false certainty, sliding down off the wagon before Rolande could help her.

"Just in case, mademoiselle, I'll wait here for you."

"There's no need…"

"Just in case."

"You're a very kind man, Rolande," she said. "I will tell his lordship to double what he's paying you."

"His lordship pays very generously. And I'm doing this for you, not him." He cast a look of dislike up at the huge house. "You go on ahead now, mademoiselle. You look very cold."

Rohan *would* have to have a broad expanse of steps leading up to his mansion, she thought dourly, starting the climb. She expected lights, gaiety, debauchery spilling out into the nighttime, but the house seemed secure and quiet.

She reached for the huge brass knocker, but before she could use it the door opened and an extremely proper-looking servant stared at her as if she was complete filth. He had to be French.

His first words confirmed it. "The servants' entrance is to the side," he said, and started to close the door in her face.

She threw her body against it, to halt him. "I'm here to see his lordship. Just tell him Miss Harriman is here."

The man's gaze flicked out at the wagon waiting for her, then back at her, and if anything, his look was even more disdainful. "I have heard no mention of that name," he said haughtily, pushing on the door.

"Just ask him…" The door slammed shut in her face, leaving her standing there, cold and furious. "All right," she said beneath her breath. "You asked for it."

She stomped back down the snow-covered stairs, mentally thanking Mrs. Clarke for her pilfered boots, and climbed up into the wagon. "The servants' entrance it is, Rolande."

She'd lived such a strange life, so many extremes, and yet she'd never ventured into the servants' quarters of a great house. From her father's country house, to the elegant Paris apartments where her mother and her lover had lived with passionate abandon—so much so that it had been up to Elinor and Nanny Maude to bring up Lydia—she'd still remained sequestered from the servants' quarters. The apartments and houses grew shabbier, but somehow she'd yet to venture into the demiworld of working people.

It was warm and clean in the back hallway. In the distance she could hear the sounds of the servants talking as they worked on what must be dinner, and Elinor wondered what it would be like to have the safety and warmth of honest labor. Perhaps she could become a servant. There was no task she particularly excelled at—she was too clumsy to be a chambermaid, too bad a seamstress to be a lady's maid and a truly terrible cook. Perhaps a kitchen maid might be possible, under the watchful eye of some stern master chef, and she could…

"Mademoiselle?" Rolande interrupted her brief fantasy. "If you go straight down that hallway you'll find stairs to the main living quarters. You keep an eye out for Cavalle—he runs this place with an iron fist."

"Bless you, Rolande," she said. "I wish I had money…"

"There is no need. I take pleasure from serving you, mademoiselle," he said, starting to bow.

She leaned forward and kissed his leathered cheek, and he gave her a dazzling smile. And then she turned and headed off in search of her nemesis.

The steps were narrow, with rough wood, clearly a servants' staircase, and she moved quietly. There was a closed door at the top, of course, and she hesitated for a moment. Once she entered the main part of the house what would she do? Start searching the rooms until she found him, obviously, but exactly how she'd start the conversation was a problem, considering that she had to sneak into his house.

That was his fault as well, for hiring a majordomo who was such a…a…polite words evaded her, and even in the privacy of her own mind she couldn't use the street words she'd unconsciously absorbed during the last few years. *Batarde* would have to do. She pushed open the door, very carefully, and stepped into the lion's den.

The space was warm, with the golden glow that came from only the best beeswax candles. The ones he had sent to her house, along with the blessed firewood and the food that she'd stormed off and missed. For a moment she felt faint with hunger. She'd eaten nothing since the toast strips in the morning and the scone less than an hour ago, and it wasn't enough to keep her sturdy frame alive. She wasn't delicate, like Lydia. She was taller, stronger, and she felt as if she'd been running some terrible, endless race. She would have given anything to lie down on one of the new beds they'd brought in and sleep for days. Anything but her sister's honor. And her own, what was left of it.

She closed the door behind her and set off, resolute. The door led into a series of formal rooms, gilded woodwork, highly polished floors, mirrors all around. She'd heard stories of Versailles and the Hall of Mirrors. Surely this rivaled those places. Despite what little she knew of Lord Rohan, she was uncomfortably aware that his fortune was enormous.

As were the marble stairs she eventually con fronted. She moved up slowly, keeping to the edge in case an overzealous servant should appear, but it was evening and most of them would be discreetly absent unless summoned. She remembered that much from her family's more affluent times.

She wandered the hallways of the first floor, peering into rooms. She found a library, redolent of leather and pipe tobacco, a pretty little salon clearly designed for the woman of the house, clearly never used, a music room with a pianoforte and harp. At the end of one hall was the ballroom, dark and silent, at the opposite end a locked door.

She pressed her ear against the door, but all was silent. Whatever that room was used for, and she shuddered to think, it was empty now.

She had no choice but to climb another flight of stairs, this one smaller but no less magnificent. What if Rolande was mistaken, what if she was wandering around the Viscount Rohan's town house with no one there? And then she heard the voices as she reached the top of the stairs. *His,* deep and melodious, and she held her breath, expecting a woman's reply.

Instead, a man's voice, the words too indistinct for her to decipher. She moved out of the shadows, heading in the direction of that room, when her rival from the front door suddenly reappeared, carrying a tray with a carafe and glasses.

"You!" the butler said in tones of extreme loathing, too much the professional to drop the tray. He set it down carefully on a table, but she was already off, racing in the direction of those voices.

A door was open, light spilling out into the hallway, with her goal just beyond it. She'd almost reached it, her booted feet no longer silent on the parquet floor, when the majordomo caught up her with her, catching her hair and yanking her back painfully.

She bit him, hard. And kicked him in the shins with Lady Carlton's boots, and she heard her dress tear as she lunged forward, skittering through the open door to greet the room's inhabitants, who stared at her in shocked silence.

9

At least the scarred man, Reading, appeared suitably shocked, Elinor thought. Lord Rohan, as always, was a different matter. He appeared to be expecting her, the wretch.

He was sitting in splendid state, in the middle of a huge bed hung with gloriously gilded curtains, his hair loose around his shoulders, and he was completely naked, at least as far as she could tell. He had covers pulled to his waist, but it still left far too much flesh exposed, and she wasn't supposed to be thinking about that when her nemesis came skidding around the corner after her.

Lord Rohan made no effort to cover himself. He merely smiled at her. "You shouldn't look so surprised, Charles. It's my darling poppet from last night. Clearly she couldn't bear to be parted from me. Did I tell you we slept together? Twice? And extremely pleasant it was."

Reading made a choking sound. "Pleasant?"

"His lordship is misleading you, as always," Elinor

said. "I fell asleep in his presence. Not everyone finds him as entertaining as you seem to."

"Do you see why she enchants me, Reading?" Rohan said. And then his gaze and voice hardened to steel. "You didn't offer Miss Harriman any insult did you, Cavalle? I should be most displeased if she were not treated with the utmost care and respect."

She glanced behind her. The majordomo was the color of parchment, and she could swear she could hear his knees knocking. There was no question that he was terrified.

"Of course he treated me with care and respect," she said in a crabby voice, taking pity on the man. "He simply wished to announce my presence to give you time to cover yourself like any decent Christian, but I was in too much of a hurry and I ran ahead."

"Indeed," he said, clearly not believing a word she said. "You always run around in torn clothes and your hair halfway down your back? You may go, Cavalle. We'll discuss this later."

"Yes, my lord," the man said, his voice quaking.

Then Rohan's dark blue eyes focused on her. "And what in heaven's name made you think I was a decent Christian, child? I am affronted."

She took a deep, steadying breath. "There is always hope, Monsieur le Comte. I wish to speak to you."

"And here you are, my precious. Is it a private matter? Reading will be more than happy to leave us. Come sit beside me." He patted the snow-white sheets. "If I am to entertain a woman in my bedroom I prefer to keep them in close quarters."

"And I prefer you to put clothes on."

"Why?" He sounded like the soul of reason.

For the first time she noticed the bandage on his arm. "You've been hurt," she said, momentarily distracted.

"A trifle." He dismissed it. "Why do you want me to put clothes on?"

"I will not have a discussion with a…a naked man. It's distracting."

His soft laugh was maddening. "Very well, my sweet. In that case Reading had best take you to my sitting room while I ring for my valet, because I'm afraid that under these covers I'm as naked as the devil made me, and if you aren't going to join me you should retire before you faint with shock."

"Come along, Miss Harriman," Mr. Reading said, taking her arm. "He's in one of his moods. It's wiser not encourage him. We'll await him in the sitting room."

He'd already begun to pull the covers away from his body, and she spun around, hoping the heat in her cheeks wasn't visible to the sardonic man by her side. The comte's soft laugh followed her out into the adjoining room.

"Have a seat, Miss Harriman," her substitute host said. "May I offer you something to drink? We can have Cavalle bring tea, or perhaps something a bit stronger. I fancy he's not overfond of the stairs, and forcing him to run up and down them would be entertaining."

"No, thank you, sir." She perched herself on the

edge of one slender gilt chair, determined not to show how exhausted she was.

"I trust your…family is well? Nothing untoward has brought you racing out into a snowy night?"

She heard that hesitation, and she repressed an inner sigh. Everyone who saw her sister fell in love with her, and Reading was clearly no exception. "My sister is fine," she said.

There was a curious sweetness in Reading's scarred smile. "If I can be of any assistance…?"

"This concerns Lord Rohan and myself," she said.

He took a seat beside her on one of the little chairs. "You're clearly an intelligent young woman—you must have realized that his lordship and I are particularly close. You can talk to me about whatever it is that troubles you."

She didn't bother to suppress her skeptical expression. "I'll await his lordship, thank you. This is between him and me."

"Oh, indeed it is." Reading smiled faintly. "In which case I'll take my leave. It's been weeks since I've been in town and there are a number of friends and establishments I wish to revisit. I do realize that it's completely rude to abandon you like this, and I assure you it has nothing to do with the vast amount of respect I hold for you, but merely because I'm a shallow soul who's a slave to my appetites. And I strongly suspect Rohan wants to be alone with you. The bonds of friendship, alas, outweigh the duties of polite behavior." He rose, took her hand and bowed low over it. She jerked away before he could kiss it, her face flaming as she remembered the last time a man had kissed her hand. And exactly what it had followed.

But Reading merely smiled at her, that peculiar, twisted smile, and was gone.

She had a moment's panic when he closed the door behind him. Her initial rage had settled enough for her to have the sudden, horrifying thought: What in heaven's name was she doing?

It wasn't as if help was coming from any other quarter. Surely she could have accepted Rohan's charity without offering her sister as virgin sacrifice. As for her own sense of honor, that was long gone. Ending up like her mother might be a step up in the world.

If it were simply a matter of reputation that had been destroyed long ago, and she was worrying for naught. That particular concern had vanished years past due to any number of occurrences, including the fact Lydia's mother was a whore and her sister…

She looked out the window into the swirling snow and shivered. Somewhere a church bell tolled eight, and she breathed a sigh of relief. It was early. Late for a social call, but early enough for her to make her objections clear, insist that Lord Rohan remove what could be taken from the house and desist from bothering them again. Her sister wasn't for sale.

There was a fire blazing in the hearth, filling the room with almost oppressive heat. She should have agreed to the offer of tea—she was so tired she could barely keep her eyes open, and she wasn't, she absolutely wasn't going to fall asleep in his presence again. She wasn't in any particular danger from him, despite his banter, but she might not always be able to count on that, and if Rohan was in the mood to humiliate her she'd be fair game.

No, she needed to stay wide-awake, and she stood up, walking back and forth in the room, her long, heavy skirts swinging back and forth. What was keeping Lord Rohan? Surely it didn't take that long to put on a shirt and breeches? Lord help her, he wasn't getting dressed in his full glory just to receive her thorough dressing-down?

Her inadvertent play on words amused her for a moment, and she sat back down, leaning against the striped silk of the cushioned seat, closing her eyes, just for a moment. She'd hear him coming, particularly if he wore those ridiculous high-heeled slippers he'd worn when he'd accompanied her back to town this morning. She hadn't been looking at his shoes, she hadn't been looking at anything if she could help it, as remembered shame and something else swept over her. Had it only been that morning? It seemed like a week ago—a month since she'd raced off in a stolen coach to find her missing mother. It seemed like forever since she'd first set eyes on the Prince of Darkness himself.

She rose and paced back across the room again. What was taking him so long? He'd be ready for a full-court presentation at this rate. She sat down again, then popped up, restless. There was no telling what he might or might not be wearing if she were to go and bang on the door, and in her short acquaintance with him she knew he'd delight in further embarrassing her.

It had already been shocking enough. Not that she hadn't seen a number of totally naked bodies in any number of acts of depravity the night before. She prided herself on her pragmatism, and some of those things she'd glimpsed still astounded her, but a naked human body was simply that. She of all people shouldn't be fragile about such things. But for some reason, what was easily dismissed in his motley crew of decadent guests was a little more difficult to deal with when it came to Rohan himself. In particular, nudity.

He had hair on his chest. Not a great deal—a mere dusting. Dark mixed with gray, which surprised her. She was aware of the oddest desire to touch it. He certainly had the body, the musculature of a young man, and...

And why in Christ's name was she sitting here thinking about his musculature? Perhaps because it was so very different from the only other body she'd seen so intimately. Though thank God she hadn't really seen it.

And she certainly wasn't going to be thinking about that either. Granted, it was enough to keep her awake, but some things had too high a price to be paid.

She brought the memory back forcefully, the good one. The one she used when things became unbearable. The wide stretches of fields at her father's estate in Dorset, the feel of the young mare beneath her as she raced along, the sun bright overhead, her hair in plaits streaming out behind her as she sped ahead of the groom. She had been twelve, just days before her mother had packed her and her sister up and taken her to the continent. The last time she'd been on a horse. All she had to do was recreate that moment in her mind and she was happy, at peace, secure in the joy of the world, that nothing could harm her.

"That's quite the expression on your face, Miss Harriman," Rohan's voice disrupted her dream. "Were you thinking of me, by any chance?"

Her eyes flew open. "Had I been considering your head on a pike, perhaps," she said coolly. He was dressed, at least partially, in silver cloth breeches, a billowing white shirt and a long black waistcoat laced in silver. His hair was pulled back in a queue, and his hard blue eyes were watching her in amusement.

"I won't bother asking to what I owe the honor of this visit," he said, coming into the room. "You're here to berate me for keeping your sister from freezing and starving to death, are you not?"

Everything inside her froze. "You're not to come near my sister!" she said, her voice rough with panic.

He rolled his eyes. "Why in the world would you think I'd be lusting after that pretty child? There are scores of lovely girls in this city, possibly hundreds, and I expect I could have them all if I expressed any interest."

"Not all of them," she said fiercely, jumping up.

"My dear Miss Harriman," he said, pushing her back down in her seat with gentle hands. "I do assure you I could have your sister as well. But I expect that would distress Reading, and I would never think of doing such a thing to my dearest friend. Not that he can have her either. He has to marry an heiress, and despite my wicked influence he's far too noble to trifle with a girl of good background."

There was a soft knock on the door. *"Entrez,"* Rohan said, and a servant backed his way into the room, carrying a heavy tray. Not the loathsome Cavalle, and the scent of cinnamon-toast strips assailed her.

"I decided I couldn't tempt you with wine and grapes, but hot tea and toast might be acceptable." He lifted one of the lids. "Ah, and eggs. Just the thing. That's all right, Willis, you may leave us."

"I'm not hungry," Elinor said.

"Don't be ridiculous, of course you are. You practically wept when I said there were eggs. Allow me to serve you."

"I'm not going to eat your food."

"Why? Are you afraid if you eat six pomegranate seeds you'll be trapped here for the winter?"

She glared at him. "You might fancy yourself the king of the underworld, my lord, but you're nothing more than a spoiled aristocrat who's used to getting his own way."

"I'm hardly likely to argue with that, child," he said, setting the plate in her lap. "Indeed, you see me quite clearly, flaws and all. I'm nothing but a decadent, useless fribble. In which case, why should you be so incensed about a small act of charity? And don't get all fired up again. Eat your eggs before they get cold. I know you want to tell me you have no need of charity, but you're much too virtuous a soul to lie. You have no money, I have more than I know what to do with and I happen to know that there's been no time for you to apply to your new cousin, the baron, for assistance. You simply have nowhere else to turn. Consider this—if I'd kept my house in better order your mother would have never gotten inside to gamble away what must have been the last bit your pathetic family possessed. Consider that I'm simply repaying a debt."

If she were the woman of principle she wished she were she never would have touched the eggs. But the scent of them, just under her nose, was unbearable. It had been weeks since she'd had an egg. Besides, her principles had been smashed beyond recognition several years ago. She could sell her own soul for a plate of shirred eggs. Just not that of her sister.

After the first bite she had to look away so that he wouldn't see the sheen of tears in her eyes. How absurd to weep over eggs. There had been times when she would have willingly traded what was laughingly called her virtue for a roasted beef. Sad to think her price had dropped so low.

She blinked the momentary dampness away and fixed her stern gaze on Rohan. He was nibbling one of the toast strips, *her* toast strips, seemingly at ease. "So, my very dear Miss Harriman, why don't you explain to me in that cool, collected voice of yours just why it is so wrong for me to decide to spread some of my largesse in your direction."

"Who shot you?"

For a moment he looked annoyed. "I fail to see what that's got to do with anything. Reading assures me that anyone who's ever met me would have reason to shoot me, so I must admit with all candor that I have no idea. Was it you?"

"If I'd shot you I wouldn't have missed," she said.

"Was that wishful thinking or are you in fact a practiced shot?"

"Desire would have made up for lack of expertise."

There was silence for a moment as she realized what her words might suggest. And then he simply smiled at her. "Oh, no," he said. "That's much too easy."

She ducked her head, refusing to meet his gaze, and continued to work her way through the pile of eggs on her plate that had somehow gotten replenished. She could feel the flush in her cheekbones again, and she silently cursed. Her skin, apart from the despised freckles, was much too pale and prone to showing her slightest agitation.

"In fact, I'm pleased you chose such a delightfully inappropriate time to visit, Miss Harriman," he said after a long moment of silence. "I have an idea that might solve both your problem and mine. A way for me to happily endow your family with worldly goods without society looking askance, and to chase away any slight stain on your name."

She almost choked on the eggs. She looked up at him, horrified. "What do you mean by that?"

"What a curious reaction, child. Why, nothing more than that your extended time in my presence is likely to tarnish your reputation. Not past repair, I would hope, since I have nothing to show for it, but still... So I have fixed things most admirably."

The eggs stayed down. "And how have you done that, my lord?"

"I've found you a husband."

She was too astonished to react. "I hadn't realized I was in need of one."

"Of course you are. It's only with a husband that you'll have true freedom to explore the pleasures life can bring you."

"How exceedingly kind of you to worry about such things," she said icily. "And you've found a husband who'll provide me such pleasures?"

"It's seldom the husband who provides the pleasure, Miss Harriman. It's the lover."

"So you've found me a husband in order for me to take a lover? Forgive me for saying this doesn't make sense. And I would think a husband would object to acts of charity on your part."

"That's where you underestimate me. I have a cousin, a stern young man who disapproves of me thoroughly. He's a doctor, and I've decided he's in need of a wife to assist him in his practice. Someone who's unafraid of life. He also happens to be my heir, since I've done my level best not to procreate, and he'll inherit my French estates. I've been supporting him for the last decade or so. It would seem entirely logical that I support his wife. Which I propose to be you."

"I think, my lord, that you must be mad," she breathed. "What could you possibly gain from such an arrangement?"

"Why, Miss Harriman, I thought that would be completely obvious."

"Not to me, Monsieur le Comte." The eggs suddenly felt cold and leaden in her stomach. His ridiculous plan would give him access to Lydia, all under the guise of familial affection.

"Then, my dear Miss Harriman, I would gain you." And he handed her a cup of tea.

10

Elinor took the last careful bite of eggs, setting her fork down beside the gilt plate that had held them. She considered retaining it as some sort of weapon, but the Viscount Rohan was hardly the sort of man to use force. Besides, despite his words, she wasn't fool enough to believe him.

"You're an accomplished liar, are you not?" she said.

He was lounging on the settee opposite her, the very picture of indolence. Lace dripped down over his strong hands and flowed from the throat of his waistcoat. The sight should have been reassuring, after that unsettling glimpse of his bare chest, but she couldn't stop thinking of what lay beneath all those layers of silk and wool.

"How could I possibly confess to that? If I'm a liar then anything I tell you will be untrue. It's a waste of time asking me such things. Now, when it comes to lovemaking it's an entirely different matter. I can assure you when it comes to matters of the flesh I am quite simply unparalleled."

She gave him her most disagreeable look. "That is of no interest to me."

"Don't lie, precious. You're secretly fascinated at the thought of it. You're wondering what your own body is capable of, after the brief taste you had in the carriage, and who would be the one to give you that kind of knowledge. And you know, deep in your heart, that I'm the one man capable of—"

"Oh, stop it!" she snapped. "You're being quite tiresome. Don't look at me with hooded eyes and pretend I'm the object of your undying lust. I'm a little too old to fall for such fantasies."

"You're a child."

"Perhaps compared to your great age, but I'm three and twenty and have seen far more than most women my age. How old are you?"

He seemed amused. "Nine and thirty. Old enough to be your father. I was very active when I was sixteen."

"And my mother doubtless was a whore even back then, but it's been pointed out to me that I bear an unfortunate resemblance to my father. The Nose, you see."

"I quite like your nose."

She looked at him with dislike. "Let me explain things in short, clear sentences since you seem unable to comprehend. I have no interest in marrying your cousin, for whatever reason you think it a good idea. You are not to send any more inappropriate gifts to our household, and most importantly, you are to keep away from my sister. Is that clear, or do you need me to repeat it even more slowly?"

"It's very clear, Miss Harriman," he said. "But what

if I don't wish to? What if I require some other kind of motivation to follow your stringent orders?"

"Such as what?" she asked, suspicious.

"I think you should come here, Miss Harriman," he said in a soft, silken voice. "And I will show you."

It was foolishness, pure and simple, but she was beyond tired, and feeling cross and reckless. He was challenging her, and Elinor had never been one to back down from a challenge. She stared at him for a long moment, her eyes meeting his with cold disdain. And then she rose and crossed the room so that she stood in front of him as he lounged on the settee.

"Yes?" she said in a cool voice. The embarrassing flush had fled, leaving her cold and determined.

He had the smile of an angel. Which made him doubly dangerous, given his devilish proclivities. "Kneel down."

She arched an eyebrow. She no more believed in his supposed passion for her than she believed in fairies or a just and loving god, but she was willing to see how far he would carry this bluff. And what kind of safety for Lydia she could claim.

She sank to her knees in her threadbare clothes, letting them pool around her. Her eyes were the level of his, and she met his hard blue gaze with a steely one of her own.

"That's right, poppet," he murmured. "And now you may kiss me."

She started to get up but he caught her arm, pulling her back, and she noticed with dismay he was quite strong. "I just want to see what a kiss from a bad-tempered virgin would taste like. I'm not asking for anything more, not at the moment. In general, I don't care much for kissing, but I vaguely remember that's part of the whole ritual with untried females."

"You really are mad," she said feelingly. "All I can assume is that you're caught in the toils of the same disease that afflicts my mother, and while I'm very sorry for you, it's simply the wages of sin. You can't fornicate with every creature who crosses your path and not pay the price."

"Poppet, you greatly overestimate my stamina. And my foolishness. In fact, I'm very careful to avoid diseased partners. Any sensible man would."

She wanted to throw up. She knew just what lengths men would go to avoid diseased partners. She kept her voice and face steady. "I rejoice to hear it. May you have a long and happy life of debauchery. I, however, do not plan to be part of it."

"My precious, I'm not asking you to. I'm merely requesting a kiss from those disapproving lips. Is it so much to ask? Don't be missish. It's not as if I'm opening my breeches for you to service me."

She should have been horrified at his words, but she knew well enough what he was talking about. It was common currency in the back alleys and the drawing rooms, though she was unable to fathom why people would want to engage in such things. That he should even allude to it didn't surprise her.

"Is a chaste kiss so much to ask? After that you may go home in my carriage and I promise I won't even demand you send my presents back."

She couldn't break away, not without an undignified struggle. And part of her didn't want to break away. A wild, reckless part of her, one that she always denied, kept wrapped up tight inside her, cried to escape. "If you truly wanted to kiss me you'd get up from the settee."

"But I don't. I have no interest in kissing you, at least not at the moment. I'm not saying that won't change, but for now I'm much more interested in what would happen if you kissed me. I'm assuming your virginal state only extends below the waist, or at worst, below the neck. Kiss me, and I'll let you go."

She looked into his ruined beauty and hated him. Hated him for a thousand reasons, most of which had nothing to do with him at all. Hated him because she wanted to kiss him, wanted those pale, beautiful hands on her body, wanted the wild, wicked things he'd promised. False promises, all of them.

She'd had enough, of him, of men in general, and with a sudden burst she yanked free, falling backward and scrambling to her feet.

He caught her by the door, moving faster than she would have thought he was capable. He took her shoulders and spun her around, pushing her back against the door. "I believe I said you weren't leaving without a kiss," he said softly. "I assure you, it's not such a difficult thing. I'll demonstrate." And his mouth covered hers.

It was a shock. The intimacy of it, like nothing she'd ever felt before. Hard and wet and deep, his mouth open against hers, demanding a response she didn't know how to give. It was a far cry from the chaste first kiss she'd dreamed of—it tasted of sex and desire and dark delight, and for the first time she began to understand why people sought such things.

He lifted his head, looking down at her, and she stared up into his hard blue eyes, half hidden by his ridiculously long lashes. "You survived that quite well, my sweet. Now kiss me back. I know you must have been kissed before—it's not near so dire as losing your innocence. I want to taste a virgin's kiss."

She froze, still trapped against the door by his bigger, stronger body. "Then I'm sorry, I'm afraid I don't fit your requirements," she said stiffly. "You'll have to look elsewhere."

"You can't tell me you've never been kissed—I won't believe it. Paris is not so full of stupid men."

"The entire world is choked to death with stupid men. I've been kissed before."

His expression would have been gratifying if she was in the mood to notice. "Indeed, it is. I should have tried it this way." His mouth brushed hers, light, soft, and she rose into it, unconsciously wanting more. He slid his arm around her waist, pulling her up and into his body, deepening the kiss, and his other hand cupped her chin, his long fingers gently stroking the sides of her face as he kissed her with the seductive, leisurely expertise of the devil himself, and when his fingers tugged she opened her mouth for him, wanting him. To her complete and utter shame, wanting him.

A moment later he set her aside, backing away, looking at her with a strange expression on his face.

No one ever suggested that the Viscount Rohan was slow to understand subtleties. There was but the slightest pause. "So you've been kissed before but still fail to meet my requirements," he murmured. "But how delightful for me. If you're no longer a virgin then there's nothing to keep you from going to bed with me. I'm even considering unfastening my breeches after all. Or doesn't your expertise go that far?"

She'd asked for it, she deserved it. For letting him kiss her, for, God help her, kissing him back. In trying to shock him, she'd only managed to degrade herself further.

"No?" he said lazily, turning away from her for an unguarded moment. "*Tant pis.* I can teach you easily enough."

She backed away from him, coming up against the table that held the tray and her empty plate. And the fork.

For a weapon it was pathetic, but it was all she had. She grabbed it, sending the tray crashing to the floor. "If you touch me again I will stab you."

He made the very dire mistake of laughing at her. "That's not going to do much damage through these clothes, poppet. And there's no need to threaten me with your fury. I haven't taken a woman against her will in decades—I would hardly be likely to start with you."

As a reminder of her lack of beauty his statement was effective enough to make her lower her arm. Even his following words couldn't break through the tightly controlled pain. "You're much too interesting to take by rape. Besides, what could you do with a fork?"

"I could stab you in the eyes," she said fiercely.

"You couldn't reach them. Besides, you don't want to. You'd much rather I kissed you again. Let me demonstrate." And he reached for her, pulling her into his arms, against his hard, warm body.

It was a different body, strong and hard, so very different from the soft, sagging flesh of the other, but she panicked anyway, struggling, and without thought stabbed the fork into his upper arm, where she'd seen the bandage.

His reaction shocked her. He merely flinched, but the hold on her changed abruptly, and a moment later she found herself on the sofa, wrapped in his arms, held tightly, and she had no idea why. He held her as a father might comfort a child, and she realized with shock that she was sobbing, loud, noisy sobs. And then she stopped thinking at all, giving in to all the grief and fear and sorrow that had torn at her life with a thousand tiny claws.

His arm was around her, and blood was seeping through the sleeve where she'd jabbed him, and she moaned and tried to say something, but he simply shifted her in his arms so that she couldn't see it, holding her head against his chest and gently stroking her hair, her tear-streaked face, as the harsh sobs racked her body. From a distance she could hear his words, soft, comforting, half in a language she couldn't understand, but then it was simply the sound of his voice that soothed her, the way he held her, strong yet gentle, so that for the first time in what seemed a lifetime she could stop fighting, she could simply let go of everything, for a brief, blessed moment. She could simply be.

She truly did have the most amazing ability to fall asleep in his presence, Rohan thought absently, stroking her tear-damp face. He'd recognized the signs of it, the slowing of her breath, the infrequent shudders, her clutch on his perfect silk waistcoat loosening. It would never recover from the wrinkles, but it was little matter—he was bleeding all over it. Another extremely expensive article of clothing ruined, thanks to Miss Harriman. Poor poppet.

He considered carrying her into his bed, to let her finish her exhausted sleep, but thought better of it. If she awoke while he carried her she'd panic, and he really didn't fancy her slamming into his wound once more. He'd probably drop her, ruining the entire, romantic effect of it.

He had to laugh at himself. Romantic gestures were as far removed from his life as this kind of tenderness. All he'd been able to do was treat her as Mrs. Clarke had treated him so many years ago. "Peace, now, love," he whispered in Gaelic, a language he'd forgotten he knew. He rose from the sofa, cradling her carefully and lay her down on it. There was blood on the silk damask. If he spent much more time with Miss Harriman he was going to need to replace his wardrobe and his furniture. She was going through things at a prodigious pace.

She slept, exhausted, and he stared down at her. Her face was blotched and puffy from the tears. With the

Harriman Nose she was such a far cry from her pretty little sister, from the beauties that surrounded him. She was a ragamuffin of misery. So why was he wasting even a moment of his time on her?

The answer was instant, obvious and reassuring. He was bored. It was that simple. She was something entirely new in his sphere of existence, and he appreciated the novelty. He'd tire of her soon enough, thank heavens. In the meantime she was entertaining.

He moved his arm, and flinched, glancing down at his blood-soaked sleeve. Such drama was exhausting, even as it entertained. She hadn't been raped—that much was obvious, or she would have reacted more strongly to his use of the word. No, it must have simply been some clumsy fool. Perhaps she'd been in love with him and he'd used her poorly and left her. Without even so much as a kiss, poor angel. He wasn't a great fancier of kisses, but someone like Elinor Harriman needed to be kissed, well and often.

A sensible woman would simply look for another lover, but women were seldom sensible. And doubtless his sleeping guest thought her life ruined after one awkward encounter.

Etienne would do very well for her. She would no longer have to brood about her lack of virginity, and while he doubted his cousin had the imagination to awaken her senses, he was, after all, French, and they were, reputedly, particularly good at that sort of thing. With luck, the good doctor could work her past her painful memories, and then he could step in and finish her education, much to their mutual pleasure.

The Revels were fast approaching. He couldn't quite see the fierce Elinor stripping off her clothes and her fears to participate in that planned debauch, though it was an enticing idea. It would make sense to put the matter to one side and take it up again once spring had arrived. Perhaps he would discover some new and mysterious beauty at the Revels and forget all about the delicious innocence of Elinor Harriman.

Because she was even more of an innocent than he'd first thought. A woman who'd simply never encountered the pleasures of the flesh held a certain amount of interest if the woman herself appealed. But one who had tried, and been disappointed, was far more of a challenge, a delicious one.

Still, it would be safer all around if he simply transferred his interest to someone more likely to join in the celebrations of the Heavenly Host.

But then, when had safety had anything to do with it?

The blood was running down his arm and dripping onto the carpet, and he cursed. She was costing him a fortune. He'd have great pleasure taking payment for it with her eventually agreeable body.

If he didn't manage to distract himself in the meantime. He headed back into his bedroom, stripping off his clothes as he went, signaling for his valet. Georges was asleep in the dressing room, and he appeared almost immediately, stifling a yawn until he looked at his master's bloody clothes.

"Milord, what has happened?" he said, shocked. "Your wound is bleeding again. I will call the doctor…you must lie down…"

Rohan batted away the valet's nervous hands. "A simple slip. I was awkward. We don't need the doctor you can rebandage me. But first I want you to go into the outer room and cover the young lady with a blanket."

Georges looked understandably confused. "A young lady? Out in the sitting room? You don't want her in here?"

Rohan allowed himself a wry smile. "I believe the young lady would object. She's asleep now—be certain not to wake her up. Take the silk throw—I don't want her destroying the fur one. I'll manage to divest myself of these bloody clothes and then you may assist me."

"But, milord…"

He raised an eyebrow. "Did I give the impression that this was open for discussion?"

Georges blanched, clearly terrified of him, as most of the servants were. With reason. He was not a good man.

"Don't wake her," he said again. "Or I'll be most annoyed."

"Yes, milord. Of course." He took the silk coverlet from the freshly made bed and disappeared with his usual silence. A moment later he was back.

"She's gone, Monsieur le Comte," he said, his voice shaking slightly.

Rohan slammed past him, into the sitting room,

162   *Anne Stuart*

but Georges had told the simple truth. She was gone. He went to the window, half expecting to see her running down the street as if the hounds of hell were after her. No sign of her.

"Take the other servants and look for her," he said in a sharp voice. "If she's not in the house, send someone after her to ensure she arrives home safely."

"Should he attempt to bring her back, milord?"

Rohan shook his head. "There'll be time enough for that," he said lightly. "Once you're done, come back and dress me. I believe I'll go out. I feel the need of company tonight. Female company."

"Yes, milord."

Anyone would do, he told himself. He should have known that oh-so-convenient sleep was feigned. Miss Harriman was, after all, a delightfully burgeoning liar. Either she had pretended to sleep, or awoken when he'd set her down but been too clever to show it. The moment he'd closed the door she would have been off and running.

He'd let her think she'd escaped. For now. It was almost time for the Revels, and he had other things to do. More than enough to keep him busy for the next few weeks. For now, she could mistakenly feel safe.

For now.

It was a great deal later when Elinor finally arrived home, half-frozen, exhausted. The fire in the front room was banked, the coals sending a warm glow through the room. In the past she and her sister had slept on pallets in front of it, but there was no sign of

Lydia. She tiptoed down the narrow hallway. The tiny storeroom that had held nothing but dust and cobwebs had been swept clean and now held a bed and a wash-stand. Her sister lay on one side of it, sound asleep.

It had been an endless day. It was hard to believe that it had barely been twenty-four hours since she'd first run afoul of the Prince of Darkness. Twenty-four strange, unsettling hours that were now over.

She tiptoed back to the living room. There was a settee, which reminded her a little too much of Rohan lounging on the one in his salon, plus two small chairs. She ignored all of them, curling up in a tight ball in front of the fire.

And forced herself to remember.

11

She'd been seventeen, not yet convinced that a happy life was out of the question, despite the Harriman Nose. She was young, strong, and hopeful. To be sure, their fortunes had begun to decline. They were living in a ramshackle house on the edge of the city, and Lady Caroline had been without a steady male companion for months.

Elinor preferred it that way. The men who came and stayed tended to treat her mother with a familiarity that made her uncomfortable, and that familiarity reached her daughters as well. When Lady Caroline was uninvolved she still went out most nights, gaming, drinking, but there were days when she was home. Sometimes she was morose, with a vicious tongue that could flay her daughter with its caustic truth. Those words never touched Lydia, thank God. Like Elinor herself, Lady Caroline doted on Lydia. She reserved her complaints and criticisms for Elinor.

But there were other times, times her mother was bright and gay and laughing, lighting up any room she entered, and that was one of those times. She'd come in from an afternoon visit, taken young Lydia's arms and danced her around the drawing room, the two of them laughing, Elinor standing to one side, enchanted. Her mother could charm anyone, and six years ago, when she'd been seventeen and Lydia eleven and Lady Caroline hadn't begun to show the signs of her illness, back then her charm had been at its brightest.

"I've met the most wonderful man, my darlings," she'd said, and Elinor had preened under the random endearment. "He's older, so he's more settled, and he's fabulously wealthy. Solange told me he'd been asking about me, and she arranged for him to be at her house this afternoon, and oh, my dears, sparks flew! I'm going to his house tonight, and if our luck holds, we'll all move in there, away from this wretched, bourgeois place."

The wretched, bourgeois place was a palace compared to their current house, but for Lady Caroline it had been a shameful comedown.

"Is he very handsome, Mama?" Lydia had asked.

"Handsome doesn't matter," she'd said lightly. "It's inner beauty that matters." And Elinor had preened once more. For all her mother's harshness, she really did love her. She really must strive to do better, to make her mother proud of her plain child as much as her pretty one.

"Who is he, Mama?" she'd asked.

"He's titled, and fabulously wealthy. Did I mention that? Sir Christopher Spatts. Isn't that a lovely name? So very English. He lives there, of course, and I'm thinking that enough time has passed that I might return. We wouldn't be accepted by some of the worst high-sticklers, but I would think more people would have forgotten. There's always a new scandal. And wouldn't it be glorious to see England again? You could ride once more, Elinor. Christopher doesn't keep a stable when he's visiting Paris, but perhaps when we move in he might consider hiring a mount for you." She did a little dance around the room, her silk skirts swinging over her hoops, her beautiful face alight with joy. "I wonder if marriage is too much to hope for? He's only a knight, not even a baronet or a viscount, so it might be possible. I wouldn't mind being a bride."

"You're putting the cart before the horse," Nanny Maude had said darkly, the one person who ever dared tell Lady Caroline the truth.

"Oh, pooh!" she'd said with her light, silvery laugh. "It's all going to be glorious."

She'd been wrong, as she so often was. Looking back on that day, it seemed to Elinor that that was the last time she'd ever seen her mother truly happy. It was one of her wild fantasies, with little connection to real life, but it had filled the house with light anyway.

Caroline had gone out that night, wearing the Harriman emeralds that she'd taken with her, the ones that were to be Elinor's, and hadn't returned for more than a fortnight. It was Elinor's first taste of real responsibility, and she managed relatively well. There'd been money, and credit, and the hope of a splendid future. Until Lady Caroline returned home.

Her skin was sallow. She wore new clothes, made of rich, expensive fabrics, and a dashing new hat, but her jewelry was missing, and she waltzed in and collapsed on a chair, declaring herself exhausted.

"Where are the emeralds, Mama?" she'd blurted out. Not only were they supposed to end up with her, they were the most valuable thing their little family owned, their something against dark times.

"What a little miser you are, Elinor," she'd said with what seemed like profound dislike. "If you must know, they're temporarily in other hands."

Relief flooded her. "They're being cleaned? Repaired?"

"I lost them in a wager. I fully expect to win them back in a new few days, so there's nothing to worry about. You're such a greedy creature, Elinor. Even if you can't be pretty like your sister you should try to acquire at least a few social graces." Her gaze was withering. "And where did you get that hideous dress?"

It was one of the two dresses she'd been wearing for the last year. It was true, she'd grown too tall and curvy for it, but there hadn't been much money for new clothes, and it was much more important that Lady Caroline look prosperous, since she was their public face to the world.

Before she could think of something to say, Lady Caroline turned her attention to Lydia. "There you are, sweetness. How I've missed you! Give your mama a kiss."

Lydia had thrown herself into her arms. "Are we going to move, Mama?"

"I don't think so, dearest," she said in a distracted voice. "I've decided Sir Christopher is not the man for me. For one thing, he's too old. For another…" She shrugged, an affectation she'd picked up since coming to Paris, one she did very well. "He'll be coming to tea this afternoon. I want both of you on your best behavior. And, Elinor, do try to look a little prettier. Don't we have anything better for her to wear?"

"No," Nanny Maude said in her uncompromising voice.

"I know what we'll do. Our neighbors have that absolute horse of a daughter. You know the one I mean—she's Lydia's age but absolutely enormous. I'm certain I can convince them to lend me one of her dresses for Elinor."

"Clothilde de Bonneau is thirteen years old, Mama," Elinor had protested. "And she's much wider than I am."

"We can fix that. Nanny Maude is a genius with a needle. Now, someone bring me my notepaper—we haven't time to waste. *Vite, vite!*" Her eyes were bright, feverishly so, and she had two dark patches on her already rouged cheeks.

No one was immune to Lady Caroline's charm, and the dress had been produced almost immediately. It had been an insipid shade of pink, with nowhere for her chest to go in the fortunately high bodice. To this day she couldn't abide the color pink.

But her mother had fussed over her, directing her maid on how to arrange Elinor's hair to her satisfaction. Never in her life had Elinor received so much of her mother's attention. It was dizzying.

When she was done she looked in the mirror. The dress was expensive, better than anything she'd worn in years, and the maid's ministrations had been expert. She'd almost looked pretty.

Her mother had clucked her tongue. "Too bad you're such a plain child, but we've done the best we can. We'll simply have to hope it works."

"What works, Mama?"

But Lady Caroline hadn't answered, moving away to focus on Lydia.

For the first time Lydia wasn't the favored one. She was instructed to wear her oldest dress, her lovely golden ringlets were plaited into such tight braids that they pulled at her skin, and Lady Caroline ordered her to sit quietly in the corner and say nothing. There was no disguising Lydia's gorgeous blue eyes, pretty mouth and perfect little nose, but she'd done as her mother asked, keeping her head downturned when Sir Christopher Spatts graced them with his presence.

He creaked when he walked. He was old, much older than their mother, and quite fat. His wig was long and elaborately styled, his complexion florid, his lips the color of liver. He had fingers like fat sausages, covered with rings, and a beauty patch rested on one sagging cheek.

She knew better than to call attention to herself in public, but in this case she had no choice, with Sir Christopher barking questions at her, all the time he was sneaking glances at Lydia as she tried to disappear into the furniture.

It seemed to go on forever. He sprinkled biscuit

crumbs all over his expansive front, and he drank his tea noisily, like a bourgeois. The thought of her mama in his bed was horrifying. She was not so naive that she didn't realize exactly what her mother did with her gentlemen friends, even though the details were mercifully unclear at that point.

Finally he rose. "She'll do," he said with a brisk nod. "I'll meet your price." His rheumy gaze swept the room. "I'd still rather have the younger one. I'd pay double."

"No, Sir Christopher," her mother said with what Elinor considered to be great dignity. "You've had my response to your offer."

He'd nodded, and his wig had shifted slightly. No decent valet would have allowed his gentleman to go out with his periwig improperly applied, and Sir Christopher struck her as a vain man. She hid her grin.

"I expect you to hold to the terms of our agreement," he'd said, clearly unwilling to have the last word.

"But of course, Sir Christopher. I am a woman of my word. Have your man of business call on me at his convenience."

He took a last, hard look at Elinor, harrumphed and departed in a wave of overpowering scent.

"Go into the other room, Lydia darling," her mother had said once their guest was gone. "I need to talk to your sister. You, too, old woman," she added to Nanny Maude.

A rare occurrence, but Elinor was no fool. She understood what was going on but hadn't been said. Her mother had arranged a marriage for her.

She'd known it would have to happen, sooner or later. She'd already known that the chance of finding someone young and handsome was unlikely. Lydia's young music tutor had never looked her way, while Elinor died of longing every time he was in the room. He was poor enough that it might have been a possibility, but he'd only had eyes for Lydia.

She should be grateful. She had never thought she'd end up with a title, and it was clear Sir Christopher possessed great wealth. With luck he'd be unfaithful, and she wouldn't have to put up with his affections very often.

Once they were alone, her mother turned to look at her, and for the first time she looked uncertain, almost guilty, and Elinor took pity on her.

"Don't worry, Mama," she said. "I understand what's going on."

"You do?"

"Of course. You've arranged a marriage for me with Sir Christopher. I understand that it's my duty. I probably won't have many choices, and I should be very grateful."

"Not exactly," her mother had said, moving away and refusing to meet her eye.

Elinor tried not to show the rush of relief that ran through her body. In truth, she would much rather die an old maid than be married to someone like Sir Christopher, but she would have done it, for Lydia. "Then what was he talking about?"

Her mother paused in front of the window, fully aware of the lovely picture she made. "Sit down, Elinor."

Elinor sat, dutifully.

"We're in a bit of a pickle, dearest," she said, finally turning around to take the chair opposite her. She still wouldn't meet her eyes. "And we're going to need your help. You'd do anything for your little sister, wouldn't you?"

"Absolutely," she replied. "Without question."

Her mother's smile was small and contained. "I was hoping you'd say that. You're a very loyal girl, Elinor. I knew I could count on you."

Elinor drew a deep breath. She'd already learned her mother was far from the most trustworthy presence in their lives—Nanny Maude had that honor. And the way her conversation was circling around was making her feel extremely odd.

"Of course, Mama," she said. "What is it you want me to do?"

Her mother hesitated. "Sir Christopher has a peculiar…interest, shall we say. You understand about men and their appetites, don't you?"

Elinor had nodded, understanding no such thing.

"Well, Sir Christopher is very much afraid of contracting the Spanish disease. His father died of it, and he's always been most particular in his choice of partners." She was staring down at her new puce underskirt, her thin fingers pleating it nervously.

Elinor really didn't want to hear about Sir Christopher's habits, particularly when it came to that most intimate of acts. But her mother clearly expected her to keep up. "I don't understand, Mama."

Lady Caroline looked annoyed. "He only beds virgins. He says that's the only way he can be sure they're clean."

Elinor laughed. "Isn't he going to run out of them sooner or later?"

Lady Caroline's gaze narrowed. "I believe he is willing to accept girls who are quite young. And if someone pleases him he'll keep her for a while, ensuring a safe outlet for his…er…masculine energy."

It had taken her a moment, but a dreadful suspicion was entering Elinor's mind, too dreadful to possibly be true. "And what does this have to do with me, Mama?" she said in a small voice.

"He heard I have two young daughters. He wants one of you in return for my IOUs, and I told him I would arrange it. He's destroying my debts, and on top of that he'll give us a thousand pounds, perhaps more if he's pleased. He heard about Lydia, but I flatly refused him, and he's willing to accept you in her place." She stopped abruptly, having run out of breath in her hurry to get the bad news out.

Elinor had grown very cold, as the last of her childhood slipped away without a sound. She stared at her mother, the mother who had just sold her for a thousand pounds and her gaming debts. "You want me to sleep in his bed?"

"Don't look at me like that. It's not as if you're likely to contract a decent marriage. We needn't worry about your virginity, and if by any chance you do find someone who's a stickler there are ways to get around it. In the meantime, we've been offered a great opportunity, a way to get out of debt and ahead a bit, and we should be grateful…"

"We, Mama?" she'd echoed. "I won't do it."

Her mother looked at her with deep dislike. "I should have known you'd be a selfish child. Then it will have to be Lydia."

"She's only eleven!"

"I told you, Sir Christopher is…odd. He'd much prefer her, but I was hoping to spare her at such a tender age. However, he did say he'd double his offer, so if you're unwilling, she'll simply have to take your place." Her mother's voice was flat, implacable. Knowing Elinor's only possible response.

"You're whoring your daughters to pay off your gaming debts?" Elinor said in an uncompromising voice. "And if I don't present myself to that disgusting old man, you're willing to let him touch Lydia? Am I clear on this?"

Her mother didn't flinch. "Very clear, Elinor. You've been given a chance to save your family, to protect your younger sister, to aid your mother in a time of great need. You can do the selfish thing, and refuse, or you can accept, gracefully. It's your choice."

And it was no choice at all. That night she lay in bed beside Lydia, her last night as a maiden, and listened as her mother and Nanny Maude argued, but in the end even Nanny had given in. The pink dress had been returned to the neighbors, replaced with one that was hers alone, made with alarming swiftness by Lady

Caroline's own modiste. Her hair had been primped and fashioned, and the wardrobe of thin, diaphanous undergarments and nightclothes should have made her blush.

But she'd lost that ability. The next evening a coach came to collect her, and the hatchet-faced woman who accompanied her said nothing, viewing her with the contempt Elinor knew she deserved.

Sir Christopher's house was alight with noise and laughter when she stepped inside, and she automatically turned toward it, when the woman caught her arm. "You're not welcome in there," she'd said in French, the words somehow sounding crueler in that language. "You're to wait for him in your room. One of the maids will assist you."

"But I thought—"

"You have one purpose and one alone, mademoiselle. Do not forget it, and do not presume to ask me for anything. Once I show you your quarters you're to keep silent and do what you're paid to do."

She would have turned around and walked out, but the memory of Lydia, her confused expression when Elinor had tried to explain she would be visiting her friend in Italy for a while, stopped her. She had no idea whether her mother would make good her bluff. It didn't really matter—she couldn't take that chance, and Lady Caroline knew it.

So she'd nodded, and Hatchet-Lady, whose name, oddly enough, was found out to be Madame Hachette, had led the way upstairs to a spacious corner room with a distressingly large bed up on a dais.

"This is his bedroom?" she'd asked.

"Don't be absurd. He'll come to you here when he feels the urge. Otherwise you're to keep to this room and your food will be brought up to you."

"But what will I do the rest of the time?"

"How should I know? Or care? Do what other whores do," she'd said rudely. "Marie will see to your needs. She's hopeless as a housemaid, but your needs will be minimal and shouldn't be beyond her limited comprehension." A young girl was standing off to one side, face downcast.

Madame had looked at them both, made a noise of disgust and walked away, and as Marie raised her head Elinor expected another look of withering contempt. Instead, Marie's plain young face was filled with such sympathy that Elinor's strong resolve nearly shattered.

"I can help," Marie had said calmly. "If you want me to."

She'd stood still beneath Marie's strong young hands as the maid had divested her of the new, frilly clothes her mother had bought her and dressed her in the sheer undergarments. "He won't ask much of you," she'd said in an even, practical voice. "You'll simply have to lie still and let him do what he wants. For anything special he can use his society women—he knows he can't get the Spanish disease from a whore's mouth. If you take opium it won't be so bad."

She'd looked into Marie's sad, dark eyes and didn't ask how she knew. It was more than obvious.

So she took the powders and climbed up into the

big bed, and when Sir Christopher came and pushed his hard, ugly thing between her legs and made her bleed she didn't move, didn't cry out. She simply closed her eyes and dreamed.

For three months she saw no one but Marie during the day, with the occasional nighttime visits from Sir Christopher. Marie would sneak her books from the library to keep her entertained, brew her teas to make certain she didn't conceive, help her dream at night when he would cover her body with his huge weight, grunting and sweating and hurting her.

And then it was over as abruptly as it had begun. She rose one morning and washed him away from her body and Madame Hachette appeared in her doorway to whisk her back home, her harsh face set in the same cold disapproval. She didn't even have a chance to say goodbye to Marie.

When she walked into the house on the edge of the city she expected everything to have changed. She stood in the hallway and looked around her. There were signs of prosperity—a new rug in the entrance, a Chinese vase on an occasional table by the stairs. But the rest was the same as always.

She found her mother in her bedroom, with Nanny sitting in a chair near the bed. There were sores on her face, on her arms, and her eyes were cloudy when she saw her daughter. "He got tired of you, did he?" she'd said in a cracked voice. "I should have known our fortunes wouldn't last, not when they relied on you." She turned her head away.

But Nanny Maude leaped up, putting her arms

around Elinor. For a moment she fought—no one had touched her with gentleness or affection in so long, and she felt dirty, ugly.

But Nanny would have none of that, and it was all Elinor could do to keep from sobbing. She let Nanny hold her tightly, as if to squeeze the ugliness away. But it was too late.

Her mother's voice had whispered from the bed. "And now I've got an ugly daughter who's a whore," she'd said. "Why is my life so wretched?"

Elinor had broken free of Nanny's gentle embrace and looked down at her mother, trying to think of something to say. But Lady Caroline's eyes had drifted closed, and there were no words harsh enough.

It had taken months for her to accept Lydia's embraces and joy in having her home again. Not until she'd had word that Sir Christopher had returned to England with his new bride, a girl of fourteen, the gossips had said, horrified.

And the last trace of regret had vanished, and Elinor had put her arms around Lydia and for the first time in a year, she wept.

12

The next ten days proved to be a challenge to Elinor's newfound determination. It wasn't simply the daily arrival of gifts from Viscount Rohan. With no other source to turn to, she had no choice but to accept his charity, and she did so with perfect grace, as long as she didn't have to see him. In fact, her nightmare had done her good. It didn't matter that she refused to be a whore like her mother, dependent on the largesse of wealthy men—she'd already accepted that role the day she climbed into Sir Christopher's bed.

Each day a new arrival of food, of firewood, of rich wool blankets and silken throws, would arrive, and she would dutifully sit down and write a polite note of thanks and promise of repayment, dispatching Jacobs with it. Each day he would return with a note in Rohan's careless scrawl, and even her sister failed to see the impropriety of his suggestions that she might visit to further discuss methods of repayment. Ones, he said, that didn't involve rats. Lydia had wrinkled her brow at that, but Elinor refused to explain. Besides, she'd changed her mind. She'd underestimated the danger of the King of Hell, and she wasn't going anywhere near him again, not if she could help it. The memory of his mouth still burned. Rats would be easier to forget.

She ate the food, rich and wonderful beyond her memory, without choking, she warmed herself by the fire his money had provided, and she slept in the bed next to her sister, holding tight to the knowledge that as long as Lydia slept beside her the girl was safe.

There'd been a time, a brief time when she'd been in Rohan's dangerous, mesmerizing presence, when she'd really believed it wasn't her sister he wanted. When he'd touched her, kissed her, and a whole new world had opened up. Not the sunshiny bright world of true love and happy endings. Something darker, more complex, infinitely more alluring.

Common sense had returned along with daylight. If he'd had even the slightest passing interest in her it was occasioned only by her unique status as an innocent. Once he learned otherwise he would have come to his senses. Assuming he had left them in the first place.

But he'd made no effort to broaden his acquaintance with her sister, and Elinor allowed herself to relax, at least briefly. And to be grateful for the most important gift of all. Etienne de Giverney.

It wasn't until the third day that there was a sudden knock on the door, and apprehension swept through Elinor. "Go in the bedroom, Lydia," she said swiftly, rising from her seat by the blessed fire. "I'll get rid of him."

Lydia didn't argue. She never did when Elinor used that tone of voice. She was far from naive, and she knew full well, without any vanity, that her looks brought her unwanted attention, and she slipped into their bedroom as Elinor waited for Jacobs to open the door, certain that Lord Rohan would be there, ready to claim his reward.

Instead, a husky young man stepped into the house, ducking beneath the low lintel. He was dressed immaculately, perhaps too much so, and he carried a medical bag in one hand. "Miss Elinor Harriman?" he said in the French of a native. "My name is Etienne de Giverney. I've been sent by my cousin, the Comte de Giverney, to provide assistance."

She stared at him, dumbfounded for the moment. And then memory flooded back, Rohan's absurd suggestion that she marry this young man. If she could go by the way he was looking at her out of flat black eyes, he was having none of it.

She was half tempted to see him on his way, but the visit of a real doctor was too valuable to ignore. "You're very kind, monsieur. My mother is quite ill— if you would see if there's anything you can do for her it would be much appreciated. But that is all we have need of."

He didn't bother hiding his relief. He'd walked into the room with the air of a man going to his execution, and Elinor wondered whether she should be amused or insulted. Either way it didn't matter—she could hardly marry in order to please Lord Rohan. The comte was clearly delusional.

"I will endeavor to do my best," he said in a stiff voice. "I'm indebted to my cousin on many levels—he paid for my education and sees to it that I'm well employed."

"His lordship is a very charitable man," Elinor ventured.

The doctor snorted. "You might say so, though whether he's actually a lord is open for discussion."

Elinor responded as he clearly meant her to. "How so, Monsieur de Giverney?"

"Another man in England holds the viscountcy, and I myself should have acceded to the title of Comte de Giverney instead of an Englishman. It was a mere accident of birth—if he were a man of honor he would have refused the title."

Such a stuffy young man, Elinor thought, bearing his full share of grievances. "I don't believe Lord Rohan is known for his more honorable qualities."

His earlier sniff became a full-blown snort. "I tell you, mademoiselle, it is very difficult for me. Very difficult indeed. That I, a true de Giverney, should toil like a tradesman while he enjoys the family château, the town house, the money…"

She made all the right soothing sounds, mentally thanking God for the Harriman Nose. Even if she thought marriage was a possibility for her, she'd prefer to do without rather than end up with this pompous young man.

She led him into the bedroom where Lady Caroline lay, still and small beneath the covers. "The Spanish disease," he said knowingly. "She is too far gone— there is nothing that can be done for her but ease her pain." He leaned over and lifted her eyelids—her eyes were dull and glassy, though she managed a muffled and obscene curse.

Elinor could feel the color stain her cheeks. "I beg your pardon…" she said.

"It is of no consequence. In the late stages the madness is fully upon them, and very little remains of the person they once were. I'm sure your mother was a kind and generous soul before becoming so afflicted. I assume she contracted this from your father. Is he still living?" He was looking at her with slightly more approval, since she'd provided him a seemingly captivated audience.

"Alas, no. He died recently, leaving us nothing. If it weren't for your cousin we would be quite destitute."

His momentary warmth vanished. "I have laudanum for your mother. You'll need to watch the dosage carefully. As her pain and agitation increase you'll need to give her more of the tincture. If she's still alive at the end of a fortnight I'll return to check on her…" His voice trailed off as the door opened and Lydia poked her head in the room.

"You don't look like the King of Hell," she said cheerfully, and Elinor groaned.

"This is Etienne de Giverney, Lydia. He was just leaving—"

Her words were cut off as the doctor pushed in front of her, taking one of Lydia's hands in his. "My dear lady," he murmured. "What a trying time for you."

Elinor blinked. Why was she surprised—most men had only to look at Lydia and fall desperately in love. The stiff-necked doctor was no different.

"Dr. de Giverney says she hasn't much time left, and we must keep her comfortable, my love," she said. "He was about to leave."

"On the contrary, Mademoiselle Harriman," he protested, not looking anywhere but into Lydia's blue eyes. "I have yet to complete my examination, and then I will inform you and your sister exactly what you may expect. She is very ill, but that doesn't mean she is past the point of all help. Please." He gestured them out the door.

It could be worse, Elinor thought, ordering tea for the three of them. He was a handsome young man, if stuffy, and he even had a trade. He would make Lydia an excellent husband. Before the disease had claimed Lady Caroline's mind their mother had had grand plans for Lydia—a title, a wealthy husband were to be expected, and there was no saying how high they might look.

All that was gone now, and Lydia had no interest in coronets or fortunes. As Madame de Giverney she would have a strong, stable husband who would give her children, keep her safe, and if Francis Rohan managed to die without reproducing, Lydia might even end up with the French title after all.

Elinor wasn't going to think about that. Francis Rohan's plans for procreation had nothing to do with her, and Lydia wouldn't care if she was a French countess or a simple doctor's wife. She smiled her sweet smile at Etienne when he came every day, listened to his lectures on modern medical practices and asked all the right questions. She could prove a helpful assistant in his surgery if he would let her, and in the meantime the stuffy young man, like so many others, was thoroughly enchanted. He would offer marriage, despite Lydia's lack of a fortune. He was too besotted not to.

And Elinor clung to that small hope as the days passed and her newfound cousin, her only hope for rescue, still didn't return to town.

She had no idea whether Etienne reported to the viscount, but with disconcerting suddenness his lordship stopped responding to her oh-so-polite thank-you notes. The first day that Jacobs had returned empty-handed she had paced the thick rug, expecting a messenger at any moment with the delayed missive. No one came.

The next morning there was pheasant and apples and a set of crystal wineglasses, and she sat by the fire and wrote her note, never mentioning his lack of response. For sure, she'd barely noticed, and it wouldn't do to have Francis Rohan think he mattered in the slightest. Not to her.

There was no return note. And yes, his lordship was most definitely in residence, and had received her note, Jacobs assured her, disapproving. Apparently his lordship was caught up in plans for some grand party, and the Harrimans had little enough claim on his attention. But the food and fuel and the small gifts kept arriving each morning, and Elinor wrote her

dutiful notes, telling herself she was relieved he'd forgotten about them. Delighted, in fact.

If Lydia proved amenable, then rescue was at hand.
In the meantime she would forget about Viscount
Rohan, even as she lost herself in the books he sent
her, and pray that the slim hope fate had dangled in
front of her wasn't to be snatched away.

Lydia slipped on her sabots, pulled the thick
woolen cloak around her shoulders and grabbed the
marketing basket. It was a warmer day in this long,
cold winter, and Lydia had been cooped up for too
long. Elinor tended to be too protective, but a trip to
the market was among her allowed single excursions,
as long as Jacobs kept an eye on her. The sun was
shining for the first time in what seemed like weeks,
and she almost thought that spring might be a possibility.

Most importantly, she needed an escape from the
tiny house, from the specter of Lady Caroline's
imminent death, from Elinor's constant worry, from
Etienne de Giverney's oppressive presence.

She knew what he wanted. She could feel the full
weight of Elinor's approval, of Nanny's concern. He
would make an excellent husband—there was no
denying it. He was handsome, not unkind, with a good
living that could support them all if need be. With the
devilish Viscount Rohan behind him, he was better
than she could have hoped for.

And she would say yes, once he brought himself
to ask for her. She would marry him and sleep in his

bed and bear his children. And no one would ever guess that she dreamed of someone else.

But that was in the future, and Lydia was a firm believer in not borrowing trouble. "Sufficient unto the day is the evil thereof" were words she believed in, and this day was filled with sunshine and blue sky and she had money enough to buy fresh bread and cheese.

Elinor would have a fit if she knew Rohan's daily largesse included French livres. Nanny had enough sense to confiscate the money before Elinor noticed, and she'd built up a tidy little nest egg, enough to cover some of the small pleasantries of life.

The great market of Les Halles was only a brisk ten-minute walk away. Lydia could almost feel sorry for poor Jacobs, struggling to keep up with her. She slowed her pace, ignoring the energy that felt ready to burst free. She'd been kept bottled up for too long, like old champagne, and soon enough she'd be put back in, to molder away. Right now she wanted to dance, to breathe, to run through the streets…

She came to an abrupt stop, her empty basket still swinging on her arm. She glanced behind her, but there was no sign of Jacobs—she'd managed to outpace him again. And directly ahead of her, staring up at a row of buildings that overlooked the busy street, was Mr. Charles Reading.

She had absolutely no doubt it was he, even though she'd only seen him on that one, brief occasion when she'd been so worried about her mother and Elinor she shouldn't even have paid attention to him.

But paid attention she had. She'd looked up into his scarred, beautiful face and felt something she'd never felt before, a treacherous softening inside her, an urge to move closer, to touch his face, to…

For his part, he'd seemed to barely notice her. Oh, he'd been politely flirtatious when he'd first arrived, but she well knew what lay behind men's eyes when they looked at her. She'd known Etienne's covetousness from first glance, she'd known Rohan's lack of interest, and she knew just how respectful or licentious men's glances were.

But Charles Reading eluded her. He'd said all the right things, smiled at her so charmingly, and yet when she'd tried to look into his dark eyes she saw nothing familiar.

What a delicious irony, she thought. She was so used to men falling all over her that she simply accepted it as her due, and the first man who didn't was the first man she wanted.

Nanny Maude would tell her, if she were fool enough to talk to her about such a thing, that she was a silly, vain girl, and the only reason she was obsessed with him was because he didn't care about her. Elinor would be practical and tell her that Mr. Reading probably only enjoyed the company of other men, carefully skirting the issue. So she didn't bother discussing it with anyone. Which probably made his hold on her imagination even stronger. If she'd simply been able to talk about her feelings she might have moved past them days ago.

And now, here he was, staring up at the rooftops across the way as if he'd find the Holy Grail up there.

She was half tempted to turn and walk the other way. She could feel an unexpected flush rise to her cheeks, and she put one gloved hand up to cool it. She was being ridiculous, she told herself. It was a very good thing that he had no interest in her. It meant she could talk to him without being worried about untoward advances.

Maybe he did like only men.

Lydia squared her shoulders, put her bonnet more firmly on her head and started toward him, a determined smile on her face.

He must have sensed that someone was approaching. He spun around before she reached him, and one hand had gone instinctively to the sword that hung at one hip. Most gentlemen wore swords as part of a fashionable toilette. She had the strong feeling that Mr. Reading knew how to use his. And then he recognized her.

"Miss Lydia," he said, sweeping off his hat. "This is an unexpected pleasure." His voice made it sound anything but. "How did you find me?"

She curtsied, wishing she'd listened to her first instinct and gone the other way. "Mr. Reading," she murmured. "In fact, I was heading for the market. I had no idea you would be anywhere near here."

"No, of course you didn't. I beg your pardon." An uncomfortable silence fell.

"What were you looking for?" she said. "Perhaps I could help you find it?"

"Unlikely," he said, replacing his hat. She wished he wouldn't—in the bright sunlight it put his face in shadow, the ruined beauty of it, and his eyes were un-readable. "Lord Rohan was shot when he was driving through this area. I was trying to figure out where the shooter stood."

"He was *shot?*" Lydia said, panicked. What would Elinor do? What would they do without his charity? Thank God Nanny had squirreled away the money. "Is he dead?"

"Of course not. Didn't your sister tell you? It wasn't much more than a graze. It happened over a week ago, just after we left your house, and he's already mostly healed. He thinks it was an accident. I'm not so certain."

"He has so many enemies, then?"

"Enough."

Another uncomfortable silence. Lydia knew she should move, should say something, should ignore this exceedingly uncomfortable pull that was drawing her to him.

Clearly he despised her. He wouldn't even look at her—his gaze was focused somewhere past her shoulder. Nanny would tell her this was good for her. At that moment it felt like pure misery. "I should continue to the market. It was a pleasure to see you again, Mr. Reading," she said, wishing she could sound as unruffled as Elinor.

Something in her voice caught his attention, and he frowned. "Surely you aren't out alone, Miss Lydia?"

She glanced around her. Still no sign of Jacobs. "Of course not. Jacobs is somewhere behind me—it was such a beautiful day that I'm afraid I was a bit too exuberant in my walking, and I lost him. I'm certain he'll catch up with me by the time I reach the market." She held out her hand. "Good afternoon, Mr. Reading."

He took her hand, but didn't release it. "I'll accompany you to the market, if you'll permit me."

"There's no need…"

"I'd be remiss in my duties as a gentleman if I allowed you'd to continue alone," he said in that polite, distant voice. "A young lady as beautiful as you shouldn't be traveling alone. I would be desolate if anything happened to you."

Flirtation by rote. She couldn't manage Elinor's icy smile either, though she could try. "There's no need to pretend you have any interest in me, Mr. Reading. I realize I'm not to your particular taste, though you say all the right things. I do assure you there's no need to accompany me—I've been to the market on my own or with Jacobs any number of times and nothing untoward has happened. If you'll release my hand…"

She tugged, but he tightened his grip, and beneath the brim of his hat she could see his smile. "Does everyone fall at your feet, Miss Lydia?"

"In truth, everyone but you, Mr. Reading," she said ruefully. "Nanny says I'm vain, but I'm not. It's simply an accident of birth that I'm pretty. It's no great accomplishment on my part. My mother was pretty, and knowing her, I expect my father was as well. So people smile on me, and men flirt with me. Except for you, Mr. Reading."

He tucked her hand under his arm, starting forward, and she had no choice but to fall into step beside him. "I flirt with you, Miss Lydia," he said easily. "If you haven't recognized it as such I must have become suddenly gauche, and I do beg your pardon. I will endeavor to improve my skills. Shall I tell you how exquisite your golden curls are? Your delicate British complexion? That you move so gracefully angels would weep in jealousy, that your smile brightens every encounter? A sonnet, perhaps?

'Miss Lydia's eyes
Are something divine
A delicate prize
'Twill never be mine.'"

"I don't think much of that," she said frankly. "It sounds as if you want my eyes gouged from my head and placed on a pillow. Or a plate," she added.

Reading made a muffled sound, which in someone else she might have thought was a laugh smothered by a cough. "I'm afraid that most of my instant poetic efforts tend toward deliberately obscene doggerel, composed for the entertainment of one's drinking partners. If you want a true sonnet you'll have to wait while I write it down. I wouldn't want to give you less than your due."

Each flirtatious remark seemed forced, but he still kept her arm captured, his hand on hers, pressing against his forearm, and for some reason she still felt as if she were dancing on air. She tilted her face up to the sunshine, drinking it in. "I give you leave to stop flirting, Mr. Reading. I still don't believe you. Tell me about Lord Rohan. Is he in much pain?"

She could feel the tension in the muscles beneath her hand. "I would suggest, Miss Lydia, that you cast your gaze elsewhere. Lord Rohan is naught but trouble, and he's moved his gaze beyond pretty virgins such as you."

"He's interested in my sister, is he not? Isn't she a pretty virgin?" If he disparaged Elinor she would happily hit him with her empty basket.

"You know as well as I do that your sister is far more than pretty."

"Indeed she is," she said, pleased with him after all. "And I do assure you, I'm not as shallow and vain as you appear to think me."

"I do not think you shallow or vain," he said in a low voice. "I find you exquisite, delightful, a wondrous…"

"Oh, be quiet," she said crossly. "You think I'm—"

He stopped, and one gloved finger haltered her in midsentence. They were on the edge of the market now, beneath the shadows of an overhanging building, and she could see his face now, see his eyes, no longer covered by drooping lids.

"I find you exquisite, delightful, a wondrous temptation and most definitely not for me," he said in a slow, deliberate voice. "You have everyone else at your feet, Miss Lydia. Why should you need me as well?"

For a moment she couldn't speak, mesmerized by the torment she saw in the dark depths of his eyes. "Because you're the one I want," she said in a hushed voice, shocked at herself. Shocked at the simple truth of it.

He stared down at her for a long moment. And then his head moved, and she knew he was going to kiss her, here in this marketplace full of people, he was going to put his scarred mouth on hers, and she was going to throw her arms around him and kiss him back.

"There you are, Miss Lydia!" Jacobs's voice broke the moment, and Reading released her arm. She turned, feeling the heat flood her cheeks.

"I thought I'd lost you, Jacobs," she said in a determinedly cheerful voice, as if she hadn't just lost her only chance for the best kiss of her life. "Mr. Reading was kind enough to escort me in your place." She turned back to him, ready to say all the polite things. And then the words, the breath left her, as she finally looked into his eyes and saw the truth.

A moment later it was gone, and he bowed over her hand. "Your servant, Miss Lydia," he murmured, and a moment later he was gone, swallowed up by the crowds.

She stood motionless, watching him until he disappeared, her heart hammering. It was no wonder she hadn't been able to read his thoughts, his feelings in his dark, shaded eyes. They were deeper, more powerful than she'd ever imagined. Too powerful to put into words. All she knew was she wanted to run after him, throwing caution, throwing everything to the winds. He'd said she wasn't for the likes of him. She didn't care. She'd follow him anywhere, she'd…

"Miss Lydia?" Jacobs broke through her momentary dream, bringing her back to reality with a thud. "We need to finish the marketing and get back home. The doctor is due this afternoon, and he was going to take you to the park for a picnic." He made it sound like an operation.

Etienne, she thought miserably. The man she was going to marry. The right man for her. If she learned to stop dreaming. "I think we need tripe," she said. "Come along, Jacobs. You're right, we'd best hurry."

She told herself to stop thinking about Mr. Reading's eyes, immediately. And she almost succeeded.

13

Elinor was sitting alone in the refurbished parlor, rereading a book of philosophy. There was a thick Persian carpet on the floor, heavy damask drapes covering the dreary windows, and the chair beneath her was sinfully comfortable. There was a good fire in the grate, the new table had fresh spring flowers, and the place no longer stank of poverty and death. It was pleasant, comfortable, even if she had to thank Rohan for it all.

She'd allowed Lydia to accompany Etienne on his rounds that afternoon, after her morning visit to the market. Lydia had returned, flushed and abstracted, retiring to the bedroom until the doctor arrived. By then she was her usual sweet, smiling self, the shadow gone from her eyes. Almost. What could have happened at the market, with Jacobs close by, that could have overset her?

It was probably her active imagination. She was so used to disaster that it was hard to believe that disaster had been averted. If things continued as they were,

Lydia would marry the doctor and bring Nanny Maude and Jacobs into their household. Elinor would even be willing to face the King of Hell in his den in order to make that possible.

And then she'd be blissfully, deliriously free. The thought was terrifying, intoxicating. One thing was certain— she wouldn't move in with her sister. She could already see the way Etienne's mind worked, and he would doubtless welcome another conscripted pair of hands, someone to work for the dubious charity of a bed and food.

She would find something, anything. She might travel back to England—surely there was something she could do. Her education had been sadly neglected— she was dismal at watercolors, her attempts on the pianoforte were painful for all and her knitting was disastrous. She could, however, translate Latin with dizzying speed, and presumably still ride a horse, if rumors were true and you never lost that particular skill.

At least her plain looks would be to her advantage if she were to apply for work as a governess. No woman wanted a pretty creature who might lure either the young gentlemen of the household or, even worse, the patriarch. Surely she could—

The knock on the door broke through these ruminations, and for a moment her stomach knotted in crazed hope, and she half rose from her chair, wanting to race to the door.

She sat back down, taking a deep, calming breath as Jacobs went to answer the summons, but she knew immediately that the caller was a stranger. As expected, Viscount Rohan had forgotten her existence.

"Baron Tolliver to see you, Miss Elinor," Jacobs announced in his most proper voice.

And Elinor rose, prepared to meet her long-lost cousin, and her last best hope for the future.

It was absolutely ridiculous that he was having such a damnably hard time putting Miss Elinor Harriman out of his mind, Rohan thought as he surveyed the decorations. The two-week celebration was usually the high point of the year, and his servants had been preparing for months. The curtains in the ballroom were hung with black, every bedroom and in fact, every flat surface, had been gone over, prepared for unparalleled lechery. Food was spilling from the kitchens, excitement was building, and a ceremony of induction had been meticulously planned. The members of the Heavenly Host were, in a fact, a relatively small, select number, but there had been a spate of recent requests to join them, and Rohan had been considering them. In particular, one name stood out, and he was more than mildly interested in how the gentleman in question would comport himself.

The newcomers were usually a greedy lot, unable to comprehend that everything was available for their pleasure. Do what thou wilt. Eat and drink and gamble with no limit. Partake of the pleasures of the flesh with any and all who were willing, and no variation was forbidden. He had one room devoted to the giving and receiving of pain, others for dedicated play. One of the most popular was the chapel, where the members could mock the notion of the devil and the strictures of the church. He'd outgrown the silliness of spitting in the eye of God, but other, more devout souls found it the epitome of titillation.

In fact, he wasn't quite sure what he was looking forward to this time around. Pain had lost its appeal, costumes felt forced, and in truth, he could think of no one he wanted, no female who stirred his blood. He leaned back, lazily considering whether he had reached a point where those of his own sex held any allure, but after a moment he dismissed the notion reluctantly. He had no rules, and he could care less where his sexual drives took him. He only regretted that right now they were taking him nowhere but to a tumbledown house in Rue du Pélican.

Reading would tell him his mind was disordered. And in fact, he did so, almost nightly, when he accompanied Rohan home from a rout or a card party or some less savory entertainment.

Because, for some quixotic reason, his coach ride home invariably included a trip past the dark streets that housed the Harriman family.

Reading had the good sense not to ask him why he ordered his coachman to take that particular route, and Rohan didn't volunteer any reason. He knew full well that Reading was pining for the sister, poor fool, and refusing to admit it, and Rohan was perfectly happy to be assured that the wretched little household was safe for the night.

Every night Rohan told himself that this would

be the last time. If he was concerned, which he would deny to his last breath, he could always send a servant to check on her. She'd already made two champions—Willis had reported that there was an underfootman who was now devoted to her, and Willis was probably smitten as well. God knows Mrs. Clarke was going to have his ears if he hurt her. Strange how everyone was drawn to such a plain, difficult woman, but maybe that would make things easier for him. He could simply charge them all with the task of making certain she and her family were well and forget about her himself.

Indeed, that was exactly what he would do. No more trips out of his way. He would head directly home from wherever he chose to spend his evenings, and rely on a servant to keep him informed. Perhaps then he could stop thinking about her and concentrate on the Revels.

There would be new guests, freshly arrived from England and the rest of the continent. There would be proper aristocratic wives who finally discovered their husbands weren't meeting their needs, lower-class women of limited experience looking for a protector and the more comfortable way of life an alliance with the Host could bring. Fresh blood was always invigorating, and while he was looking forward to the approaching festivities with mild irritation and a great deal of boredom, who knows who might appear to distract him? Someone else equally…inspiring… would most likely appear.

This plain woman had done nothing but distract

him, irritate him, unwillingly enchant him since she'd appeared in the anteroom at the château, and if he had to choose between his unwanted obsession with her and boredom, he'd gladly choose ennui. After all, he was used to it.

He leaned forward in his chair, reaching for a glass of claret, and paused for a moment to admire the Mechlin lace that graced his strong wrist. He had a ridiculous fondness for his wardrobe, and the new cuffs had been particularly fine. At least she hadn't been around to destroy his clothes recently. And he wondered what Elinor Harriman would look like, stretched naked on his bed, wrapped in nothing but delicate white lace.

He drained the glass of wine and set it down carefully, resisting the impulse to fling it across the room. Much as he wanted to shatter something, break something, it would simply be more proof of how disordered his mind and his desires had become. Marianne would be in attendance this week, and after the last interruption at his château, he realized it had been quite some time since he'd been able to fully enjoy her. Surely she'd manage to distract him for a few good hours. She was an expert, graceful, practiced, intuitive as to what he did and didn't like.

So why was he suddenly desiring awkwardness? He should be concentrating on other, more important things. Like who had shot him? Was it his so-dear French heir, the disgruntled Etienne? Or someone else he'd managed to offend during his long, wicked life?

As Etienne had said, one had only to meet him in

order to want to kill him, though he did think that was a trifle harsh. There were any number of his acquaintances who would gladly sell their souls for him. Unfortunately he had no belief in the existence of any force willing to buy those souls.

At least there had been no more attempts on his life. Perhaps that had simply been a stray bullet, a random event. And perhaps he'd forget all about Elinor Harriman. Whether he believed in any kind of god, there was always the possibility of miracles.

The new Baron Tolliver was a handsome man. Despite the fact that he had the unmistakable Harriman Nose, it fit far better in a masculine face, Elinor decided. He had bright blue eyes, a full-lipped mouth, a strong body just above-average height and a pleasant smile.

"Miss Harriman," he'd said, coming up to her and taking her hand. "I'm devastated that I was out of town when you sought to meet with me. Mr. Mitchum should have gotten word to me and I would have returned to Paris immediately."

His gloved hand was firm and reassuring, and she blinked, momentarily distracted. "There was no need, my lord," she lied. "I was simply hoping to discuss—"

"Oh, my dear cousin, and I hope I may call you cousin. And please, you must call me Marcus. We are, after all, distantly related."

Elinor blinked, not expecting such forceful graciousness, and then she pulled herself together. Perhaps because of The Nose, he looked very much like her father, dispelling her distant hope that he might be an interloper. Not that that would have been to her advantage—the estate would presumably have gone on to an even more remote relative, or returned to the Crown.

"Cousin Marcus," she said, sinking back into her chair. "You're very gracious. Please sit, sir. May I offer you tea? Perhaps something to eat?"

"You are more than kind," he said, taking the seat opposite her with a flourish of his elegant coat. "Tea would be delightful. I am so pleased to see you living in such obvious comfort. I confess that when I reached the neighborhood I was sorely distressed that my cousins should have fallen upon such poverty, but I am relieved to see that things are not so dire. Tell me how I may assist you, cousin, and I will endeavor to do so."

He had a warm, confiding smile, and she told herself to breathe a sigh of relief. "Mr. Mitchum mentioned that there was a small legacy left to me. I'm afraid our current circumstances aren't as comfortable as they might appear—we are living on the charity of a wealthy benefactor, and that help might disappear. I would prefer not to have to rely on others for our well-being, and I wondered what the nature of the legacy might be." She chose her words carefully, determined not to sound greedy.

She hadn't been careful enough. "Wealthy benefactor?" he said, frowning. "And who might that be?"

The King of Hell. The most profligate man in France and probably England as well, the Lord of the

Heavenly Host. If she told him the truth, her cousin would walk away in disgust and horror.

"He prefers to remain anonymous," she said. Astonishing how easy it was to lie when it was necessary. In truth, Viscount Rohan probably did prefer that people didn't know he was supplying them with both the necessities and the elegancies of life and so far had sought nothing in return. Their knowing would destroy his ruthless, soulless reputation.

"Ah," said the newly minted baron. "I wish I could thank him myself for his kindness to my kinswomen. And may I ask where the rest of your family is? My lawyers inform me that your mother still lives, though she is quite ill."

"Not for much longer. She's not conscious, but extremely agitated, and it might be for the best if you didn't see her."

"Nonsense," he said, having acquired a lordly manner in very little time. "I must pay my respects to the former baroness." He rose, and Elinor rose as well, inwardly cursing him. She could throw herself in front of him in an effort to stall him, but in the end it would do her no good. So she simply nodded.

"Of course," she said, resigned. "This way."

It was scarcely a long walk in their cluttered little house, made worse by the comfortable furniture Lord Rohan had sent them. Her cousin made a muffled groan when he accidentally rammed his hip against the sideboard that held the exquisite glassware that had arrived four days ago. She moved ahead of him and pushed open the door of the sickroom, bracing herself.

They'd taken the restraints off Lady Caroline over a week ago, as her state of malaise seemed to deepen. Nanny Maude would coax a little chicken broth down her throat, and every now and then Caroline opened her eyes. Nanny was perched in the comfortable chair beside the bed, the chair thanks to Lord Rohan, as well as the warm, rich blankets that covered her mother's frail form.

"Nanny Maude, this is our cousin, the new Lord Tolliver. Cousin Marcus, this is Nanny Maude, who's been with us all our lives and takes excellent care of us."

Nanny rose painfully, her dark eyes narrowed as she assessed the newcomer. "Good afternoon, my lord," she said, managing a sketch of a curtsy. To the casual observer it was all right and proper, but Elinor had the strange sense that something wasn't right. Nanny was staring at him with an odd expression on her face.

He gave her a polite nod and moved to stand over Lady Caroline. To Elinor's amazement, her mother opened her eyes, focusing on the man in her room.

"Who are you?" she demanded in a voice that was little more than a croak. They were her first lucid words in more than a week.

"Your late husband's heir, Lady Caroline," he said pleasantly. "Marcus Harriman."

"Marcus, eh?" She struggled to sit up, and Nanny quickly moved to her side, trying to calm her, but the glint of madness was back in her eyes. "Come here. Closer."

"Don't," Elinor muttered, uneasy.

"You're being absurd, Cousin Elinor. She's hardly in any shape to hurt me." He moved next to the bed. "Is there any way I can assist you, Lady Caroline?"

"Closer," she said.

He leaned over her, taking one clawlike hand in his, and before Elinor could cry out, her mother managed to pull him off balance, so that he tumbled onto the bed with her, and one of her gnarled hands clawed at the front of his breeches as she began to curse and shout, terrible, filthy words, animal words.

Marcus scrambled to his feet, horrified, and Elinor took his arm, pulling him from the room. "She's not well," she said helplessly.

He was bleeding—she'd managed to scratch his face, and as Elinor shut the door firmly behind them she could still hear her mother's screams, followed by Nanny's soothing words. She half expected him to brush off her offer of assistance, to storm from the house in disgust, but he simply looked at her with pity.

"You poor girl."

It was almost enough to make her weep. Almost. She'd shown that weakness only once in her memory, in front of the worst possible person. She wasn't going to succumb to it again.

"We manage," she said briskly. "The doctor says she hasn't long left, and these bouts of excitation simply mean the end is coming closer. Nanny Maude is wonderful with her, and Lydia and I are fine on our own."

"And your own father left you nothing? Unconscionable!"

She managed a wry smile. "Indeed, you'd know more about that than I do, sir. I gather the entire estate was entailed and there was nothing set aside for his children."

Cousin Marcus looked faintly uncomfortable. "In point of fact, I don't believe your sister actually is..."

"My sister was born in wedlock to my mother and father, and by rule of law she's a legitimate offspring," Elinor said shortly, her temper getting the better of her.

"You know your law well. You're an educated woman. I wonder at that, given your ramshackle upbringing."

He meant no disrespect, she reminded herself, even as she resisted the temptation to snap back. "I like to read," she said stiffly.

"And you're an intelligent woman. You cannot believe how admirable that is, in this day and age of silly young misses. I would much prefer the companionship of an older, plainer woman of sense than a pretty, shallow young thing."

She just barely managed a smile. "Too kind," she said through her teeth. "I'm afraid Nanny's too busy right now to make us tea." The screams were muffled but ongoing, and Cousin Marcus had a labored expression.

"This is clearly a difficult time. I'll return when things are more settled..." He was already edging toward the door.

"But you haven't told me of my father's bequest. And your face is bleeding—at least let me see to your wounds before you go out in public," she protested.

"We can discuss this all at a later date," he said, dabbing at his face with a lacy handkerchief. "As Mr. Mitchum told you, it's only a token, but I wish to do your father's bidding as best as I can." He didn't wait for Jacobs to reappear and open the door—he was already halfway out it. "Adieu, dear lady."

She watched him go. He walked well—he wore boots instead of the elegant shoes that Rohan favored, and if he had the trace of a swagger he was doubtless justified. He was a peer of the realm, a strong, handsome man in the prime of life. He had every reason to strut.

She closed the door behind him. Her mother's screams had finally quieted now that Cousin Marcus had left, and she moved quietly to Caroline's bedroom, opening the door a crack.

Her mother had slipped back into a drugged sleep. "Shouldn't we tie her to the bed again?" she whispered to Nanny Maude.

The old lady had a troubled expression on her face. "No need," Nanny said. "These fits are followed by bouts of sleep. She won't move or speak for days. Who was that gentleman again?" She changed subjects abruptly.

"I introduced you. He's our cousin, Marcus Harriman."

"I don't remember any Marcus, and I lived on that estate for the first fifty years of my life."

"He's distant kin. The closest they could come up with, but I'm sure it's all as it should be."

Nanny shook her head, still not satisfied. "I didn't think there were any other branches of the family."

"Well, there's no doubting he's got the Harriman look. And if it wasn't him, the estate would be going to someone else. At least he seems willing to meet with me."

"Indeed," Nanny said, not sounding happy. "Next time he comes to visit we'll have Jacobs stay with your mama, I want to ask him a few questions."

The thought of fierce little Nanny Maude interviewing the new Baron Tolliver was entertaining enough to lift the dark cloud that had settled around her heart. She was contriving as best she could—for now she could try to be patient.

She moved back to her seat by the fire and picked up her book. It was a collection of improving sermons by a zealot monk who'd spent time in the Americas, and whose notions concerning bathing, women and religion were extreme and uncompromising. The good brother was a proponent of the theory that women were an unpleasant necessity, and once they'd fulfilled their procreative duties they should be sent to convents to reside with other women and endure a vow of silence.

Rohan had sent it on purpose, just to annoy her, but the written word was scarce enough that she even read this wretched book, alternately cursing its giver.

And she tried not to think about Francis, Viscount Rohan or his Heavenly Host.

14

In the end Lydia didn't buy the tripe, though not because of any lightening of her spirits. For all that she wanted to wallow in unhappiness, tripe was carrying it a bit too far, and Nanny was far from an inspired cook. It would be up to Lydia to prepare it, and she'd never had much of a fondness for offal. She bought fresh farm eggs, leeks and cheese as well as a loaf of the freshest bread. If Nanny Maude couldn't conjure something delicious out of all that then Lydia could.

And would, once she'd gotten over her stupid fit of the sulks. It wasn't as if Etienne would help. After a riveting, arousing, frustrating encounter with the man she was foolish enough to…to be interested in, she had no choice but to follow it up with three hours of listening to Etienne go on and on. He had only two subjects of conversation: his brilliance as he worked through medical cases that he recounted in stomach-turning detail, and the great injustice served him by his cousin.

Fortunately he never needed much more than a word or two to encourage him, and Lydia was able to sit in the park eating cold chicken *à la diable* and pretend she was somewhere, anywhere, else. Until a word caught her ear.

"Jacobite?" she repeated, wrinkling her forehead.

"Ah, I forgot how young you are," Etienne said fondly. "That was before you were born. The stupid English were arguing over who should be king, and they tried to put the true Catholic ruler on the throne, a Scots prince."

"I know about Bonnie Prince Charlie, Etienne," Lydia said with just a trace of asperity. "What has he got to do with my lord Rohan?"

The look that crossed Etienne's handsome face might almost be called a sneer. "He's not a lord according to England. He's a traitor. He and his family fought for the Scottish king, and when the rebellion failed, his father and brother were killed, he was stripped of everything and exiled. If he ever returns to England he'll suffer a traitor's execution on Tower Hill. That's a day I'd be happy to see."

She couldn't hide her horror. "You want to see Lord Rohan beheaded?"

"You forget, I am a doctor. I see death every day. Seldom is it a death I think just. Rohan escaped to France and claimed the title that should have been mine, and he's gone to the devil ever since." Etienne sniffed. It was an unfortunate habit of his, and she could imagine it getting worse as he grew older. With her trapped beside him.

"How old was he when this happened? He's not terribly old now, is he?" she said.

"When he was exiled? When he fought in England? Seventeen, I believe."

"Oh, God," Lydia said in a hushed voice. Both Nanny Maude and Jacobs had Scots relatives, and they'd been firm Jacobites. Nanny had told her all about the true king, and the hideous massacre that was Culloden, when Butcher Cumberland had slaughtered thousands. That a seventeen boy had endured that bloody conflict and the savage aftermath was both cruel and enlightening. Living through a time like that would change someone forever.

"I almost wish he'd find some reason to try to go back," he said. "I would make it my business to alert the English authorities, and his execution would clear any last lien on the French title. The woman who married me will be the Comtesse de Giverney. Sooner or later."

She ignored his meaningful look. "But Lord Rohan has no interest in returning to England, I believe."

"No," he said sadly. "We shall just have to wait, *ma chère.*"

We. The idea was demoralizing and inescapable. By the time he returned her home she had a raging headache. Elinor was clearly bursting with news, something about her cousin, but Lydia couldn't listen, and she stumbled into the darkened bedroom and lay down on the soft, comfortable bed that Lord Rohan had given them. There were too many things beating at her head. Etienne's monotonous, self-serving voice.

Charles Reading's haunted eyes. The thought of a lost boy caught in the grisly horror of the rebellion. Mama was talking again, though none of it made any sense, and some of the words made her blush, while others were entirely unknown to her, and she thanked God for that. She pulled the pillow over her head to shut out the sounds and tried to sleep.

It wasn't much of a relief. In her dream Charles Reading stood there, ready to kiss her, when Etienne ran up and slashed his face with a lance. He fell, and as he lay on the ground his life's blood drained from him, and she found she was looking down at a much younger version of Francis Rohan, without the mockery or the faint sneer. And when she woke up she was crying.

She was being absurd. She dragged herself out of the room, ready to help with dinner, only to find Nanny Maude was just setting it on the table. "There you are, lass," Nanny said. "We weren't going to wake you— you looked exhausted, poor thing."

"I'm fine," she said. Elinor was already seated. "I gather we had a visitor today?"

The four of them sat down at the old table, a terrible breach in protocol that Elinor insisted upon. They were a family, she would say, and she wasn't going to have half her family eat in a kitchen. "Our cousin Tolliver," she said. "He seems a good man, but Mama was so disturbed by him that she scared him away."

"Harrumph," said Nanny.

"Just ignore her," Elinor said. "Nanny's got a fixation about the man. Swears there are no distant cousins and he's some kind of impostor. You have only to take one look at him and know he's no impostor."

"The Harriman Nose?" Lydia inquired.

"Exactly."

"Don't listen to me," Nanny said darkly. "I'm an old woman, what would I know? But you mark my words, there's something wrong with that Master Marcus Harriman."

"I certainly hope not," Elinor said in that stiff voice she sometimes used, the one that Lydia hated. "If he won't help us, it leaves us entirely at the mercy of Lord Rohan, and a useless degenerate is unlikely to—"

"I wish you wouldn't insist on vilifying him," Lydia said, staring down at the cheese-and-leek pie Nanny had made.

They all turned to look at her at once. "My dear," Elinor said, and Lydia couldn't miss the fear in her voice, the ridiculous fear that had been plaguing her. "He's not at all the right person for you—"

"How many times must I tell you I have no interest in Lord Rohan, and he has none in me? Having spent an entire afternoon with Etienne has made me a great deal more sympathetic with the viscount than I was before."

"Why?" Elinor said flatly.

"Do you know why he lives in Paris?" Lydia said.

"I really don't care, dearest. I imagine he's here because the world knows that Paris is the center of a society that is, to put it mildly, indulgent. And since Lord Rohan has an interest in indulgences, it only makes sense."

"He's exiled from England. He can't go back or he'll be executed."

Elinor raised an eyebrow. "Oh, really? Whose husband did he murder?"

"No one," Lydia said.

"He's a terrible man, miss," Nanny Maude said. "Consorts with devils, he does, and drinks blood, and…"

"He was at *Culloden!*" Lydia blurted out. "He was not even twenty years old, fighting for Bonnie Prince Charlie, and he saw his entire family slaughtered. He barely escaped with his life."

There was a shocked silence. And then Nanny Maude cleared her throat. "I always said there was good in the lad. Indeed, and I tried to tell you so. Handsome, too, and I expect a good woman would put a stop to these parties of his."

Jacobs said nothing, merely nodding his head approvingly. Finally Elinor spoke, and her voice was raw.

"Does that excuse him for the rest of his life?" she said. "Does that give him the right to destroy other lives?"

"Whose life has he destroyed?" Lydia demanded.

And she could hear her sister's answer as if she spoke it out loud. *Mine,* she cried. *Mine.*

Lydia's muffled coughing woke her, and for a moment Elinor lay there, not moving. Something was wrong, she felt it in her bones, and she sat up, squinting in the darkness around her. Her eyes burned, her throat ached, and she heard the ominous crackling sound, far too close. Horror filled her—fire in these rickety old parts of town were disastrous, spreading through streets and alleyways, and there was nothing anyone could do to stop them.

She shook Lydia, scrambling from the bed, her eyes burning. "The house is on fire," she said. "We have to get out."

Lydia was already alert, grabbing her robe and pulling it tight around her as Elinor went for the door. Smoke was pouring in under the doorjamb, but the wood itself was still cool, and she yanked it open, only to be momentarily blinded by the wall of smoke that billowed in.

"Nanny!" she screamed, fighting her way through the smoke, stepping out into the hallway just as Jacobs stormed by. He was heading for Lady Caroline's bedroom. She heard the laughter then, her mother's silvery voice chuckling merrily, and the sound raised the hairs on the back of her neck.

Jacobs kicked the door open, and flames poured out of the room. He didn't hesitate, charging into the fire, and a moment later he emerged, a small figure bundled in his arms. He headed for the front door, looking back at them. "Follow me!" he shouted from above the noise of the crackling flames.

"Mama!" Lydia cried, but then from beyond the flames the voice came again, singing a bawdy sailor's song in a hoarse, scratchy voice.

"He's got Nanny Maude," she said. "Go with him. I'll see to Mama."

"No, I won't leave you!" Lydia said, but Elinor simply shoved her toward Jacobs, and he was strong enough to catch her arm and drag her to the door, even as he held Nanny Maude's slight figure. He seemed to be having trouble with the flimsy front door, and a moment later he simply kicked it down, charging out into the cold night air with the two women.

"'There was a jolly tinker, who lived in Southern France...'" her mother sang, the hoarse sound a shadow of the once-light soprano that had captivated so many men. Ignoring the flames, Elinor pushed into the room. Lady Caroline was curled up on the floor, crooning, as the flames ate through the silk covers of her bed and started up the bedposts.

"Mama!" Elinor cried, trying to move closer. There was a river of flame between them, and if she jumped across there was no guarantee she could get back. Her mother was so slender and frail she could easily pull her to safety, if she could just be persuaded to reach out.

Lady Caroline's glazed eyes focused on Elinor. "Where's my daughter?" she croaked. "Where's my Lydia?"

"She's safe, Mama. You need to come with me, and I'll bring you to her. Just stand up and come to the edge there, and I'll lift you over."

Lady Caroline's cackle matched the noise of the fire. "You look like him. Like your father. He wants to kill me, and you do too. Get me Lydia. I'm not going anywhere without Lydia."

The path of flames widened, eating up the flooring between them, and Elinor's panic increased. "You don't want to hurt Lydia, Mama. If she comes back in this house she could die. Just stand up and walk over here and I'll bring you out safely. Trust me, Mama. I've never done anything but love you."

"Love?" She laughed heartlessly, and by a cruel twist of fate she was once more lucid. "What do you know of love? No one's ever loved you in this life. No one ever will. I won't go where it's cold. It's warm here, and it's cold outside."

"Mama!" The smoke was so thick Elinor could barely see her, but her bare feet could feel the flames getting closer, and if she waited much longer she wasn't going to get out of the house alive. She couldn't leave her there, wouldn't…

A strong arm came out of the darkness, snaking around her waist and lifting her up. She shrieked in protest, but the stranger paid no attention, scooping her into strong arms and moving through the burning house. Rafters fell behind them, and she could hear her mother's screams of laughter as they burst through into the cold night air.

She found herself dumped down on the snow with little ceremony, and she tried to run back into the house, but the hands that hauled her away were painful, and she turned in rage, and even the sight of Francis Rohan looking back at her had no effect on her. "I have to save her!" she cried as her mother's screams and laughter echoed into the night.

"She's not worth dying for, child," he said, his voice cool and practical, and she hated him. "And I'm afraid it's too late."

He spoke the truth. The burning house collapsed in on itself, and her mother's voice was shut off, gone completely, and she heard Lydia's sobs.

She tore herself away from him, going in search of her sister. Lydia was kneeling in the snow by Nanny Maude, and she'd covered her face, weeping. Elinor knelt beside her, putting her arms around her, holding her tight. There were tears on her own face, she realized with surprise. She'd given up on her mother long ago, and the King of Hell was right, she wasn't worth dying for. Even at the end she'd rejected her, and yet still Elinor wept.

He had moved to stand over them, and she ignored him, hugging her sister more tightly.

Jacobs appeared out of the shadows, white runnels of tears against the soot-dark face. "We need to get Nanny someplace," he said in a voice choked with pain or the fire. Or both. "She needs a doctor."

"Put her in my coach," Rohan said, his orders crisp and clear, and Elinor wanted to pull away from Lydia and scream at him. She had no choice. Lydia's grief was more important than her rage. "We'll have my cousin come to check on her," Rohan said. He moved away from her, wisely, and raised his voice. "Reading, why don't you see to Miss Lydia. I'm sure she'd appreciate your strong arm. She needs to get out of the snow and into the carriage before she freezes to death."

Elinor considered holding on to her, but Charles Reading had appeared out of the darkness and Lydia went to him, letting him fold her into his arms, leaving

Elinor alone on her knees in the snow. Alone with Rohan.

"You can't stay there all night," he said.

"You let her die."

"I kept you alive. You can get up on your own or I can carry you, whichever you prefer, but I expect you'd rather have me keep my hands to myself," he said in a weary voice. "Make up your mind. I'm cold, and I've ruined another pair of shoes. You really are wreaking havoc on my wardrobe."

She forced her head to turn, to look up at him, and she didn't disguise the fury in her eyes. She was awash with pain, and there was nowhere else she could direct it but at her cool nemesis.

He looked down at her, and his smile was crooked. "But how charming," he murmured. "You despise me. Feel free to, poppet, but I'm getting you out of the snow and into my carriage now, before my feet turn to icicles." He held out a hand to her, waiting for her to take it.

She didn't want to touch him. She wanted to curl up in a ball and weep, but Lydia was waiting for her. She put her foot out, expecting to rise gracefully, but the pain in her feet was excruciating, and her legs wouldn't hold her.

He caught her before she fell, and scooped her up into his arms again, carrying her toward the waiting coach. He dumped her in, unceremoniously, and Lydia reached for her, pulling her onto the seat beside her.

Rohan closed the door behind them, remaining

outside the crowded carriage. And a moment later they were off, leaving him behind, standing alone in the snow beside the still-burning grave of their poor, lost mother.

15

Elinor fell back against the tufted seat of the carriage, too shaken to move. The carriage was made for four, and with the five of them crammed in tightly there was scarcely room to breathe. There were tiny silver candles in each corner, encased in glass holders, and they shed enough light that Elinor could see Nanny looking very bad indeed.

She wanted to throw her hands over her face and scream, she wanted to hide and weep. She could do no such thing. This was her family, what was left of them, and she was needed. She straightened her back.

"How is Nanny Maude, Jacobs?" she asked, her voice rough from the smoke she'd inhaled. "Was she burned?"

Jacobs shook his head. "The shock, more like. And the smoke. She's an old lady—this will be the death of her—"

"It will be no such thing!" she said sharply. "His lordship's cousin is a doctor, and I expect he'll be waiting for us as soon as we get there." Get where? she asked herself. Though she knew the answer.

"She's not breathing too well," Jacobs said gloomily. His voice broke. "Her ladyship's gone, and now Nanny Maude…"

"Stop it!" Elinor said. "We're not going to lose Nanny Maude." She turned to Lydia and froze. Perched on the very edge of the narrow seat, Charles Reading held her in his arms, and she was sobbing quietly into the elegant shoulder of his coat, one hand clutching the fabric in a fist.

Elinor reached for her, to pull her away, and then her eyes met Reading's, and she froze, in shock. She'd never seen such naked pain, naked longing, in anyone's eyes. She hadn't even known such depth of emotion existed. He was holding Lydia so tenderly, her curls tucked beneath his chin, and he was murmuring comforting words to her. Words Lydia needed to hear, words that Elinor didn't have, not then.

She could sort that out in the morning. At the moment she couldn't begrudge her baby sister any comfort she could find, no matter how unsuitable it might be. Reading was a member of the Heavenly Host, a libertine and a reprobate. He was no fit match for Lydia, but at that moment she couldn't bring herself to care. Let her take what comfort she could.

"Do you know where we're going, Mr. Reading?" she asked politely.

He cleared his voice. "I believe we're heading to Lord Rohan's town house. It's quite close, and Dr. de Giverney should be waiting for us when we get there. I know this is not what you want, but if you would accept it for the time being…"

"I have no choice," she said wearily. "Where else can we go?" The coach was well-sprung, and she was able to slide off the seat and kneel by Nanny Maude, taking one limp hand in hers. Her breathing was labored, and Elinor glanced into Jacobs's grim face. "She's going to be fine," she said fiercely. "We all are."

"But Miss Elinor, your mother…"

"Is gone. There's no way we can change that, and she hadn't much time left as it was. At least we can hope she went quickly, that the falling rafters killed her before…" She stopped talking, realizing what she was about to say.

It was too late. Lydia raised her tearstained face. "Oh, love, you did what you could."

She considered rising from her knees on the floor of the carriage, but it was as good a place as any. "She wouldn't come," she answered simply. "I did every-thing I could to get her to move, but she just screamed at me. The madness was in full force—I can only assume she set the fire."

"Must have," Jacobs said solemnly. "I made sure the hearth fire was banked before I went to bed, and there was no way a stray spark could have escaped. And Nanny was locked in the room with her—I had the devil's own time getting to her. Begging your pardon, miss."

Elinor knew if she began to laugh she wouldn't be able to stop. Her mother's foul language still rained in her ears, and they were being rescued by the devil himself.

The carriage pulled to a halt, and the door was

opened, opposite her, a liveried footman waiting to help them alight. Hands reached out to help Jacobs with his tender burden, and Reading leaped down before he reached for Lydia, holding her close as he guided her into the house. Leaving Elinor alone, on her knees, in the deserted carriage.

For a moment she was tempted to stay there. Just let them take the carriage around to the stables and see to the horses, and no one would know where she was. She could curl up on one of the seats and manage to sleep relatively well....

"Miss Harriman?" Etienne de Giverney stood in the open doorway, looking at her curiously. "May I assist you?"

Too bad, she thought. It had been a lovely idea. "No, you may not," she said briskly. "You have two patients inside. Nanny Maude collapsed, and she has need of your expertise. And Lydia is understandably shattered—she needs your comfort." And to get away from Mr. Reading, she added mentally. "Go ahead—I'll follow in a moment."

A footman remained by the open door to attend to her, though Elinor wished he would go. She scrambled forward, pulling herself to the seat. The pain in her feet had passed, and they were blessedly numb. She realized with sudden shock that she wore nothing but her thin cambric night rail, so old that it was practically transparent in places. Lydia had had the presence of mind to grab a wrap and shoes. Elinor had been so distraught that she hadn't even thought of slippers.

The enormity of their loss hit her like a blow to the stomach. They were penniless, homeless, without even clothes on their backs. What in god's name was she going to do?

She climbed down from the coach, the snow cool on her bare feet. It was snowing harder now. Why had it waited to do this until all their possessions had burned away? Not that snowflakes would have any effect against a fire like that. It had been an angry, hungry inferno. She could only hope her mother's madness hadn't burned anyone else's home

The fire had come from everywhere. The living room had been ablaze, their mother's room with a river of flame holding them apart, the flames licking through the kitchen door, Nanny trapped inside. Had her mother done all that while they slept? There could be no other explanation. And yet...

The coach pulled away immediately, heading out into the snow-covered street, and she wondered where it was going. Had they really left Viscount Rohan standing by the ruins of her house? It appeared so. How had he happened to come by their house, just as a fire broke out? Accidents like that simply didn't happen.

She looked ahead, at the front door of the mansion. Someone had closed the door to keep the storm out, and she moved slowly, wondering if she was going to face the nasty butler from that trip that seemed so long ago. Perhaps he would recognize her as the woman who bit him and not let her in.

But of course the door swung open promptly as

soon as she approached, and the servant standing there looked vaguely familiar. She'd seen him before, at least once, and he greeted her by name, his rough Yorkshire accent unmistakable.

They'd taken Nanny to a small room at the back of the house, one that Elinor assumed was used for illness. Nanny lay still in the bed where she'd been placed, her color ashen, her breathing labored, with Lydia sitting on the far side of the bed clutching her hand. Someone had made an effort to clean the old lady up, swaddling her small figure in warm shawls, but she looked like death, and Etienne de Giverney's face, when he turned to look at her, was grave.

"She's suffered a great shock," he said solemnly. "And her heart isn't strong."

"She's *not* going to die," Elinor said fiercely, sitting on the bed beside her, taking her other hand.

"I'm afraid she is, but as to when, I cannot say. I've done what I can for her—the rest is in the hands of God," Etienne said, the pompous prig. Elinor wanted to scream at him, but he'd already dismissed both his patient and Elinor, turning to her sister. "Miss Lydia, surely you need to rest. Your sister is here now—she can keep your old nursemaid company."

"I'm not leaving either of them," Lydia said in a tear-filled voice.

Elinor looked up at her. "Dearest, he's right. It wouldn't do for you to become ill."

"Come, Miss Lydia," Etienne said. He took Lydia's hand in his and drew her away from the bed. "My cousin's housekeeper will have already seen to a room for you. You're a frail, sensitive creature and you've suffered a great shock. Your sister is far more sturdy—she can keep your nursemaid company with no ill effects."

"Indeed," Elinor said with just a hint of dryness. "After all, I'm sturdy."

"I'm just as strong as my sister, and I'm not leaving her," Lydia said mutinously, trying to pull back from Etienne's hands. "Where is Mr. Reading? He accompanied us back here, but I haven't seen him…"

"Mr. Reading has returned to fetch my cousin," Etienne said, and there was no missing the disapproval in his voice. "You have no need of him."

Lydia had tears running down her face, and she made a hiccupping sound. "Of course not," she said, sounding somewhat hysterical. "No need at all."

No, Elinor wanted to cry as she looked at her sister. She couldn't be in love with Charles Reading. It would lead to nothing but disaster.

But now was not the time to deal with it. Elinor pulled herself together. "I will take the first watch, my love, while you rest," she said gently. "Then you can come and take my place once you've regained some of your strength. I couldn't bear it if you were to become ill from this night's work. And you needn't worry about Lord Rohan or his friend. They will return safely."

Lydia looked at her in mute distress, and then she closed her eyes. "Of course," she said, calmer now, and this time when Etienne de Giverney took her hand she didn't pull it away.

He cleared his throat. "Then if Miss Harriman is in no need of my assistance I'll take you to my cousin's housekeeper," Etienne said. "Once she's settled I'll return to see if there's anything that can be done for your servant."

"Not our *servant*..." Lydia said beneath her breath, and the look she cast Etienne, the look he missed entirely, was filled with dislike.

Elinor didn't miss it, and her heart sank. Her sister loving the wrong man was hardly the worst thing that had happened this dismal night, but it was bad enough. Hating the man she should marry was far worse.

But Etienne put a gentle arm around Lydia, leading her carefully from the room, and at the last minute Elinor could see Lydia's shoulders drop, as the anger left her.

Elinor looked down at herself, at her soot-covered nightgown. At least the room had a hearty fire going, warming it against the cold night air. Her feet had moved beyond hurting her, though she tucked them beneath the hem of her nightdress to make certain no one would notice. For some reason she didn't want Etienne touching her.

The doctor was far from her favorite person in the world, but if Lydia could learn to accept him he would be an admirable brother-in-law in all the ways that counted. Even if he'd let her drop dead in front of him while he was admiring her sister.

She turned back to Nanny Maude and knew she was looking into the face of death. She rose, ready to call Etienne back, then thought better of it. He had the right of it—there was nothing more he could do for her. Nanny was very old, and the shock of the fire would likely be too much for her to withstand.

Elinor raised her voice slightly. "Jacobs?"

"Yes, miss." He appeared immediately from his position just outside the door. He looked down at Nanny's still figure and bowed his head. "May I stay, miss?"

"Of course you can. There's a chair behind the door. She might like us to hold her hands."

"Not me, miss. She always said I had the hands of a butcher. Clumsy."

"I don't think she'll mind tonight," Elinor said gently.

Jacobs brought the chair forward, sitting gingerly and taking Nanny's other hand in his.

She opened her eyes only once in the next few hours, and her gaze fell on Elinor.

"You're being quite ridiculous, Nanny Maude," Elinor said in a voice thick with tears. "Lollygagging in bed when we need you. You must decide to get better this instant or I shall be very cross with you indeed."

Nanny Maude smiled, squeezing her hand gently. "There's no need for me to stay any longer, Miss Nell. I'm tired, and more than ready. You're safe now, lass… Your mama can't hurt any of you again." She closed her eyes for a moment, restless. "But I have to tell you something," she said. "I can't remember what it was, but it's important. There's something I remembered."

"You can tell us in the morning, Nanny," she said soothingly.

"Won't be a morning for me, child," Nanny said, a trace of her usual asperity in her faint voice. "It's danger, that's what it is." She began coughing again, her small body shaking. "He's not who you think he is," she said after a moment.

"Who isn't, Nanny?" she said.

But her eyes closed, and she fell back, her grip on Lydia's hands loosening, as she sank into an endless sleep.

Hours later Etienne poked his head in one last time, coming no closer. It was already too late to help Nanny, and she had to trust that there was nothing he could have done if he'd returned sooner. "Your sister's asleep. I had the housekeeper give her laudanum—she'll sleep till midday."

"Thank you, Etienne," she said. Lydia wouldn't be as grateful. She would have wanted to be there with them, with Nanny as she slipped away.

And that was what she did, as the beginning of dawn light began to climb over the window, a gray, murky light. Her breathing slowed, with longer pauses between each one, and then finally there were no more.

Jacobs let out a harsh, choking sob, and she went to put her arms around his hulking shoulders, to comfort him. "To lose them both in one night, miss," he said, tears streaming down his face. "It's too much."

"Yes," she said with unnatural calm. "It is."

After a moment he lifted his head. "I'm going to go get drunk," he announced. "I'm going to get so drunk that you won't find me for days, and then maybe I'll get drunk again."

Elinor was too weary to smile, though she was tempted. "That sounds like an excellent idea, Jacobs. Just be certain you remember to find us when you're done with such a noble activity."

He didn't recognize her irony. And indeed, getting roaring drunk was a fitting tribute to her mother, even though Nanny Maude would have abhorred it.

He strode wearily out of the room and was gone, and she was alone. For the first time since she could remember, she was alone. The number of people in her care had suddenly been cut in half, and yet there was no relief, only guilt.

She looked about her. The house was still and silent—a few candles were burning, enough to light her way into the broad hallway. It didn't look familiar to her, but then, this house was huge, and she'd only seen a small portion of it. It stood to reason they'd brought Nanny to the servants' quarters, though the room had been large and comfortable. And this certainly wasn't a servants' hallway, with its rich carpets and paintings on the damask-covered walls.

She needed to find someone, to tell them Nanny Maude had died. She would need to be washed and laid out properly, a decent burial seen to. But she had no money. Nanny would end in a pauper's grave. Unless she asked Rohan to pay for a decent funeral.

Which she would. She would have thought she'd never ask him for anything, but she knew right now she was wrong.

At least she didn't have to make arrangements for her mother, she thought, half in a daze. She really should try to find some help, but right then her mind couldn't concentrate. There were stairs to the servants' quarters somewhere, but she couldn't remember where they were. If she could just find where Lydia slept she could crawl into bed beside her, filthy, soot-stained clothes and all, and sleep. She'd need none of Etienne's laudanum to help her. She just needed to find the right place to go.

She moved down the shadowed hallways, her nightgown flowing about her. She was becoming alarmingly light-headed. She ought to sit down before she fell down, but her feet had begun to hurt again, her legs felt weak, and she was afraid that if she sat she would never rise again. And she was…for a moment she couldn't remember where she was, which was truly absurd, and she ought to laugh, but she wasn't supposed to laugh, was she? All she could do was keep moving, through the long, endless hallways of this mysterious place.

A door opened, and a young girl backed into the hallway, a tray in her arms. She turned, took one look at Elinor and screamed loud enough to wake the devil, loud enough for reality to come crashing back as she remembered exactly who and where she was.

"It's a ghost!" the girl babbled in French. "God protect me, it's a ghost!"

Suddenly the hallway was filled with a great many more people than she could have wished. All she'd wanted was one sensible person to help her find her sister and suddenly there were servants in various stages of dress and undress, holding candelabra, and what must be the housekeeper coming in one direction, and the evil Cavalle coming from the other, a murderous expression on his face, and she suddenly thought she'd better run, and she tried to spin around, but her feet tripped her up, and she felt herself falling toward the heavy carpet, when strong hands caught her. And even without looking up she knew whose strong hands they were. Just as she'd known in the smoke and the darkness who would have snatched her up, no matter how little sense it made.

"I have always had a dislike of screaming servants," Rohan said in a mild voice that held a note of steel. "Would someone please smother that girl?"

The maid was still screeching about a ghost, and the housekeeper made quick work of her with a harsh slap and an even harsher reprimand.

"Thank you, Madame Bonnard. And could you please tell me why my guest is wandering around the house in rags when I had assumed she'd been properly seen to? Is this the way I wish to have my guests treated? And where is her sister, scrubbing floors in the kitchen?" To a stranger his voice might sound almost genial, but the servants looked uniformly terrified.

He was behind her, still holding her up, and since her feet weren't working she couldn't turn and look at him. "It's not their fault," she said, and she almost didn't recognize her own voice. It was raw from the fire, raw from tears, both shed and unshed. "Someone needs to see to Nanny Maude. She's dead." The words were so short, so harsh that she couldn't stand it anymore. She needed to disappear into the darkness, to pull the shadows around her. "I need to sleep…"

And then the blessed darkness folded down around her, and she opened her arms and embraced it.

He caught her as she fell, and when several footmen rushed to assist him he snapped at them like a caged tiger. The thought would have amused him if he weren't in such a cold, towering rage. He had a tendency to keep his temper and to view things with a distant amusement. But at the moment he would have happily seen all his incompetent servants whipped and turned out into the streets.

This was the third time tonight he'd had to scoop her up in his arms, and the thought of how much she would have hated it brought a smile to his lips. As far as he was concerned she could swoon all she wanted—he was more than happy for an excuse to put his hands on her.

Madame Bonnard had the temerity to approach him. "I will send two of the maids to see to her woman. I am sorry, monseigneur, I had no idea she hadn't been properly seen to. I promise you, I will dismiss those responsible."

"And will you dismiss yourself, madame?" He said in a silky voice. "I'm taking her to the green bedroom.

I will require hot water, enough for a bath, some clean clothes and some French brandy."

"Sir, should she be having brandy when she's fainted?" Madame Bonnard was foolish enough to ask.

"The brandy is for me, you idiot," he said in his most amiable voice. The one he used before he destroyed someone.

The servants immediately scattered in every direction. His way was lit to the green room, and lights were placed all around the elegant bedchamber. The first pails of hot water appeared almost before he'd set her down on the high bed, and a moment later Madame Bonnard read his mind and presented him with a basin and a cloth. Perhaps he might let her live after all.

He took the wet cloth and began to clean the soot from Elinor's face. There were salt trails of tears there, which oddly surprised him. She was such an Amazon, he didn't expect her to ever cry or show weakness, even at the loss of her mother. That old bitch was well and truly gone, and he could only view that circumstance with relief. The glowering nurse/housekeeper he could have dealt with—after all, he'd managed to fend off Mrs. Clarke's efforts to reform him for all these many years—and for Elinor's sake he was sorry she was dead. It was too much a burden for one night.

He was gentle with the cloth. The filth was on her clothes, down her neck, and he unfastened her chemise as he absently ordered the footmen from the room. "My lord," Mrs. Bonnard began, scandalized. "Let me do that."

He looked up at her. "How long have you served me, Madame Bonnard?"

She flushed. "Seven years, my lord."

"And did anything ever give you the impression that I wasn't entirely capable of undressing young ladies on my own?"

"No, Monsieur le Comte," she said. "It wasn't your capability I was questioning. It was the young lady's feelings on the matter."

His housekeeper was treading dangerously close to disaster. "Ah, Bonnard," he said in a silken voice. "You remind me of my better self. Unfortunately, I have no interest in listening to that part of me, and I'm much more interested in taking care of my own best interests than the young lady in question. If you're so worried about her, go see to her dead nursemaid. When Miss Harriman wakes she'll be distraught if her friend hasn't been seen to."

A moment later the door closed, and he was alone with his awkward poppet.

She looked like hell. It was interesting washing the soot off her face, discovering the creaminess of her skin, admiring once again the faint tracing of freckles across the Harriman Nose. It really was a lovely nose. Narrow and elegant, it made her much more striking than her pretty little sister. By the time she was forty she'd be magnificent, and he couldn't wait...

He pulled back. He might not even be alive when she was forty. He'd be fifty-six, an old man, and even if he were still alive he was unlikely to be anywhere near her. He wouldn't even remember her existence.

He rinsed out the cloth and drew it down the side of her neck. She was in a deep, untouchable sleep, shock and exhaustion and grief having overwhelmed her. He hated seeing her defeated, but he had no doubt whatsoever that she'd be ready to fight back tomorrow. To fight him. She was like an angry Roman goddess—nothing could defeat her for long.

He set the cloth down and put his hands on either side of her thin nightgown, pulling it apart to look at her. He was a degenerate bastard to do so, but he had no illusions as to who and what he was. He was surprised Madame Bonnard still did.

Her breasts were quite lovely. Small and perfect, and the nipples were pleasingly dark, not insipid pink. He'd always had a weakness for dark nipples. He should have known she'd be hiding such a treasure.

He stared at them, and he could feel the beginnings of arousal stir in his cynical body. What other treasures might her flesh provide? He reached out to tear the gown down to its hem, and something stopped him.

It was hardly decency, he told himself, pulling the gown back together, covering her breasts reluctantly. He was finding himself quite stimulated at the sight of her, and at the moment there was no one he was interested in…er…spending that stimulation on. He'd have to do something about that.

And he was hardly likely to make love to her while she was unconscious. It would be like making love to a corpse, something that had never appealed to him.

He rang the bell. Bonnard appeared immediately,

which annoyed him. "You didn't think I meant what I said?" he said in a silken voice.

"Of course you did, monseigneur. I was merely counting on the fact that you're easily bored."

He found he could laugh. "You know me rather better than I thought," he said. "I'm not sure how comfortable that makes me."

"Monsieur?"

"Bonnard, you know as well as I do that it wouldn't be boredom that stopped me, and that I'd need some shallow excuse to salve my wounded *amour propre*. Which you have done admirably. Send chambermaids to finish taking care of Mademoiselle Harriman while I go get drunk."

Bonnard didn't argue. *"Oui, Monsieur le Comte,"* she said, dipping into a curtsy.

Rohan took one last look at Elinor, lying still and silent on the bed. Not for him, he thought. And taking his glass of brandy, he left the room, closing the door behind him.

16

If it hadn't been for her sister, Elinor would have refused to wake up. She heard the noises from a distance. It seemed the great house was in a state of complete chaos. Furniture was being moved, servants were chattering in lowered voices. Those things she could have ignored. If she opened her eyes she'd have to face reality. That her mother was gone, burned in the flames of her own making. And far worse, Nanny Maude was dead, the last person she could even think of turning to. All their possessions had gone up in smoke, and they had nothing, only each other, for comfort.

Lydia would need her. She couldn't stay in bed, the covers pulled over her head, and pretend none of it had happened. She would need to make plans. Accepting charity from the notorious Viscount Rohan was bad enough; actually living underneath his roof would destroy any chances of Lydia making a decent marriage.

Unless Etienne came through, and there was no guarantee of that. He'd given every indication of being smitten. Unfortunately she'd seen Lydia in Charles Reading's arms, heard her piteous cry for him. She might be too blinded by infatuation to see Etienne's worth.

Except that Lydia had never been easily swayed. Despite all the men, young and old, who'd been naturally smitten by her charm and beauty, she'd viewed them all with impartial affection.

That was not how she viewed Reading.

Elinor opened her eyes to the gray-green light that filled the room. She closed them again for a moment, her nerve failing her, and then opened them once more, resolutely, and made herself sit up in bed.

And what a bed it was. The sheets felt like silk. She looked around her slowly. She had no idea how she'd gotten there—her memory of the night before was hazy and jumbled. She remembered that Nanny had died, slipping away peacefully. And she'd gone in search of Lydia, in this vast, dark house. And then nothing.

She was no longer wearing her shabby nightdress. Someone had stripped it off her, replacing it with something made of the finest cambric. She no longer stank of soot and smoke—she'd been bathed as well, and when she swung her legs out of bed she saw that her feet had been bandaged.

For a moment the notion startled her. The thought of being stripped and bathed when she had no knowledge of it was unsettling in the extreme, but then she reminded herself that her unwilling host would have had no part in it. He'd have waved a pale, careless hand to have his servants take care of her and forgotten her existence.

She climbed down from the high, impossibly comfortable bed and limped toward the window. The room was huge, a fact which startled her. Such elegancies made her uncomfortable. She pushed open the curtain, letting in the murky light. She had no idea what time it was, and the light outside was no help. They were in the midst of a blizzard. The snow had piled up everywhere, and it was coming down at a fierce rate, blasting against the windows. She could feel the cold radiating from outside, and she pulled the curtains shut again, shivering.

The fire was glowing brightly, sending forth waves of heat, and she turned and moved toward it. There was a robe laid across the foot of her bed, and she pulled it around her.

She felt as if the blizzard had entered her brain as well—she wasn't thinking clearly. She'd slept too long, or not long enough, but she could no longer afford such weakness.

She pushed open the door to a corridor filled with servants. One of the maids immediately ceased what she was doing and came to the door. "You're awake, mademoiselle," she said, stating the obvious. "Last time I checked on you, you were still sound asleep. If you go back to your room I'll bring you some dinner…"

Elinor looked past her at the hallway. The servants were busy wrapping black cloth around the portraits and windows, a singularly odd procedure. "I need to see my sister," she said. "Could you take me to her?"

The young maid hesitated. "His lordship said you were to keep to your room and not wander...."

"If you take me directly to my sister I wouldn't be wandering," she said reasonably. "And if you won't take me there I'll find her on my own."

The maid looked doubtful, but she nodded. "Would you like to dress first, mademoiselle?"

"I have no clothes."

"I've filled your closet, mademoiselle. His lordship's orders."

And now she was going to have to be grateful to the King of Hell for the clothes on her back. The alternative was not acceptable, not at this moment, but the last time a man had provided clothes for her had been six years ago, and the memory still had the capacity to make her ill.

"I'll see my sister first, thank you...?"

"Jeanne-Louise," the girl offered. "As you wish, mademoiselle. If you will come this way." She started toward the stairs, and Elinor pulled back.

"My sister's room isn't near mine?"

"No, mademoiselle."

That seemed extremely odd. She could feel the servants' eyes on her as she followed Jeanne-Louise up the winding stairs. Even with the bandages her feet were painful, but she was determined not to limp, not with so many people watching her. The marble staircase was hard and cold beneath her feet, and she gritted her teeth and climbed. Why would Lydia have been put on a different floor entirely? It made no sense.

They reached the next flight, and then Jeanne-Louise turned right, heading into another wing of the huge building. Elinor was having a hard time keeping up with her, but kept on. At that point she would have walked over coals to see her sister. In fact, it probably would have been less painful.

This wing of the house was older, smaller, the ceilings lower. The maid stopped in front of a door and knocked, then pushed it open, and Elinor quickly took stock of her surroundings.

It was a small salon off an even smaller bedroom. Pretty and comfortable, it was a far cry from the opulence of her own bedroom, which at this point seemed half a mile away. Why in the world had he separated them? And why the disparity in their rooms?

Lydia was sitting by a window, dressed in dove-gray, and she turned at the sound of the door.

"Oh, Elinor," she cried, and rushed to her, flinging her arms around her and bursting into tears. Elinor rocked back for a moment from the strength of her, and then hugged her tightly, murmuring soft, comforting words.

After a moment she nudged her toward the sofa, afraid her feet wouldn't hold her anymore, sinking down on it with gratitude. She glanced back at Jeanne-Louise, but she'd closed the door behind her. So much for finding her way back, though in truth, there was no reason for her to return to the gilded green room she'd woken up in. She'd left nothing behind.

It was a long time before Lydia's tears shuddered to a halt. Elinor had already discovered a fine lawn handkerchief in the pocket of her dressing gown, and she gently dabbed at Lydia's face. "You know, dearest, you're the only person I know who can cry for an hour and still look absolutely radiant," she said fondly.

"Oh, blast that," Lydia said forcibly, and Elinor managed her own weak chuckle. "What are we going to do, Nell?"

For a moment Elinor closed her eyes as the enormity of their situation washed over her. And then she pulled herself together. "Don't worry, sweetheart. I'll see to everything. I have a plan."

"You do?" Lydia said hopefully.

"I do," she said, hoping to God that Lydia wasn't going to ask for details. She'd come up with something soon enough, even though right now her mind was a total blank. "Have you seen the doctor today?"

"Etienne keeps asking for me," she said, and there was no missing the reluctance in her voice. "I've pretended to be asleep."

The panic she'd squashed down began to rumble in the pit of her stomach. She'd forgotten Lydia's look of dislike. "You did?" she said carefully. "I thought you liked Etienne."

Lydia managed a weak smile. "Oh, I do. I like him very much. But I know what he wants, and I cannot give him the answer he's looking for. Not yet."

"What does he want, sweetheart?" she asked gently, trying to keep the despair from her voice. If

Lydia hated the thought of Etienne then that was the end of it.

"To marry me," Lydia said, making it sound like a death sentence.

All the language of the stable came roaring back to Elinor's head, but she kept her face passive. "You don't wish to marry Etienne? I thought it would be a good match. He's handsome, dependable, he adores you."

"Yes, he's all those things," she said sadly. "The problem is, I'm not in love with him."

"Love is…" Elinor trailed off, words failing her. She swallowed, then continued. "Love is highly over-rated, my sweet."

Lydia turned to look at her, her eyes still swimming with tears. "Do you want me to marry him, Nell? Because I will, of course, if you think it's the best thing to do. I know I've been selfish, daydreaming. If you want me to marry him then I certainly will. You're right, he's all that's kind and proper, and I should make a very good doctor's wife." She even managed a sunny smile, one that didn't quite reach her eyes.

For a moment Elinor didn't move. It was the wise thing to do. Hadn't she learned in the last, increasingly hideous few years that you had to take the lifeline when offered? Here was safety dangling in front of them. She had little doubt Etienne would welcome her into their household as well, simply because she could be useful. They would never have to worry about where the next meal came from, which creditors to duck, whether they'd freeze to death in the night.

She looked down into dear Lydia's face, at the determinedly cheerful expression. "Except that he's so damn stuffy," she said.

Lydia exploded with laughter. "Your language, Nell!"

"I haven't got Nanny Maude to keep me in line anymore. You know I spent too much time in the stable when I was young. Don't marry Etienne, Lydia. Tell him no, in the most gentle of ways."

Lydia looked at her. "Are you certain? What else shall we do? I hadn't thought it through clearly. We seem to be out of resources and possibilities."

"You forget, there's Cousin Marcus. I have yet to find out what our small bequest is, but with luck it's enough to keep the two of us and Jacobs. If not, our cousin might be disposed to be charitable."

"Dearest," Lydia said, "you know as well as I do that the bequest is for you, that the cousin is yours."

"Dearest," Elinor responded fondly, "you know as well as I do that everything I have is yours."

"I could still marry Etienne. I think he'd have me."

"Have you?" Elinor scoffed. "The man would be lucky to kiss the hem of your garment. In truth, I don't want you to marry Etienne. His lectures would drive me mad. I expect we can rely on Cousin Marcus. Otherwise…" She failed to think of any way to complete the sentence.

"Otherwise we'll become adventuresses!" Lydia said. "Why not? We have no reputations to lose. We'll travel Europe and be very mysterious and very gay, and men will adore us and women will want to be like us. We'll dress in the finest clothes and be very witty. I think we should go to Venice first."

Elinor blinked. "And how are we to support this new life?"

"We'll have to find protectors, of course," Lydia said brightly. "Wealthy men in need of a mistress. We'll pick and choose, of course. Only the most handsome and most amiable of men should be allowed anywhere near our bedrooms. They'll give us fabulous jewels, which we can sell off when times are difficult. Don't you think it would be glorious?"

"Glorious," Elinor echoed. "And totally impractical. I'd have you married to Etienne before you became a courtesan, no matter how stuffy he is."

Some of the wicked light left Lydia's eyes. "You're right, of course. And a few months of passion is no fit trade for a lifetime of safety and sobriety."

She could blame the shocks of the last few days and her own exhaustion for not having put things together before. Lydia's fanciful idea hadn't been plucked from thin air. It took Elinor but a moment.

"You're in love with Mr. Reading."

Most people would have believed Lydia's light, silvery laugh. Elinor was not most people. "How absurd, Nell! I barely know the man, and while there is no denying he's very handsome he's far from agreeable and not very flattering, and he's hardly the type of husband one could look for."

"Hardly," Elinor echoed, remembering him from her night at the château. "He would, however, make a fitting partner for an adventuress. For a month or so."

Lydia's smile still didn't read truthful. "Don't worry, Nell. You said you had another plan as well as applying to your cousin. What is it?"

Her stomach dropped, but she managed a cheery smile. "Let us see if I can get in touch with Lord Tolliver first," she said. "He was most amiable when I met with him, and I would think he would be the answer. If I could convince him to give us a small cottage on one of the estates, perhaps a tiny stipend that we could augment with pianoforte lessons. And you'd be bound to marry, and there'd be no financial incentive to force you into making the wrong choice."

"And he said he'd offer you this cottage?" Lydia asked, looking skeptical.

"We didn't get that far...Mama—" oddly enough her voice seemed to have developed a catch "—had one of her fits, and he left. But I have no doubt he'll hear of our misfortunes and be more than happy to provide assistance. He would have no reason not to help us, and he would dislike the disapproval of society if he abandoned us."

"If you say so," Lydia said, looking unconvinced. "What shall we do in the meantime?"

"In the meantime I shall speak to my Lord Rohan about sending a message to my cousin. I despise having to rely on Rohan's charity, but I cannot decide which would be worse, sleeping in his house or taking money to sleep elsewhere."

Lydia looked around her. "If this is hell, it's quite cozy," she said. "Where are you sleeping? I asked for you, but no one would give me a clear answer."

"This house is massive—I'm on another floor and in another wing. I'm certain they'll have no objection to my joining you here." She was certain of no such thing. She was certain of nothing at the moment, and the lack of control was making her mad.

She prepared to rise, dreading the pain. "I'll go speak to our host. Perhaps he's already made arrangements—he could hardly want two properly brought-up young females in his household when he's about to commence on a…" She let her voice trail off.

"About to commence what?"

"Something neither of us need to know about."

"You know, for the King of Hell he's quite charming."

"No," she said flatly.

"No, what? I've told you, he has absolutely no interest in me. I'm not naive. I know when someone has lustful thoughts about me. Lord Rohan treats me like his sister."

Now it was ice forming in the pit of her stomach, freezing away the panic. "How many times have you seen him?"

"Just twice, dearest. Once at the house, and then this morning. He told me about Nanny and he was very kind."

"Ha," Elinor said. "The King of Hell doesn't know what kindness means. He was doubtless being ironic."

"Perhaps he was. You certainly seem to know him better. All I know is he calmed me down, expressed his sympathy and made certain I was well taken care of."

"He's good at that," Elinor grumbled.

Lydia said nothing, looking at her sister for a long moment. "You might consider looking at the truth," she said.

"What truth?" Elinor said, alarmed.

"You are far from uninterested in the man. If I didn't know you so well I would say you've fallen in love with the King of Hell. But that's impossible. You're much too levelheaded, when such a thing would lead to disaster." She peered more closely at her sister. "Aren't you?"

"Absolutely," Elinor said truthfully. "The very notion horrifies me. He's a man who likes to play games, and on occasion his malicious interest alights on me. Particularly since I do my best not to let him win. But trust me, there is nothing I would like better than to get as far away from him as I possibly could."

"Indeed," Lydia said, watching her. And then she shook her head. "I believe you. He's a fascinating man, but you're not interested in fascinating men, are you? You want someone strong and stable. I'll give you Etienne," she offered.

Elinor laughed. "In fact, he was sent for me in the first place. Rohan thought I should be married. But Etienne took one look at you and forgot Rohan's games."

"He was trying to arrange a marriage for you? But why?"

She wasn't going to tell her sister the truth, particularly when truth was a subjective matter in the House of Rohan. "If I were comfortably married, he would no longer have to waste his time on charity."

"But he doesn't have to now. We have no claim on him. And do not tell me that the founder of the notorious Heavenly Host is a charitable man. I suspect he has a reason for everything he does."

Elinor rose to her feet, refusing to wince. The only way to avoid this turn of conversation was to leave. Besides, she was going to have to face Rohan sooner or later. She might as well get it over with.

"If he has any reasons, I doubt he'll share them, my love. I'll go speak to him. I'm certain that at the very least I can have my room moved closer to yours."

"That would be a comfort." Lydia rose as well, pressing a kiss on Elinor's cheek. "Don't worry about facing him. You're more than a match for the most devilish of gentlemen."

Elinor managed a calm smile. She opened the door and stepped out into the cool hallway, to see her maid waiting. Accompanied by an immense footman— taller and broader than anyone she'd ever seen.

"Are you ready, mademoiselle?" he said.

"Ready for what?"

"To return to your rooms," Jeanne-Louise said.

"Yes, but—"

The footman swooped her up effortlessly, holding her with such easy strength that it almost felt as if she were floating.

"His lordship said you weren't to walk. Antoine is very strong," Jeanne-Louise said, moving down the hall beside them.

It was an extremely odd sensation. "This is unnecessary…" she began.

"His lordship has insisted," Jeanne-Louise said, as if that was the end of the matter.

Elinor bit her lip in frustration. "I would like to be closer to my sister. If you could move my things…" She suddenly remembered she had no things, other than what he'd provided. "If I could be moved…"

"That isn't up to me, mademoiselle. You'll need to speak to his lordship about that."

"Then perhaps you could take me to him."

Jeanne-Louise shook her head. "He is having a dinner party and is not to be disturbed. I will leave a message that you wish to see him, but I doubt it will be before tomorrow. There are women at the party."

"Of course there are," Elinor said, remembering the woman stretched out across his arms when he first saw her, that woman's breasts exposed to the night air. Since then she'd only seen Rohan on his best behavior, assuming the guise of a perfect gentleman. She couldn't forget the real Viscount Rohan, the strange and terrible man who directed the most depraved behavior imaginable.

17

The hulking footman set her down on the brocade-covered settee in the salon that led from her bedroom, treating her like precious crystal. "Does mademoiselle require any other assistance?" he asked.

"No, she does not," Jeanne-Louise said, leaving Elinor with the impression that she wasn't simply a chambermaid, she was a prison guard. It didn't matter. As long as she knew Lydia was safe, she was content, at least for the time being.

And as far as prison guards went, Jeanne-Louise was very kind. She bathed and rebandaged Elinor's feet. Blood had soaked into her old bandages, and she dreaded to see the damage, but already the cuts and burns had begun to heal. "You need to stay off your feet," Jeanne-Louise said severely.

The room was brightly lit with candles—night had fallen sometime during her visit with Lydia, and for the first time she looked in the mirror. And then froze.

She'd known her dark brown hair was loose down her back. She hadn't realized how very pretty it was, or how flattering the clothes Rohan had provided for her. For them. It was unsettling.

She rejected the offer to put on one of the frocks in the closet, all rich, elegant gowns in demimourning. She had no doubt they would fit her, just as Lydia's dress had been perfect. Rohan had almost supernatural powers when it came to getting what he wanted. Instead, she bathed and changed into a fresh night gown. They were all thin cambric, and she wore the combing robe over it to hide anything that shouldn't be seen. Combing robes tended to be cumbersome, made to be worn while one's hair was arranged, but Elinor didn't care. She'd wrap herself in a blanket if that wasn't enough coverage.

Dinner was brought to her on three trays—an impossibly rich assortment of foods, from roasted squab to salmon à l'anglaise, well-cooked mutton to a fine puree of turnips. More than she could possibly eat, and it wasn't until she got to the final tray that she saw the small plate of toast strips. She didn't know whether to laugh or cry.

She wasn't hungry. She ate half the toast strips and drank the tea, sending the rest back. Every time she thought of her mother and Nanny Maude her stomach would clench, and she'd want to throw up. Anything to get rid of the helpless pain she was feeling. Even Jeanne-Louise's blandishments couldn't get her to try anything more.

There were books there as well, and for the first time since she'd seen Lydia she felt a glimmering of pleasure. He'd given her a fair assortment, but she picked up the novel first. She wanted dark, Gothic delights rather than philosophy at that moment, and she curled up in bed, reading with pleasure.

When she awoke, her room was pitch-black except for the coals on the fire. She rolled over on her back in the huge, soft bed, luxuriating in the richness of the covers and the way it cradled her. She glanced over at the windows, wondering what time it was, but the small amount of light that came in was clearly from the streetlamps. She reckoned it was somewhere between dawn and dusk, but she had no idea which was closer.

He moved out of the shadows, like the dark creature he was, and Elinor didn't have time to scream. For a moment it had seemed like an illusion, but then she realized he'd simply been waiting for her. For how long? she wondered.

"You wished to see me, poppet?" he inquired in his silken voice.

She cleared her throat. "I thought you had guests for dinner."

"It's well past dinnertime—I sent the rest of them home."

"All of them?"

"What are you asking, my precious? Reading is still here, but have faith—he's miles away from your darling sister. The rest have gone." He paused. "Except for Madame de Tourville, who lies naked in my bed, awaiting me. What is it you need?"

It was a vast relief that he'd forgotten about her, she told herself. Even as it shut off one avenue of escape, an unacceptable one, it was all for the best that he no longer seemed interested in her but had Madame de Tourville instead. "I didn't wish to disturb your entertainment, my lord. It could have waited until morning."

His smile flashed white in the darkness. "My pet, you are never a disturbance. Simply tell me what you want and it shall be yours."

"For one, I wish to be nearer my sister."

"Alas, I'm afraid that is quite impossible. The rooms in the south wing are being renovated—your sister resides in the only room completed."

"She can certainly come and sleep with me here, then. There's plenty of room."

"Indeed, but there are problems with that," he said softly.

"And those are?"

"Lent is approaching, and it's carnival time. I'm afraid the Heavenly Host is particularly perverse when it comes to such occasions. Instead of feasting and rioting the weeks before Lent like most good Christians, we tend to choose the time of fasting and repentance for our time to indulge in the pleasures of the flesh. Gluttony, lust, sloth, all some of our favorite activities. I would think you'd prefer your sister not be near while such things are going on."

"I could stay with her."

"Her room is too small. Besides, that wouldn't suit me."

She froze. "Why not?"

"Because I wish to have you closer, my pet. I've

told you before, your sister doesn't interest me. You do. Unfortunately for you, I thought I might hold her hostage."

For a moment Elinor was unable to breathe. "Hostage for what?" she finally said evenly. "You know we have no money."

"Hostage for your good behavior. Or your bad behavior, if you want to be specific. As long as you do what I wish, your sister will be safe and protected like the beautiful English virgin she is."

She felt hot and cold at the same time. She couldn't see him clearly—the shadows seemed to flow around him. "Permit me to clarify this, Lord Rohan," she said in her most practical voice. "My sister will be safe and well cared for if I get in your bed?"

He laughed. "Acquit me of being quite so gauche, child. I have innumerable women to satisfy my carnal urges."

The ice vanished and she was hot, hot with shame. Of course he didn't want her. How foolish could she be? "Then what do you want from me?" Her voice showed nothing of her raging inner torment.

"You manage to keep me from being bored. That's far more valuable than what's between your legs."

She made a hissing sound at his deliberately shocking words, and once more she could see his smile. "You see," he said, "that's just the sort of thing I find so enchanting."

"You could find any young lady to shock, my lord."

"But you're not missish. You're not even a virgin. You're quite an original, my dear Elinor. A prim-and-proper, starched-up young woman of impeccable morals who nonetheless has already relinquished her maidenhood. I'm counting on you to tell me all about it."

"Over my dead body."

"No, my sweet. Over your sister's virginity."

She stared at him through the shadows. "You wouldn't! Even you aren't that depraved."

"Oh, precious, I am absolutely that depraved, and more. But in fact I would give the task of deflowering the fair Lydia to Charles Reading, who seems to be oddly enamored of your sister."

She couldn't help it, the tiny sound of distress that bubbled up from inside her.

"I beg your pardon, my precious? Did you say something?" he said with exquisite courtesy. She didn't—couldn't—answer, and he continued smoothly. "Unfortunately, Charles seems infatuated with your sister, though he denies it. It can go nowhere. He needs to marry a rich woman, and your sister won't do, and he knows it. He's got a disturbing streak of decency, but I know he won't be able to resist if I offer her. I'm afraid she'll be ruined."

"I'll warn Lydia. She's no fool."

"Indeed, she's smarter and more resilient than I gave her credit for. But you won't warn her. You won't be going anywhere near her until we come to an agreement." There was a sudden flare of light as he lit a taper, and she could see his face then, beautiful, brutal, a fallen angel reigning in hell.

"I have a cousin—" she began.

"Marcus Harriman will be of no use to you. My lawyers will ensure it."

Ice again. Her only recourse was not to show it. "Indeed?" she said coolly. "Then pray tell, what are your terms? What kind of agreement do you wish to come to?"

"You should be glad, my precious. I'm being quite reasonable and almost gentlemanly." He waited a moment as she laughed in disbelief. "I have no designs upon your so-lovely body. It's your mind I want. Now, any wise person would understand that that's a much greater sacrifice, but women tend to be valued for their cunts, and as long as I leave that alone you won't be totally ruined."

"Your language is foul."

"I'm foul, darling. Haven't you discovered that yet? But as long as you willingly keep me company your sister will be safe."

"For how long?"

He appeared struck. "I hadn't thought of that," he said. "Clearly you are used to haggling in the market-place—I salute you. How long?" He tapped his long white fingers against his chin. "In truth, I can't imagine growing tired of you, but I'm bound to, sooner rather than later. And I'm a fair man…don't scoff, precious…I should pick a reasonable amount of time. Shall we say until the end of Easter? It has a certain lovely symbolism. At the time your God has risen from the dead you get to go free."

"Not my God," she snapped.

"You continue to amaze me," he said. "Consider

this—your sister will join Mrs. Clarke at the château, where she will be well looked-after. You will stay here with me on some pretext. You're a more experienced liar than I am—I don't usually have to bother. You'll come up with something. You keep me company during Lent and the Revels of the Heavenly Host and come Easter morn you get to rise from the dead and start a new life. With a generous stipend from me to ensure that life is prosperous. How does that sound?"

"Blasphemy is far from attractive."

"I thought he wasn't your God?" he murmured. "And I'm not particularly worried about you finding me attractive, pet."

"Because you have no designs on my body," Elinor supplied.

"No, sweetness. Because you're already completely fascinated by me, and nothing's going to change that. It doesn't matter what I say or do. You're trapped, like a sweet little moth in a spider web."

"You may find you're mistaken, my lord. You may have a wasp in your web."

"Oh, I do hope so, child," Rohan said, rising. He blew out the candle, plunging the room into darkness again. "I'll have the agreement drawn up for your signature tomorrow morning."

"Drawn up? You expect me to sign something?"

"But of course. That way, if you renege I have merely to show the contract to a few influential people to destroy you completely."

She looked at the shadowy form in the darkness.

"I'm not sure there's much difference between my current position and total destruction."

"Your sister is the difference, my pet. Do we have an agreement?"

She wanted to scream at him, rage at him, beat at him with her fists. She did nothing. Later, when she was alone, in the darkness of her bedroom where no one would see or hear, she would give in to grief and rage. For now she would show him none of it. "We do. Now may I sleep? I find I'm quite fatigued." She even managed a creditable yawn.

"Indeed. Madame is waiting for me and she tends to be quite insatiable. I can only hope that I have not stayed away so long that three men have taken my place."

"Why three?"

"Darling, it takes that many to replace my skills."

To her astonishment she felt a brief caress against her face. An impossibility, because he'd already gone. With shaking hands she lit the candle beside her bed. To scare away the shadows, perhaps. She peered through the darkness, but she was alone.

Elinor slipped out of bed, cursing at the pain in her feet. She'd forgotten about it, but in truth, it was already improving. She limped over to the salon, but there was no sign of him. There were two doors leading into her room—she went to the first to lock it and found it was already bolted from the inside. She hobbled across the room to the second door, the one that led to the dressing room, to find that it, too, was locked from the inside. How had he managed to get in, to materialize through locked doors?

It didn't matter—he wasn't going to do it again. She dragged one chair and shoved it under the door handle, then took another chair and tucked it under the other. No one would get past her barricade. She went to the windows. The heavy snow had almost stopped, with only gentle flakes still drifting down, and she could see the rooftops of the building quite well. If need be she could go out that way. She wasn't going to stay trapped in this room if he chose to disturb her again...

But she was fooling herself. She had nothing to run from. As long as she agreed to his rules Lydia would be safe and she herself would simply suffer the annoyance of his company. Not the insult of his physical attentions.

So why did it feel as if his lack of interest was the true insult? Where did she get these sudden silly ideas, that she might be desired, wanted?

She'd gotten them from him. Part of the games he played, the games she would have to endure for the next six weeks if she remembered her liturgical calendar correctly. But nowhere in his rules did it say she couldn't fight back He could play his games all he wanted –that didn't mean he was going to win.

She limped back to bed, taking a look at the bandages on her feet before she blew out the candle. No fresh blood seeping through—they really were improving. Before long she'd be able to walk. To run. To dance rings around Francis Rohan, who foolishly thought he'd have everything his way. She wouldn't let him win. She would ensure that he sent Lydia away to the country where she'd be safe, and then she'd start in on him.

She could make his life so miserable he'd be begging to send her away.

Two hours later Francis Rohan lay naked and stretched across his current lover's equally naked body. Juliette had always been inventive, and he'd found himself particularly inspired tonight. It was a great shame that he was imagining Elinor Harriman's body naked beneath, above, in front of his, but Juliette wouldn't mind as long as he gave her the mind-numbing pleasure she demanded. Indeed, even dear Juliette was worn out this evening, taken to her limit and beyond, until she had to beg him to stop.

It was troublesome, this fascination with his reluctant houseguest. A great deal too bad that it was bordering on obsession. His friends, if he could call them that, would be astonished.

He knew his reasons were simple. He was denying himself, when he usually took what he wanted like the rakehell he was. Normally Miss Harriman would be seduced and forgotten by now. But something had stayed his hand. Perhaps it was her calm, pragmatic air, or the curiously vulnerable streak that broke forth occasionally. There was no denying that he was enjoying himself, enjoying the wanting, enjoying spending that need on others while the ultimate prize awaited. Unless he came to his senses before he actually managed to bed her.

He had no idea whether that was going to happen or not. He'd never gone through anything like this, so he had nothing to compare it with. All he knew was he hadn't felt more alive in years, perhaps decades. He couldn't remember.

He slipped out of bed, away from Juliette, and frowned for a moment. He was totally unacquainted with guilt or regret—they were the emotions of fools. Nevertheless, as pleasantly exhausted as he was, there was the oddest sense that he'd done something wrong.

Nonsense. Do what thou wilt. He'd wanted a female, quite badly, and Juliette was more than available. Life was too short to stint on pleasures, and if Elinor Harriman started interfering then he'd simply have to ship her back to England where she belonged. He wasn't about to let anyone or anything interfere with who and what he was.

Juliette stirred, whimpering slightly as she moved, and she could thank him for that. Would he really consider making Elinor submit to the deliciously perverse things he sometimes fancied? Perhaps he wanted to make love to her chastely, like a careful bridegroom.

He was nobody's bridegroom. He'd have her on her knees in front of him, taking him in her mouth. He'd have her every way he could, and then think of new ways to try it. The Heavenly Host was keeping a chapbook of positions and variations, often named after the lady first willing to attempt them. Perhaps ten years from now he'd open the book and be reminded of the Harriman.

There was something displeasing about that, though he wasn't going to brood about it. There were no rules in the Host, but the generous sharing of partners was expected. He rather thought he'd skip that with the enchanting Miss Harriman.

When he was done with her he'd probably send her back to England, along with her sister. He knew very little about her cousin, but there would be some way to pass along a comfortable stipend without anyone knowing and becoming offended. There was something rather delectable about a starched-up creature like Elinor actually being a kept woman.

Juliette moved again, and her eyes flew open. She looked at him in the candlelight, and she smiled slowly, holding out her hand.

He moved back to the bed.

18

"I don't understand," Lydia said, staring at her sister in dismay. "Why in the world should I go into the country while you stay here?"

Elinor looked uncharacteristically nervous. Lydia's darling older sister held the fond belief that Lydia couldn't tell when she was prevaricating, as she was now. "I told you, dearest, I'm helping his lordship with his library. Actually he's been very kind," she said, and Lydia said nothing. "He needs someone with a knowledge of Latin who can write a good hand, and that's one thing I can do. He's been given a score of very valuable old texts, some more than a hundred years old, and he needs someone to ascertain what they're about and make a record of them."

"He doesn't know Latin?" Every young man of quality had endless years of Latin drummed into him, and despite Lord Rohan's dissipated character, he still struck Lydia as someone conversant with the classics.

"Of course he does," Elinor replied. "He simply

doesn't have time to do the work. He has a very busy social calendar…"

"Indeed," Lydia said with an unbecoming snort. "Everyone in Paris knows about his social calendar."

"You know how people gossip, Lydia," Elinor said, trying to sound reasonable and failing. "I doubt his parties are any worse than what goes on at Versailles. People love to make up stories and spread rumors, the more vile the better."

"I thought you arrived in the midst of one of his notorious parties," she pointed out. Why in heaven's name was her sister suddenly changing her severe disapproval of the man? Was it possible that she was beginning to see what her baby sister had known all along? That her sister, her practical, unromantic older sister, was drawn to the beautiful and dangerous Viscount Rohan?

"I did," Eleanor said stoutly. "And I didn't see anything untoward. Surely you don't still think that Lord Rohan has any feelings for me? He can have any female in Paris, up to and possibly including the queen. He finds me entertaining, nothing more."

Lydia surveyed her sister. She was wearing a gray gown that fit her slender figure beautifully, exposing more of her chest than Elinor usually allowed. She'd tucked a fichu around her shoulders in an effort to hide herself, but it was a failure. With her rich dark hair flowing down her back, her brown eyes nervous, her lips red, color in her cheeks, she looked absolutely lovely, and Lord Rohan was connoisseur enough to recognize it. "You are naive," Lydia said severely.

"For all that you're older than I am, in many ways you're much more innocent. I don't want any man taking advantage of you."

Elinor's smile was forced. "I think that's unlikely to happen. I swear to you that he has no interest in me apart from my mind," she said flatly, and her words had the ring of truth.

Lydia recognized it. Or at least that Elinor believed it. "Then he's a blind fool."

Elinor laughed. "Darling, you're more than a bit partial. Look at it this way, it's to my advantage to be plain. It enables me to work for his lordship without running the danger of any importune advances. I never thought I would come to bless the Harriman Nose."

"*Blast* the Harriman Nose," Lydia said crossly. "You're not plain and you never have been. Just look at yourself in the mirror."

"You're a true sister," Elinor said, clearly not believing a word. "You'll love Mrs. Clarke—she's kind and welcoming. And after Easter I'll come and get you and we'll go home to England. We'll find a nice, small cottage. It might be on Father's land, perhaps in a village, perhaps just outside of one. We'll have a garden and we'll grow peas and lettuce, and we'll raise chickens. And maybe ducks."

It was a fairy tale, Lydia thought, but she wasn't going to point that out to her sister. "I love ducks."

"But no geese. They bite."

"What about swans?"

"That depends whether we're on water. It would

be nice to be near a river or a pond or something," Elinor said.

"Since we're making this up out of whole cloth, let's simply decide we'll have water," Lydia said. "I say a stream leading into a pond, where we can have swans and ducks and absolutely no geese, and we'll live very happily, two old-maid sisters. I do think we should have cats, a great many of them. They won't go after the ducks, will they?"

"We'll have cats that are afraid of ducks," Elinor said. "But I'm not certain how long we'll get to be two old maids together. You're sure to get married."

"Not if I don't want to," she said firmly. "And I suspect I'm not going to. I've always been stubborn, you know, and faithful in my affections. Once given, I don't change my mind."

"The trick to that, darling, is don't give your affections," Elinor said lightly. "Just wait until we arrive home and you catch the eye of some dashing gentleman with comfortable means. I'm going to want nieces and nephews, you know."

"I'm afraid it's too late, love," Lydia said. She quickly changed the subject before Elinor could respond. "I'll agree to go to the country if that's what you wish. A little seclusion would probably be good for me. As long as you absolutely swear to me that you aren't staying behind to be a…a…" Words failed her.

"Fallen woman?" Elinor suggested helpfully. "Courtesan? Lady of the night? Don't be ridiculous, child. Do I look like a light-'o-love?"

"You look very beautiful," Lydia said truthfully. "I don't want you staying behind to be hurt."

Elinor had deep reserves of calm good sense, and a remarkable ability to weather crushing blows. She smiled at her sister. "I'll be fine, you little goose," she said with a laugh. "When have I lied to you?"

Lydia just looked at her. "More often than I suspect." She didn't want to leave Elinor. She didn't want to go out to the countryside, far away from the temptation of Charles Reading. Not that he was any danger—though he'd held her so tenderly the night of the fire she hadn't seen him since, and she doubted she would. Going out of town would ensure that, doubtless one of her sister's reasons for encouraging it.

Elinor was still looking at her, anxiety beneath her calm exterior, and guilt swamped Lydia. "I'll go," she said, and Elinor's relieved smile was reward enough.

As long as her strange, irrational faith in Lord Rohan wasn't misplaced. He wouldn't hurt Elinor. He wouldn't dare.

If he did, he'd have Lydia to deal with, and she would ensure that he was very, very sorry.

Elinor slept late the next day, waking with a guilty feeling. She dressed quickly, not waiting for Jeanne-Louise to assist her, and started out her bedroom door only to run into the oversize footman from last night. Before she could say a word he'd scooped her up. "His lordship said I was to transport you, mademoiselle."

"I'm entirely capable of walking on my own," she said. She refrained from squirming for the sake of the poor footman, who was pink from either embarrassment or exertion.

"I have my orders, mademoiselle. His lordship bade me carry you and I will do just that. If you please, mademoiselle." There was just the faintest note of pleading in his voice, and Elinor took pity on him. Disobeying Rohan was not something to be done lightly.

"I want to see my sister."

The footman looked even more uncomfortable, as if he was struggling with something a great deal more weighty than her not inconsiderable body. And then he nodded, starting off.

"You're going in the wrong direction," she said.

He nodded again, signifying God knew what, and Elinor took pity on him. Lydia must be waiting for her elsewhere.

The vastness of the house once again startled her, as they seemed to tread through miles of halls, many of them decorated with black cloth. It was a good thing she wasn't walking herself—she'd doubtless get totally lost. Once Lydia left, Elinor had every intention of staying in her room. With luck Rohan would be so distracted by the lascivious temptations of the Revels that he wouldn't remember she was there.

Except she recognized the last hallway they turned into—she'd been there before, two weeks ago, when she'd confronted him in a righteous fury. "I don't think my sister is in Lord Rohan's bedroom," she said, beginning to struggle. "At least, she'd best not be."

The footman ignored her, knocking gently on the

door without losing his grip on her, and then pushing the door open.

Rohan stood there, still in shirtsleeves and small clothes, as two valets dressed him. He glanced at her, unmoved. "My dear Elinor. What a delightful surprise. What brings you here?"

"Your so-helpful footman," she said in a tart voice. "And I didn't give you leave to call me by my name."

"I thought you might prefer it to endearments," he purred. "But if you want me to use more intimate terms…"

"You may use my first name," she said hastily, just imaging the terms he could come up with. "I asked the footman to take me to my sister. He brought me here. If Lydia is anywhere around your bedroom, I'll cut your liver out."

He blinked. "What a delightfully bloodthirsty image, Elinor. Would you then eat it? I didn't know you had such a violent streak."

"I do where my sister is concerned."

"Your sister is safe," he said. "You may set her down, Antoine. I would suggest the bed but she would fight you. The green chair should suffice."

She found herself settled gently into one of his chairs, and she jumped back up immediately.

"Someone restrain her," Rohan said in an unconcerned voice. "Without hurting her," he added, and the footmen took her arms and forced her back in the chair, careful not to be too rough. She sat back, knowing when a battle could not be won.

"Where is my sister?"

"Where I promised she should be," he said as the two valets helped him into the rich satin coat that fit him perfectly. "She should be arriving at the château by now, and Mrs. Clarke will welcome her by taking her to her bosom. She'll thrive in the good country air, and by the time the Revels have concluded she'll be delighted to rejoin you and return to England."

"Why didn't you let me say goodbye to her?"

He smiled thinly. "Dare I say I didn't trust you? I gather you were very delicate when you first told her what the future held, but you have a ridiculously tender heart beneath that calm mien, and I think your sister's tears would have broken through that admirable self-control."

"She was crying?" Elinor picked up the salient point.

"Of course she was. She just lost her mother and her old nanny, not to mention whatever meager possessions she still had, and her sister, the person she thought she could count on, has abandoned her."

Elinor clenched her hands, hiding them in the folds of her skirt. "Why would she think I've abandoned her?"

"My dear Elinor, do you really think she believed that ridiculous story you told her about becoming my amanuensis? Yes, I made certain someone was listening and reported to me—no, don't jump up again. You should have realized I would do that. It's wise not to underestimate me."

She did her best to hide her bitterness. "Indeed, I shall endeavor not to."

He turned away to survey himself in the mirror. Clearly the vision met with his approval. "Your sister is much smarter than you give her credit for," he murmured. "Right now her imagination is running riot, coming up with all sorts of wicked things you might be getting into. You'll have to write her and set her mind at ease. And I have no doubt that Mrs. Clarke will manage to make her feel better—she could cheer up Satan himself."

"She cheers you up?"

He laughed softly. "Oh, no, my precious. I'm not Satan. Merely one of his fallen angels." He waved away the offer of a wig, letting his luxurious silver-streaked black hair be tied in a neat queue. He held out his hands and his servants slid rings onto his long, elegant fingers, then he cocked his head, looking at her. "In truth, I'm glad you came in search of me. I had some questions for..."

"I didn't come in search of you," she snapped. "I would be happy if I never saw you again. I was looking for my sister. Since she is no longer here I will repair to my room, on my own two feet. You may call off your footman."

"Once I ascertain that your feet have healed, certainly," he murmured. "Do you want me to undo your bandages or would you prefer to handle the honors yourself?"

She immediately tucked her feet under her voluminous skirts. "Don't be ridiculous."

"I've already seen your bare feet, poppet," he pointed out, the soul of reason. "And quite delightful they are. But I can assure you that unlike the Chevalier du Corvalle I find other parts of the body to be far more stimulating. Although you do have exquisite arches."

She looked at him with clear dislike. "I should have known better than to have trusted you. We made a bargain and you cheated."

"I would call a man out for saying such a thing." His voice was silken. "Do not trespass on my good nature."

"You're not going to call me out. Indeed, I would be happy if you did. Shooting a gun couldn't be that difficult, and I would like nothing more than to put a bullet in you."

"I think I liked the cutting out of my liver a bit better, child," he said critically. "Firearms are so tediously impersonal. Not to mention loud."

She glared at him. She had been determined to keep her face and voice calm—she'd certainly had years of practice. During their slow descent into the lower echelons of Paris society she'd managed to convince her sister and indeed, the entire household, that things were not as dire as they seemed. She could lie quite handily, hide her fear and other roiling emotions. And yet Lord Rohan seemed to knock them down as swiftly as she erected them. "You truly are a despicable man, aren't you?" she said, no longer mincing words.

His smile was charming, exquisite, as he looked down at her. "I am indeed, my precious. A true villain—you'd best remember that. As well as remembering that you had no choice when it came to your sister's safety. If you wanted her away from here while my friends break almost every commandment then you must agree to whatever terms I offered you. It is that simple."

She didn't bother to argue. He had the upper hand, which was both unsettling and infuriating. Fighting against him got her nowhere, and he probably enjoyed it. She needed to plan her battles more wisely. She took a deep, calming breath, forcing her hands to release their tight grip.

"So tell me, how are you feeling after the death of your dear mother? I expect the sense of relief is almost overpowering."

She glared at him. "You are such a despicable man," she repeated.

"Give it o'er, child," he said wearily. "She was in the midst of dying a protracted, painful death. I would have said this was God's mercy if I believed in mythical creatures. You can't expect me to believe you truly mourn her."

"I don't expect you to believe anything," she said calmly, looking around her. The large, hulking footman had remained in the room during their conversation, and she signaled for him to come forward. "You may take me back to my room, Antoine," she said, having learned his name the day previous. "I've finished with his lordship for the time being."

She'd hoped to see Rohan's eyebrows snap together in anger. Instead he merely smiled. And Antoine made no move in her direction. "You haven't eaten yet, have you? Neither have I. I'll have the servants lay for both of us and we can set forth the rules of our little truce."

"I'd prefer to return to my room and eat there."

"But I'd prefer you to join me," he said in the sweetest possible voice, with absolute steel beneath it. "Antoine, you may transport Miss Harriman to the green salon."

"*Oui,* milord," Antoine said, coming forward to scoop her up again.

She fixed him with a look, and Antoine halted, clearly torn. "Touch me and you'll regret it," she snarled at the poor boy. He looked so frightened she almost took pity on him, but that had gotten her into this mess in the first place.

"Terrorizing the servants, my dear? You're learning from me." He waved an elegant white hand in Antoine's direction. "You may leave, boy. Clearly the lady would much rather I carry her myself."

She had played piquet in the past, and recognized herself outplayed by a master. "*Repique, monsieur,*" she said. "Antoine, you may assist me."

Antoine didn't move until Rohan gave a slight nod. "You disappoint me, *ma belle,*" he murmured. "You're no featherweight, but I've managed to carry you on more than one occasion, and I believe I'm up to the challenge. But if you prefer young Antoine, so be it."

Antoine had already scooped her up with due deference. "When have you carried me?" she demanded.

"Out of your burning house, my sweet. And when you fainted in my hallway."

"I've never fainted in my life," she protested.

"You needn't worry, poppet. I carried you into your bedroom and for the most part the servants undressed you. Your virtue was safe with me."

"For the most part?" she said in an icy voice. "I remember none of this."

"Just as well," he said airily. "Take her away, Antoine. I have a small bit of business to conduct. I'm certain she'll manage to entertain herself well enough while awaiting me. Make certain you see to it."

In other words, keep her prisoner. There was nothing she could do. She was well and truly trapped, and she'd put herself in his hands. At least his interest in her seemed as base and uncomplicated as a cat playing with a mouse. He would let her escape, just a bit, and then slam his paw down on her to hold her there.

But mice didn't snarl and fight back. As she most assuredly would. He wanted entertainment, and respite from boredom? She would provide it. So thoroughly that he'd be afraid to go to sleep at night, for fear she'd stab him.

She could play games as well. She wasn't strong enough to challenge him to a duel, she had no resources. But she had every belief that she could make his life a living hell.

And she had every intention of doing just that.

Mr. Mitchum was a troubled man. He dealt with estates and finances, not the cruder business of trials and criminals, and he'd been fortunate enough to spend most of his busy life dealing with the émigré population of Paris. To be sure, young men of quality were a feckless lot, and it had been his duty to ensure that their spendthrift ways didn't land them in a French prison, but by and large it had been a good living.

Until this recent case. Clients lied to him all the time, he expected it. But he was unused to full-out fraud, to attempted embezzlement, to crimes on a scale quite unexpected. So unexpected that he had no notion what to do about it.

He could scarcely turn the man over to the French authorities. He had the Englishman's distrust of the French, combined with a nationalistic shame over one of his countrymen perpetuating such a lie. He was certain that once he confronted the gentleman the situation could be handled with diplomacy and tact. The impostor would simply have to withdraw his claim and disappear.

Really, it was astonishing that he had gotten as far as he did, and he thought less of his colleagues back in London that they hadn't noticed something irregular in the situation. Had it not been for his own diligence the man would have gotten away with it, a notion that chilled Mr. Mitchum's legal soul. He believed in the sanctity of marriage, the superiority of the British race and the infallibility of British law. That someone would attempt to contravene it was a blow to all he held most dear.

He'd sent his clerk home for the day. The fewer witnesses to the man's disgrace the better. He sat behind his desk and waited, patiently, as the snow fell outside. He was going to be late getting home, and his dear wife would scold, out of worry rather than temper, and he would drink a glass of burgundy and tell her, just a little, of what had been troubling him for the last few days. And she would kiss his forehead and tell him he was a good man and he would feel better.

The man finally showed up, half an hour later. Mr. Mitchum despised tardiness, but he had a moment's sympathy. Though he couldn't quite make the leap and put himself in the gentleman's position, he thought it likely that if he'd been caught in wrongdoing he would be reluctant to face his accuser.

He glanced outside his window. A storm was brewing—indeed, the winter and late spring had been unusually harsh. The sooner he got home the better.

His client was all charm and apologies for his tardiness when he arrived, shaking the snow from his hat. If he had any idea what was troubling Mitchum, he didn't show it.

After a moment, not wanting to waste time with conversational niceties, Mitchum forged ahead. "I'm afraid," he said, "that I've come across a grave problem, Mr. Harriman. Your papers are forged. You are no more the heir to Baron Tolliver's estate than I am."

Marcus Harriman was a handsome, affable man and he smiled at Mr. Mitchum. "I think you must have made some mistake, Mitchum," he said pleasantly. He'd refused a seat, and was standing near the window, looking out into the gathering storm. "Has someone been slandering me? Who knows of these accusations?"

Mr. Mitchum drew himself up, all offended dignity. "I believe I know how to be discreet, sir," he said with a sniff. "So far I have passed my suspicions on to no one. I thought it only fair to give you a chance to right the situation."

"Only fair," Mr. Harriman echoed in his warm voice. "I do appreciate the chance to set things right, Mitchum. Perhaps you might show me where in the papers you find a flaw?"

Mr. Mitchum was well prepared, and he spread out the various proofs of identity on his desk as Mr. Harriman came round behind him. "Here," he said, pointing to one clear forgery. "And here," he added as Mr. Harriman leaned over him.

Mitchum saw his blood first, before he felt a thing, and he put his hands to his neck in a vain attempt to stanch it. There was no pain, a blessing, he thought. His wife's face swam in front of his vision. A moment later he slumped forward, dead.

Marcus Harriman wiped the blade of his knife against the old lawyer's coat, then slid it back under his waistcoat. He moved swiftly, scooping up the blood-soaked papers and stuffing them in the fire. He waited while they burned, then took the small shovel and scooped up some of the bright red coals, sprinkling them over the rug and the wood floor. The fire caught almost immediately.

He took a step back, admiring his handiwork. He hadn't dared stay long enough in Rue du Pélican after he'd set the fire—it had been a rush attempt and in the end it had failed. This would be easier.

He glanced back at the lawyer. His wig had slipped from his head and landed in the pool of blood. He looked ridiculous, and Marcus laughed softly. Served the old fool right.

And a moment later he let himself out the door, closing it, and the fire, behind him.

19

Rohan moved through the candlelit hallways, threading his way around entwined couples. He knew he looked exquisite—he'd spent many hours on his toilette, and everything was as it should be. From the top of his perfectly curled and powdered wig, down the front of his gray satin coat encrusted in black pearls. His clocked stockings were made from the finest silk, and his evening shoes had diamonds on the high heels to match those on his fingers and in his ear.

He was of mixed feeling about those shoes. They were quite magnificent, and had cost a small fortune. One of many he could afford to waste. They matched his evening dress perfectly. And the heels added to his already considerable height, making him taller than any member or guest of the Heavenly Host. The problem was, he'd never managed to master the perfect, mincing walk. He had too much a tendency to stride, and half a lifetime living in the scented drawing rooms and bedrooms of France hadn't been able to change that.

Early influences were often the strongest, he knew. And the first decade and a half of his life had been spent alternating between his father's vast estates in Cornwall and his grandfather's lands in Scotland. Cities were virtually unknown to a young boy with far too much energy, and he'd roamed the countryside, coming in each day covered with mud, an equally filthy spaniel or two by his side, sometimes with a brace of pheasant, sometimes with a string of trout from the nearby stream. He would dream, at times, of stretching out by that stream, his line in the water, a spaniel snuffling in the grass nearby, and he would think he was back in that well-nigh-perfect time in his life. And then the water would turn red with blood, and men were dead and dying all around, and he'd be holding his brother in his arms, trying to staunch the flow of life's blood as Simon's eyes slowly glazed, when he saw the pike just as it was thrown, and there was no way he could duck.

He'd wake up screaming, covered in sweat. It had been a great many years since he'd had that reaction, and the blessing was he'd never been sharing his bed with anyone who might ask questions. He'd come to the reasonable conclusion that if he was able to exhaust himself with the soft form of a woman the nightmares would keep their distance, and he'd acted accordingly.

It was a good thing he hadn't gone the way of Elinor's mother. Though in fact the English disease, as well as other, lesser misfortunes, were easy enough to avoid if one was careful in one's choices. When in doubt he simply walked away—he'd never wanted someone enough to put himself in danger. There was always someone just as charming with a more trustworthy history.

He was willing to change that careful plan, however. He had no idea exactly who and what had occasioned Miss Harriman's deflowering, but in truth it didn't matter if she'd been raped by a boatload of infected sailors. He wanted her. It was that simple. And there were contraptions to avoid illness, envelopes made of sheep guts or linen soaked in chemicals. He'd never used one, but for the sake of partaking of Miss Elinor Harriman he'd be willing, and he'd sent his valet to procure a goodly number. He had the strong suspicion that once was not going to be enough with his charming, so-unwilling houseguest.

In truth they ought to be available to the Revels of the Heavenly Host, but proper caution was such the antithesis of "Do what thou wilt" that he imagined his fellow members would ban them. There were times when their games seemed remarkably foolish.

The formal start of the Revels was not till tomorrow night, but members had already begun to arrive. Including the new applicants. There was one of them who interested him mightily, though he pretended to have no knowledge of him. Marcus Harriman, Lord Tolliver, had been brought to their gatherings by Sir Henry Pennington, which was far from a recommendation. Sir Henry was an annoying little toad with a particular affection for the giving of pain, but he had enough friends in their close circle that Francis simply chose to ignore him. But the Harriman name had caught his eye, and he was most curious to meet the heir whose inheritance had forced Elinor into his wicked toils. Not that he would see her. He had every intention of keeping Elinor well out of sight of the Heavenly Host. Still, he would have to find some way to express his gratitude.

He'd had word from Mrs. Clarke. Lydia had settled in well enough, as he'd no doubt she would. If Elinor stopped to think about it she'd know that giving Lydia over into Mrs. Clarke's tender care was a boon worth any sacrifice. Her warm, practical affection could heal any sort of wound.

He'd been three years into his exile in Paris when she'd simply shown up, husband and infant daughter in hand, and proceeded to dig him out of the dark, wretched place he'd retreated to. She hadn't been able to bring him all the way back. No one could, not after the things he'd seen. It was of no consequence. She helped him keep his life neatly partitioned, and when the dubious pleasures of the Heavenly Host grew too wearisome he could always escape into the world Mrs. Clarke had created for him.

That was what Miss Lydia needed right now. Fate had not been kind to her, but then, fate was a fickle jade. If her sister was determined to provide her with some kind of happy ending the cards were stacked against her.

Interesting, that his poppet might even consider that a happy life was possible. She certainly didn't think one would be available for her, and he once more considered Etienne. He was a humorless bore, but Elinor had the ability to charm even one as world-weary as he. After a few years perhaps she could get Etienne to laugh.

One thing was certain: Etienne was not going to get his wish. He was not going to have Miss Lydia Harriman, no matter how sweet she was to him. He expected Charles Reading would be seeing to that.

And Etienne was not going be inheriting the title of Comte de Giverney, along with the considerable estates, until Rohan chose to die, and he had no intention of doing so for quite a long time. No intention of reproducing, so Etienne would most definitely end up as a wealthy count. And Elinor a comtesse. Would she like it? He'd have to be dead for that to happen. Would she think of him, and what he'd given her?

It was a great deal too bad that Mrs. Clarke's civilizing influence hadn't extended very far. Etienne had presented his lawyers with a simple way to turn over the estate and the title. He'd inherited it on a fluke, and if Etienne had had the money he could have contested it, and chances were the French king would have favored his own countryman over the exile. After all, they'd driven the Young Pretender from their shores in record time, once he became a liability.

Which was just as well with Rohan. He'd only seen Bonnie Prince Charlie from a distance, that red-gold hair shining in the cold sun, not near enough to see the famous blue eyes. He'd lost everything for the man whose arrogance had led to disaster at Culloden, putting them at the mercy of Butcher Cumberland, and he was perfectly happy never to see him again. Rome was too close.

"Care to join us, Francis?" a woman's voice lured him. Juliette was lounging on a sofa, a man kneeling beneath her voluminous skirts, and her eyes glittered in the candle light.

He shook his head, so as not to disturb the young man servicing her. He was guessing by the sight of his rump that it was milord Valancey, who was a good fifteen years younger than her most recent bed partner, and he allowed himself a small smile. She was indefatigable. It was good that she was choosing a young man bursting with energy. She would be less likely to come looking for him.

He heard the shrieks of laughter coming from the smaller ballroom. At least, he assumed those whooping noises were amusement. Whatever they were, they were not his concern. Right now he was going to visit his captive princess, to see if he could convince her to let down her hair.

There was music playing, a recent conceit of his. He'd discovered the surprising pleasure of coupling whilst listening to music, and the habit had spread among the members of the Host. A small quartet played in what he preferred to call the evening room. Long ago it had been a morning room, complete with a chaise for a young lady to recline on, a desk at which to write her letters. There were no young ladies in his household. The chaise was still there, and had seen much vigorous usage, but the desk was gone, and the east-facing windows were covered with black cloth, to keep the curious from peeping inside.

He moved past the gaming room, resisting the urge to play a few hands of piquet. The focus was not on the game, and he was ever a man who preferred to do one thing at a time and do it extremely well. Besides, it was far too easy to win when people had other things on their minds, and he found winning under those circumstances to be an utter bore.

He climbed the flight of stairs to the second floor. The numbers of guests would reach above this one, filling most rooms on this floor and the next, with even some in the east wing that had previously held Miss Lydia Harriman. Of course, he'd lied about their previous occupancy—he'd had no interest in letting Elinor spend too much time with her sister.

The luncheon they'd shared had been…interesting. She'd watched him like a wary fox, certain he was about to attack. And he'd been his most amiable self. Any other woman, and she would have been put entirely at ease. Which was why he didn't want any other woman. Elinor simply watched him out of her warm, brown, skeptical eyes, waiting for him to cross the line.

He didn't, of course. The sturdy Antoine carried her back to her bedroom, where, in her absence he'd had books and sweetmeats delivered, and since then he'd heard nothing. Reports came that she had asked for a light supper, but apart from that she was entirely self-sufficient in her apartment.

He was about to change all that.

Paris was a noisy city at the change of the hour—bells from every part rang in the cold night air, and as he approached her door the hour of eleven o'clock announced itself. To his astonishment he could feel his arousal stirring. While his body parts worked perfectly and reliably, no matter what he demanded of them, it had been many years when anticipation had caused a reaction. An anticipation that might not be met.

Eleven o'clock. A lovely hour. The girl he'd assigned to be her maid was sitting in a chair outside her room, wise enough to be awake at his approach. "You may go," he said softly.

"Where, milord?" she asked, startled.

"Do I look as if I care?" he said, caustic. "Far enough away that you won't be listening to every bit of our conversation, close enough that you will arrive if she calls for you."

"Yes, milord," she said, ducking her head quickly. She scurried off, and he watched her go, impatient.

The door was locked from the inside. The key was still in the lock, keeping him out, and he suspected there might be a chair in front of it as well. He laughed to himself, and the pleasant tension in his body grew. He liked to play games.

There were two doors to the suite where he'd had Elinor placed, as well as two covert entrances. The rooms had once belonged to his great-aunt, whose appetite for lovers had astounded even the jaded French. There was always a way for an enterprising man to make his way inside the fortress.

She'd found the first one and blocked it, and his interest grew by measurable accounts. It was a panel in the hallway that would slide open if one touched the right part of the cherub that perched on the molding. *Tant pis,* he thought, moving on. There was one more entrance, this one through a cupboard in the adjoining room, opening up beside the massive, curtained bed. If she'd found that one he'd simply call for Antoine to beat down her door.

The adjoining room was still and quiet. In the daytime the damask covers on the wall were a peaceful gray-blue, while the faint light from his candle rendered everything into shades of black and gray. It was a large apartment, almost as large as his own, and he made the sudden decision to have some of his clothes moved in here.

The moon was almost bright, filling the darkened room with enough light to see his way. He blew out his candle, opened the cupboard door and reached for the latch.

There was a satisfying click. He pushed open the door and moved into her bedroom, as silent as a ghost.

She was sitting on the chaise, a candle by her side, a book in her lap. And the same, lovely little pistol pointed directly at his black, black heart.

"How in heaven's name did you manage to regain that nasty little weapon?" he murmured, moving into the room.

"Charles Reading returned it to Jacobs. He thought we needed protection, living where we lived. And where is Jacobs?"

"Who, may I ask, is Jacobs?" He strolled across the room. The pistol didn't waver.

"Our coachman."

"You had no coach."

"Don't be pedantic," she said briskly. "At one point we had any number of coaches. He came with us to France and stayed with us over the years, looking out for us."

"Ah, the larcenous coachman. May I point out that his caretaking abilities fell short?"

"He did the best he could. Where is he?"

"I rather believe he's accompanying your mother and your nursemaid's bodies back to England for burial."

She almost dropped the gun, which might have been unfortunate if it had gone off. "What?"

"I assumed both of them would rather be buried on English soil. I made arrangements for them to be brought back to your father's estates and buried there."

"And you didn't think to ask me?"

"Obviously we had to move with a fair amount of speed, although winter made such a gesture more reasonable. You don't think that's what they would have wanted?"

"Nanny Maude, of a certainty. She always missed England. My mother would be rolling over in her grave to be buried with my father."

"There was always that advantage as well," he said solemnly. "You think your mother deserved eternal peace?"

"I think my mother had her own hell in this life-time," she said.

"True. However, she was more than generous enough to share it with her daughters, her older one in particular. I don't happen to believe in heaven or hell, so I can't imagine it will make any difference where she's buried, but you'll have to allow me my quixotic gesture."

"I don't really have a choice in the matter," she said tartly.

"True enough. May I sit?"

"No."

"Which leaves me with a quandary. If I sit anyway, will I simply be rude, or will you shoot me? You've been quite hard on my clothing so far, and I'm particularly fond of this toilette. I would hate to have it marred with bullet holes."

"Why don't you try it and see what happens." She had the most delicious amount of menace in her voice. It would almost be worth it, just to see how far he could push her.

"Thank you, I will," he said, spreading the voluminous skirts of his coat out and sitting on the end of her chaise.

She quickly pulled her legs up, away from him, and her grip tightened on the gun. "You certainly do like tempting the fates, do you not?"

"Are you my fate, poppet? I've had that uneasy feeling ever since I saw you, huddling beneath your rags out at my château. Most men would run in the opposite direction, but I must admit I'm inordinately fond of risk. Are you really going to shoot me?"

"It's quite possible."

He smiled at her. "Why? Simply because I annoy you? That's a bit extreme. Do you think I'm going to rape you?"

He felt the sudden jerk of her body, so near to his, and he allowed himself to be grateful that her finger hadn't jerked on the trigger of the pistol that was still pointed in the general direction of his belly. And he could feel the effort she made to calm herself.

"No," she said.

"Why not? I've made it very clear that I intend to have you, even though you've chosen not to believe me."

"You said you wanted me to stay for conversation. To entertain you," she said.

"And you believed me? Silly child. You're talking to a libertine, a member of the Heavenly Host. I don't believe we're known for our love of good conversation."

She grew very still. "So you are going to rape me?"

"Good heavens, no," he said with a soft laugh, and some of the tension left her body. "I never take by force what I can have by charm."

Her astonished laughter was genuine, and it might have wounded a more sensitive soul. It just made him want her more. "If you're relying on your charm you'll have a long wait, my lord," she said tartly.

"Perhaps," he said. "Why don't you put that pistol away. I'd take it from you, and you'd let me, but then we'd simply have to go through the rigmarole of getting it back to you. Set it down, poppet. You know you don't want to shoot me."

"You're wrong. There's nothing I'd like more than to pull this trigger," she said, her voice uncompromising.

He laughed. "I do concede that part of you would like nothing better than to put a very large hole in me. But I hold that the rest of you would much rather have me in one piece."

"I don't want you at all."

"Now, that, my precious, is a lie." He took the pistol from her hand, uncocked it and set it down on the parquet floor very carefully. He hadn't thought she'd had it properly primed. He really shouldn't underestimate her.

She said nothing.

Now that she was no longer clutching a gun, her hands lay in her lap, and he picked one up, letting his thumb rub against the inside of her wrist, letting his long fingers slide around hers. She tried to curl it into a fist but he stopped her, and she didn't fight him.

She took a deep breath, forcing herself to relax, and he could have told her that was a mistake. One needed to be wary around a member of the Heavenly Host when he wanted something. She pulled her hand free, and he let her, and she leaned back against the chaise, surveying him out of those deliciously practical eyes.

"I think, my lord, that you haven't thought this through. For some bizarre reason you decided you wanted someone innocent and untried in your bed. Perhaps you have the French disease and think a virgin would cure it. Perhaps the novelty of it, after so many whores, was irresistible. But I'm not the woman you want. I'm not innocent, I'm not inexperienced, I'm not a virgin."

Poor darling. Virginity be damned, he didn't know when he'd met a more innocent female. It almost, almost made him feel guilty.

"You'll give me leave to doubt you," he said, not doubting her for a moment. "The fact that you've freely said this twice now makes me think you're lying to distract me."

"I'm not lying."

"Prove it," he said. "You've made a devil's bargain, Scheherazade. Tell me the story of your love affairs, and perhaps I might let you go."

He could practically see her mind working as she balanced her options. The truth, or an elaborate fantasy? He waited patiently, entirely at ease.

"My first lover was my sister's music teacher," she said after a moment. "We were still living in Faubourg Saint-Martin—my mother had several generous friends and we were...happy. He was my age, seventeen, and quite beautiful, with long blond hair and blue eyes and the most gentle touch. He loved me," she said simply.

"And what was this paragon's name?"

"Pascal de Florent," she said without hesitation, and for a moment he almost believed her.

"Move over."

She glared at him. "Why?"

"Because you're going to tell me all about this and I want to be comfortable. This chaise is big enough for the two of us, unless you'd rather we retire to the bed. No? Then move over."

She hesitated, but clearly he'd managed to still her fears. She moved over, and he slid up beside her.

"Ouch!" she said. "Do you have to wear so many blasted jewels?"

"Of course not, my dove." He unfastened the diamond-studded buttons of his coat and pulled it off. He'd chosen one of his less severely tailored coats for the evening, wanting to be certain he could divest himself of it without help. He dumped it on the floor, smiling faintly as he thought of what his valet might say.

He leaned back again, very close to her. "Shall we continue?" he said.

She turned to look at him. Even in the candlelight he could see her quite clearly, the gold flecks in her rebellious brown eyes. He wondered if they ever softened.

She leaned back beside him, their shoulders touching. She tried to move away, but there was no place for her to go. "Well, then there was one of my mother's young admirers…"

"Not so fast, my precious. You're telling me a story. The adventures of an impure maid. I want to hear about it. Did you fall in love with the music teacher?"

"Of…of course." She paused. "He was beautiful and he was very kind."

Not the words to describe a lover, he thought. "So. Tell me about it. Where did you manage your assignations?"

This should be fairly easy for her. He had no doubt the music teacher had existed, that he was beautiful and very kind. No doubt that she'd spent hours fantasizing about him. No doubt that he'd never touched her.

"My bedroom at first. He would sneak in there after he finished with his lessons."

"How did it feel, precious? Did it hurt?"

She turned and gave him a look of real dislike. "Of course it did. But that doesn't matter when true love exists."

"Of course not," he said soothingly. "So he deflowered you on your bed, and it was tender and beautiful. And painful. How many times did you do it?"

Her brow was wrinkled. "Once."

"Once the first time, or only once with the music teacher?"

He could practically feel her annoyance. Unfortunately her body was pressed up against his, and no matter how she tried to keep her distance the warmth of his leg against hers, the feel of his body next to hers, even through the many layers of petticoats and cloth, was loosening some of her tension.

"Many, many times," she said between gritted teeth. "We did it in my bedroom, in the music room, in…"

"Where in the music room?"

She looked at him with real dislike. "Underneath the pianoforte. On top of the pianoforte. Unfortunately Nanny Maude caught us, and my mother dismissed the piano teacher, and I never saw him again."

"Very tragic," he murmured. "But I'm encouraged by your inventiveness. Who came next?"

"There was an actor at the Comédie-Française. His name was Pierre duClos and he was quite beautiful—with dark hair and an angelic smile."

He was enjoying himself immensely. Scheherazade was doing an excellent job with her stories. Which were just that—stories. "Apparently you favor beautiful men. How fortunate for me."

She looked at him. "You don't suffer from an excess of self-doubt, do you?"

"Why should I? It's a waste of time. You and I both know I'm exquisite." He flicked his flowing lace cuff. "My valet puts a great deal of effort into making me look glorious—it would distress him greatly if he somehow had failed. Perhaps I should get rid of him."

"He hasn't failed," Elinor said in a disgruntled voice. "You're very beautiful. So much so that you put everyone around you to shame, like a strutting peacock surrounded by little brown hens."

"Do you see yourself as a little brown hen, my sweet?"

"Thinking of me that way might be a very grave mistake," she said, appearing unmoved.

He leaned back against the side of the chaise and smiled at her. "I seldom make mistakes, precious. And I haven't underestimated you since the moment I first saw you. I know just how dangerous you are."

"Then why don't you let me go?"

"Let you go? I wasn't aware that I was imprisoning you. Exactly where was it that you wanted to go?"

She bit her lip, which annoyed him. He wanted to

be the one biting her lip. "Perhaps you could be kind enough to offer me shelter at the château?"

"I could most certainly do that," he said gravely. "I can have Charles drive you out there first thing in the morning."

"You can?" She actually looked hopeful. He almost hated to dash that hope.

"It doesn't do to underestimate me either. You may go, and Charles will bring your sister back in your place."

Her eyes narrowed. "You're a bastard, you know. A heartless, manipulative monster."

"Oh, surely that's too harsh. I'm not a monster. I wouldn't even say I'm a bad man. I'm just not a very good one." He picked up one of her cool, limp hands and brought it to his lips before she jerked it away. He kept his grip on it, letting her drop it into the covers, but his fingers were like steel, unbreakable.

She took a deep breath, clearly trying to calm herself, and he could almost imagine her counting to ten to try to settle her temper. It was simply too bad for her that he liked arousing her ire. He liked the thought of arousing everything about her, and intended to do just that. Slowly but surely.

"So tell me about this handsome actor of yours. I have seen him onstage. He is indeed very pretty, though his performance was at best mediocre. How did you happen to form a liaison with him?"

"Easily. I sent him a note praising his acting ability and suggested we meet. And we did."

"And what did you do?"

She looked at him calmly. "Fuck," she said.

He laughed softly. "I wasn't aware that you even knew that word, my darling."

"I spent time in the stables."

"And exactly which positions did you prefer?"

He could see the momentary blankness in her eyes, and he hid his smile. "Er…anything he fancied. I was very amenable."

"I'm most certain you were," he said in a soothing voice. "And who after him? The assembled court of King Louis?"

Her warm brown eyes could glare at him, but they could never grow as cold as he knew his could. "You don't believe me?" she demanded, clearly affronted.

"Oh, I imagine there's a grain of truth in your intricate tales. You most likely had a crush on your sister's music tutor, perhaps shared a kiss or two. As for duClos, he quite adamantly prefers the company of men."

"So you persist in thinking I'm a virgin?"

"Oh, I know you are not, my sweet. You simply are lying to me about how you lost that particularly useless bit of your anatomy."

"What exactly is it you want, my lord? Why don't we simply stop this charade, you tell me what you want and I'll give it to you."

"But where's the fun in that, poppet?"

She bit her lip again, and he couldn't stand it anymore. "Don't do that," he said sharply, putting his fingertips on her lower lip to stop her.

She bit him. On purpose. He should have pulled his hand away, but he didn't.

She had very strong white teeth and she bit down hard. He didn't move.

"Child," he said in a deceptively weary voice, "if I didn't still retain a tiny, unwanted shred of decency I would shove you back on this chaise, push your skirts above your head and take you here, immediately, ignoring your struggles. Didn't your oh-so-many lovers teach you that biting is highly erotic?"

She immediately released him. He smiled at her quite pleasantly. "Please go away, Monsieur le Comte," she said in a polite voice. "You must have tired of your absurd, inconsequential games by now."

"My games are never inconsequential, as long as they entertain me."

She closed her eyes in frustration for a brief moment. "This house is filled with beautiful women…" she began.

"Oh, not quite filled," he said frankly, leaning back. "The Revels won't start for another day. At this point there are no more than half a dozen beauties in residence."

"Then why don't you go bother one of them?" she said in a tart voice.

"Because I don't want one of them, my sweet. I want you."

She made a low noise that was deliciously close to a snarl. "No, you do not."

He still had possession of her hand. Before she had any idea what he planned he picked it up and placed it on his lamentably hard cock. She tried to yank it away, but he bore her hand down, giving her no choice.

"That's not the member of a man who doesn't want you, pet."

For a moment she ceased her struggles, and her eyes met his. It was a moment of rare intimacy, something he usually avoided. It was part of the piquant danger of her, and she froze, staring at him, her breath coming in short, rapid pants.

"Hold very still," he said in a soft voice.

"Why?" she whispered.

"Because I am going to kiss you, just once, and then I'll leave you be for…oh, perhaps a few hours. If you move around too much I might be inspired to move beyond a simple kiss, and that—"

His drawling words were silenced by her mouth against his. It was the first kiss she'd initiated, and it was clumsy, endearingly so, her soft lips against his, not quite on the mark. His cock jerked in her hand and she jumped away from him, startled. "Now go away," she said. "You promised."

He smiled thinly. "I wasn't aware that it was exactly a promise, but that's enough for now. Perhaps next time you'll tell me the truth about your deflowering."

She met his limpid gaze defiantly. "And why should I?"

"Because I want to know. And I always get what I want, my sweet." He leaned over and brushed a gentle kiss against her mouth, clinging for a moment, then removed her hand from between his legs and rose. "*À bientôt.* We'll continue this on the morrow."

She stared up at him, and her lowered eyelids hid

her expression. "Perhaps tomorrow your conscience or your sanity will have returned and you will arrange for me to join my sister."

"My conscience has been lost to the fires of hell for lo these many years."

"And your sanity?"

"I am," he said, "quite mad about you, poppet. And I doubt anything will change that until I finally have you. But you needn't worry I'll force anything. The chase is as delicious as the capture."

He set her hand down, oh so gently, and strolled to the door, unlocking it and pocketing the key. "Good night, my dear."

She had been reading when he first disturbed her. She threw her book at him, a charming display of temper. He blew her a kiss, and disappeared into the hallway, a smile still lingering on his usually cool face.

20

Francis Rohan mounted the dais in the grand ballroom, slowly, surveying his assembled guests. He could recognize most of them. There were a number of new members to be welcomed into their hallowed halls, and he'd long ago lost interest in vetting them. Rolande was in charge of such things, and the newcomers were lined up, dressed like monks, with the ropes around their waists tied to each other. They alternated male and female, conveniently, though he doubted it would remain that way for long. He would sit in his chair and try to keep from drumming his fingers beneath the flowing lace cuffs, and watch while they went through their silly rituals, drinking from the sacred cup, a tacky piece of glass that was shaped like a phallus. He wasn't quite sure what Rolande had planned next and he didn't particularly care, as long as he wasn't required to watch. He would stay long enough for his guests to scatter to their various pastimes and then he would visit his unwilling guest for more interesting sport.

There was only one thing that caught his attention. Marcus Harriman, Baron Tolliver, appeared to be missing. He was supposed to be one of the new members. Apparently he'd been a guest out at Château de Giverney during their last festivities, and acquitted himself well. And yet he'd suddenly chosen not to partake of the legendary pleasures of the Spring Revels? It didn't fit with what Rolande had said.

Still, he wasn't going to worry. Elinor had only met him once, and there'd been no offer of help forthcoming. If he felt any responsibility as head of the decimated Harriman family he appeared to have forgotten it, or doubtless he would have demanded that Elinor remove herself from his lustful clutches.

Except that Lord Tolliver had just as much interest in lust as he had. Perhaps more. All Rohan's lustful feelings went in one direction and one alone. According to reports, Tolliver was more generous.

All this—*frolicking*, hadn't Elinor called it?— would be going on for two weeks. The thought wearied him. At least he wouldn't have to make an appearance more than once a day, to proclaim the motto and begin the Revels. He did so now, rising, his cloth-of-gold coat magnificent in the candlelight.

"Fais ce que tu voudras," he pronounced the ancient words. "Do what thou wilt." The resounding cheer made the candles waver, and he smiled faintly.

And then he turned around and left, as the adjoining doors were opened, and the festivities began.

Charles Reading was in the library, sitting crosswise on one of the leather chairs, his booted foot swinging, a glass of claret in his hand. "You didn't stay?" he inquired idly.

"As you see. You didn't attend?"

"As you see," Reading replied evenly. "Are we getting old, Francis?"

"My boy, you're a child compared to me," he protested.

"Oh, give o'er, Francis!" he said in a lazy voice. "I'm eight years younger—scarcely a child. I wonder why you like to fancy yourself older and wiser than anyone else. His grace the Duke of Leicester is in attendance tonight, and I believe the old gentleman turned eighty."

"I gather his main pleasure at that advanced age is to simply watch," Francis said, pouring himself a glass.

"Nothing wrong with that."

"Then why aren't you there, watching? It might keep your mind off other things."

Charles sent him a dangerous look. "Other things such as what?"

"Such as your pathetic affection for Elinor's sister."

"Elinor, is it? I hadn't realized the two of you had become so…intimate," he said with just the touch of a sneer.

Rohan refused to be offended. "I'm enjoying the approach to the summit, my dear. Once reached I imagine I'll quickly lose interest, so I'm putting it off as long as possible. And you? I trust someone a bit more…approachable has caught your eye?"

"No."

"No?" Rohan echoed in mock horror. "My dear boy, you are ill. 'Tell me no more of constancy, that frivolous pretense.'"

"You know nothing about it," Reading said in a less than equable voice.

"Faith, I'm 'as constant as a northern star,'" Rohan quoted back cheerfully "For 'there is nothing as constant as inconstancy.'"

"I'm not in the mood to swap poets with you, Francis," Charles said.

"My dear, that voice could almost be called surly. Perhaps you should ride to Château de Giverney and give in to temptation," he suggested.

"And be her ruination?"

"When has our kind ever cared about such things? *Fais ce que tu voudras,* child. Do what thou wilt. She won't object, I promise you."

Reading swung his head around, gimlet-eyed. "What do you mean by that?"

"Are you going to call me out, Charles? I meant nothing but that the poor chit is enamored of you, and if you choose, you could take advantage of that fact."

"No," he said shortly. "Let us talk of other things."

"Certainly. Do what thou wilt," he said mischievously. "Did I just hear you growl?"

"I went and looked around the street where you were shot," he said grimly, changing the subject. "And we will resist discussing whether I wish the bullet had come a little closer. You are damn irritating at times, Francis."

"It's part of my charm."

"I could see no way the shooting could have been an accident. It would have been a tricky shot to make, and I wonder at anyone even attempting it. It could have just as easily hit whoever else rode in the carriage with you, and it was woefully inadequate."

"Woefully so," Rohan echoed lightly.

"So who would most like to kill you?"

"Apart from you at this particular moment? The two men who covet my titles come to mind. My dear French cousin Etienne would be delighted to see me dead. He'd come into the title, the estates, and he'd no longer have to sully his hands with common people. He really is the most insufferable snob. He thinks the canaille are subhuman, made only to serve him."

"Don't we all?"

"Oh, heavens, don't tell me you're a reformer?" Rohan said with deep distress. "I much prefer my creature comforts to a fair and just world. My servants are rightly terrified of me, and I never have to do a thing to prove how heinous I can be."

"Everyone is rightly terrified of you, Francis."

"With the exception of you, dear boy." He thought for a moment. "And Elinor. I imagine that's a great deal of her charm. Is Miss Lydia terrified of you?"

"We will not discuss her," Reading said in a flat voice. "So tell me, do you think Etienne was behind the assassination attempt?"

"Probably not. He strikes me as someone more likely to use poison. I won't say it's impossible, but he wouldn't be my first choice." Rohan rose and poured himself another glass of wine. He held the decanter up in a silent question, and Reading responded by raising his glass to be filled as well.

"Who else?"

"There's my dear *English* cousin, the one who currently thinks he holds my title." Rohan's lip curled. "The so-charming Joseph Hapgood."

"If you were dead there'd be no claim on it. He'd have it free and clear," Reading pointed out.

"He already has it free and clear, as long as I'm exiled from England upon pain of death," Rohan said lightly. "And I don't fancy ending up on Tower Hill, separated from my head."

"Something could be done about that. You could apply to the king…"

"I doubt the so-called king has forgiven the rebellion. And my case might strike a little close to home. One man with a stolen title and the true heir wishing to claim it?" Francis shook his head. "I think his clemency is unlikely."

"Francis," Reading said in an uncharacteristically gentle voice. "Culloden was over twenty years ago."

"A blink of the eye, dear boy. Shall we make a bargain? I will refrain from discussing Miss Lydia if you keep away from the subject of my lamentable ancient past. It is of no importance to me. Lost causes are distressing. Let us return to whoever is trying to murder me. It's not going to be Joseph Hapgood. Did I tell you he visited me a few years ago? I don't remember where you were at the time. Delightful fellow. Hates Yorkshire. He's a farmer, you know.

Already had vast estates in Cornwall, a plump wife and eight children. Probably more at this point—he seemed exhaustively procreative, both in agriculture and offspring. He says he never really wanted the title or the responsibility."

"And you believed him?"

"Most certainly I believed him. I believe he still had a whiff of cow dung clinging to his boots. He would give up the title most happily if he could."

"And what did you tell him?"

"That I never considered him to have it in the first place," Rohan said sweetly. "Not the most tactful thing to say in the circumstances, but he's the annoying kind of man who refuses to take offense, no matter how hard I tried to give it. So no, he wouldn't kill to ensure there was no other claim on the title. He'd much rather do without it."

"So we eliminate one suspect. Who else?"

Rohan shrugged. "I have no idea. I did have an entirely contrary theory, one that has absolutely no substance in any kind of common sense, but the idea has stayed with me. Suppose I was not the intended target?"

"You think someone was trying to kill me?" Reading raised an eyebrow. "I have to say, Francis, that I do not boast the number of enemies to your credit."

"Not you, my boy. My dear Miss Harriman. I'd just delivered her in that selfsame carriage less than an hour beforehand. What if the assassin thought she was the one in the carriage beside me and was aiming for her?"

"And why should anyone want to kill Miss Harriman?"

"I have no idea. But you know I was ever a fanciful creature, and the idea has stuck. I wonder about the fire as well. Lady Caroline could barely move or speak except in moments of extreme agitation, and her bed was well removed from the fire. How did she manage to escape and start the conflagration?"

"Is that what they think happened?"

"It is. It was quite clear the fire was started by artificial means. Which means your sweet Lydia was put at risk as well."

He could see Reading stiffen for a moment, then deliberately relax. The man was pathetic, Rohan thought. In love, like a calfling, besotted by a pair of blue eyes and a pretty face. Lord save him from ever becoming so obsessed.

"Which still begs the question," Reading said. "Why would anyone want to kill Miss Harriman?"

"What do you know of the new Baron Tolliver?" Rohan countered.

The contract lay on the table, elegant foolscap written in a fine hand. Miss Elinor Harriman agrees to remain in residence at Maison de Giverney until the end of Lent, while her sister resides at the château. And her signature on the bottom, written with a hostile flourish.

It was far from the first contract she'd signed. While most of working-class Paris made do with a handshake, there were still any number of issues involving her mother and their motley family that had required contracts of one sort or another.

And she was about to break one.

She could tell herself it was *his* fault. He'd forced her, blackmailed her into this position, and she was simply doing what she had to do. They were his just deserts.

So why did it feel so dishonorable?

It didn't matter. Someone in this vast household had taken pity on her. The ordinary cloak and new boots had appeared hidden in her bed, like one of the pillows, with a note and purseful of coins. *Escape when you can,* the note read, and Elinor would be a fool not to.

She had friends in this household. She could even count Willis and Jeanne-Louise as people with sympathy toward her situation.

But it was unlikely that any of them could write, particularly with a fine, masculine hand.

And then it came to her. Mr. Reading. He was enamored of Lydia, though for some reason he'd kept his distance. Maybe rescuing her gauche older sister was his way of winning Lydia's favor. Except as far as she could see, Lydia's favor was a foregone conclusion, and it was Mr. Reading who was diffident.

Escape was all well and good, she thought, feeling particularly cranky. But where did one go, if one managed to actually leave the house? Obviously she'd head for the château and extricate Lydia. Mrs. Clarke certainly wouldn't stop her. But how did one leave in the first place when one was a prisoner? She had no idea how to get out without running afoul of Jeanne-Louise, or, heaven spare her, Rohan himself. He seemed to roam the halls like a bat, waiting to pounce.

She had no idea whether bats actually pounced or not. And Rohan wasn't at all like a bat, which were horribly ratlike and not to her preference at all.

Rohan was like some kind of cat. When she was very young Nanny Maude had taken her to an exhibition of wild animals in Hyde Park, and there were all sorts of huge, exotic cats. Rohan wasn't a lion, he was one of the others. Sleek and black and dangerous, with hard eyes and a strange beauty. Rohan was like some kind of cat.

And she was a mouse. A mouse who snarled. And had teeth. An angry little mouse who fought back.

For the first time in what seemed like forever she giggled.

"What's so amusing, my precious?"

She jumped. She'd given up locking and barring her doors—he always seemed to find a way past them. This time he'd simply strolled in from her dressing room, moving as silently as…a cat.

She couldn't help it, she giggled again. Once started, it was very hard to regain her composure. "I was thinking about you, my lord," she said in a dulcet tone.

He raised an eyebrow. He looked particularly elegant tonight, and she remembered it was the beginning of the Revels. "You were thinking about me and laughing? How very damaging to my self-esteem."

"Actually I was laughing about me. I was envisioning you as some kind of cat, playing games with me, but that, unlike a timid little mouse, I fought back with hisses and fangs."

"Hisses and fangs, dearest? Oh, surely not. You really do have the strangest notion of your charms."

Elinor snorted, an act Nanny Maude had always deplored. "To what do I owe the honor of your visit, my lord? Your vast orgy begins tonight. Shouldn't you be planning on ruining some innocent?"

"But you see, poppet, I am." He took a seat on the divan, glancing around him with great interest, and she could only thank God she'd had the sense to hide the clothes and money. "How have you been entertaining yourself? I sent an array of books to entertain you."

"And lovely they were, though certain illustrated volumes were not to my taste. I don't know what antiquities those drawings were taken from, and I doubt that such interesting contortions could actually take place. And I took leave to doubt the size of various portions of the anatomy of some of the people represented." She managed to keep the flush of color, which had flooded her face when she first opened the volumes, away.

"Well, many of them were gods," Rohan said carelessly. "Those were drawings taken from Roman ruins and temples in India. If you like, we can look at them together and I can explain which are exaggerations and which are not. I do believe most of the positions are feasible. I could be persuaded to attempt some of the more unlikely."

It did no good to glare at him. "I found the books

very…instructive, but now you may take them back. They are irrelevant to the life I intend to lead." She could feel some of the color begin to creep up. Unfortunately she was remembering a particular plate, where the young lady, dressed in nothing but a silver girdle, was astride an Indian gentleman of quite astonishing proportions. She seemed quite happy about it, and Elinor inadvertently pictured Rohan in the place of the Indian gentleman.

"Indeed," Rohan murmured. "You don't intend to procreate?"

"Those books aren't about procreation, they're about…" Words failed her.

Rohan was ever helpful. "Lechery? Degeneracy? Ruination?"

"Pleasure," she said.

She'd managed to startle him, which was almost worth bringing up such a dangerous word. "I beg your pardon, my dear Elinor. Did you just equate pleasure with coupling?"

"It must provide pleasure," she said frankly. "Otherwise why would they continue to do it? Why would you hold these ridiculous parties where people can fornicate in public, if they don't find pleasure in it?"

He smiled at her, an enchanting smile that must have seduced a hundred women. Or more. "There *is* great pleasure in it, child. I've offered to show you more than once."

"It's a pleasure I can do without, my lord," she said.

"I don't think so," he said softly. There was a gleam

in his hard blue eyes, at odds with his faint, charming smile, and she was held captive by that look for a long, breathless moment. And then it was past. "So why don't you tell me the truth about your lurid past, my dear? You know I don't believe your tales of music teachers and actors. You would be far more receptive to my delicate overtures if you'd ever consorted with…how did you put it…pleasure?"

She was going to escape, she reminded herself. She would have enough money to get away from him, enough to book passage back to England if that's what she wanted. He could never return to those shores— she would be well and truly safe.

If telling him the truth, which she'd never told another living soul, would keep him occupied for the evening, then so be it. She took a deep breath, determined to be calm and unemotional.

"My mother sold me as a bed partner to a friend of hers, a gentleman who was so terrified of the clap that he only bedded virgins. I remained in his service for three months before he found a replacement."

"Indeed," he said, not sounding particularly shocked. "Was he kind to you?"

"No. He didn't speak to me. He rutted."

"And how old were you, my pet?" His voice was silky soft.

"Just turned seventeen. There's no need to feel sorry for me. I agreed to it. Agreed to become a whore."

"And why was that?"

"My mother said he preferred Lydia."

"Ah. And what was this gentleman's name?"

If he'd shown pity it would have been unbearable. His calm curiosity had the desired effect—it kept her recital calm and matter-of-fact. "Why would you want to know that?"

"Simple curiosity, my pet. His name?"

"Sir Christopher Spatts. He went back to England, I believe, and married."

"Did he indeed?" Rohan was very still and calm, almost unnaturally so. "And did your mother continue to barter you to her acquaintances?"

"Hardly. I've lived a life of blissful celibacy ever since. I'm not made to be a courtesan. My only value to Sir Christopher was my virginity. Without that and lacking a pretty face I had no value to anyone."

For some reason she wanted him to say something. To tell her she had value to him. God, she wanted him to tell her she was pretty! How pathetic!

He rose, graceful in his cloth-of-gold coat. "I was going to continue your education, my dear Elinor, but I find I have something more important that has arisen. I know it will desolate you to know I'm not going to teach you about your breasts tonight, but there will be other times."

Odd, but his words set a sudden, ridiculous tingling in her breasts, almost as if he'd touched them. In the pictures, grown men had suckled on the breasts of women, something that surprised her. Now, with the sudden tight sensation his words had inexplicably caused, she could begin to understand.

He crossed the room to her, graceful as ever, and

she didn't move from her chair, managed not to jerk away when one slim, elegant hand reached out to touch her face. "Poor poppet," he said softly. "With no one to avenge her."

She wanted to turn her face into his hand, to press her lips against his palm. She was mad. "My mother is dead, sir. I believe she was the one who sold me."

"Indeed," he murmured noncommittally. "I'll let you rest tonight. Tomorrow is time enough to continue your education."

"What if I don't want to learn?" she said, trying not to tremble at the gentle touch.

His smile was genuine. "You will, my child. I assure you, you will."

21

Francis Rohan moved through the vast hallways of Maison de Giverney, his jeweled heels clicking on the parquet flooring. He no longer bothered to pace himself, to achieve the perfect mincing walk. Most of his guests had retired to places of privacy, and those who were still cavorting in public would be far too interested in their partners to notice the King of Hell striding through their midst.

He found Charles at one of the gaming tables, staring at his hand with a complete lack of enthusiasm. He turned inquiringly when Rohan came to stand over him, and with one look at his face he immediately turned his cards over and rose, following his friend to the empty hallway.

"You look like death," Charles said. "Was your 'poppet' that bad in bed?"

Rohan gave him a measured look. "Do you really want to be discussing the sister of your true love in such a crude manner?"

"She's not my true love," Charles said. "And considering all the blasted effort you're putting into having Elinor Harriman, I would assume a question would not be out of line."

"Phrase it better." There was a note of steel in his voice.

Charles looked at him for a long, thoughtful moment. "You, too," he said ruefully. Before Rohan could respond he went on, "Was your time with Miss Harriman less than you hoped?"

"We held a short conversation. I have something I must do, and I need your help for it."

"And what is that?"

"I need to kill a man."

Charles's sleepy eyes opened more widely. "Anyone in particular?"

"The fat man who joined us tonight. Sir Christopher Spatts."

"I'm not objecting, mind you," Charles said. "He's a slovenly creature, and there are rumors about some of his less savory activities."

"Such as what?"

"Such as his preference for children, the younger the better. He was quite disappointed when he heard you don't allow children to be part of the Revels, but decided there were other ways to find pleasure. Why?"

Rohan didn't answer. "Do you have any notion where he is at the moment?"

"I believe he went off with young Wrotham."

"Where?"

"Dear me," Charles murmured. "What did he do?"

His eyes narrowed. "Good God, man, are you wearing your sword? You can't fight him. He couldn't possibly be any kind of match for you. It would be murder."

"Good," said Rohan. "Where is he?"

For a moment Charles didn't move. And then he nodded. "Come with me."

Now was as good a time as any to leave, Eleanor thought. He'd already made his nightly visit, though departing without touching her, even attempting to, was different. She understood completely. She'd told him the truth of what had happened six years ago and he'd been disgusted. Whatever kind of exotic allure she'd held for him, and while she hadn't understood it she'd come to accept that it existed, had vanished.

She moved to the window, looking out into the street. She was probably being foolish, escaping when there was no earthly need. It was more than likely she'd be taken to a coach tomorrow morning with no explanation, just sent on her way.

As it had happened so many years ago when she'd been trapped by that horrible man.

This had been a different kind of imprisonment, and she told herself she was delighted that Rohan had finally seen the error of his ways. She just didn't want to face him when he set her free.

No, she would leave now, when the house was relatively quiet. She could hear the sounds of gaiety and something else drifting from a distance, and she remembered the frenetic energy as Rohan had led her, blindfolded, through the rooms in the château.

Rohan would clearly be partaking of that gaiety, and for the time, perhaps forever, she was forgotten. Once she was out she had more than enough money to hire a coach to take her out to his château. There, she would collect Lydia and they would run, back to England where no one—at least, one particular person—could follow.

She pulled the cloak around her shoulders. She'd managed to braid her thick hair and tie it with a strip of ribbon. For some reason hairpins and the like had remained absent from the many elegancies provided. She took the plainest dress, since she could scarce leave in her ripped and shredded night rail, and the sturdy boots provided. Tucking the purseful of coins in her pocket, she started for the door, then stopped. The contract lay out on the table, the quill and ink still beside it. She reached for it, planning to tear it into pieces, but something stayed her hand. For some crazed, silly reason she took the pen, dipped it in ink, and wrote "I'm sorry" at the bottom of the page. And then she slipped out into the deserted hallway, heading for the servants' stairway.

It was quick. How could it be anything but, Rohan thought dazedly. He was a gifted fencer, light on his feet, entirely ruthless. Sir Christopher Spatts was slow and fat and stupid, unable to comprehend that he was staring death in the face. He thought it was one more game played by the Heavenly Host, mocking the rules of life and death. It wasn't until he began to realize that he was going to die that he started to fight in earnest, slashing with the sword that had been provided him.

Murder. Plain and simple. They were no match, and when Rohan drove the blade into his heart the man squealed like a pig, and Rohan wanted to shout in triumph.

Sir Christopher crumpled to the floor, and Rohan turned and walked away, throwing his sword across the room. The man was dead, executed, as he should have been years ago.

He walked out onto the snow-covered terrace, staring up at the night sky, trying to control his racing heart, the dark, murderous rage that had yet to leave him. Sir Christopher had managed to pink him a couple of times, probably luck driven by sheer terror, and there was blood staining his billowing white sleeve and seeping through the shallow cut on his chest. Another set of clothes ruined, he thought, shivering.

Charles came to stand by him, saying nothing. Finally Rohan brought himself to speak. "He's dead?"

"Thoroughly. The seconds are satisfied. It was a fair duel."

Rohan's laugh was harsh. "What was the fairness in that? It was like fighting a child."

"You should have let me do it," Charles said. "I have no qualms killing those who need to be killed."

Rohan looked at him. "How do you know I have such qualms?"

"Francis, I know you," he said. "You've abhorred death and violence for as long as we've been friends. Have you ever killed your man before?"

"I don't fight duels."

"Then before?"

Rohan turned his head away, looking out past the high wall of the stables. "It was Culloden, Charles," he said wearily. "What do you think? I watched my father and brother slaughtered. I saw good men bayoneted after they surrendered, I saw death everywhere. I saw what men could do, and I swore I would never take a life again, no matter how evil he was."

"So you changed your mind," Charles said. "Why didn't you let me handle it?"

"It wasn't your fight." He looked back at the house, filled with self-loathing. "I want you to take…"

"Who's that?" Charles said, interrupting him.

"Who's what?"

"Moving along the edge of the stables. Someone is sneaking around. I'm not sure if it's a thief or someone's outraged spouse, but I think…"

He saw her quite clearly, though she hid in the shadows, certain he couldn't see her. He recognized her walk, the way she moved, even covered in that hideous cloak. He'd killed for her, betraying everything he believed in, and she was leaving.

The cold anger settled down about him, a rage that should have burned hot if it were a little less powerful. He looked down, expecting to see blood on his hands. Fittingly enough, it was his own.

"Go on in, Francis," Charles said gently. "Go find Juliette, or perhaps Marianne. I'll bring Miss Harriman back safely."

He didn't hear him. His rage blinded him, and

nothing seemed to make sense. "Go away, Charles," he said, his voice like ice. "This is my business."

Charles grabbed his arm, trying to stop him. "I can't let you hurt her, Francis."

Rohan slapped him. The same challenging slap he'd administered to Christopher Spatts's soft, pink cheek after he'd tossed his glass of wine in his face. "Anytime, anyplace," he said in an evil voice.

"Now."

Rohan's smile was ugly. "No. I'm busy tonight." He started after her, and Charles made one last attempt to stop him, grabbing for his arm.

"You can't hurt her," he repeated somewhat desperately.

Rohan stopped, turning to look at his old friend who knew him so little. "I wouldn't think of hurting her." Everything unbearable in this life had narrowed down to focus on Miss Elinor Harriman. He'd been a fool, and he'd waited too long. The waiting was over. "I merely intend to finish what I started."

Elinor kept close to the sides of the buildings. It was unlikely anyone would see her. Lights spilled from the windows on the upper floors of the house, but the ground floor was mostly dark. Anyone still awake would hardly be looking outside, not when there was such decadent entertainment to be had inside. She was probably worrying needlessly.

Maison de Giverney was huge, the size of an English country house in the heart of Paris. Her newly healed feet were freezing, the night sharp and cold and clear, like Rohan's heart. She pulled the cloak more tightly around her and moved on. The high walls ended in a narrow gate, and she almost thought she saw a carriage there. In the dark and shadows she couldn't be certain, but it seems her mysterious savior wasn't content with simply helping her escape the house.

She moved away from the shelter of the stables, when a familiar, drawling voice sent chills through her body. "Did I give you permission to leave?"

She spun around, like a fool, when she should have simply run. He was standing in the darkness, a mere silhouette, but there was something about his voice that sent shivers through her body. Something was wrong, something very bad had happened, and her first, mad instinct was to reach out to him, to reassure him, to hold him…

She knew insanity when it blossomed in her heart. She turned to run, but it was already too late. He caught her as she fled, and there was no gentleness in his hands as he imprisoned her wrists, hurting her.

"Your broke your contract," he said in a cool voice. "I find I have a great dislike of cheats, Miss Harriman."

"I'm not a cheat," she said hotly.

"Are you not? You agreed to remain here with your sister as hostage for your good behavior. And now I find you running off in the middle of the night. Though perhaps I was wrong, and it wasn't actual escape you were seeking. Perhaps you were just meeting a lover for an assignation and then planned to return to your room, once more presenting yourself as the proud demivirgin wounded by a cruel life."

His voice was mocking, cold. Different. She'd heard him speak in that voice before, when a servant had displeased him, and she remembered the terror in their eyes. She had the same unexpected fear inside her heart.

It was a waste of time but she said it anyway. "Let me go." She tried to pull away, but his hand tightened on her wrist, so hard she cried out.

"I think not." He started back toward the house, ignoring her struggles. She had one last, despairing glimpse of the coach waiting for her, and then he yanked her forward.

She stumbled once, falling to her knees in the snow, but he simply hauled her up again, barely pausing. There were servants waiting to open the doors for him when he approached, and she expected him to release her, to order one of the footmen to accompany her to her room, more prison guard than servant. But he didn't, dragging her after him along the wide corridors, up the broad marble stairs, past some of his more flagrant guests. She heard catcalls, a few cries of encouragement, but Rohan ignored them all, ignored her stumbling attempts to slow him down. He was intent, cold, furious, and for the first time since she'd met him she understood the ferocity behind the name. King of Hell. He terrified her.

She tried to talk with him once more when they reached the second floor, tried to reason with him, and he halted, dragging her in front of him. The sight of his face sent a chill through her. It was cold, blank, emotionless. "Pray refrain from making excuses, Miss Harriman," he said in that cold, angry voice. "I have yet to hit a woman unless she's requested it in sex play, but I'm always interested in trying something new. Be silent."

And then he yanked her after him, down the hallways that grew narrower, darker. He wasn't returning her to her rooms, nor was he taking her to his, a small consolation. But there were no lights, only the candelabrum he'd taken from a waiting footman, and the Revels hadn't penetrated this deep into the house. They were alone, beyond sight, beyond hearing.

It wasn't until he kicked open a door that she realized how very dangerous things were. Imperturbable, elegant Lord Rohan had never evinced emotion in her presence, and his anger at his servants had been cold and remote. His rage right now was hot and wicked.

He set the candelabrum down, kicking the door shut behind him, and this time when she tried to pull away he released her, so that she sprawled on the floor. He made no effort to help her up; he simply stood there looking at her out of hooded eyes.

"Oblige me by removing your clothes, Miss Harriman," he said, his voice cool and clipped, at odds with the wildness in his face.

She could see him clearly now, and the sight shocked her. He was wearing his long waistcoat and billowing shirtsleeves, and he was bleeding. The sleeve was torn and stained bloody red on his arm, and there was a slash on his chest through the layers of clothing, and she stared at him, uncomprehending. What had happened to him?

He moved to stand over her, reached for the cloak and ripped it off her. "And who provided the means for your escape?" he inquired in a silken voice. "This hardly looks like the cloak I provided for you once your house burned down. I tend to have more extravagant taste than this." He pulled it from beneath her and tossed it away. The purse that had been tucked in one of the pockets spilled on the floor, the gold and silver coins bright in the candlelight. He looked at it contemptuously. "That's your price, Miss Harriman? It seems fairly paltry to me—I would have been willing to pay a great deal more for your relatively untried favors. Assuming you haven't been lying to me the entire time you've been here." An expression crossed his face, so dark and bleak that it shocked her. A moment later it was gone, leaving him calm and cold. "You had best hope you haven't been," he said. "I couldn't answer for the consequences. Who gave you the cloak and the money?"

She started to pull herself together—she wasn't going to stay sprawled at his feet like a harem girl. "I don't know," she said, starting to rise.

"Did I give you leave to get up?"

"I don't need your leave," she said, anger overriding her fear.

"Yes. You do." And with one strong, pale hand he pushed her down onto the rug again. "I would recommend you stay there until I tell you otherwise. I'm not ready to touch you, and you would only have yourself to blame if you anger me more than you have already."

"*What* have I *done?*" she cried. "You should have known I'd try to escape if I had the means. I have no idea who helped me, but I would have been mad not to take the chance."

He moved then, walking around her in a slow, deliberate circle, and his eyes were hard and merciless in the shadows. He reached up and began unfastening the heavy silver buttons of his vest, using his left hand. "Did I not tell you to remove your clothes?"

For a moment she watched, almost in a dream, as his strong, pale hand moved down the buttons of his waistcoat. "You told me you hadn't raped in decades, my lord," she said in a measured voice. "Are you so devoid of novelty that you want to experience that particular unpleasantness?"

"Unpleasantness for you, Miss Harriman, not for me," he said smoothly. He shrugged out of the waistcoat. The blood on his chest was darker, and it looked as if it had slowed or even stopped. His arm was still dripping blood, soaking into the linen sleeve. "But no, I'm not going to rape you."

She stared at him for a long, indecisive moment. "Why should I believe you?"

"Because unlike you, Miss Harriman, in matters like these I keep my word."

She was beginning to hate the sound of her own name, particularly when spoken in that contemptuous voice. But she knew he'd spoken the truth.

He took a seat, still watching her. "Your clothes, Miss Harriman," he said again, in that silky voice that still made her uneasy.

She was wearing a high-necked demimourning gown of pale gray, with narrow hoops and lacing up the back. "Then I assume you simply want to make certain I don't attempt to leave again, and leaving me in my undergarments should ensure that. Not that half your household doesn't wander around in undergarments or even less, but they don't attempt to leave the house."

"Your assumptions don't interest me, Miss Harriman."

"Then what does?"

"Your obedience."

As nervous as she was, she laughed. "Never one of my strong points. And I'm afraid I can't take my clothes off. I need a maid to unlace me."

"You forget the vast amount of experience I have divesting women of their most elaborate toilettes," he said. "Come over here and I'll unlace you."

The very idea was repugnant to her, but she wanted this horrible nightmare to be over quickly, so she nodded, starting to get to her feet.

"On your knees, Miss Harriman." His voice was calm, almost bored.

Her choices were not many, and they were all unappealing. She could move on her knees like some kind of supplicant. She could rise and run—he'd left the door unlocked and in this deserted corridor she ought to be able to find a hiding place, at least for a while. Or she could gather her lost dignity around her, rise and let him decide what he was going to do with her. Surely his fury must be fading. But his eyes still looked empty, as if someone else inhabited his body.

She made the calm, sensible decision not to incite him further. She slid across the floor, turning her back and presenting it for his hands, pulling her thick braid out of the way.

He pushed her hand aside, catching the heavy braid and pulling it, and she saw the flash of the knife. She cried out, putting her hands up to her head, certain she'd find nothing but short strands. Instead, her heavy mane of hair flowed loose around her shoulders. She let out a small sobbing sound of relief, hating her own weakness.

He pushed the hair over one shoulder, and she could feel his hands on the back of her dress, the knife slicing through the laces. "What did you think I was going to do, Miss Harriman?" he said in a silky voice. "I'm hardly likely to stab you."

"I thought you'd cut off my hair," she said.

His hands paused their work. "How interesting. Why should you care?"

She turned her head to look at him. "It's the one pretty thing about me."

"And why should you care whether you're pretty or not?" He went back to cutting through her laces, and she took small comfort in the fact that he was taking his time, being careful not to cut her skin. He was favoring his wounded arm, and she wanted to ask him what had happened, but she was afraid to. Whatever it was, it had set this whole nightmare in motion.

She looked straight ahead, into the darkness. There was a bed, she could see the outlines of it. He'd brought her there for that, she thought, whether it be rape or not.

Her chest felt tight, and there was a low twisting in her belly that she realized with shock wasn't fear. It was something far more shameful and elemental. It was longing.

"Every woman cares whether they're pretty or not, my lord," she said in a low voice. He'd finished with the dress and he pushed it off her shoulders. She slid her arms from it and let it pool around her, all without asking, knowing what would come next, but he expressed no approval. He was cutting through her stays, closer to her skin, with the same exquisite care.

"Not you," he murmured. "You insist no man would ever want you. You pretend you're above such things, you ignore who you are and what you want."

"What do I want, my lord?"

The corset dropped around her, and she was wearing nothing but the thin cotton shift and her stockings and garters and the ugly shoes.

"You want me, Miss Harriman. You have since you first saw me. You are simply too dishonest to admit it. Take off your shoes."

She'd been kneeling in front of him, and she sat back, reaching for the sturdy shoes that had been part of her escape. They were the wrong size for her, too big. The shoes that Rohan had supplied had been perfect. Whoever her aborted savior was, he didn't know her very well.

She took off the shoes and set them to one side, then looked up at him. He was unbuttoning his shirt, and she knew this was going to happen, nothing would stop it. And she knew he'd spoken the truth. She wanted him, in ways she hadn't realized she was capable of feeling.

She started to rise, and he caught her, keeping her down. "Where do you think you're going?"

"I was going to lie on the bed," she said. "You needn't worry, I won't fight you. I promise I won't move and disturb you while you do it. It would help if you had laudanum—I was lucky enough that one of Sir Christopher's housemaids gave me some the nights he chose to visit. But I'll try hard to lie very still and not make a sound." She even managed a shaky smile.

He froze. He'd pulled his shirt free from his small clothes, and he paused in the act of unbuttoning it, staring down at her in disbelief. And then he closed his eyes. "Oh, poppet," he said, and put one hand to the side of her face, and she let out a choked sob of relief, turning her face into his hand.

"I'm so sorry," she said in a raw voice. "If it were only about me I never would have tried to leave, but I'm responsible for Lydia. I have to take care of her, and I couldn't be sure…I can take risks for myself. Not for her. Please, my lord…"

"Don't," he said. "I've hurt you." His voice was filled with self-loathing. He rose, pulling her with him, and clothes fell about her feet, leaving her covered with only the light chemise. And then he stepped away from her. "Cover yourself. You'll get cold. I'll call your maid."

She stared at him in disbelief. "Why?"

"Why? Do you need to ask? I was about to take out all my anger and pain on you. I hurt you, I know I did, and I didn't care. You're just fortunate I came to my senses. There are blankets on the bed. Go get under the covers until someone comes."

"No."

He was in the midst of turning away when her flat, simple word stopped him. "No?" he repeated.

"Not unless you get on the bed with me."

"Child, I'm not in the mood to provide comfort," he said shortly.

"I'm not a child. And I don't want comfort." She wanted to move closer, but the mound of clothing lay between them. "If I have to do…that…again, then I want to do it with you."

She was starting to see traces of the old Rohan, as he smothered a laugh. "As flattering a confession as that is, I believe you'd be better off if I forgo the honor. Get in bed," he said, and moved away from her toward the door, leaving her trapped in the welter of discarded clothing. "There are no servants allowed in this hallway, so it will take me a moment to find someone to assist you. I'll leave you the candles." And before she could stop him he went out the door, closing it quietly behind him.

She stood there, frozen in disbelief. And then she kicked the clothes out of her way and went to sit in the middle of the bed. She counted to ten, and then began to scream at the top of her lungs.

22

It was only a few moments later that Rohan slammed open the door, looking as if he was ready to battle demons. Only his own needed defeating. "Are you all right? What's happened?"

Elinor's voice was raw from screaming, and she cleared her throat. "Rats," she said.

"Rats?"

"I saw a huge rat in the corner. The size of a hedgehog, and he was staring at me out of his evil little eyes, and if I hadn't started screaming he would have…"

Rohan had closed the door behind him by then, moving slowly toward the bed. "And you're terrified of rats," he said in a voice devoid of inflection.

"Absolutely terrified. There's nothing worse than rats. Nothing. And this room is infested with them. They're everywhere. I need you to rescue me."

She saw the smile curve his mouth, slow, reluctant. "Do you know what you're telling me, poppet?"

"Yes, my love… Come have your wicked way with me." And she lay back, closing her eyes, bracing herself.

She felt the smoothness of the covers against her body as he slid in next to her. His hand on her face made her jerk, and she opened her eyes, startled. This wasn't part of it. He was looking at her with such tenderness.

"You really are such a virgin," he murmured in a soft voice, his long fingers stroking the side of her face.

"No, I'm not," she protested. "I've done this many, many times before."

"I beg to correct you. You most certainly have never done what we're about to do. Permit me to demonstrate." And he leaned down and kissed her, holding her face still for his mouth.

He was so gentle at first. His lips barely brushed against hers, featherlight, soft and sweet, and she moved up into the kiss, wanting more.

He opened his mouth, tugging hers open as well, and she felt the astonishing touch of his tongue in her mouth. His hand still held the side of her face, and she knew nothing of this kind of kiss, but she closed her eyes and sighed in pleasure, liking it. Liking it very much. Loving it.

She lifted her own hands, to reach up and touch his face, and then froze. She'd forgotten that this was coupling, this was when she was supposed to lie still, and she started to put her hands back at her sides, when he caught them, drawing them up, and as her fingers cradled his face he deepened the kiss, and for a moment she couldn't think, she could only feel, and she slid her fingers into his long, loose hair and pulled him closer, making a soft sound of need.

He pulled his mouth from hers, and she could feel the tension in his body. "Sweet poppet, I can't do this.... Not the way you need it." He started to pull away, and she simply put her arms around him, sliding underneath him.

"This is the way I need it," she said. He'd put her hand on that part of him last night, and it had been hard with wanting. It had to be something he liked, so she did the unthinkable, sliding her hand between them until she touched the hard, hard length of him.

He groaned, pushing into her hand, and she knew she was right. It gave him pleasure. She slid her fingers along the shape of him, stroking, caressing, and when he reached down and freed himself, the warm flesh was even more wonderful. How could something be so soft and so iron hard at the same time? It would hurt her, she knew it would, and accepted it, because this time she would welcome it. Because this was part of him, elemental and powerful, and he would give it to her, and she finally understood why women wanted this.

He moved to his side, just a little bit, and she let him, as he wrapped her fingers around him, encircling him, and he moved his hand over hers, showing her what he liked, the rhythm of his grip, her grip, the way his hips bucked into the feel of her, and this was one more thing she loved.

His eyes were closed, and she could feel the tension running through his body, building, building. She was wet between her legs and she didn't know why, but it didn't matter. Nothing mattered but the feel of him, his body sliding against hers, his life pulsing in her hand.

And then with sudden startling clarity she realized what he planned to do. He planned to finish in her hand, leaving her body inviolate, and she froze.

"Don't...stop..." he groaned.

"I want you inside me," she whispered. "I want you to finish in my body."

His groan was powerful, and his need was great. Without another word he rolled over on top of her, shoving her shift up to her waist and pulling her legs apart, and she was just about to brace herself for the pain when he pushed inside her, hard, sliding deep into her with a smoothness that left her breathless, hungry.

She put her feet on the mattress, arching her hips into him, wanting more, and he reached his hands under her rump, moving in deeper still, and she cried out, not in pain, but in some confused need that she didn't understand.

"It's too late," he gasped. "I shouldn't have...You won't..."

"Finish it," she whispered in his ear.

Her words released him. He surged into her, his strokes smooth and hard and deep, and she felt something tight in her throat, in her chest, her breasts, her stomach, but most of all between her legs, and she thought back to the feel of him in her hand, and he reached up and put his mouth on hers, his kiss plunging, possessive, and she knew he was ready for his release, and she was going to love it, every sensation, every sound, every—

Her own explosion hit her so hard she cried out, her body suddenly going rigid in his arms, and she knew she was sobbing with some kind of dark need, wanting more and more as everything spun out of control, light and dark, hard and soft. She made a choking sound, and a moment later he was there as well, spilling into her body, flooding her emptiness.

She was holding him so tightly her muscles felt locked, and then she suddenly let go, falling back against the mattress, soft and boneless, and he fell on top of her, his strong body covering hers, and she welcomed it. It was power, it was longing, it was safety, it was unimaginable pleasure. He was still inside her, and she wanted him to stay that way forever. For the first time in her life she felt part of something, of someone else, and she wanted to laugh out loud with the joy of it.

He pulled away from her, and she tried to pull him back, desperate to keep him with her. He wrapped his arms around her and smoothed her wet face with his fingers. "Dearest, you're crying. I hurt you."

She shook her head, but for some reason she was totally unable to speak. She managed to smile through her tears, and she pulled his head down to kiss him, and he laughed against her tear-damp mouth. "You're going to have me crying too," he said. He rolled over on his back, taking her with him, and his hands were busy, stripping the chemise off her, so she was wearing nothing but her stockings and garters beneath the linen sheet. He was still wearing his clothes—his shirt and his breeches were open, and he divested himself of them quite handily, all without losing hold of her. And then he tucked her under his arm.

"You need to rest, poppet," he whispered, his mouth against her ear. "I promise to do a much better job of it in a little while."

Her sleepy eyes flew open, and she found she could finally speak. "We're going to do it again? Tonight?"

"Trust me, we could do it again immediately, but I think you need to rest. But we're most certainly going to do it again tonight. And tomorrow morning, and midday, and early afternoon. And teatime, and…"

"I won't be able to walk," she said, alarmed and enchanted at the thought.

"Then I'll carry you. Sleep now."

And she closed her eyes and slept.

She woke in the darkness, hours later, to see him leaning over her, an intent expression on his face. "You sleep too long," he murmured. "I've been waiting for you."

"You could have woken me."

"Believe me, I tried," he said ruefully. "We have work to do, my precious. There are all these delicious parts of you that I was in too damn much of a rush to appreciate. So now your turn. Though in fact, I may enjoy this even more than you do."

"Enjoy what?" she said, curious.

"Lie back, poppet, and I'll show you."

She remembered the last time he showed her something, in the carriage so long ago, and she wondered if there could be anything more interesting than that.

He kissed her mouth, slow and deep, and she felt tremors vibrate through her, as if he were still inside her. He moved his mouth across her cheek, and when he reached her earlobe he bit, hard, and the tremors grew stronger. He moved his mouth down her neck, biting the base of her throat lightly, and she reached her arms to pull him down on top of her.

"No, my sweet," he said, placing her hands down on the bed beside her. "This is the one time when you do have to try to lie still. Trust me, you'll enjoy it more that way."

Enjoy what more? she thought, confused. The act of sex? How could that possibly be more enjoyable?

And then his hands touched her breasts, and she tried to sit up, but he was very strong. "Lie back, poppet. We hadn't gotten to your breasts yet, and they are absolutely delicious. Did I tell you I love your nipples? So dark, like black cherries." His hands cupped them, and one thumb flicked across the center. She jumped, keeping her eyes closed, as the sensation speared down between her legs.

"How do you know what color my nipples are?" she said in a raw voice. "It's dark in here."

"You know I'm a very bad man, poppet. I may have peeked when you were asleep. Believe me, I've suffered for my sins. I haven't been able to stop thinking of them in days." His thumb flicked the other nipple at the same time, and she let out a small squeak of shy pleasure. "Oh, you like that, do you?" he murmured. "I thought you might. This will probably be even better." He leaned over her, and she felt his long hair on her breasts, and then his mouth went where his thumb had been, latching on to her breast and sucking it deep into his mouth.

She jerked, stunned at the pleasure rippling through her. He had told her to keep her hands at her sides, and all she could do was clutch the sheets to keep from moving as the first swirls of something dark and dreamy began to stir through her body.

The more he sucked at her breast, the more she wanted, and when he moved to the other one she cried out, until he covered the abandoned breast with his hand once more, using his thumb and fingers to make her half-mad, and she could feel the sheet in her hands as she clutched it.

He lifted his head, and then blew softly on her wet nipple. "I want to put my mouth everywhere on your body, poppet. I want to taste you all over. And then I want my cock to follow. I want to do things to you no one has ever dreamed of doing. I want to have you so completely that no one else has ever existed, only you and me."

She made a soft, whimpering sound. He slid his hand over her stomach, and then down between her legs, in that wet, messy part of her, and she tried to close her legs, to keep him away, but he just laughed. "This is us, precious. Nothing to be shy about." And he slid his finger inside her.

She arched off the bed with a muffled shriek. His thumb touched her, higher up, and she began to writhe, feeling the darkness pulling closer, dark and sweet and rich, and he pressed harder, so cleverly, and she hid her face against his shoulder and let go, as wave after wave convulsed her body, sharper and harder than last time.

He moved, and he was between her legs, and just as the last tremor died down he slid inside her. She was so slick from their earlier time that nothing stopped him, and he went in deep, so deep, and the tremors started all over again, and she could feel her body squeezing him tightly as he held still inside her.

They slowed, those wicked tremors, and just as they died he began to move, thrusting inside her, taking his time now, moving slowly, deliberately, pacing her, pacing him. He seemed to know just when she was about to explode again, and he would back away, slow the pace, then build it up again, so that she was no longer able to control herself. She let go of the sheets and clawed at him, begging him, and finally he lost his restraint, thrusting into her, over and over, and the final release caught her just as his did, and she opened as he filled her, her hands digging into his hips, trying to take even more of him. Greedy, selfish, wanting more.

This time he was the one who fell asleep, still inside her. She lay still, feeling some of the wetness leak out, and she wanted to reach down, push it all back into her. She didn't want to lose anything of him. But she stayed still, and while he slept he grew hard inside her again, bigger than he'd been before, and he was already moving when he awoke, stroking into her as he held her, his hands covering her breasts, his thumbs rubbing the tips, and as this final climax swept over her she gave in, to the darkness, to the rich, dark dream, and she was lost.

He was lost. He felt it ripping through him, and he pulled out of her arms, shaken. She slept on. He'd worn her out, and they'd had nothing but the most pathetic of traditional sex. Her on her back, him on top. And he felt as drained as if he'd just survived a week-long orgy.

Worse. He'd never felt like this. He was empty, shaken, and he took his clothes and threw them out into the hallway so as not to wake her, closing the door behind him. He didn't want to, couldn't look at her anymore. If he looked at her he'd touch her, if he touched her, more of him would disappear, until there was nothing left at all.

He was a bad man. A heartless bastard, a rakehell, a libertine, and he made no apologies. He had never been faithful in his life and he didn't intend to change. He could feel himself strangling on the sticky-sweet strands of emotion she was awash with. She probably fancied herself in love with him. The sooner he put a stop to that the better.

He yanked on his breeches and shirt. What would she expect of him? Nothing, if she had any sense, and Elinor Harriman had always had more than her share of common sense. He had no reason to feel guilty. He hadn't taken her maidenhead. That was long gone to the man he'd ruthlessly skewered. If by any chance he felt a twinge he could ignore it. By killing Sir Christopher Spatts he'd more than earned the privilege of sharing her bed for one night. She didn't happen to know that, and he'd prefer she never find out. She might read too much into a gesture that was merely…

He could come up with no excuse for it. He still had the man's blood on him. He smelled of sex, of the full erotic flowering of her desire, and he was growing hard again, curse it. He had to get away from her—she'd bewitched him, and he would be dependent on no woman.

He moved down the dark hallways, almost at a run. His servants could come and clean up the mess that he'd left behind. He'd keep her back there, away from everyone, until he figured out what the hell he was going to do with her.

In the meantime, he needed to wash the blood, the sex from his body. Wash away her touch and her scent. Wash away the memory of weakness.

He needed to remind himself who and what he was. Francis Rohan, Comte de Giverney, Viscount Rohan, Baron of Glencoe. The Prince of Darkness, the King of Hell. A thoroughly bad man.

With no room in his life for a good woman.

When Elinor awoke she was alone, and the sun was up. It looked to be early morning, and someone had come in and lit a fire. There was even a pitcher of lukewarm water on the dresser. But there was no sign of Rohan.

She sat up, dazed. She was entirely naked save her stockings and garters. She'd forgotten she had them on. One of the garters had come untied, lost somewhere in the tangled bedclothes. She looked down at her body, timidly, and then frowned. She had blood on her. Rohan's blood. She hadn't even asked him what had happened.

She sat in the middle of the bed, naked, unmoving, while she considered the strange turn her life had taken. It wasn't so much that she had fallen in love with a libertine, a rakehell, a Very Bad Man. That had happened weeks ago, and she hadn't been alert enough to nip it in the bud. Now it was full-blown, and she had no idea what, if anything, could destroy it.

She also discovered exactly why everyone wanted him. The pleasure he had given her last night was astonishing. If he could do that with anyone it was small wonder the world was ready to worship the King of Hell.

He must have had hundreds of women. And now he'd had her, body and soul. The question was, would he want her again? Or had she served her purpose, like so many others before her? The novelty had been experienced, there was no reason why he'd still want her. Not a man who was constantly looking for new and different sensations.

She reached for the cloth, slowly washing him from her skin. She didn't want to. She didn't want to wash anything away, she wanted to keep it all. The blood, the seed, the touch and the sweat. She was being ridiculous, she told herself, striving for her usual common sense. Though where her common sense had disappeared to last night she couldn't begin to guess.

She finished washing, pulling on the fresh chemise some thoughtful servant had brought her.

There were clothes as well, though no sign that Rohan had ever been here, except for the various stains on the sheets and her body. Someone, presumably Jeanne-Louise, had chosen a dress that was simple to put on by herself, though she had a bit of a struggle doing it up. Her entire body ached, in places she didn't know she could hurt, and a brief, worried smile crossed her face.

She'd seen it happen with her mother so many times she knew how these things worked. The blush of attraction, the wild, irresponsible passion. And then parting. And Viscount Rohan was known for his partings.

There was a pair of sturdy shoes, as well. And, she noticed with sudden horror, her cloak. Not the cheap one that she had tried to sneak out with. But the one provided for her. The money had been collected and put back in the small purse as well. She stared at it all for a long moment.

Did he want her to leave? Now that he'd had her, was he done? It certainly looked that way. And did that mean that Lydia was free as well?

If he thought she was now going to slink away like a soiled dove he was mistaken. If he wanted her gone he would have to tell her to her face. She picked up the cloak and purse and opened the door.

A footman was waiting, not her friend Antoine. "Good morning, mademoiselle. Do you need some assistance?"

"I need to find my way back to my rooms."

"I beg your pardon, mademoiselle, but those rooms have now been filled by his lordship's guests."

She didn't know if her face whitened. It felt like it. It felt as if all the blood had drained from her body.

"Then I wish to speak to his lordship. Can you take me to him?"

"Of course, mademoiselle. I am not quite sure where he is right now, but I will take you to his library and send word that you wish to speak to him. May I tell him what it is about?"

"You may not," she said, clutching the purse tightly. And she followed the footman down the long, dark hall.

Rohan was sitting at his desk, looking through papers, when Charles Reading stormed in. "What did you do with her?"

Rohan looked up, deceptively calm. "What do you think I did with her, Charles? Exactly what I said I would." He reached for his glass of burgundy. "Would you care for a glass?"

"No. I need to know what you're going to do now."

"My dear Charles, are you enamored? I thought it was the silly chit of a sister you wanted," Rohan said in his silken voice. His hand didn't have a tremor, he noticed. He had moved past the debacle of the last twelve hours quite well, he thought.

"Don't play games with me, Francis," Charles said bitterly.

"In truth," Rohan said, "I'm much more interested

in what happened after I…decamped last night. Is the late Sir Christopher stinking up one of my rooms?"

Charles shook his head. "Of course not. Your cousin came and took him. He'll see to it that the man gets a decent burial."

"Knowing Etienne, he'll probably cut him apart and observe his organs first," Rohan said in his light, airy voice. "So no unfortunate aftermath?"

"Only that your guests are at fever pitch. They seem to like the smell of blood."

"I'm so glad I could be of service," he said smoothly.

"What are you going to do with her, Francis? She's a gentlewoman. You can't treat her like one of your whores."

"Oh, my dear Charles, that's exactly what I did, and I assure you she liked it enormously." He gave Charles his most angelic smile. "There are two choices, I suppose. Send her on her way with enough money to support her for a reasonable amount of time. After all, one night's tup shouldn't equal a lifetime of support. But perhaps enough to get her to England."

"And the other choice?"

"Well," he said thoughtfully, "I had considered introducing her to some of the Host's more moderate behaviors. Veronique was extremely interested in her, and you know how she likes an audience. And I'd be more than happy to see her drifting around here in scanty clothes, enjoying herself with some of our young bucks."

Charles looked at him, long and hard. "I don't believe you," he said flatly. "You're lying to me."

"My dear Charles, why should I lie? Miss Harriman means absolutely nothing to me. Since I'm a charitable man I have no problem with seeing her safely settled elsewhere if she's not interested in our revels."

"Last night she was Elinor."

"Well, today she is Miss Harriman."

"And her sister?" Charles demanded, barely containing his temper.

Some good could come of all this, Rohan thought wearily. He smiled at Charles. "I think I might have her after all. Miss Harriman makes the most delicious noises when she comes, and it would be interesting if Miss Lydia did the same."

He barely got to finish the sentence before Charles flew across the desk, crashing onto the floor with him.

It was what he needed. A violent outlet, to hit and be hit. The battle was short and immediate, punctuated by grunts and curses seldom heard outside a stable. They were too-well matched, and eventually they both lay on their backs, bloody and bruised and struggling to catch their breath.

"Hardly a fair fight," Rohan wheezed. "I'm still recovering from a duel."

"You bastard," Reading said, his chest going up and down. "You touch Miss Lydia and I'll kill you."

"Perhaps, dear Charles, I wouldn't mind," he said, and then laughed at himself. "My, how maudlin I'm being." He managed to sit up, groaning. "There's only one way to keep her safe from me, Charles. Marry the chit. If you're worried about money I suggest that is a mere trifle in the face of nauseating true love. I expect you will find a way to manage things."

Charles stared at him. "Never in all my life have I ever heard you advocate marriage."

"Of course you have! I thought Etienne should marry Miss Harriman. He thought he should marry Miss Lydia. If he does, I get her. And I don't think you want that, do you?"

Charles sprung to his feet with an agility Rohan could envy. "I won't let you touch her."

"So you said. Well, do something about it."

Charles slammed out of the office. With luck he wouldn't realize he'd been manipulated until he arrived at the château. Any earlier and he might turn around and come back. He expected one look at Lydia Harriman's exquisite face and tear-filled blue eyes and the last amount of his reserve would leave.

Love was a tedious thing, he thought wearily, reaching for his ale. He was heartily glad he was above such things. He'd been ridiculously sentimental last night, but then physical pleasure on that level caused its own kind of madness. *Amour fou,* the French called it. Mad, passionate love, the kind that drove one crazy and made no sense.

He was very lucky he was able to put all that aside. It was going to be difficult, handing Elinor the money to get away. And whether she'd go without her sister was always a question, but he expected, once she was certain Lydia was well taken care of, that she would be more than happy to quit these shores. Secure in the knowledge that she'd be in the one place he couldn't reach her.

Sanity would hit her as it had hit him, and her disgust would be total. Anything would be better than fancying herself in love with him. Love was the one thing he couldn't tolerate.

Perhaps he could count on Charles to make the arrangements, once he realized that Rohan had no real interest in his virgin bride. In the meantime he needed to stay away from Elinor. *Amour fou* was for the young and resilient.

Not for the old and jaded, who knew there were no such things as happy endings, true love, or the dangerous, deceptive peace that had swept over him last night.

Best to dispense with it before it crumbled beneath his touch. She would be far better off without him. His hands and his soul were stained with too much blood, and there was no washing them clean.

He leaned back in his chair. In the distance he could hear the sounds of the Revels, going full tilt. And he closed his eyes and began to curse.

Elinor backed away from the door. "You can't treat her like one of your whores," Charles had said.

And his devastating reply: "That is exactly what I did, and she liked it enormously…one night's tup shouldn't equal a lifetime of support."

She listened until she could listen no more, each word like a sharp stone thrown at her, until she felt as if she were dying from the constant, cruel blows. She backed away, too numb to cry, until she knocked into someone.

She turned, ready to snarl at the first hapless libertine she saw, but instead found herself looking up into her cousin's handsome face.

"Cousin Marcus," she said, astonished. "What are you doing here?"

He was still wearing his cloak, and he gestured for her to move away with him, to a deserted alcove far out of hearing. "Dear Elinor, I've come for you. I know that Rohan has some kind of hold over you, and I thought to help you escape. I had servants smuggle in a cloak and shoes for you last night, and my carriage was waiting, but you never arrived."

"That was you?" she said, disoriented.

"Of course it was me," he said. "Why else would I be at such a foul place? Do you know your host murdered a man last night?"

The blood on his shirt, on her nightgown. "He did?"

"It was the pretext of a duel, but it was more wholesale slaughter. The poor man was no match for him, he just happened to be in the wrong place at the wrong time. Rohan was so angry he wanted to kill someone, and that poor man was the first one he came to."

And she was the second, she thought miserably. She looked up at her handsome cousin and his Harriman Nose. "I would be most grateful if you would take me out of here," she said in a low voice.

"I shall indeed, cousin. I have several things I wish to tell you that you might find interesting, plus a proposal you might not find unappealing."

"I need to see my sister," she said, trying to control the utter misery in her voice.

"Of course you do, Cousin Elinor. We'll discuss that. Come with me."

She had Rohan's fur-trimmed cloak with the matching muff. She would have preferred the rough one, but that was gone. She pulled the new one around her neck. "Yes," she said, and put her hand in his. "Yes."

23

Lydia sat by the window, staring out at the gray day. She'd trained herself not to cry. It always grieved Elinor so, and besides, it did no good. It didn't change things. It wouldn't bring Nanny Maude back, it wouldn't erase the fire and her mother's agonizing death. It wouldn't even give her back her sister when she needed her. Tears were a waste of time, and she had no intention of indulging herself, not when Mrs. Clarke and Janet were so good to her.

And it wasn't as if she was actually worried about Elinor. Lord Rohan couldn't keep his eyes off her, and despite his swagger, she knew he wouldn't hurt her. It was too much to hope for a good outcome, but if Elinor could claim even a small portion of happiness then Lydia could only be glad for her.

Though why she should think happiness would come from a rakehell like Rohan was quite ridiculous. If she had any common sense she'd be terrified for her sister and her future.

But she had something better than common sense.

She had her almost infallible instincts when it came to people. She knew who were the good ones and who were the bad. Not by society's rules—if you went by them you'd know that Rohan was despicable and the man she had once thought was her father to be stalwart and upstanding.

That man had abandoned his real daughter as well as his false one, and while Lydia never held grudges, she knew that a truly good man wouldn't turn a child away no matter how dubious the parentage. Rohan wouldn't have.

No, Rohan wouldn't abandon, wouldn't force. And Lydia knew that Elinor was more than a match for him, or she never would have left Paris peaceably. They would have had to carry her out screaming. For a few short weeks, or even days, Elinor was going to have the novel experience of being charmed, courted, even seduced. She was going to have to face the fact that she was beautiful, outside as well as in. And if her virtue was the cost it would be her own decision, and well worth it. Elinor wouldn't give up anything she didn't truly want to.

And if truth be told, she wasn't certain that Elinor was still a maid. Oh, she knew Elinor would never have given herself willingly to anyone in the past, but there were secrets, whispers and lies that had moved beneath the surface of their small family. Angry comments Nanny Maude had made, the grief and loss on Elinor's face when she'd disappeared for a time when they were younger. Whatever had happened, it had been bad, and for her sister's sake Lydia had chosen not to pry.

She'd instinctively known who to blame. The one person she could never forgive, the one person who had doted on her to the exclusion of everyone else. The author of their destruction. Their mother.

Somewhere along the way Lady Caroline had lost her right to the compassion Lydia held for everyone else. Not for her feckless ways and the disaster she'd drawn them into. But for her sister's sake. Lydia could overlook anything, forgive anything. Except when it came to Elinor.

If she was wrong about Rohan, if he hurt Nell, she would find a way to make him pay. But she wasn't wrong. She had seen him look at her when he thought no one was watching. Bad man or not, Lydia had faith in him. He might be the King of Hell, but there was redemption slipping past the brimstone.

And Lydia could do her part. She'd made up her mind, and indeed, as far as sacrifice went, it was little indeed. She'd learned long ago that bright pretty things were all well and good, but settling for dull and sturdy was the wise, the generous thing to do.

Not that anyone would consider Etienne de Giverney dull and sturdy. He was a very handsome man. A little lacking in humor, perhaps. A bit stiff, and most of his understanding had gone into his study of medicine and little into the rest of the world. There was something else beneath the surface, something she didn't quite understand. It disturbed her, but she decided that was simply her own reluctance. A reluctance she had every intention of ignoring.

Which would be no problem. Her mother had been

the same, and she knew just how to deal with it, fashioning conversation around them, rearranging life and the past to best flatter them. Etienne saw her as a pretty ornament to his life, and he would treat her well, never hit her, give her children and a secure life.

But even more important was what he would give Elinor. The freedom from worrying about her baby sister.

It was a small enough sacrifice after all Nell had done for her. And it wasn't as if she'd had any choice. Charles Reading had never said or done anything to suggest she was of any importance to him. She only knew that he was beautiful and scarred and that she was no possible mate for someone in need of an heiress. She'd seen him only a few times, and for some reason when it came to him her instincts failed. She couldn't read anything in his stormy gaze, in his polite behavior. Not admiration or desire or even regret. And she was mad to dream about anything else.

Etienne had been the one to bring her out here, when she'd been secretly hoping Charles Reading would appear by the carriage, and he'd come to visit each day, drinking tea and giving her such long accounts of all the ways Viscount Rohan had robbed him of his birthright that Lydia ought to be outraged at the injustice of it all. Lydia had listened to the repeated litany of offenses and murmured all the right things, and Etienne had slowly begun to calm himself and even preen a bit.

And surely that was a good role for a woman in life.

He was a doctor, a man given to helping people. And she could help him, by soothing him, bolstering him, tending to his feelings of ill usage and resentment.

It just wasn't what she wanted.

But what she wanted didn't matter. At least, not to her. She'd never been able to do much for Elinor, to help shoulder the burden of living with Lady Caroline, and for all Elinor's efforts their mother only had eyes for Lydia. She could only assume her dislike for Elinor's father had been passed on to his daughter, but it was cruel and wicked and Lydia had hated her for it.

Now she could finally pay her sister back, just a little. How could she possibly resent such a choice?

She'd left her bedroom door ajar. Mrs. Clarke poked her head in, her plain face smiling. "You've got a visitor, dearie."

Lydia rose. Etienne again. He'd said he wouldn't be able to come today, announcing it with the air of a great treat to be denied her. She'd said all the right things, of course. She knew her duty, she owed it to Elinor. She smoothed the front of her dress, one of the pretty ones that Rohan had provided, put the perfect smile on her face and followed Mrs. Clarke down the broad staircase of the château with its odd architecture.

It was bisected—one half was kept locked, and Mrs. Clarke warned her against wandering into *those* parts. Her imagination had gone wild, and she'd tried to peek through windows when she'd walked out on the grounds, but it all looked distressingly normal. A little ornate and ostentatious, unlike the comfortable quarters of the rest of the house, including her bedroom.

"He's in the library, miss," Mrs. Clarke said, barely concealing her smile. Lydia paused by the door, just for a moment to remind herself why she was doing this. Clearly Mrs. Clarke approved, though she hadn't seemed to have much of an opinion of Etienne before, and Etienne treated the housekeeper like a peasant. But if Mrs. Clarke had decided she liked him then clearly there was more to Etienne than Lydia had at first imagined.

She pushed open the door, breezing through. "Etienne, I had no idea you'd be able to make it today…" Her words trailed off, and Charles Reading turned to look at her, and she froze where she was halfway across the room.

"I'm sorry, I'm not Etienne," he said, his rueful smile twisting his face.

Oh, merciful heavens, she thought, swallowing. How was she going to get through this? If she was just assured that she'd never have to see Charles Reading again, never be alone with him, never look into his dark, unreadable eyes, then she might be able to do what she needed to do.

"Why…why are you here?" she stammered. "I'm sorry, that's unforgivably rude. It's just I was so surprised. May I have Mrs. Clarke bring you some tea? You've had a long ride. Perhaps something to eat? It's no trouble, I assure you, I can just…"

While she nattered on he crossed the room to her, taking her hand. "Hush," he said. "Hush, Lydia."

She stared up at him, and a sudden dread filled her. For him to have used her name meant dire things were afoot. "Has something happened to Elinor? Is she all right?"

"She's fine. Rohan says she may leave, and I thought I would see if you wanted to return to Paris."

"He's letting her go?" The panic did a quick dip into pain. Elinor loved him. Lydia knew it as well as she knew her own heart, hopeless as it was. She'd hoped for some kind of happiness for one of them. If he was letting her go then that hope was dashed.

"He is."

She suddenly realized he was still holding her hand in his gloved one. She pulled it away quickly. "And where will we go?"

"He's an honorable man…"

"Lord Rohan?" Lydia said, walking away from him. Her earlier approval had vanished with his release of Elinor. Clearly she'd mistaken his interest. "I take leave to doubt that."

"He has an honor of his own. He'll see to it that she has enough money to return to England and live there."

"That's a high price for a short-term whore," she said bitterly.

"You shouldn't call your sister names."

"It's not my sister's fault. And you, you're part and parcel of this. Did you take your turn at her as well?"

The ice had built up in his eyes again, and his expression was blank. "Hardly," he said.

"Oh, that's right, the Revels were in full swing. You probably had half a dozen other women to service."

He looked at her long and hard, and then a light came into his eyes. "No," he said simply.

"No? Don't tell me you've reformed?"

"I wouldn't go that far. But I lost interest in whores long ago, I'm afraid."

"How noble." She didn't know her voice could sound so harsh. "And what do you do instead?"

"Fall in love with unsuitable young ladies."

That silenced her for a moment. And then she rallied. "How many?"

"How many what?"

"Unsuitable young ladies have you fallen in love with?"

"Only one."

She was halfway across the room from him, the settee in between them. She liked it that way; he wouldn't see that her knees were trembling. "And what do you intend to do about it?"

He turned, so she could see only the ruined side of his face. He did so deliberately, the foolish man, not realizing that she loved both halves of him. The whole of him. "I thought I'd be stupid enough to see if she would marry me anyway, instead of the wealthy doctor and heir to a title. She'd be a fool to do so, and I don't think she's a fool, but something Francis said convinced me that I couldn't possibly be as stupid as he's planning to be and turn my back on my heart's desire."

She took a deep breath. "So we've established that she'd be a fool to have you, and you'd be a fool not to have her. How in the world do you reconcile such a dilemma?" She kept her face sober and concerned, while inside her heart was singing.

"I would think I'd have to ask her, just to make certain I'd done everything I could. But I'd warn her. I have no money, no prospects, an exceedingly ugly face, and my dearest friend is the King of Hell."

"You think that would stop her?"

"I have no idea. Would it, Lydia?"

She looked into his eyes, the eyes she could never read, and shock washed over her. Of course she hadn't been able to read the look in his eyes. She was used to admiration, lust, flirtation, acquisitiveness. She'd simply never seen love before.

"Nothing would stop her, if she loved you," she said. "And she does, Charles. She loves your pretty face and your scarred face. She loves your past and your present and she most especially loves your future. Just ask."

"Marry me, Lydia."

Nanny Maude would have been most distressed. Lydia leaped over the low-backed settee and threw herself at him. He caught her, quite handily, and kissed her, more thoroughly than she'd ever been kissed, with such tender longing that she wanted to weep. When he lifted his head to look down into her eyes she knew they were swimming with tears.

"I'm sorry I'm fool enough to want you, dearest," she said, looking up at him. "But since you've suddenly become so wise you'll have to instruct me."

He kissed her again, and no instruction was needed.

Her cousin's carriage was warm and well-sprung, though a far cry from the elegance of Rohan's equipage. The coach took off immediately once they were inside, and within moments they were far away from Maison de Giverney. Away from Rohan, with his cold, cold words.

She still felt numb inside. She sat back in the corner, the cloak pulled tight around her, pain and sorrow threading through her body. She sat silent, lost, until she saw that they were following the river, the wrong way to the château.

"Where are we going? You said you'd take me to Lydia," she said sharply. If one more man betrayed her—

"My dear cousin," he said smoothly, "I told you I had much to report. Your dear sister is fine, staying with her fiancé, Etienne de Giverney. You needn't worry, there are proper chaperones, and they're planning a small wedding as soon as they can manage it. She sends you her love, and tells you not to worry about her."

"She's going to marry Etienne?" Elinor said, doubtful. It had seemed the best solution, but she remembered Lydia's wailing confession that she loved Charles Reading. Something had brought her to her senses—love was a trick, a trap, an illusion. Etienne would take care of her—there was no need for this sudden apprehension.

"Apparently he's been visiting her out at the château every day, pressing his suit, and she finally agreed. It's just as well he took her from under Rohan's roof, don't you agree?"

"Absolutely," she said numbly. "Can I see her?"

"It would be wiser not to at the moment. You haven't yet asked me about my proposition."

She forced herself to evince an interest. "Of course, cousin. I'm very interested." Perhaps he had an elderly aunt who needed a companion, or a cousin who needed a governess. Except that he had no family—his family was hers.

"I know this will sound unexpected, but I've thought it through in great detail, and it seems as if it would answer everything. It might not be what you want, but I suspect it would work out very well indeed, and…"

"Cousin," Elinor interrupted him, some of her old fire coming back. "What are you trying to say?"

He took her hand and got down on one knee in the swaying coach, and she watched him in utter horror. "I'm asking you to marry me, Cousin Elinor. I believe we should get on very well together, and I can't help but feel that all the grand things I've inherited really should be yours, but for an accident of birth. I want to share them with you."

"Cousin…" she said gently, trying to hide her annoyance.

"Indeed, I have the utmost respect for you, dear lady, and…and fondness. I think we can grow to love each other very deeply, and I beg you will consider my offer."

She stared down at him for a long moment, all the while he attempted to keep his balance as the coach rattled along the rough roads. It would answer everything, she thought numbly. Rohan would hear she'd married, and promptly forget all about her, which is what she wanted. If she couldn't have him then she wanted it over, completely.

She looked at her handsome cousin, holding her hand in his. "Yes," she said in practical tones. "But I would like to return to England immediately."

His smile was beatific. "Dear girl! I have a small ship waiting for us at Calais. We can be in England by tomorrow."

Tomorrow. She'd be far away from this place, the country where she'd lived for the last ten years, the place she'd grown up in, the place she'd lost the only mother she'd ever known. Not to mention Lady Caroline.

He could never follow her. It didn't matter if he suddenly came to his senses, remembered the long hours in each others' arms, the heat, the tenderness. He couldn't come after her. To follow her would be to risk his life. His miserable, ill-begotten life. "And my sister?"

"We'll have her and her new husband to visit us as soon as we're settled," he said. "We can get married by special license almost as soon as we reach Dorset. You don't know how happy you've made me, my dear. I was afraid it was too much to hope for."

He rose up, taking the seat beside her, and she immediately jumped up and took the seat opposite him, oddly unwilling to have him so near.

"There is something I must tell you, Cousin Marcus," she said, "which might cause you to change your mind."

"I can't imagine what, my dear."

"I've lived a…a difficult life for the past few years."

He nodded vigorously. "I know you have. It angers me that your father couldn't have aided you when you most needed him."

"I'm afraid…Marcus, I'm no longer a maid."

He didn't even blink. "I'm sure it wasn't your fault, my dear. I am certainly not one to hold blame. You will be modest and faithful to me, and that is all that matters."

For a moment she didn't move. "Yes, Marcus," she said finally. "Then I will marry you."

"Darling cousin," he said, beaming at her.

It wouldn't be too awful, she thought, leaning back in the corner of the coach. He knew enough not to try to sit beside her again, not to touch her or kiss her. He would be polite, patient. And in truth, she could lie beneath him and let him rut on her body, because she knew with utter certainty that that was all he would do. There would be no touches, hard and then gentle, no kisses. And she would be fine.

She would just need to find someone who would dispense laudanum. Perhaps her new brother-in-law would be so kind, she thought mirthlessly.

She looked over at her husband-to-be. He was quite handsome, all in all, despite the Harriman Nose. His colorless hair was thinning slightly, very different from Rohan's luxuriant black mane, and his mouth was…

She had to stop thinking about that. She had to remember the cruel, heartbreaking words and hold them close to her, in case she should ever waver, ever long for him. That man was a lie. The truth lay across from her, dozing slightly as they made their way through the night, heading for Calais.

24

Maison de Giverney was dark and silent. Charles Reading looked up at the huge building in astonishment. It was only five days into the two-week Revels, and the place looked abandoned. He'd been gone for only three days, and he knew a moment's dread when he surveyed the darkness.

He'd waited too long, selfishly assuring himself and Lydia that Elinor was safe under Rohan's protection. Francis had compromised her—that had been in the cards since the moment he'd laid eyes on her, but despite his threats Charles knew he wouldn't hurt her. And he'd simply swept Lydia off to the nearest English parson he could find and married her out of hand before anything or anyone could stop them, including his own conscience. He wasn't good enough for her, and it was totally impractical, and he didn't give a damn. He was in love, and all the rationalizations couldn't make it go away.

The nearest English parson had been half a days' ride outside of Paris, and they'd spent their wedding night in a tiny inn in the countryside. The next two days had passed in a blaze of desire and a burst of tenderness, and it was only after they'd arrived back in Paris, returned to his rooms in the Place des Vosges, that they'd both emerged from their cocoon of happiness to think about Elinor's rescue.

His wife was safely ensconced there, drowsy-eyed and naked in his bed, and he'd been more than loath to leave her. The only thing that could distract them from their dazed delight in each other was the nagging question of Elinor, and he'd come to retrieve her, take her away from Rohan before he could dispense with her.

He'd known perfectly well that despite Rohan's threats he'd make no move to get rid of her until after the Revels had concluded, and he would cushion the blow. For all that Rohan strutted around thinking himself the Prince of Darkness, his battered soul contained a bruised nobility that would appall him. Rohan much preferred to fancy himself heartless.

Charles had no idea how Elinor Harriman would take her dismissal. From what he'd seen of her she was a most resilient young woman. If anything, she might come back and smash a vase over Rohan's elegant head, but she wasn't the sort to sit in a corner and weep.

Then again, she wasn't the sort to succumb to Rohan's notorious powers of seduction, and she had. And Rohan's usual methods were totally at odds with his current behavior. Reading wasn't certain if he'd ever seen his friend the way he'd been that night, the savagery of his one-sided duel with the unlamented Sir Christopher, the anger when he'd gone after Elinor during her aborted escape. Something was very wrong in his friend's life, and the darkness at Maison de Giverney was a clear sign.

He was relieved to see some light behind the windows surrounding the vast front door, and it opened upon his approach, a dour Willis standing there. For a moment he'd wondered if the Heavenly Host had some new conceit—Revels in dark and silence, but he knew immediately that his first surmise had been correct. The place was deserted.

"Is your master here, Willis?" he said.

"He's here. Everyone else is gone, though, including half the servants," he muttered. "I'm glad you're here, sir. He needs you."

"Where is he?"

"In the library. Drinking or drunk, if I make my guess. No one's to go near him, and since he almost blew Cavalle's head off with his dueling pistol the servants, what's left of them, are keeping their distance."

"He won't shoot me," Charles said, heading off through the dimly lit hallways.

The house was spotless—all signs of the recent party had been swept away. Charles couldn't imagine how he'd done it—once the Heavenly Host were in full swing it was almost impossible to distract them until excess had exhausted them.

The door to Rohan's study was closed, and for once no footman sat waiting for a summons. He knocked on the door.

"Go away, damn it," Rohan's voice came from behind the door. There was just the faintest suggestion of a slur in it, another astonishment. In their years of heavy drinking he'd never heard Rohan sound anything but cool and in control.

"It's me."

"Get the hell out of here, Charles."

That was welcome enough. He pushed the door open and stepped inside.

The last time he'd been in this room they'd been trying to kill each other. Obviously Rohan had continued that pursuit on his own.

The room was destroyed; a madman had clearly taken a firepoker to every possible surface, smashing and destroying in a blind fury. The massive desk was overturned, chairs were splintered, paintings torn off the walls and sliced through. And Rohan was in the midst of it. On the built-in window seat that even he couldn't destroy, a bottle of Scots whiskey in his hand.

He looked like holy hell, and Charles could only surmise that he'd been doing nothing but drink and smash things since the moment he left.

One of the overturned chairs looked to have four intact legs, though one arm was gone, and he picked it up and righted it, then sat in it, looking at his old friend. "What have you done with the Heavenly Host?" he inquired politely.

"Got rid of the lot. Drove 'em out of the place, and they won't be coming back."

"No, I expect not. Not with their Revels disrupted,"

Charles observed. "And where is Miss Harriman? I assume you sent her on her way as well?"

"It didn't come to that," he said with an ugly turn to his mouth. "She left on her own."

Reading's eyes narrowed. "How?"

"Someone saw her departing soon after you left. Were you fool enough to go after the sister?"

"You knew I would," Reading said.

"Indeed. You're still young and foolish enough to believe in love."

"And you don't, Francis?" he said gently. "I think Elinor loved you."

"I didn't give you leave to call her by her given name," Rohan snapped drunkenly.

"I wasn't aware that it was your permission I needed," Reading said wryly. "Where is she?"

"Damned if I know."

"You most certainly are." Reading kept his voice pleasant. "How do you know she's gone?"

"Went back to her room. Rooms. I put her away from the riffraff, and when I went to find her she was gone."

"Perhaps she knew that was what you wanted."

"How the hell did she know what I wanted?" Rohan argued with drunken logic. "I didn't know what I wanted."

Reading looked at him in frustration. "You've cocked this up badly, Francis. It isn't at all like you— you have more finesse. I can only think there must be something else at play here. Perhaps something on your part."

"I beg you, Charles, spare me your sentimentality," Rohan said.

Reading shook his head. "I need to find her, Francis, for her sister's sake if for no other. I would think you'd feel some responsibility…"

"None," he said succinctly, taking another drink from the bottle. "She may go wherever she wishes and tup anyone she chooses. I'm done with her."

Charles rose, crossed the room and grabbed the bottle, smashing it in the fireplace. Rohan leaped from his seat with drunken fury, murder in his eyes, and then his face went blank as he stood there for a moment, then gracefully passed out in Charles's arms.

Charles let his old friend down carefully on the littered floor and went to the door. Willis was already waiting, with coffee and food on a tray, a bowl of warm water and fresh clothes over his arm.

"What happened to her, Willis?"

"It's uncertain, Mr. Reading, but I had word that she was seen leaving in the company of a gentleman."

Alarm swept through Reading. There was no member or guest of this devil's retinue who was a fitting companion for Elinor Harriman.

"I believe it was Baron Tolliver. He's a relative newcomer, and I gather he has some relation to the lady."

"So she's safe."

Willis looked torn. "As for that, I'm not certain, Mr. Reading. I took it upon myself to see what I could find out about the situation. He'd hired a carriage to transport them to Calais, from whence I can only assume he's planning to return to England. With Miss Harriman."

He should be relieved. If she was with the titular head of her family then he should have nothing to worry about. Except that this was the very man that Rohan had been gathering information about, though he'd been damn secretive about it.

The time for secrets had passed. "Bring some very cold water, Willis. I think it's time for Lord Rohan to face the mess he's made of his life."

"Indeed, sir." He nodded, bowing.

Charles didn't wait for Willis's return. He opened the doors to the snowy terrace and went back to Rohan's unconscious body. He was too big to lift, so Charles simply dragged him across the floor to the door, hoisting him over the doorjamb until he went face-first in the snow.

He came to quite quickly, heading for Charles once more. "Enough," Charles thundered, holding one arm out to keep him at bay. "You've spent enough time feeling sorry for yourself. It's time for you to sober up and do something."

"I could do your intended," Rohan said evilly in a deliberate attempt to get Charles to hit him.

"She's my wife, you degenerate bastard. And you know perfectly well she's not the Harriman you want. Elinor went off with that new cousin of hers—she's probably in England by now. We're going to have make absolutely certain she's—" He stopped as Rohan began to curse. "What?"

But Rohan seemed to have shaken off the vast

amount of whiskey he'd had. He rose to his full, impressive height. "Get my valet," he snapped. "And order my coach."

"Willis is bringing water and fresh clothes," Charles said warily. "But why bring your coach? She's already back in England by now, and you certainly can't even think of going there."

"Can't I, Charles?" he said in a grim voice, stripping off his torn and stained waistcoat and shirt. "I'm not convinced she's safe with him. I had him removed from the property at the beginning of the Revels, but he must have somehow gotten to her anyway."

"And she's safer with you? Allow me to doubt that," Charles said derisively.

"You don't understand. He's not her cousin. He's not the true heir to Harriman's estate, but he presented papers that Harriman's daughter had died in France."

Charles froze. "How did you discover this?"

"I can get any information I need, you know that," he said, his voice dark. "Young Marley, the Duke of Mont Albe, all had knowledge of the so-called Marcus Harriman. He's a fake, Charles. He's her bastard half brother, and I can't believe his intentions have anything to do with Elinor's well-being."

Charles felt the ice that he'd dumped Rohan in begin to form in his veins. "Bloody hell. That would explain a lot. Neither you nor I were satisfied that Lady Caroline started that fire, and you yourself said the attempt on your life might have been a mistake. Miss Harriman had accompanied you only minutes earlier, and it would be simple enough for him to have hired a marksman, one of the disaffected soldiers who roam the streets."

Rohan was splashing water on his body. "If he's taken her back to England it's in order to kill her. And I've been sitting here for days, drinking."

"We could be worried for nothing," Reading said. "After all, the estate's entailed. What could he hope to gain?"

Rohan shook his head, then moaned, putting his hands to his temples. "Devil of a headache," he muttered, momentarily distracted. Then he looked up, steely-eyed. "The estate isn't entailed. Not even the title. She inherits it all, and if she marries, her son inherits the title. I don't think our so-called Baron Tolliver is going to let that happen."

He strode to the door, filled with feverish energy. "Willis, damn you!" he shouted into the darkened hallway. "What's taking you so bloody long?"

"I'm coming, my lord!" Willis's voice wheezed from a short distance away.

"Tell me what to do, Francis," Charles said urgently. "You have no choice but to stay here, but I can go after them, catch up with them before anything happens."

"It might already be too late. He could have tossed her over the side of the boat," Rohan said bleakly. "But no, he didn't do that. I'd know. In my heart, I'd know."

Charles stared at him, stupefied. "You have a heart, Francis? Surely not."

Rohan turned to look at him. "We still haven't settled our duel," he said in an evil voice.

"You really wish to waste time with such inconsequentialities?" Reading said. "Don't glower at me—I've known you too long to be intimidated by the *King of Hell*. You'll have to give up that title, you know. You'll be drummed out of the Heavenly Host."

"God deliver me from their tiresome playacting," Rohan said wearily.

"Lord save us, first you have a heart, now you have a god? Will wonders never cease?" Charles said, turning back to close the door that was still blowing icy air and snow into the library. "One thing is certain. I'm not letting you go anywhere near England. Not that you'd be fool enough to even think of it, but you're out of your mind already, and it would be just like you—"

Something crashed down on his head. One moment he was lecturing his old, dissipated friend, the next he was falling toward the littered, snowy floor of Rohan's library, and then everything went black.

Rohan didn't stop to consider what drove him, what he was risking. There wasn't time. He had no idea when Marcus Harriman had departed with his half sister, but any kind of head start was unacceptable. He'd done nothing but drink for the past three days—they would have left anytime, while he'd be feeling sorry for himself.

He tied his old friend up deftly, bitterly amused at the realization that the only reason he knew how to bind someone was for some of the Heavenly Host's more interesting games. Charles would be ready to kill him when he awakened, but at least Rohan would have a head start. He knew full well that there was no way Charles would stand by and let him put his life in jeopardy by returning to England. He also knew there was no way he could stop him.

He moved quickly. He had no line of credit or bank in England, necessitating that he take a large amount of cash from his Paris bank. He sent Willis ahead to Calais to hire a boat—he needed one ready to sail at the first tide, and he had his valet pack his plainest clothes. He left the Maison de Giverney less than an hour after Charles had arrived, taking his horse and riding toward the coast hell-for-leather.

He stopped only to change horses, pushing on at a madman's pace. It was sheer luck that he decided that one more change was necessary, and he stopped at a small inn some ten miles from the coast. Sheer luck that when the man accosted him he didn't simply shoot him and move on.

It was the Harrimans' erstwhile coachman, though his name escaped Rohan. It didn't matter—the man knew who he was.

"Begging your pardon, your lordship," the man said. "Miss Elinor and Miss Lydia—they're back at your house, aren't they? They're safe?"

Rohan looked at him. Jacobs, that was his name. The question was, who did he serve? The Harrimans? Or the new heir? "Why do you ask?" he said in a more civil tone than he usually used with servants. "Weren't you supposed to be in Dorset, seeing to the burial of Lady Caroline and the old nanny?"

"I didn't wait, your lordship. I came back here as soon as I could. There's trouble a-brewing at the old estate. The man who says he's her cousin—no one knows anything about him. He's turned off all the old servants, and when I tried to find out what was going on no one would talk to me. They were all scared, my lord, even with the man hundreds of miles away in France."

"Indeed," Rohan said, his face a mask. "And what do you suggest I do about this?"

"Make sure he doesn't come sniffing around my lady again," the old man said with some dignity. "I don't trust him. There are stories—people have gone missing. I don't want her in any danger. I promised Nanny Maude."

Rohan looked at him for a long moment. "I'm afraid we've failed," he said finally, deciding to trust him. "He's already got Miss Harriman."

"Oh, no, my lord," Jacobs wailed. "He can't...I..."

"I'm going after her, though I pray it isn't too late. I've got a boat waiting for me in Calais. Am I correct in assuming you wish to accompany me?"

"Yes, m'lord," he said, nodding vigorously. "I can show you the best way to get to Dunnet. I know places where..."

"Do you have a horse?" Rohan interrupted him.

"Me, sir? No, sir. I've been riding on the stage."

"Get this man a horse," he ordered the nearest hostler. "And be quick about it." He looked at Jacobs. "You can ride, can't you?"

Jacobs drew himself up as tall as his stooped figure

could manage. "I'm a Dorset man, born and bred. Of course I can ride."

"Then stop talking and get moving," he snapped, his voice icy.

It took but a moment for a fresh horse to be saddled and brought forward. Long enough for Jacobs to peer into Rohan's face. "Er…your lordship?" he had the temerity to begin. "Are you allowed back in…?"

"I fail to see how that's any of your concern," he said, mentally cursing the Harrimans and their talkative family. Did he have no privacy left? "Concentrate on Miss Elinor, and I'll worry about myself."

"Yes, my lord. And Miss Lydia?"

"Happily married," he said, waiting impatiently as Jacobs scrambled onto the horse.

"To that doctor fellow?" He sounded disapproving.

"To Mr. Reading."

A broad smile wreathed his face. "That's all right then."

"That," said Rohan, "remains to be seen."

To his amazement Jacobs kept up with him. It was close to midnight by the time they reached Calais, and three hours till the next tide. Rohan paced the deck of his hired yacht, unable to sit still, when he heard a voice from the quay. He strode to the side and looked down into Charles Reading's determined face.

He should have known. He leaned over the side. "You're not going to make me have to kill you?" Rohan called. "I'd really prefer not to."

Charles stood looking up at him. "I've got orders from my wife. I'm supposed to bring you both back safely, or it won't be worth coming home at all. At least I can watch your back while you commit suicide."

Rohan grinned at him, sober, clear-eyed, determined. For the first time he had the sense that this desperate, crazy mission might not fail. "Then welcome aboard, old friend."

"You're going to end up on Tower Hill, minus your head," Charles grumbled as he followed Rohan onto the deck.

"Then you'll have two Harriman women to look out for," he said lightly.

"Presuming we get there on time and presuming we manage to get back to France without running afoul of the King's men, what do you plan to do with your Miss Harriman?"

Rohan looked out past the harbor, into the dark sea. "Is it your business?" he inquired coolly.

"It is. She's my responsibility now that I've married her sister."

Rohan gave a hollow laugh. "Oh, my dear Charles, she is not going to want to hear that."

"It doesn't signify. What do you intend?"

"I suppose I intend to marry the girl," he said, unable to sound too cheerful about the prospect.

"Why?"

"Holy Christ, Charles, do I have to explain myself to you? Isn't it enough that I'm doing the honorable thing?"

"It is not. If she doesn't want to marry you she doesn't have to."

Rohan turned to look at him then. "I suggest you don't involve yourself," he said. "Because she's going to marry me whether she wants to or not. I don't intend to give her a choice."

"Why?" Charles said again.

Rohan cursed him, snarling. "You know as well as I do, damn you. Like it or not I seem to have grown a heart. I have absolutely no use for the damned thing, but there it sits, demanding Elinor. I can't live without her."

Charles clapped his hand on his old friend's shoulder. "Welcome to the family, old boy."

There were times when it seemed to Elinor as if she'd been traveling forever. The crossing had been rough, and her cousin had spent the time in his bunk, casting up his accounts, while Elinor stayed on the deck, reveling in the stormy waves. They suited her dark and stormy mood. By the time they reached Dover, Marcus was little better, and he spent the first day of their journey stretched out on the seat of their capacious Berline coach, moaning softly.

Elinor sat primly on the opposite seat, her eyes lowered. She should scarcely feel pleasure in another man's discomfort, but Marcus's sensitive stomach served her well. She wanted no signs of affection, as he'd seemed inspired to attempt before the sea afflicted him. There was something about his diffident kiss that felt dreadfully wrong, indecently so.

She knew why, of course. It was simply because he wasn't Rohan. The thought of lips other than his touching hers naturally felt wrong. Just one more thing she'd have to grow accustomed to.

They were to be married when they reached the village of Dunnet on the Dorset coast, the site of her father's comfortable country estate. It had been twelve years since she was last there, yet she found she had no sentimental curiosity about returning. The world had gone from blazing color to muted black and white, and she expected it to continue that way until her death. It had been that way before she'd run afoul of the King of Hell, who'd shown her the colors of the universe.

Bastard pig spawn Rohan, she thought, glancing at her cousin as he reclined on the seat opposite her. Cousin Marcus was a well-looking man, to be sure, with taller than average height and a sturdiness that would eventually run to fat. It was a shame she found tall, elegant men with lean, golden bodies more appealing. Marcus was covered with a thick pelt of hair, so much that it peeped beneath his cuffs and tufted above his severe neck cloth, and every time she looked at it she shuddered. She had gotten over her infatuation with Rohan, she would get over that as well.

The best possible cure was a quick wedding and a quick bedding. The sooner she lay beneath him the sooner she would get past her maudlin longings for what had never been real in the first place.

By the time they arrived at the old house she was so weary she felt dazed. Marcus's excitement had grown as they drew nearer, his lingering illness finally vanishing. "Things haven't changed much since you've been here, Elinor," he said smoothly. "As I've only just taken possession of the house I haven't had time to put my own stamp on it." What was clearly an unpleasant thought crossed his face. "And of course you'll want to have some say in things."

"No," she said wearily, "I won't. I'm sure you know the place far better than I ever did. And indeed, it's your house, not mine."

There was a look of deep satisfaction in his dark eyes. "Indeed, it is. But once we're married it will be *our* house."

He didn't sound as enthusiastic about the idea as she would have thought, but the house and estate were the least of her concerns. In fact, she doubted she'd ever give a fig for it. All she wanted was a bed and for the world to stop moving.

They arrived at dusk, and as liveried footmen helped her down she glanced up at the old house, waiting for some sense of relief, of familiarity, to lighten her bleak spirits. There was none. She looked around her, hoping to see some of the old servants including Nanny Maude's much younger sister, Betty, among the staff that was lined up to greet them. There was no sign of her, or any of the servants she had once remembered with fondness. Everyone was a stranger, including the man she'd traveled with, and a faint shiver crossed her spine.

A moment later she was swept inside with a great fuss, taken upstairs to her mother's old rooms, and she knew a moment's distaste. Like the rest of the house, those rooms had been redecorated, presumably for her short-lived stepmother, who clearly had appalling taste. Everything was new and faintly gaudy, and she wondered that her father had married such a tasteless woman. The one thing that could be said for Lady Caroline—her judgment in such matters had been exquisite.

Elinor looked about her, at the rich velvet hangings that were just the wrong color, and there should have been no memories attached. Indeed, brooding over her childhood would give her welcome respite from the current subject of her dark and longing thoughts. The maid who came to wait on her was young and nervous, and once Elinor had washed some of the travel dust from her, she rejected the notion of napping. She'd been trapped in that coach for too long. She needed to stretch her legs, to walk around the grounds and see if those too had changed as dramatically.

Here at least she found familiar ground. She walked past the winter-dead orchards, the spring gardens that were beginning to show just the barest tip of buds reaching through the ground. She remembered playing with Lydia in better times, well out of sight or attention of their parents, and she knew a sudden fierce longing for her sister, so powerful she wanted to weep. She should be happy—her sister was by now safely Madame De Giverney, she thought as her mood began to quickly deteriorate. She'd married that pompous, self-satisfied idiot and it was Elinor's fault; all this was her fault, and she'd ruined her sister's life as badly as she had her own.

She fought back the tears. Tears were a waste of

time, and in no short order she'd be a married woman as well, mistress of the household she thought she'd left behind forever. She had pined for England, secretly, for the house and grounds, for the life that was gone forever. It now seemed as hollow as her dreams.

She let herself back into the house by a side door she'd used when she was younger. Neither the new nor the old Baron Tolliver lived with the formality evinced by the Viscount Rohan. There were no footmen stationed at each door, ready to assist. In fact, the house seemed oddly understaffed, she thought as she wandered through the shadowy, deserted hallway.

Marcus was standing in the hall, looking impatient. "I wondered where you disappeared to, my dear," he said smoothly. "I was worried about you. You've seemed a bit disconsolate lately."

"Really?" she said, surprised. She'd been putting a great deal of energy into being amiable and even-tempered. Perhaps her fiancé was more sensitive than she gave him credit for. "All the travel has been wearying."

"Of course," he said swiftly. "And my trials aren't over yet. I wanted to tell you that I've been called to London for the rest of the week. Some business to do with the estate. I hope you don't mind, dear Elinor. I should be back on Monday, and the arrangements are set for our marriage to take place that very day."

She summoned an agreeable smile. "That sounds lovely." Why in God's name had she ever agreed to this mad proposal? She'd been so desperate to leave France she would have jumped into the channel and swum.

He leaned over and kissed her hand with a wet, smacking sound, and it took all her determination not to pull back. "I'll miss you, my dear," he said, looking down at her. "It won't be long now."

"I'll miss you too, Marcus," she replied. Holding her breath until she was finally alone.

She'd thought the house would feel more familiar with Marcus elsewhere, but it didn't. Some rooms were still the same—whoever had done the massive redecorating had been uninterested in the kitchens and stables. But no matter how she looked, she could find no one who had been there in her father's time, and she eventually stopped asking.

Indeed, there was little that interested her. Not food, since the new cook seemed to favor heavy sauces swimming in fat. Normally she would have found something to read even in her father's narrow library, but the written word couldn't hold her attention. In fact, she wanted to do nothing but doze by the fire. Her dreams were bizarre and colorful, but most of the time Rohan didn't appear in them, and when he did he was suitably contrite. When she awoke, her face was still wet with tears, but she couldn't blame herself. She would have thought the more time passed, the less she felt like crying, but for some reason she'd become a total watering pot.

The next few days passed in a blur, and she was almost glad she didn't see Marcus until the morning of her wedding. To her surprise there were to be no witnesses or guests apart from those at the registry office, but she dutifully dressed in the fussy day dress of puce and lavender and was handed into the carriage by her husband to be.

She surveyed him critically from across the small carriage. He was indeed a handsome man. His lips were full, almost overgenerous, and his color was high and healthy. He would kiss her with those lips, later today, she thought. And she would let him.

Or perhaps, like Sir Christopher, he wouldn't kiss her at all. She would find that a great deal more preferable.

The marriage ceremony went quickly, with only the parson's wife and clerk in attendance. Marcus spent an unexpected amount of time making certain that the marriage was duly recorded, that all the paperwork was in order, and by the time he was finally ready to escort her to a celebratory lunch her appetite had gone from nonexistent to flirting with nausea. Perhaps her new husband hadn't suffered from sickness of the sea during their travels but instead a stomach illness that had now transferred to her. The thought was hardly reassuring.

Nor was his kiss once they were alone in the carriage. She could scarce complain—he had every right to put his hand on her breast, to breathe into her mouth and chew away at her lips as if they were his last good meal. The thought that she'd spend the rest of her life with this didn't help matters, but she simply remained still, grateful at least that Marcus, like Sir Christopher, preferred her to be still.

"I thought we might go for a walk along the sea,"

Marcus said after finally releasing her. "Unless you prefer to go back and retire…"

"A walk sounds divine," she said hurriedly, trying to avoid the sight of those lips.

"The bluffs overlooking the harbor are particularly delightful, don't you think?" he said.

"Indeed," she said. She remembered those bluffs. They were high over the rocks near the ruins of the old abbey, commanding a spectacular view of the coast, and if it were up to her they'd be hiking until midnight, despite the less than clement weather.

The abbey overlooked the bluffs, and the place had served as a most excellent picnic spot in her youth. A brisk wind was blowing when she alit from the carriage, and she pulled her cloak more tightly around her as she glanced up at the darkening sky. It was still the same cloak Rohan had provided, and it had gone from being despised to giving her a nameless comfort. She took her husband's arm, and he put his gloved hand over hers as they started over the stubbled grass.

She looked down at his hand. It was so very different from Rohan's pale, languid, surprisingly strong one. This was undistinguished, with fat fingers and a hamlike appearance, and she quickly looked away. Those clumsy hands would be touching her tonight.

One wall of the old abbey still stood, the gaping windows an eerie sight on a gloomy day. They walked past it, heading for the bluffs. She and Lydia would play hide-and-seek among the ruins when they were younger. There were innumerable places to hide, and in retrospect Elinor shuddered at the thought. The cliffs were far too steep for two children to be playing there unsupervised, but Nanny Maude's painful legs had precluded her accompanying them, and the chambermaid that had charge of them was far more interested in flirting with one of the undercoachmen who'd driven them.

The wind grew stronger as they approached the bluffs, and she sensed an odd excitement in her new husband. She glanced up at him. His eyes were shining with anticipation, and he licked his thick lips…and Elinor's heart sank. He was clearly looking forward to the coming night with a great deal more enthusiasm than she was. Men were indeed odd creatures. He scarcely knew her, and yet he wished to perform that most intimate of acts in her body.

The ground grew uneven beneath her light shoes, and she slipped. His hand was there to catch her, and she laughed lightly. "Had I known we were going to go hiking I would have worn boots to my wedding," she said.

"I should have warned you."

There was the strangest note in his voice. "Had you planned this, Marcus?"

He smiled down at her. "In a way." They were at the edge of the pathway, close to the edge, closer than what she deemed comfortable. While she had no particular fear of heights, the bluffs at Dunnet were well-known as a place where unsuspecting hikers could fall to their deaths, and she had a healthy respect for the crumbling ledge.

"Come, my dear," he said, tugging her.

"This is quite far enough," she replied firmly, trying to remove her hand from his grip.

She couldn't—his hamlike hand was like iron. She looked up into his handsome face and felt a moment's dizziness. There was no love in his eyes, so like her own in shape and color. There was malice.

And murder.

Suddenly everything was made clear. She froze, looking up at him. "I've been very stupid, haven't I?" she said softly.

"My dear?" He was tugging her closer.

"You're going to kill me, aren't you?" she said, her voice deceptively calm. "I cannot imagine why, but that's what you've planned all along, isn't it?"

"Dear Elinor," he said, pressing her hand. "Where did you get such a strange idea?"

"From your eyes, Marcus. I know your eyes."

His smile changed then, going from solicitous to something verging on evil. "I was hoping for your sake you wouldn't realize until it was too late, my dear Elinor. You've been so distraught over your titled lover that you've barely looked at me, and I was afraid I couldn't contain myself on a number of occasions. It has taken a great deal of time to get to this point, and you'll allow me a moment of pride."

"Should I?" she responded calmly. "But why do you want to kill me, cousin?" He was pulling her closer and closer to the cliffs, and the ground was rough beneath her slippers. She was going to die, and for some reason she couldn't view that probability with anything more than distant curiosity.

"My dear, I'm afraid that I lied to you. And most everyone besides. I've almost managed to convince everyone that I truly am your distant cousin, Marcus Harriman. Your marriage to me ensures that any remaining questions will be answered."

"If I die on my wedding day?"

"It will be a great tragedy," he said in a solemn voice. "But you were ever known as a daredevil in your youth. Plus you've been moping around most conveniently, and I've let it slip that you've suffered an unfortunate love affair. I've managed to get rid of most of the old servants, but a few of the families remain in the area, and they remember you. It will be viewed either as one of those unfortunate, freak accidents or a melancholy suicide. I don't really care which, but I always like to have a backup plan."

"I could pull you down with me," she said in a cold little voice, feeling the first stirrings of anger.

"No, my dear, you could not. I'm a great deal stronger than you are." He patted her numb hand again. "Come along, Elinor. I'd hope to be back home in time for tea."

Madness, she thought. This was real madness, not the crazy joyousness of falling in love. "If you're not my cousin then who are you?" she asked.

His smirk was most unpleasant. "Haven't you guessed? I must confess you've been surprisingly slow about all this. I'm afraid our relationship is much closer. In fact, I'm your half brother—unable to inherit by English law, while your sister, with her unknown father, has more right to this place. Surely you can see how wrong this all is? I had to do something about it. By all rights this place should be mine, not yours."

The shock of his words was enough to give her the strength to pull away. "You *married* me!" she said in horror. "You *touched* me…"

"And I would have happily bedded you. I'm not at all picky about such things. You spread your legs for Rohan, you could do the same for me. But since you were willing to come out here it seemed wiser to simply have done with it." He looked over his shoulder and frowned. "It looks as if we're about to have guests. We'd best hurry this up." He moved toward her, but he'd underestimated her.

She didn't want to die. It was simple, clear, and she wasn't going to simply let him kill her. She held very still, and then at the last minute she moved, slamming her reticule against the side of his head. There wasn't much inside, but it gave her the element of surprise. She ducked under his arm and began to run down the pathway toward the old ruins. There were a thousand places to hide back there. Pray God she could find at least one.

Francis Rohan had never been so terrified in his entire life. Not when he followed his father and brother into battle at the age of seventeen, facing almost certain defeat. Not when he'd cradled his dying brother in his arms and looked up to see one of Butcher Cumberland's men bearing down on him with a pike.

Not during the long, endless night he'd escaped across the channel, curled up in the bow of a small boat, determined not to cry, trying very hard not to wet himself.

They'd been moving nonstop, racing across the southern coast. They'd lost Jacobs outside of Dover, but by then he'd told them all they needed of the layout of Dunnet and the great house. He only would have slowed them down, and Rohan had given him money and sent him back to Paris to watch out for Lydia, assuring him that they would bring Miss Elinor home safely.

He and Charles went directly to the registry office, only to find out they were mere hours late. Harriman had already married her. Which meant that Elinor would be a dead in a few short hours...or, if they reached her in time, merely a widow.

The local inn was just as helpful. The happy couple had headed toward the cliffs for a walk before returning to the Harriman estate—if they hurried they could reach them and offer their felicitations. Rohan hadn't waited for Charles—he'd leaped onto his horse and taken off in the direction of the cliffs.

He could see the figure of a woman up ahead on the bluffs, racing across the grass with someone close on her heels, and his blood froze. They were almost too late.

He spurred his horse just as Charles caught up with him. He had no idea whether Harriman was planning on raping her or murdering her, and it didn't matter. He was going to cut his heart out and make him eat it.

Rohan barely waited for his horse to stop before

jumping down. They'd disappeared into the ruins, and he started after them, sword drawn, Charles close behind him. And deep inside his cold, black heart, he prayed.

Marcus was fast behind her, too close, and Elinor was sobbing with fear. In the distance she saw a dead branch lying on the ground and she allowed herself just enough time to snatch it up, whirling around as Marcus overtook her and smashing it across his face.

He let out a howl of pain, momentarily blinded, and she ran. The foundation of the old refectory was on the right, and she'd hidden down there any number of times. Lydia had never wanted to venture down there to find her—she firmly believed it was haunted by all the dead monks that King Henry had burned alive. She raced down the ancient corridor and found the small well she'd once used as a hiding place.

Climbing over it, she ducked down, crouching in the shadows, pulling the hood of her cloak over her face so that he wouldn't see her fair skin in the darkness. It was smaller than she remembered, or more likely she was larger. She waited, listening to the hammering of her heart.

She heard his booted footsteps first, ringing on the old stone. "You're down here, aren't you, sister mine?" he called out in that smooth voice of his. "It's useless to run—you may as well make it easier on yourself and come out now." The footsteps faded for a moment, but she didn't dare move. And then they approached once more. "You know, you were very unwise to run down here, though I do thank you for it. I'll simply break your neck and leave your body until the place is once more deserted, and then I'll toss you over the cliffs. If the witnesses are produced and they ask where we disappeared to I can always tell them we were consummating our wedding vows."

The faint nausea that had been plaguing her for the last few days grew worse. She clapped a hand over her mouth and waited, praying, wordless prayers winging up. She had the errant thought that she must believe in God after all, no matter how ill-used she felt. Perhaps this time, when she most needed it, help would be forthcoming.

Closer, closer. He had a particularly heavy footfall, and Elinor shut her eyes in despair. He was coming closer, and there was nothing she could do. No ornate pistols in this dim place, nothing like the one she'd threatened Rohan with. Nothing to defend herself with but her hands.

She had a brooch on her cloak, a large, ugly thing that her…brother had given her as an engagement present. With shaking hands she unfastened it. If nothing else she could try to jab it in his eyes, anything to slow him down.

And then there was no more waiting. He stood over the small place where she hid, and she knew he'd have that affable smile on his thick lips. "There you are, wife," he said genially, and put his ugly hands down to haul her up.

Rohan, she thought, clutching the pin, the sharp

side out. If she were to die, the last thing she wanted to see in her mind's eye was Rohan. Marcus drew her up, out of the small well, and she lashed out with the pin, aiming for his eyes.

He howled with pain, dropping her, and she went down hard on the ancient stone floor, the pin flung from her grasp. She looked up, and saw *him* —saw Rohan, and she wanted to cry. Death was merciful, and he would truly be the last thing she'd see. A vision or a dream, it didn't matter.

"Get away from her."

The voice was low, deadly and very real. She lifted her head. He was there, he really was, with Charles Reading behind him. Rohan looked like the wrath of God, and she tried to get to her feet, to run to him.

Marcus's meaty hand caught the edge of her hood and hauled her back. "I don't think so," he said.

"You can't get away with it, Harriman," Rohan said.

"Lord Tolliver to you," he said stiffly. "And I certainly can. If anyone finds out you're in this country you'll be executed as a traitor. And who's going to believe a scoundrel like Reading when it's his word against a peer of the realm?"

"The title's stolen," Reading said. "It belongs to Elinor's son."

Marcus had a thick arm around her throat, choking her, and she struggled, fighting him. *Elinor's son,* he said, and she knew, with sudden blind, crazy certainty, that she was carrying a son. Rohan's son.

She felt a surge of fury, and she slammed her elbow into his soft stomach. Marcus grunted in pain, but his hold didn't loosen. She struggled, kicking back at him, and his grip tightened until she felt the blackness beginning to close in. She reached up to claw at his hands, raking her fingernails into his skin, but he was impervious.

"Don't be a fool," Rohan said in his lazy, elegant drawl. "You really can't hope this will work. If you hurt her I'll disembowel you while you watch, and Reading will help me. I'll be on my way back to France before they even find your body. But I'm prepared to treat you like the gentleman you profess to be." His voice dripped contempt. "You do fancy yourself a gentleman, do you not? I'm willing to fight you for her. Surely you wouldn't refuse a challenge."

"So you can skewer me like you did that poor fat bastard?" Marcus laughed. "I'm no fool—I'm a better swordsman than Sir Christopher Spatts, but I'm no match for the likes of you. I…"

The sound of that hated name shocked her, her response so visceral that she kicked back, somehow managed to connect with something sensitive. He let out a yelp of pain, releasing her, and she scrambled away, running toward Rohan, needing him.

But Charles moved in front of her, grabbing her arms and pulling her out of the way, and Rohan's hard blue eyes didn't even glance at her. "You'll fight me, Harriman," he said. "Or I'll kill you anyway. This way you have a chance."

There was silence from the end of the ancient hallway. And then Marcus spoke, his voice full of bravado. "I'm afraid I don't have a sword."

"Charles, be good enough to lend this man your sword," Rohan said lazily. There was murder in his eyes, deliberation in his movements. "And then remove your sister-in-law."

Charles withdrew his sword, still managing a restraining hold on Elinor, and handed it to Rohan, who tested it. "A good blade, Harriman. More than you deserve."

"Come with me, Elinor," Charles said, pulling her away.

She tried to fight him. "No," she cried. "What if something happens—"

"Something will happen," Rohan said without looking in her direction. "Your false husband will die. Leave now." His voice was like ice.

"No," she cried. Not wanting to leave him, terrified that Marcus might win. And then there was a part of her, a dark, ruthless part, wanting to see Harriman's blood spilled.

"If you stay here you'll distract me and that could cause my death," Rohan said calmly, not even glancing at her. She had no choice.

Charles pulled her out of the underground hallway, and in comparison the overcast day was blindingly bright. She had managed to twist her ankle in some part of her flight and simply not noticed, but Charles put his arm around her, supporting her until they reached a place to stop. She rested against one of the many overturned stones, looking up at Charles in despair.

"What if he kills him?" she said in a choked voice.

"He will," Charles said.

"No, I mean…Marcus. What if he hurts him?"

"Not a chance in hell." He looked at her with his twisted smile. "You haven't had to listen to him for the last week. The man was dead from the moment he dared a look at you." Before she had time to digest this he continued. "And I'm sorry, but I'm your brother-in-law. I'm afraid neither Lydia nor I could stomach the notion of Etienne."

She managed a brief smile. "To tell you the truth, neither could I." She tried to rise, but her ankle twisted beneath her and she was forced to sit again. "Are you certain Rohan won't be hurt? And what did Marcus mean about…the man he killed."

"Sir Christopher Spatts," Charles said with a note of grimness. "I have no earthly idea why he did that. He came down into the…er…one of the rooms being used for the Revels, singled out Sir Christopher and threw a glass of wine in his face. The man was no match for him—I've never seen Rohan more vicious or more deadly."

A faint smile touched Elinor's lips. "Good," she said softly, managing to startle her new brother-in-law.

He didn't ask, however. "I'm afraid Rohan didn't think this through. You'll have to take Marcus's carriage back…"

"No," she said with a shudder. She looked back at the entrance to the ruins. "Should it be taking this long?"

Reading shrugged. "That depends."

"On what?" she tried to keep from shrieking.

"On his opponent's skill. And just how Rohan wants to make him suffer. I imagine he'll want to make it slow and painful."

"I'll be patient," Elinor said grimly.

"You're a bloodthirsty creature, aren't you?" Charles said.

"On occasion."

Charles shook his head with a faint laugh. "You two are a better match than I would have thought."

They began the slow walk back to the horses, Elinor leaning on Charles's arm. Her panicked flight into the ruins had taken what seemed like moments, but the walk back felt endless. She kept looking behind her, desperate for a sight of Rohan.

They finally reached the horses. The sun had moved lower in the sky, the wind had died down, and overhead she could hear the wheeling and cawing of the seabirds as they soared above the cliffs.

When she looked back, Rohan had emerged from the underground cavern and was shrugging back into his coat. She waited, her fury building as she watched him saunter down the pathway to where they were waiting.

He was in one piece, unharmed, and he didn't look at her, merely handed the sword back to Reading.

"What are you doing here?" Elinor demanded, her voice shaking with tightly controlled rage.

He glanced at her, and a faint smile curved his mouth. "I believe I was saving your life."

She ignored the treacherous softening that his smile always seemed to start. "Why? *'A one night's tup isn't worth a lifetime of support.'* It should hardly be worth a trip across the channel." She might have almost laughed at the look of dawning horror on his face. "Fortunately it appears that I have inherited my father's estate after all, so you won't be obliged to pay for your momentary weakness."

He didn't move for a moment. And then he simply turned and started walking toward his horse.

Furious, she said, "Is that it? You seduce me, insult me, and then you simply walk away when I throw your appalling behavior in your face."

He paused, then turned. He looked tired, and there was blood on his sleeve. Not his blood, she knew. The blood of her enemy, and she felt a secret joy. "I don't believe there's anything I can say."

He didn't want her. It hit her with crushing misery. It didn't matter that he'd come all this way to save her life, the truth was he truly didn't want her.

She made a strange, gulping noise. He would leave, and she could wail to her heart's content. In the meantime she would be stoic, calm. She would show no weakness.

The sob somehow escaped, and she tried to cover it with a cough. She was so caught up in trying to control her own misery that she didn't realize Charles Reading was suddenly at a discreet distance, and Rohan was standing in front of her.

"What do you want from me, Elinor?" he demanded, his voice rough.

"Nothing…you can ever give me…" She choked

back another sob. "It's all right, I understand. You don't want me, and why should you? But I don't understand why you killed Sir Christopher, and why you came all this way, when you really don't care…"

"Stop it!" His voice was sharp.

"No!" she said, her voice unfortunately close to a wail. "You're a miserable rotten pig and I hate you."

"Of course you do," he said grimly. "You have every reason to and you've always been a most reasonable female."

"Well, I do," she said uncertainly. Her face was wet now, damn it. "So just go away."

"I was attempting to do exactly that," he pointed out.

"Well, who's stopping you?"

"You are."

"This has been…an extremely difficult day," she said, trying to control her voice. "I've been married, kissed by my brother—" she allowed herself a shudder "—almost murdered, saved from a nasty death, and you just stand there saying nothing."

"What would you have me say, child?"

"I'm not a child!" she shrieked, stamping her foot like a two-year-old.

A faint smile quirked his mouth. "I'll ask you again, what is it you want from me? Would you have me grovel? That would hardly be punishment enough. I was cruel and stupid and a coward, three things I most despise. I scarcely deserve to get the one thing I need most in this world. What is it you want?"

I want you to love me, she wanted to cry. She wiped

her tears away. "I'll have you know I don't usually cry. This has just been a bit…trying."

"Indeed," he said politely. "Are you going to answer my question?"

"It doesn't matter," she said. "You don't want me, and I'll be just fine on my own."

He stared at her, and some of the grim tension began to leave his body. It was more than a faint smile by now. "Why, poppet, whatever gave you the impression that I don't want you? I must point out that in this country there's a price on my head, and I came after you anyway. I'd have to be mad not to love you, and for all my sins, I've never been considered mad."

She stared at him. "You love me?" she asked in disbelief.

"More than life itself," he said simply, and took her in his arms. There was a light behind his hard blue eyes, one that danced. "Mind you, no more wickedness. I've given up my allegiance to the Heavenly Host, and I intend to be the most staid, honorable gentleman. You'll have to marry me now."

She stared up at him. "And what if I think you're doing this out of a misguided sense of decency?"

"Oh, any sense of decency I possess is most definitely misguided," he said cheerfully. "I never do anything unless I want to."

"And what if I don't want to?"

"Look at it this way, poppet. You can spend the rest of your life making me suffer." And he kissed her.

It was rapture, astonishing, bewildering, and his hold on her was so tight it felt as if he'd never release her. She sank against him, letting go of the last of her anger, the last of her fears, the last of her sorrow. She slid her arms around his neck, pulling him closer, and kissed him back. He was hers, and she was his.

"I think we'd best get going," Charles Reading interrupted them.

Rohan moved his mouth to Elinor's ear, biting it lightly, and a shiver of delight swept down her body.

"Did I tell you, dear Charles, that you are most definitely de trop?" he murmured against her skin.

"Not as de trop as the king's men should anyone discover you're here. Come on, you two. The yacht's waiting for us in Bournemouth. The sooner we're out of here the better."

Rohan threw back his head and laughed. "He's right," he said. "Come, my love. That is, if you'll have me, miserable bastard that I am." There was just the slightest look of uncertainty in his hard blue eyes. It was probably the only time she would ever see it, and she would treasure it for the rest of her life.

"Oh, I'll have you, my lord," she said in a dulcet tone. "After all, it's better than rats."

* * * * *

REQUEST YOUR FREE BOOKS!

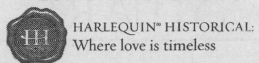

HARLEQUIN® HISTORICAL:
Where love is timeless

2 FREE NOVELS PLUS 2 FREE GIFTS!

YES! Please send me 2 FREE Harlequin® Historical novels and my 2 FREE gifts (gifts are worth about $10). After receiving them, if I don't wish to receive any more books, I can return the shipping statement marked "cancel." If I don't cancel, I will receive 6 brand-new novels every month and be billed just $4.94 per book in the U.S. or $5.49 per book in Canada. That's a saving of 20% off the cover price! It's quite a bargain! Shipping and handling is just 50¢ per book.* I understand that accepting the 2 free books and gifts places me under no obligation to buy anything. I can always return a shipment and cancel at any time. Even if I never buy another book from Harlequin, the two free books and gifts are mine to keep forever.

246/349 HDN E5L4

Name _____ (PLEASE PRINT) _____

Address _____ Apt. # _____

City _____ State/Prov. _____ Zip/Postal Code _____

Signature (if under 18, a parent or guardian must sign)

Mail to the Harlequin Reader Service:
IN U.S.A.: P.O. Box 1867, Buffalo, NY 14240-1867
IN CANADA: P.O. Box 609, Fort Erie, Ontario L2A 5X3

Not valid for current subscribers to Harlequin Historical books.

Want to try two free books from another line?
Call 1-800-873-8635 or visit www.morefreebooks.com.

* Terms and prices subject to change without notice. Prices do not include applicable taxes. N.Y. residents add applicable sales tax. Canadian residents will be charged applicable provincial taxes and GST. Offer not valid in Quebec. This offer is limited to one order per household. All orders subject to approval. Credit or debit balances in a customer's account(s) may be offset by any other outstanding balance owed by or to the customer. Please allow 4 to 6 weeks for delivery. Offer available while quantities last.

Your Privacy: Harlequin Books is committed to protecting your privacy. Our Privacy Policy is available online at www.eHarlequin.com or upon request from the Reader Service. From time to time we make our lists of customers available to reputable third parties who may have a product or service of interest to you. If you would prefer we not share your name and address, please check here. ☐

Help us get it right—We strive for accurate, respectful and relevant communications. To clarify or modify your communication preferences, visit us at www.ReaderService.com/consumerschoice.

HH10R

ANNE STUART

MIRA®

www.MIRABooks.com

MAS0810BL